REVIEWS
Tiernan's Wake

"An intelligent yet lighthearted mystery, with the added appeal of academia. In the same vein as Dan Brown's *Robert Langdon* series, the reader goes on a historical adventure while remaining grounded in the present through history lessons and captivating tidbits of information on theology, symbology, art and more. Make sure to keep an eye out for this one in 2018!" Rebecca Skane, *The Portsmouth Review*

"An amazing historical mystery, guaranteed to keep you compulsively turning the page until the very end. Highly recommended!" Susan Keefe, *The Columbia Review of Books & Film*

"Exciting and fun to read! Well written and highly imaginative, *Tiernan's Wake* offers a wonderful historical mystery set against the growth and self-realization of a group of people thrown together by more than chance, people who complement one another and develop deep and rewarding relationships. Art, cryptology, the European history of the Elizabethan and Nazi eras, and family secrets all come together enjoyably in this fascinating book." Melinda Hills, *Readers' Favorite*

"A compelling mystery thankfully bereft of car chases and gun battles … A book rich in history, but even richer in humanity … Writing with humor, and a style which doesn't try to draw attention to itself, (Rook's) choice of words fit snugly into each character's individual persona. Subplots also blend seamlessly into his story, and one continually remains interested in what happens to both tangential and prominent players." Joe Kilgore, *Pacific Book Review*

"Not your ordinary piece of fiction ... The narrative has a unique blend of eloquent, thought provoking and amusing one-liners. The characterization is decisively written and, whether living or dead, each character has unique attributes that give meaning to the story. The plot is perplexing, humorous and challenging." Cheryl E. Rodriguez, *Readers' Favorite*

"A rewarding storyline, and a compelling cast of entertaining characters ... A satisfying and entertaining novel ..." Mindy Hood, *SPR Reviews*

TIERNAN'S WAKE

A Novel

Richard T. Rook

TIERNAN'S WAKE

A Novel

Richard T. Rook

ISBN 978–0–244–05133–4

Published by AudioArcadia.com 2018

Cover photo and design by Dyan Rook

This is a work of historical fiction. Except for the well–known actual people, events and locations that are described in the novel, all names, characters, places and incidents are the products of the author's imagination or are used fictitiously. Any resemblance to current events or locales, or to living persons, is entirely coincidental.

4

INSCRIPTION

"Our history is their history, and theirs is ours."
Rosemarie Geraghty

ACKNOWLEDGEMENTS

It takes a village to write a book. I couldn't have done it without much help and support.

Deepest thanks to my wife Dyan (a female pirate descendant) and daughter Caitlin for their love, patience, ideas and encouragement. To the real–life John Carroll and his Irish family, for lighting the Grace O'Malley flame. To Anna Lynskey, for teaching me wonderful things about our Irish family and making me feel really part of it. To Rosemarie Geraghty and Phil McIntyre at Ionad Deirbhile Heritage Centre on the Mullet Peninsula in Mayo, for their kindness and impressive work documenting the stories of Mayo emigration, connecting descendants and generally keeping the flame burning.

To Andrew Shiff and Richard Gingras for helping turn this into a real book. To my very literate friends Debby Hess, Nikki Kermish, Dennis Finlay and Gene Reilly for the time they spent looking over several drafts, their sometimes painful honesty, and all the excellent feedback. To my editor, Lindsay Fairgrieve, for saving me from myself.

Special thanks to the late Edwin O'Connor, who visited my (and his) high school in 1964, and asked an English class to promise that each of us would someday write a novel. It probably won't win a Pulitzer Prize like his did, but better late than never.

AUTHOR'S NOTE

Grace O'Malley was a real pirate, but much more. She was an educated noblewoman of the Irish Clan system, a competent CEO, a skilled political operative, an Irish patriot and overall a major player. She may have been a spy. And she certainly is a symbol of the Irish thirst for independence, and the strong Irish woman in a male–dominated world.

With little help, Grace held off the completion of England's Irish Conquest for years, and appears to have stared down the powerful Queen Elizabeth when they finally met in 1593. It's a shame her story is not more widely known outside Ireland. There is little known about her, even in Ireland. No identified portraits have been located, but there are tales, and rumors of her buried treasure. That's where this novel begins.

Be warned, though, this isn't really a pirate story. I hope It's an entertaining historical mystery with some twists and turns that will make readers laugh. (Nothing Irish can take itself too seriously.) But on another level, it's a story of damaged and scared adults confronting their mortality and looking for the "missing portraits" of themselves. And it's a story of how our past speaks to us and shapes our present and future. Sometimes important messages are best delivered by ancestral spirits. Real spirits, not genetic memory. The Irish know that the spirits of our past live in us, whether we believe in them or not. We just have to know how to handle them.

NORTHERN
IRELAND

ROSSES
POINT

CLARE
ISLAND ● CASTLEBAR

● GALWAY

DUBLIN ● HOWTH

IRELAND

CHAPTER ONE

The day that changed so many lives said hello with a crooked red shamrock. I never thought I'd say that. I never thought I'd meet the Irish Pirate Queen, Grace O'Malley, either. As my wife, Sara, says, life gets weird.

I looked forward to Saturday mornings in the law office. There was no need to pretend you were working hard, especially on a stinking hot summer day. It was already bumping ninety degrees in Boston and the sun had barely dragged itself over the horizon. Even Trumpkin climate change deniers were getting a little worried. Could be a record heatwave, gloated the television weather ghouls. Bostonians do love their records, even the ones they boil in. I had driven in before dawn to watch the hazy fireball rise from the Harbor. I wasn't planning on being in Massachusetts for the end of days. This might be like watching a free preview.

There would be plenty of time today for family history research. Everyone who could escape the city had already left. This was my Saturday ritual now, "obsession", Sara jokingly called it. She wasn't really joking any more. I thought there was a special vibe to doing research in the office. I could see the dock where my Tiernan ancestors landed in 1883. They probably walked down the street in front of my office, heading to the train that would take them to new lives as railroad and mill workers. Names morphed into shadowy figures in the haze. I could hear them. Were they talking to me? Could they ever have dreamed I'd be looking out my window at them?

It always began the same way – fire up the desktop Wayback Machine and light the candle. I hated the candle. An elderly Irish client, Mrs. Boyle, told me you had to light a candle if you wanted your ancestral spirits to reveal themselves. It showed respect. "Did ye' not learn a feckin' thing in school?" She said this with such conviction it almost made sense. She would also tell me her checks were in the mail and she probably believed that too. People were starting to think I lit the candle to cover up something I didn't want them to smell. I told Mrs. Boyle the candle wasn't working. I wasn't getting a lot of messages. Maybe I'd offer the spirits a snort of Jameson Green Spot instead. Mrs. Boyle's husband recommended it. How could the spirits not appreciate the good stuff? "Save the candles for power failures," he smiled. "And drink the Jameson yourself if the spirits are away for the day."

Mrs. Boyle wouldn't give an inch. How did I know it wasn't working? Spirits aren't trained seals. If they felt disrespected, they might invite me over the divide to discuss it face–to–face. "You're not ready to take that trip yet, are you?" In Mrs. Boyle's world, it was clear. If I wanted to keep my spirit communications long–distance, humor them and keep lighting the candle. I told her I set my wastebasket on fire last week. "Good. The spirits responded by turning on your sprinklers. They gave you a sign." It just didn't seem to be something a spirit would do.

Mrs. Boyle played her ace. If I started a spirit custom and abandoned it, a terrible curse would surely be visited upon me and my family. "What kind of curse?" She couldn't say, because nobody

10

had ever dared discontinue a spirit tradition. It would probably involve eyeballs being plucked out, a common spirit curse. They weren't known for their sense of humor. They were Irish. Seldom forgive, never forget. And spirit traditions are antibiotics. Once you start taking them, you have to finish the whole bottle. I'd keep lighting the candle. "Smart lad," she crowed. "A little cheap insurance never hurts. Hedge your bets." It was her own Boyle's Law.

The checks never arrived ("damnable postal office"), but Mrs. Boyle taught me how the Irish manage risk. Every blessing is a curse if you look at it from a different angle. It's usually safe to blame the post office. And have a reliable saint on speed dial to save your ass if you guess wrong. Even better, an archangel, if you can find one accepting new clients. Mrs. Boyle was partial to Gabriel. He could blow his horn and make a problem go away. Mrs. Boyle said that as a young girl she could make her family go away by playing her trumpet.

I meant to ask Mrs. Boyle what would happen if you never began observing the spirit custom. Would the curse even know about you? I didn't get the chance. She was killed by a falling icicle while sneaking out of Sunday Mass early. Gabriel must have been booked at another gig that morning. There were rows of lighted candles at her wake, my first Irish wake. The mourners smoked the traditional clay pipes dipped in poitín. Mr. Boyle laughed, sang and broke into a sprightly jig or two around the table where Mrs. Boyle was laid out. The whiskey flowed as freely as the tears. Good tobacco, better whiskey and the best music. I was pretty sure Mrs. Boyle felt respected.

I'd often stare into the lighted spirit candle. After thirty–four years of legal trench warfare, my own flame was burned out. I'd rather spend time with dead ancestors than most living people. I was escaping into the distant past for hours every day. What was I running away from? It wasn't always like this. I had great clients along the way, people who did more for me than I could ever do for them. There was the always–smiling Auschwitz survivor who joked about getting her tattoo free before they became fashionable. And the scowling Nobel laureate who grew up with nothing, scaled a scientific Everest, and spent his retirement teaching inner–city kids about math and life. You'd never find them humble–bragging on Facebook or polishing their personal brands. They had no time for crap. And the Mrs. Boyles, for the sheer entertainment. But there were never enough of those people and most of them were gone. I had been moved to Table One, soon to be called up to the afterlife buffet.

Okay, I wasn't pulling rotten potatoes out of the ground the way my ancestors did. They didn't get to spend time trying to find their happy place. A good day was when they had enough to eat. A lot of years didn't have many good days. I knew their seething determination made my soft life possible. I just didn't want to become the pathetic old guy who hangs on too long and thinks he's still a player, the guy everyone laughs at when he's not around. The one they're probably laughing at today.

My law partner Glenn Bradley thought I was crazy. When I lit the candle, he'd chant "Ommmm....," usually followed by, "Dude, can you spare some weed?" I wasn't sure why Glenn associated a Hindu mantra with marijuana. It was probably a Republican thing. And Glenn wouldn't know what to do with a joint if you stuck it in his mouth, lit it for him, and handed him a copy of the Stoner Manual. On the other hand, Glenn could identify fifty different brands of Scotch, blindfolded and by smell alone. We live in a world of legal specialists.

Glenn and I had been friends for thirty–two years. We met when we were both cannon–fodder associates at big law firms. We were usually on opposite sides of a case, but we hit it off from the start. I once remarked to Glenn we'd make better law partners than sparring partners. He looked up and replied let's do it. It was one of the few impulsive things I had ever seen him do. He could spend an hour deciding on a coffee mug. And it all sure worked out well for us.

Glenn came from a wealthy, socially connected Boston family. Not the A–list, but solid A–minus. He had reddish hair, brownish eyes, bluish blood and the athletic build of the star high school football player he once was. He probably always gave the impression he had stepped off the cover of a preppie clothing catalog. Now he was the distinguished patriarch in the back, not the sullen punk fondling the tennis racket in the foreground.

Glenn walked with a slight limp. I could tell it hurt. He told me it was an old football injury. They don't play much football in Vietnam, where he got the limp. You don't pump a Vietnam vet for details, but sometimes they have chatty clients. Glenn enlisted right out of high school, three days after he turned eighteen and a few months before the war ended. On his second patrol, he left a safe position to drag an injured boy to safety. The kid panicked and stabbed him in the knee. Glenn pulled him to safety anyway.

Glenn dated attractive women, but wasn't married. I didn't ask about it. I knew he gave away big chunks of his inherited money to charities, always anonymously. Guys like Glenn almost give old money a good name. Almost.

Glenn wasn't perfect. He had been a precinct captain for Ronald Reagan. But hey, we Catholics once had a Pope in Hitler Youth. You have to forgive mistakes from coercion or the developing adolescent brain. And Glenn was on the road to recovery. He listened to Dylan now and remembered the lyrics. Even Dylan didn't remember the lyrics. Glenn still kept an autographed picture of Reagan on his office wall. I figured it was similar to a recovering alcoholic keeping an empty liquor bottle in view, to remind himself how far he's come.

I tried to interest Glenn in genealogy and he tried to interest me in Scotch. We each had limited success. I preferred Irish whiskey. It tastes better. And Glenn's roots went back to the Mayflower, but he hadn't done the digging himself. He bought a certificate of ancestry for roughly what it cost to build and outfit the Mayflower. Where's the fun in that? I told Glenn I thought the Mayflower was a prison ship taking grifters to a penal colony off Long Island. It was blown off course and the grifters became Boston Brahmins. They married siblings or pets and began to talk funny. Glenn started chanting "Ommmm…" I guess we agreed to disagree.

I often wonder if America would have been better off if my people made it here first and shot Glenn's ancestors and their friends as they stepped off the boat. The Irish wouldn't have been as trusting as the Native Americans. I never dwelt long on those thoughts. They took me back to the fifth grade. Sister Mary Catherine, Sister Diabla, when she was out of hearing range, would have said those thoughts were mortal sins. I had some doubts. No bodies were ever produced.

And as my Irish Grandpa Tom told me on my twelfth birthday, if you're going to burn in hell anyway, commit the sin and enjoy it, then have yourself a smoke and a drink. Why be a human torch for eternity for a desire you never even acted on? It seemed to me there should be some extra penalty for committing the sin after you've already sinned rehearsing it. I didn't want to discuss it with Sister Diabla. The parochial school Penal Code was etched in stone, and she'd wonder why I was asking.

I decided to go with Grandpa Tom. He had given me other advice that impressed me as sound, or at least fun. Leave unfulfilled desires to the Methodists.

By 9:30 I had worked through a pile of correspondence. I tried to make some telephone calls, but nobody was answering. Maybe all the phones had melted. My 9:30 appointment called and asked if we could meet by Skype instead. Her car was searing hot and she thought it might explode if she turned the key in the ignition. We watched each

15

other sweat for twenty minutes. I did a quick check of my email. Nothing interesting, except one I didn't understand: 'Anxiously awaiting your response, Aedan Burns'. I didn't know an Aedan Burns. It was probably a Nigerian banking scam.

There was a knock on the door and Glenn stuck his head in.

"Good soggy morning to you, Michael. Here's your mail. And a strange manila envelope that just came for you by courier. What century are you in today? Ommmm…"

"Thanks, Glenn. I didn't think you were in. And would you please cut the chanting crap? Isn't there a Spawn of Mayflower meeting you can go to?"

"No, we don't meet in the summer. So many of us are in the Hamptons."

"Not you? Maybe your family were Mayflower stowaways? No, waitstaff."

"Ah, the always amusing class envy of the downwardly mobile Irish–American."

"Bet your ass I'm downwardly mobile. I wound up being your law partner, didn't I? Look, how much do I have to give you to get out of here? Name your price."

"Nothing. It's damn hot. My butt is sticking to my new leather couch. I'm heading up to Montreal to cool off. See you next Friday. You've got my cell phone number. Try not to use it. Is there anything else you need to know?"

"Two things. First, it's a really nice couch. Did the office pay for it?"

"No, it was a gift. A client was having a problem with a business permit violation. I called a friend at the Enforcement Division and the misunderstanding went away. I think the file did too. Next day, there's a leather couch with a smiley face note being delivered to my office."

"Glenn, the IRS wouldn't consider it a gift."

"Only because satisfied customers don't have leather couches delivered to their offices. Hey, I never asked the guy in Enforcement to do anything. He took pity on a hard–working business owner. It's way too hot to chat about tax law. What was the other question?"

"It's a bigger one. How much longer are we going to keep doing this?"

"Doing what? Comparing office furnishings?"

"No, practicing law. We've been partners for what, thirty years? And I wouldn't have wanted to do this with anyone else. Glenn, we'll both be getting Medicare cards in about five years. We've changed, not only in the mirror. I'm fried, and I don't want to drag you down with me. Should we be thinking about an exit plan?"

"We've been together thirty years, three months and thirteen days as of yesterday. I've been thinking about it too. We might have to get that plan in place pretty soon."

"I don't like the big red flag I just saw. What's wrong?"

"I may have an inoperable tumor. They're still running tests, but it doesn't look good."

"Christ, Glenn, I can't think of anything to say. I'm so sorry."

"Thanks. You don't have to say anything. Let's not worry so much until I know for sure. Some heavy hitters are working on my case. If anything happens to me, keep the couch and don't tell the IRS how it got here. I have to go now. Montreal beckons."

He smiled, but it wasn't much of a smile. And he closed the door too softly on the way out.

Damn it to hell. I switched off the computer and stared into the lighted candle. Let's play a long shot.

"Okay, Mrs. Boyle, there has to be someone over there you can talk to about this. I swallowed a great deal of your blarney and at least a tuition–year of your bills. It's time to put up or shut up."

Actually, Michael, she had shut up two years ago. She was dead, remember? You've got to keep those things straight.

Glenn stuck his head back in.

"You understand I didn't mean some of what I said, right? Unfortunately, the tumor part is real. I'm talking about the other shit."

"The Irish class envy and downward mobility? That shit?"

"No that's all true. My family saw a lot of it in the servants. It was sad. I meant the part about the Sons of Mayflower vacationing in the Hamptons. We're Bostonians, Michael. Yankees suck. Nantucket is our summer turf. Give me lobster and a nice white wine, or give me death. Au revoir and stay cool."

His smile looked a little better, almost genuine.

But I still hurt. I decided to sort through my mail and call it a day. I could use some of that Jameson Green Spot Mr. Boyle swore by. You're sitting there minding your business, wallowing in a little self–pity, then life sneaks up behind you and kicks you in the ass. Just tell me what you need, you fucking spirits.

18

There wasn't much mail. A will questionnaire I had asked a client to fill in and return about thirteen months ago. I hoped he was still going to the gym. A request for a political contribution, with a cheery too–personal note written by an unpaid intern. A legal newspaper to add to the pile of legal newspapers in the corner.

The in–box was down to the lumpy manila envelope the courier delivered a few hours ago. It had been mailed from Castlebar, Ireland, to a local courier by International Registered Post. The sender was one Aedan Burns. So much for the mystery email. There was a crudely–drawn, crooked red shamrock on the outside of the envelope. I could be almost sure Aedan Burns wasn't an art teacher. He must have given the courier instructions for delivery to me. Why would anybody send a package that way? And why should I open it? It could be a prank or much worse.

What would Sherlock Holmes do? It was always one of my first questions when I was trying to solve a mystery. Right, let's see what I can find out about Aedan Burns. Too bad you didn't have computers, Sherlock. It took two hours on the internet, but I liked doing research and it would take my mind off Glenn until the watering holes opened.

There really was an Aedan Burns living near Castlebar. He was twelve years older than I was, and a retired lawyer. Aedan started his own law firm in Westport, Ireland, about twenty–five years ago, and built it up to a pretty decent size. Ten years later, he just quit.

Aedan didn't retire the way most lawyers do. No four weeks' notice, no farewell dinner with people making up nice things to say about you. He did everything on his own terms, with a flair for the dramatic.

Aedan was known for his regular routine. Every morning, he left his Westport house at the same time, walked to his office and arrived at the same time. He left his office in the afternoon and arrived home at the same time every day. Same routes, opposite directions, same pace. Shopkeepers set their clocks as he walked by. If their mobile phones showed a different time, they went with Aedan. Better to trust Solicitor Burns than some atomic clock they knew nothing about.

One morning, Aedan reached his office building right on schedule and kept walking. He went to the bus station, bought a ticket to Dublin, and called his office to tell them he wasn't coming in to work, ever again.

The shopkeepers along his route would have to make the necessary adjustments. Aedan had some regrets about that. Mr. McGarry the tailor was wheelchair–bound and refused to use a mobile phone. He thought it would give him a brain tumor. Aedan always felt bad watching him struggle to set his wall clock when he walked by. So he left a package to be delivered to Mr. McGarry – a mobile phone with a note: 'You're ninety–four years of age, Mr. McGarry. You've beaten the bastards. Use this. It's almost as reliable as Aedan Burns'. I was starting to warm up to this guy.

Aedan was an only child. He inherited a substantial amount of money immediately before he bailed on his law practice. Sweet. People wondered how his simple parents accumulated such a vast sum. His father Liam was a laborer who didn't labor much, and his mother never worked outside the home. Aedan told people his father was a good investor. The truth was Liam's brain was an IBM Watson computer. He could eyeball a horse as it was being led to the starting gate and know exactly how the horse would run that day. His brain would then instantaneously identify and process every actionable inefficiency on the betting board as odds were posted.

Liam would watch the board, smoking a cigarette, nursing a beer, running algorithms through his alcohol–lubricated cerebral mainframe. When the time was right, he would explode to the betting window, getting there as it closed. Liam had a finishing kick Jamaican sprinters could only dream about. Sometimes he would look up at the board mid–stride, re–crunch the numbers, and change his bets as he was throwing money down. Warren Buffett, meet Usain Bolt. When Liam passed, he was waked at the racetrack. There was an open bar for his "colleagues" and buckets of fine imported oats for the horses. It was the only pre–paid human funeral the racetrack ever handled.

Aedan was a widower who never remarried. The newspapers said his wife died in childbirth and his only child died of pneumonia a few months later. Aedan took degrees in history and accounting at one of Ireland's best universities, then went to law school. Now he wrote books on Irish history and taught courses at two universities. His 'Western Irish Histories and Mysteries' was the most popular course at each university. You signed up a year in advance if you wanted to take Aedan's course. Students considered him to be an exceptional teacher, but "a bit daft."

Aedan would often show up for class dressed as an historical or mythological figure, and teach the class from that person's point of view. His favorite historical character was the Irish pirate, Grace O'Malley. She taught many a class with Aedan. After each lecture, discussions with students would continue for hours at a nearby pub. The only recent picture of him I could find showed a man with a fierce smile and a shock of white hair with a life of its own. He looked vaguely familiar, but I couldn't quite place it. I hadn't expected so much information to be available online. My curiosity had won out.

There was something loose in the envelope. I opened it carefully, keeping it inside an empty storage box. I wasn't sure why I thought that would do any good if there was poison or an explosive. It just seemed I should do something.

Two smaller sealed envelopes fell out, both with my name on them, scrawled with a bright red marker. One said, 'Open me first'. The other was thicker and had another crooked hand–drawn red shamrock, with: 'Are you the man I have been looking for?'.

I opened the first envelope. It contained one sheet of paper with neat block printing, signed by Aedan Burns at the bottom. I held it up to the light, what Sherlock Holmes would have done. Then I read it.

Good day, Michael.

I expect it's Saturday and you're in your office trying to flush out your ancestors. I have met some of your people, so please allow me to give you a little hint. Check the pubs. I asked the courier to deliver this on Saturday morning. It would be appreciated if you respond by email shortly after you read this. I enjoy finding out if I've hit the nail on the head. But please don't respond yet to the rest of what I have to say. You'll want time to think about it and talk to Sara. You can reply on Monday.

I know quite a lot about you, Michael. I'm an historian, as you are. And our families go back hundreds of years in Western Ireland. You caught my attention on some family history message boards you frequent. I enjoy reading your posts. It's how I learned you come into your office Saturdays and gaze over at the dock where your people landed one hundred and thirty years past. You hear your ancestors' voices as they walk by your office and wonder if they are speaking to you. I believe they are. You wouldn't understand them, not yet. They spoke in an almost incomprehensible Irish dialect. But one of your ancestors was an educated poet, fluent in Latin, Irish and the Queen's English. I'll wager you did not know about him. He may be part of a great historical puzzle I hope we shall solve together. I need to meet with you to discuss it.

If I am right about you, you shall find my proposition rewarding in many ways, and nothing illegal, I assure you. It will mean working closely with me. Some consider me a bit eccentric, so you'll be well compensated.

We can go over everything when we meet in Ireland. I don't much travel any more. Bad things happen when one leaves home. And coming here will give you time to poke around the local cemeteries. I may be able to direct you to some churches with relevant family history information. If you spread grease on the palms of many Irish clergy, they'll show you fascinating records they keep to themselves.

Think it over. If you're not interested, have the other envelope returned unopened to the courier. I don't think you'll do that. I look forward to meeting you, and I insist you bring Sara.

Best wishes, Aedan Burns

Was someone playing a game? Glenn? No, this wasn't Glenn's style. It would be an elaborate hoax to pull while he had so many other things on his mind. And I doubted Glenn would send communications pretending to be from a lawyer who really existed. That was a lawsuit waiting to happen. It was probably just a scam. Or was it? I was feeling a rumble. My life had to switch tracks. Maybe it would start today. I went back to his email and hit the reply button.

Good day to you, Mr. Burns.

You were right on all counts. I will open the second envelope and get back to you. If I can comply with your request, I would be delighted to discuss it in Ireland. And I'm sure I can interest Sara in coming. She's an artist and says Irish landscapes are the best she's seen. I am flattered you consider me to be an historian. I know something about you now as well, and I am not at your level as an historian or writer.

Regards, Michael Tiernan

The reply came within two minutes.

Splendid, and please call me Aedan.

   I am impressed you have spent the last few hours on your due diligence. I know exactly what time your package was delivered. And I am delighted to be dealing with a brother puzzle—solver. As I expected, you know now I have written three books on Irish folklore and history. I hope you read them. As Sara uses paints, I use words. Now please open the second envelope. You should find its contents enriching. And you will be able to comply, but I suppose a good lawyer always leaves an escape hatch. Such a guarded response, Michael.

   I have learned today you enjoy your waffles.

Cheers, Aedan

I needed a few minutes to think this over. He knew about Sara. He had checked us both out online. Do it, Michael. You're not getting any younger. I ripped open the second envelope. A sheet of paper fell out, and two bundles of currency tied with rubber bands. The sheet of paper had a hand—drawn red shamrock at the top, and was written on a computer.

Hello again.

   I knew I did not misjudge you. I am inviting you and Sara to spend the first week of August in Mayo as my guests. If things go well at our initial meeting, then I shall have a business proposal for you. I have a project I think would benefit from your skills and background. It involves your Irish ancestors, so we need to discuss your research. I believe your files contain a clue that will enable us to solve an Irish mystery. It is a clue you would never recognize on your own. Does this intrigue you? I'll give you a taste. You've heard, I'm sure, of the Irish pirate, Granuaile Mhaol. You know her as Grace O'Malley, the Pirate Queen of Connacht, feared by anyone who had the misfortune to cross her path. Some say they see her ghost on Achill Island almost four hundred and fifty years later. Perhaps it is just wind. Do you believe in spirits?

Grace, as I'll call her, was real enough. She was an important historical figure, indeed, a symbol of Ireland itself. She resisted the efforts of England to subjugate us. And she appears to have intimidated even formidable Queen Elizabeth when they finally met in 1593. Grace was a political operative of the first rank, perhaps more than we know. And her ability to raise money quickly on the high seas would make a fine case study at your best business schools. I believe her techniques are still used by investment bankers.

Grace is also a neglected historical figure. The world knows little about her, not even what she looked like. No portraits of her have been conclusively identified. All we have is a portrait of her great–great–granddaughter, Maud Burke. Historians argue whether she spoke English, but we know she spoke Latin. Don't you think there must have been portraits of such a wealthy, educated and notorious woman? I do. And there must have been documents, perhaps her own journals or diaries.

26

The real story of Grace O'Malley must be told, Michael, her treasure discovered. It is not a chest of gold I seek. It is buried history, the warp and weft of Grace's life. Those are more valuable to me than precious metal. Oh, there may be real gold too. Grace is rumored to have amassed a substantial fortune, never located. Maybe we'll find a map to it. I care little. My Holy Grail may have less monetary value, but its historical value cannot be computed, especially by an old historian who now has reason to believe Grace is his direct ancestor.

The story of Grace is the story of the strong Irish woman and our thirst for independence. This is not pulp fiction, Michael. The world must know the reality. I have concluded the best way for me to fulfil my quest may be with you at my side. We shall bring Grace O'Malley back to life. Any records or portraits we find must be transferred to an Irish museum. It will be my crowning achievement as an historian. If there is any pecuniary benefit to be derived, we shall be equal partners. First, I need to know I am dealing with the right man.

I do not expect you to disrupt your life for free. Please examine the enclosed bundles. They contain what you American lawyers call testimony from Mr. Green. One bundle is in dollars and the other is in euros. There's no particular reason except to make me seem more mysterious. Both bundles are all yours for meeting with me one time. There is no further obligation if our first meeting does not go well or you do not wish to proceed further. And in such case, you and Sara will have had a pleasant vacation in Ireland at my expense.

If you are not interested in taking our adventure to the next step, please put the bundles back in the envelope and call the courier for a pickup. I realize you could just keep the cash and destroy this letter. You won't. I trust you, Michael. Trust is the most valuable currency of all. I know when and where to spend it.

I expect you'll want to meet me and things will go well. If so, Mr. Green will testify again that day and you shall find his testimony even more persuasive. And there shall be more testimony in the future. I am a man of considerable means and I can recognize a good investment. I shall furnish your plane tickets, very agreeable accommodations and meals and a car for you to use. There's a lovely B&B near Castlebar. The proprietor gives me a generous discount. It goes back to an irksome matter of unpaid taxes I was able to resolve for her. Sometimes the good citizens of Mayo get busy and forget to render unto Caesar what is Caesar's.

If you are interested, please meet me at the White Stag Pub outside Castlebar at noon on Saturday, 1st August. I shall be sitting at a table on the deck, wearing dark glasses. It may strike you as unusual because it will be raining. This is Western Ireland, so that's a safe wager. If our adventure is ever turned into a film, the initial meeting will make a good scene. Perhaps the Depp fellow will portray me. After all, this is a tale of piracy, up to a point. But it is much more, as you shall see.

Please assemble your family history files before we meet. I'm only interested in your Connacht ancestors. Put all of the files on a flash drive. I no longer trust my cranial hard drive and I have no room in my library for more paper.

Fair warning, Michael, I intend to change your life. So it's best not to come if you think your life needs no changing. Please let me know on Monday if you and Sara will be joining me. I shall make the arrangements and send you the details.

With much anticipation, Aedan

I flipped through the bundles. One had eighty–five crisp hundred–euro notes. The other had eighty–five crisp hundred–dollar bills. Maybe eighteen thousand dollars total, quite a bit more than I usually got for an initial meeting. There was a note on the bottom hundred–dollar bill.

I know you are wondering. Eighty–five is my lucky number. Both my parents were eighty–five when they passed and made me a wealthy man. Please consider me a client for now so our discussions are confidential. And I have heard how honest you American lawyers are. I'm sure you'll tell Glenn about the eighty–five hundred dollars.

That's a little lawyer joke, of course.

Cheers, Aedan

I had heard of Grace O'Malley from my father, but it was time for an online refresher course. She was born in 1530, the daughter of an Irish chieftain and shipping magnate. Shipping magnate as in maritime racketeer. Dad was an Irish toll plaza, collecting protection money and cargo from ships that tried to pass through or fish in waters he controlled. Grace inherited land and cash from both parents and didn't need to be a pirate to put food on the table. But a girl has to make waves of her own. Her father had brought her into the family business at a young age, and Grace expanded it. She recruited Scottish Gallowglass mercenaries to join her homegrown crew of leg–breakers. She controlled the waters off Western Ireland for more than forty years until she died around 1603, rich, undefeated and thumbing her nose at England.

Depending on whom you listened to, Grace was either a freedom fighter, who almost single–handedly fought off English control of Western Ireland for decades, or an un–ladylike thug. The Irish favor the first description and the English the second. She certainly had the Irish knack for survival and for playing everyone against everyone else. Her victims included rival clans, the English, the Moors, ship captains who didn't share her vision of maritime wealth redistribution, and even an unlucky vessel from the Spanish Armada that strayed off course in 1588 and paid the price.

As part of her conglomerate, Grace ran a semi–legitimate and lucrative merchant trade with other western European countries. Her trading partners included countries whose ships she plundered. She would sometimes steal their goods, sell them back, and then steal them again. Not a bad business plan. As a female role model, Grace might not have been a Joan of Arc, but she got things done.

Where was the connection to my family? I had traced my ancestry into Mayo back to about 1600, and into Sligo sixty years earlier. It was all within a small circle of coastal towns in the heart of Grace

O'Malley country. My ancestors were poor and illiterate farmers, with a fisherman or two thrown in.

I never came across the name Grace O'Malley or any of her family names in my own family research. What was this clue Aedan was talking about? And why wouldn't I recognize it, especially since Aedan had told me so much? I guess he'd have to tell me that when we met. I was ready to have my life changed.

CHAPTER THREE

Sara and I had much to talk about that afternoon. She was devastated to hear about Glenn. Sara had known him almost as long as I had. He was best man at our wedding, the same year we opened our office. He would occasionally visit Sara's art gallery, usually with a lady friend. Sara called them Glenn's "misses." A former Miss California, a former Miss New York and so on. The misses weren't arm candy. Miss California was a Stanford grad with a doctorate in physics. She worked as a lead engineer in the space program. Glenn liked people who challenged him.

Glenn often complimented Sara's work. He'd ask a lot of questions and apologize for being so ignorant. Sara loved it when people studied her paintings and asked questions. She said Glenn had a good eye, and not only for the misses. He bought several of Sara's paintings for himself and more to donate to his charities for fundraising drives. Sara would give him and his miss du jour a gallery tour and then we'd all go out to dinner. It was fun chatting about gravitational pull with Miss California.

Sara was a full–time artist now. Her studio and gallery were in a converted warehouse down by the few remaining fish piers. It was only a matter of time before the warehouse was converted into cookie–cutter condominiums for millennial masters of the universe. The same assholes who would then complain about the city losing its character, flip their condos and move on to devour another neighborhood. Puffed–up locusts in Armani suits.

For now, there were other galleries and studios in the building, a quirky oasis of art as long as it could hold out.

Sara was excited about Aedan's offer. We were empty–nesters now, and Sara was getting restless too. I could feel it. Our only child Emma would be starting graduate school in a month. We both could use a jolt, something to get the juices flowing again. She could close her gallery and studio for a week or two in the summer. It was an easy sell.

And Sara particularly liked the Grace O'Malley part. I had traced her own ancestry back to another female pirate from the 1300s, Jeanne de Clisson, the Lioness of Brittany. Grace and Jeanne were on the shortlist of all–time bad–ass pirates. Sara thought Aedan might enjoy comparing their ancestors' numbers. I told her I didn't think Aedan was envisioning a body count competition, but it wouldn't surprise me if he had actual figures.

I reviewed my calendar for the weeks around August 1st. There was nothing I couldn't move around. But I wanted to look into one other thing first. Was Aedan contacting me because we were related? Why else would he be following me on family history message boards? I went over my files. There were no ancestors or connections named Burns, nobody named Burns on my DNA match lists. I'd do more research later when there was time, but for now, I'd presume Aedan had other reasons. I got back to him Sunday night.

Good evening, Aedan.

I've discussed everything with Sara, and we accept your kind offer with much appreciation. I insist that we pay Sara's expenses. I'll meet you at the White Stag on Saturday 1ˢᵗ August at noon. I'll load my files onto a flash drive.

Best wishes, Michael

The response came within a minute.

Good evening to you as well.
I am pleased this is progressing nicely. But I shall pay Sara's expenses, as one artist to another. You will be pleased with the room you are staying in. It has a lovely view if the rain ever stops. The proprietor, Mrs. Carty, swears James Joyce stayed in the room to rest his fevered brain between books. It might be fantasy, the Irish equivalent of your 'Washington slept here'. We Irish have some trouble sorting truth from fiction. Mrs. Carty has particular difficulty. Perhaps it would be best if you and I met alone for a few hours. Sara might be bored by the initial conversation. I hope she will join us for dinner at the White Stag, say at 17:00? A package will arrive at your office in a few days with tickets and details.

Sláinte, Aedan

As I rode the commuter train into Boston Monday morning, it occurred to me I didn't know how much Glenn had told Anna Danos, our secretary, office manager and so much more. Anna had been with us for twenty years. She didn't welcome surprises.

Anna was at her desk, crying softly. She knew. We held each other's hands for a moment and said nothing. There are some situations where words get in the way. Then she put on her game face and

34

announced it was time to get to work. God will do what God will do, but she didn't have to be happy about it when God was an imbecile.

Anna was more Secretariat than secretary, impossible to keep up with when she hit full stride. Even I knew enough not to use a horse analogy to a woman's face. They don't like it, even if the horse is Secretariat. I would have considered it a very high compliment.

In her mid–forties now, she was slender, striking and a bit north of six feet tall. She had dark green eyes and long jet–black hair, with a few streaks of gray she made no effort to hide. You noticed Anna. Maybe I noticed her too much. It's a good thing she never chose a life of crime. She would have been easy to pick out in a police lineup.

She was soft–spoken and reserved, but not at all aloof. She had, as my grandmother used to say, a smile to make the crabby angel do back–flips. But Anna didn't smile much and almost never laughed. A misty sadness clung to her. If she ever wanted to talk about it, we were there, but it hadn't happened and we figured it never would.

Anna had a magnificently vulgar sense of humor, totally at odds with her elegant appearance. It would blow in without warning and disappear as quickly. Even her voice changed. She was embarrassed by it and thought there must be a medical reason why she turned into Bad Anna. Maybe it was an allergic reaction to candles, or a spirit curse that missed me and turned her into a potty–mouth demon. Whatever it was, Glenn and I hoped she never found the cure. Good Anna kept Bad Anna locked up in a desk drawer while Good Anna concentrated on being professional. She said someone had to maintain proper office decorum, and she didn't see anyone else volunteering. Point taken.

She dressed simply but stylishly, always in black, white and soft gray. I could see where the Annas of this world don't need to be flashy, but there didn't seem to be enough colors or casual Fridays in her world. Not that any sane person would ask Glenn or me for fashion advice.

Anna's family came to the United States from Hungary a few months before she was born. Her father was a university professor who incurred the wrath of the communist secret police by writing approvingly about the 1956 uprising. The family was ordered to leave Hungary immediately. So she was conceived in Hungary and born in the United States. I wondered if that gave her Catholic dual citizenship.

Anna didn't have an easy life before we met her. Her father was never able to match the status and income he had in Hungary. The family struggled. I knew she married right after high school. Her husband died five years later in a construction accident and left her with two young daughters. She never remarried, although I had to think there was a long line of men applying for the job.

She kept pictures of her daughters, both now in their twenties, on her desk. Anna lived with her older daughter in an apartment north of Boston. She was very proud of her daughters, who had recently graduated college. Anna never talked about herself, her late husband or anyone else in her family. I didn't know much else about her, except she was the best thing that ever happened to our office.

Anna walked in off the street twenty years ago and asked if she could apply for a job. We had no idea how she found us. It must have been right after her husband died. She was uncomfortable, and we guessed she really needed work. Her only office experience was some typing and filing she had done for an uncle with a small trucking business. Glenn and I weren't looking for office help, but we both knew immediately that Anna was something special. The firms we had worked at would have hired her on looks alone and used her as a reception area ornament. We could tell Anna didn't want to be stared at, and we didn't have a budget for ornaments. *Bradley and Tiernan* was scraping along quarter–to–quarter. It was crazy to even think about hiring her. Thank God for life's crazy decisions.

Glenn suggested we give Anna a secretarial test and, if she did well, offer to hire her for a few weeks to see how it worked out. She got close to a perfect score on the test and accepted our offer on the spot. No negotiating minuet, no playing hard to get. Let me show you what I can do. If you're unhappy for any reason, I'll walk away with no questions asked. Anna was at her desk two hours after she walked in. Piles of work started to disappear. She came in early, stayed late, and took home books from our library to read up on the things she was doing.

And clients loved her. One of our best clients, an elderly woman, told us if we weren't smart enough to keep Anna, she was going to find smarter lawyers to handle her business. She wasn't kidding. We offered Anna a permanent job. We'd find the money to pay her. A month later, our other secretary Christine unexpectedly left for California to "find her bliss." Glenn and I decided not to replace her if Anna would agree to run our office herself, at twice what we were then paying her. Before this morning, it was the only time I had ever seen Anna tear up. Christine wound up in a mani/pedi salon in Encino. Maybe that's bliss in California. All I know is hiring Anna was the personnel equivalent of buying a boatload of Amazon stock at the IPO.

If there was anything Anna couldn't do well, we never found it. And she almost never lost her cool, although Glenn and I gave her every opportunity. She would look at us, tilt her head, make a gesture with both hands as if breaking something, and say a couple of sentences in Hungarian. It was probably a compliment, but we thought it best not to ask for the translation. Things get lost in translation.

After she had been with us six months, Glenn remarked, "Anna certainly has a nice even keel, doesn't she?" Glenn didn't talk like a yacht club commodore, and I didn't think he was talking about Anna's composure. I told him whatever he meant, the answer was yes, she certainly did. It was usually a safe answer when Sara asked me something.

Anna called herself our secretary. Her title was office manager. The reality was she became our partner in everything but name. If she ever graduated law school, we would gladly have made it official. Glenn and I made sure Anna got paid well and first. We made few big office decisions without giving her an equal vote. Political correctness wasn't a factor. We weren't crazy. We knew we couldn't afford to lose her. The woman with the nice even keel also had a nice level head, and a gift for discreetly sweeping aside any obstacles we threw in front of her. As she modestly put it, it wasn't hard for her to triangulate to common sense when the other two legs of the triangle were certifiable. She might have phrased it a little better, but it was hard to deny.

I thought it was worth seeing if I could arrange for the Archangel Gabriel to discuss Glenn's situation directly with God, maybe over a glass or two of wine. Wine is probably all they drink in heaven. Maybe my Confirmation Saint Timothy could set up the meeting. I had never asked Timothy for any favors. Truth be told, I didn't know who he was. I picked Timothy as my role–model saint because it was the first name of my favorite college basketball player at the time. The basketball player wound up doing ten to twenty for armed robbery, but he remains the school's all–time leading scorer. Maybe Saint Timothy had something to do with that, but I hope he wasn't betting on the games. Gabriel and Timothy weren't going any place soon, so I told Anna I'd call Glenn first to see what we could do for him in the next few days.

As I was getting ready to make the call, I heard Anna engaged in an increasingly irritated telephone conversation. She was never loud. Usually I couldn't hear her from my office. Sometimes I couldn't hear her when we were in the same room. Something unpleasant was going down. Maybe she was talking to God about Glenn. Don't call him an imbecile, Anna. We might be asking for a miracle.

"Fine! If you don't hear from me in five minutes, come in at eleven. I'll see if an attorney is available."

She slammed down the phone and yelled something in Hungarian. This one certainly was not a compliment. There were only two attorneys in our office, and one of them said he was in Montreal. So maybe I should mosey on down to the men's room and talk to Anna as I passed her desk. She was fingering an unlighted cigarette. Anna didn't smoke. This wasn't going to be pretty.

"Sorry, Michael. It was that shithead John Bennett, Glenn's worst client. He made an appointment months ago for a will update. He canceled the day before, rescheduled, and never showed up. Then he called to schedule for this morning, canceled last Thursday, and now he's changed his mind and absolutely has to come in this morning. He says he's so busy and can't believe how hard it is to meet with an attorney around here. I told him Glenn isn't here, but he doesn't believe me. I should have talked to you first. He'll probably cancel in ten minutes anyway."

"Not a problem, Anna. It's only a will update. I'll talk to him if he shows up. If you don't mind me saying so, unfiltered cigarette is a good look for you. It's quite European."

Her eyes narrowed. Blow retreat, bugler.

"So, would you please grab the Bennett file?"

"Are you sure you want to do this? You're bucking for sainthood here."

"Ah, if Sister Diabla could only have heard you say that. She wrote me off as a lost cause. Now I might be Saint Michael of the Shithead Clients, patron saint of lawyers everywhere. Before we start the canonization paperwork, let me call Glenn." I dialed his cell number.

40

"Bonjour, mon ami. I was in the shower. I'm buck naked and dripping. This hotel doesn't have towels. How are things in balmy Boston?"

"They all have towels, Glenn. Put the phone down and find one. And it's two degrees cooler here than when you left, which takes it down to the mid–nineties. I love this global cooling. Is it better in Montreal?" Maybe he'd bite.

"Oh, much better. A little cold, even. I'll be wearing my wool sweater this morning. What can I do for you?"

"It's more what can we do for you. Anna and I want to move as many of your cases as we can while you're away. You don't need more things to think about, and it will take our minds off the heat. The first lucky client is John Bennett. He wants to come in this morning for that will update. Is it okay with you if I meet with him and draft whatever it is he wants? You can review it when you get back."

"Holy shit, not Bennett. Did he talk to Anna?"

"She took the call. She's sitting at her desk now, talking to an unlighted cigarette. Her eyes are flashing red. I'm afraid she'll spontaneously combust."

"Michael, I appreciate what you're doing, but don't meet with Bennett. He's a whack job. We were in Lions together and he glommed onto me. His late wife was a sweetheart. I did some estate planning for them. She passed away and now I'm stuck with him. He hates lawyers, but thinks he is one. He used to have one of those talk radio shows for conspiracy nuts and the forever outraged. Grunt radio. I was hoping to pay him off to go somewhere else, or at least get him in while Anna was on vacation. Bennett drives her over the cliff."

"I see that. Can you tell me why, so I can avoid lighting any fuses?"

"It's too late. Bennett makes appointments and cancels at the last minute or never shows up. I guess every office has clients like him, and we deal with them, right? He takes it to the next level. He'll call Anna, pretend to pull out his calendar, and run through various times he has available. Eventually, he hits one I can't make. It becomes the appointment he absolutely has to have. When Anna says it's not possible, he screams at her about how busy he is, how tired he gets having to deal with low–level staff, and could Anna please let him speak with her supervisor? I've told him Anna is the office supervisor. He can't get his brain around a woman in charge. Calls from Bennett always end with Anna slamming down the phone. Last time he called, we had to replace it. Good grief, who could possibly not want to talk to Anna? I've never seen anyone else get under her skin that way. But it's been a while since she pulled out the unlighted cigarette. That's DEFCON 2. He's well into his eighties and spends all day watching television. His only calendar is a TV Guide. You'd be canonized for meeting with him."

"That's the second time I've heard about sainthood today. Not likely, but I'll hedge my bets."

The infamous Mr. Bennett walked in promptly at eleven. At least when he shows up, he's on time. Then again, he lived only four blocks away.

42

I expected him to be larger than life, but Mr. Bennett was very short, very wide, and very unhappy. It was not quite a homo sapiens body, but I couldn't place it. I once saw a fish at the Aquarium that looked like him, a grouper, I think it was. Our office lights reflected off the top of his bald head and made me squint. I blocked him immediately after he walked through the door so he couldn't make it any closer to Anna's desk. There was no sense asking for trouble. I tried to position myself so they couldn't even see each other.

Anna was making a throaty sound that was unsettling. The last time I heard it, a German Shepherd bit me.

"Good morning. Mr. Bennett, is it?"

"It's eleven o'clock. Who else would it be? And who are you?"

"I'm Michael Tiernan, Glenn's partner. Glenn is away for a few days on urgent personal business. He's agreed to have me help you, if you wish."

"Are you a real lawyer?"

"For thirty–four years, Mr. Bennett."

"I don't care for lawyers. Human ticks. Have you ever written a will?"

"You mean start to finish? Maybe fifteen hundred, more or less, and I don't care for most lawyers either. Would you care to step into our conference room and tell me what you have in mind?"

I had to put more distance between Mr. Bennett and Anna. The throaty sound was getting louder. And I needed to move the top of Mr. Bennett's head out of the lights. I was getting dizzy.

We went into the conference room down the hall. Usually I offered to get clients coffee from our kitchenette, mostly so I could get some myself. I wasn't going to leave Mr. Bennett alone or ask Anna to bring us coffee. He would think he had put her in her place. Anna would never forgive herself if she caught a heel on the rug and spilled scalding coffee on him, accidentally of course. But Mr. Bennett made it clear he was not there to socialize in any way.

"Let me get to the point, Mr. Tinman. I'm a busy man. And I know you lawyers turn on the meter and then talk very slowly. I have one change I want made to my will. Clean and simple. I don't expect to pay a lot for a few words. Your partner overcharged my wife's estate something terrible, billed exorbitantly for things he never did. It was disgraceful and unethical. I've discussed his conduct with my professional friends in the Lions and they agree with me. I have their statements in writing in case I ever have use for them, so I know what I'm doing. Don't try anything. Do we understand each other?"

Mr. Bennett was quite the charmer.

"We do indeed. Glenn is honest and keeps good records, Mr. Bennett, but that's a discussion for another day. And I know exactly how busy you are. Rest assured my goal today is to get you out of here as quickly as possible. What change do you want?"

"In my present will, I disinherited my brother Henry. I have no children and left everything to my brothers and sisters, except Henry. You don't have to know why. Now I want to make one specific provision for Henry. Don't try to upsell me on anything else. I know how you bloodsuckers work."

44

Maybe I'd let Anna come in and show him what blood really looks like.

"Certainly, Mr. Bennett. We usually keep notes for the file, but I'll just say you didn't care to explain. I will ask you to write down Henry's full name, address, and a brief summary of how you wish to provide for him. It's so I can be sure I'm following your wishes exactly."

Yes, it was. And because I don't trust you as far as I can throw you, obnoxious little fish–man.

I forced myself to smile at him.

Mr. Bennett glared back at me, took a piece of paper, wrote on it for about twenty seconds, and slid it across the table. The paper had Henry's name and address, and the words 'He gets my fifty gold Krugerrands and not a goddamn thing more'.

"You certainly stated your wishes clearly. Fifty gold Krugerrands. They would be worth over sixty thousand dollars today. Will Henry know where to find them when the time comes?"

"What are you talking about? He'll never find them. That's the whole point."

"You're losing me, Mr. Bennett."

"They don't exist. Never did and never will. I don't even know what a Krugerrand looks like. I don't give a damn about shitbox third–world countries and their currency. It will drive the bastard crazy hunting for them. Henry doesn't respect me, thinks he's better than I am. Can you imagine? I'll get the last laugh from my grave. Now make the change."

I closed his file and stood up.

"I think we're done here, Mr. Bennett. I can't help you. You're looking for an accomplice, not an

45

attorney. No charge for the meeting. I'll show you out."

Mr. Bennett turned a glowing shade of crimson. It reminded me of sunset over Harvard Yard on a humid day. Even the top of his bald head went red. A pulsating red cue ball. How did he do it? He stood up slowly, made a sound similar to a hot–air balloon taking off and stretched up to the full majesty of his slightly under five feet, well, in platform heels. He sputtered for a few seconds, then hissed in the general direction of my navel. Sputter, hiss, sputter. The man was a walking steam radiator. I recalled the sound from grammar school and waited for the clanking pipes and the snow flurries of asbestos dust falling from the cracked ceiling tiles. It was a nice little trip down memory lane.

"This is the most unprofessional office I've ever dealt with, and you are nothing but a shyster. You agreed to change my will, and now you refuse. That, sir, is breach of contract. I know my law. You may expect to be hearing from the Board of Bar Overseers."

"Mr. Bennett, I think I would rather enjoy discussing our meeting with someone at the BBO. If I'm as unprofessional as you say, they must have quite a thick 'Michael Tinman' file by now, don't you think? Perhaps a staff person assigned only to me."

"Don't make fun of me. You're bluffing. You can't tell them anything. It's protected by attorney–client privilege. Did you sleep through professional ethics class in law school?"

"Mr. Bennett, there are so many things you don't understand, including the privilege. However, I do recall something else we went over in a class I was awake for. You told your faux Lions Glenn ripped off your wife's estate, lied about what he did and took money for it. And they agreed, even put it in writing. You can think whatever you want about Glenn. But when you start sharing your fantasies with other people and passing them off as facts, well, it becomes what we shysters call defamation. A serious tort, especially when you're spewing venom at one of the most respected lawyers in Boston. So you'd better be sure you can prove what you said about Glenn. Otherwise, there could be a large judgment against you, and maybe the rest of the Cowardly Lions too. Beaucoup Krugerrands. Get Judge Judy to explain it to you. I've seen the light, hallelujah, and I don't mean the one blinding me from the top of your skull. Now get your sorry ass out of here. If you have any trouble reaching the door handle, let me know."

Mr. Bennett never looked at Anna as he raged through the reception area. She raised the unlighted cigarette from between the middle fingers of her left hand and wished him a good day. Nice touch there, Anna. We braced ourselves for the slamming door and Mr. Bennett did not disappoint. He knocked two mugs off a nearby bookcase and left a third wobbling on the edge. A two–mug slam, so close to a triple. Not bad for an eighty–something swamp creature.

Our last memory of Mr. Bennett turned out to be a pleasant one. Anna stared at me for a moment, laughed, and threw the unlighted cigarette into her wastebasket.

"Michael, you're doing an amazing job so far taking care of Glenn's practice."

I did feel good. I made Anna laugh on an awful day for us, solved the Bennett dilemma and even defended the integrity of the legal profession. That must be enough miracles for a backstage pass to heaven's Inner Circle, and it wasn't even noon. Hello, Timothy, my man. You're looking good. Been working out? It's nice to finally meet you. Can I buy you a drink? I hope you have something up here stronger than wine.

I'll tell you what, God. Let's make a deal. Oh, sorry, it's Saint Michael, one of the new guys. No, I haven't been sworn in yet. I think I have to die first. How about you wipe my slate clean on miracles and we'll call it dead even? Make Glenn better. You can do that in your sleep. Think about it, and have your people get back to me. I'm in the book.

The lion in winter can still be a force to be reckoned with if he doesn't go to the well very often. It's time, Michael. How many lightning bolts do you need? And who ever thought I'd run into Mr. Bennett on the road to Damascus? Do it. You think too much and not all that well. Do it and don't look back.

But I had seen something unsettling, something I never saw before. Anna always wore long–sleeved blouses, even in heatwaves. I sometimes wondered why. When she gave Mr. Bennett her farewell salute, the sleeve of her blouse came unbuttoned and slid down close to her elbow. There was a long, nasty scar on her left forearm.

CHAPTER FOUR

I started thinking about my conversation with Glenn that morning. He said it was almost cold in Montreal. I went online and checked the Montreal weather. They were in a heatwave too, only a few degrees cooler than Boston. Unless he had signed up for the Meat Lockers of Montreal tour, there was no way Glenn was wearing a wool sweater today. Something wasn't adding up.

Glenn knew I fancied playing detective. He knew I would check out the Montreal weather. Was he telling me he wasn't in Montreal, or that he was dressing for winter in a heatwave? Tough call. Glenn had been known to make some strange fashion statements. When I called him later, I'd see if I could get him to give me an address or a local telephone number.

I had to start clearing my own calendar for the Ireland trip. Before I got into that, Anna and I would review the files on Glenn's desk. They might give us a clue as to what was going on.

The top two files were simple. The first was a cash real estate deal for the sale of an empty lot. Glenn represented the seller and all the information we needed was in the file. We could easily draft a deed, get it signed, run the closing numbers, and have everything waiting on Glenn's desk when he got back. I could notarize the deed, and I drove by the client's house every night on the way home from my commuter train stop. Piece of cake.

The second file was even easier. A small–estate probate – just one form to be signed and notarized for the Probate Court and one affidavit for recording at the Registry of Deeds. The fiduciary named in the will lived fifteen minutes from the other client. Two quick stops on the way home, and there would be two fewer distractions for Glenn when he returned. I'd take care of the filing and recording.

I called Glenn again.

"Hey, Glenn, sorry to bother you. I hope you're dressed, but spare me the details. I met with Mr. Bennett. I don't think you have to worry about him pestering you or Anna. I didn't even have to pay him off to go somewhere else. We'll need to replace a few mugs, though."

"Do I want to know the details?"

"Probably not."

I explained to Glenn what Anna and I were planning to do on his two files. And would he mind if we went through his other files to see if there were things we could do?

"Michael, I appreciate this, but I don't want you and Anna to go through a lot of trouble for me. I'm okay, promise."

I wished he could say that and mean it.

"No problem at all. I'll leave the files on your desk, or maybe on that new leather couch. It should get some use."

"You've been a good friend, better than I deserved. Thanks, and use the couch for anything you want. Just clean it."

"A weak stab at Brahmin humor there, Glenn? I'll share it with Anna. Now would you like to give me an address or phone number where you're staying, in case we have to reach you?"

"Send an email or text to my phone. I'll be back Friday morning. You worry too much."

Right, Glenn. As I began to sink deeply into bad scenarios, Anna appeared, holding a manila envelope.

"This came for you by courier. There's no return address. I'm afraid it might be from Bennett. Do you want me to run it under some water?"

I looked at the envelope. Same courier, but there was no red shamrock on this envelope.

"No, I think I was expecting it. On the other hand, it's missing something, so I suppose it could be from Bennett. Do you think we should offer someone down the hall ten bucks to go into an alley and open it?"

"Give me twenty and I'll do it. Less liability for you."

"Fifteen. And you can open it in the conference room. Close the door when you go in."

"You'll pay up front?"

"Why? What are you going to do with fifteen dollars if you're dead?"

"Ten now and seven if I come back. Final offer."

Anna was so much fun when she got into one of these moods. Why couldn't she do it more often? I pulled out a ten–dollar bill and handed it to her.

"Anna, if anything goes wrong, I'll miss you."

"That's sweet. And if anything goes wrong, you'll probably come into the conference room and take the ten dollars back. I'll see you in two minutes. Have another seven dollars waiting."

It was closer to ten minutes. I was starting to worry. Anna came back with the envelope opened.

"I can't believe how tightly this was sealed. I had to use my special tool. You owe me seven dollars."

I paid her and offered to throw in a three–dollar tip if she told me what the special tool was.

She said she'd rather take the seven dollars and not tell me.

The envelope contained a note from Aedan and a neatly–typed single sheet with names, account numbers, addresses, phone numbers, and email addresses. The crooked red shamrock was at the bottom of the note. It was smoking a crooked red pipe. If there's anything worse than a bad drawing, it's an embellished bad drawing.

Top of the morning to you, Michael. Such a dreadful expression. You'd never hear it in Ireland, save from an intoxicated Russian street vendor in a green cardboard hat.

I'm enclosing information on tickets and accommodations. You'll see my Aer Lingus account number. Book the best available flights and seats for you and Sara. They know me well and it's all authorized. Be sure to ask for premium seating. Quicker deaths if the plane goes down. Then please email my personal assistant, Aoife Mullaly, with the details. A delightful woman she is, what you Americans would call my fixer for many years. She'll make sure a decent car is waiting at the airport and finalize your accommodations at the B&B, all on my account, of course. And she'll see to it that a bottle of whiskey is delivered to your seats, a worthy peated single malt. Airline stock whiskey is piss, smells like it was distilled in an Ulster barn. I suppose it could serve as extra jet fuel in an emergency.

52

I'm sorry I must ask you and Sara for your passport information. The old biddy who runs the B&B insists upon it. She fears that Muslim terrorists will stay at her place and steal the towels. The fact is, we see few Muslim terrorists here. Western Ireland is not fertile ground for jihad, or anything else. If the roundabouts didn't get them, the pub food would. Martyrdom by potato. Don't you think that might be worth fewer virgins in paradise?

We'll humor Mrs. Carty, not that we have a choice. I've tried to convince her there are decent Muslims with better towels at home. She will hear none of it. So if you would please email that page of your passports to me, Aoife will handle Mrs. Carty.

Warmest regards, Aedan

Sara was home that afternoon. I called her and asked her to pull our passports out of the safe, scan the information pages, and email them to me.

"You have two passports. Which one do you want to use?"

I had recently gotten an Irish passport and had never used it. I was eligible for dual citizenship because my grandparents were born in Ireland.

"I think the Irish passport would be appropriate, don't you?"

"Absolutely. Once an Irishman, always an Irishman, isn't that what you say?"

"I say a lot of things. They don't all make sense. My Irish passport it is."

I forwarded the scanned passport pages to Aedan, with my thanks for his package. The response came back immediately.

An Irish passport, excellent. I knew you were eligible for Irish citizenship by ancestry. I'm pleased to see you availed yourself of it. We'll tap all the bases again before you leave, as you say over there.

Best, Aedan

Tap all the bases? Do we say that over here?

"Anna, let's put a dent in Glenn's files. Could you please draft up an affidavit of no tax due for the probate case? While you're doing that, I'll run the title for the real estate closing and then you can draft the deed. And please call both clients to see if I can swing by their homes after work this week for signings. It will save them a trip into the city."

Anna looked happier. The starting gate had opened.

"Certainly. Anything else I can do?" She had probably already done it.

"Yes, and you should do this one first. There was a note in Glenn's file that the real estate closing is next Monday, but I didn't see anything in his calendar. Could you please call the other lawyer to see if she knows what's going on here?"

"Sure. And he didn't tell me about the closing either. He never forgets to do that."

Ten minutes later, Anna was back. How does she do these things so quickly?

"The closing is on for 10:00 Monday at the Registry of Deeds. The other lawyer will do the settlement sheets and bring a certified check. You can email her a copy of the proposed deed. She said we could do the whole thing electronically, but she

54

likes to get out of her office now and then or she goes nuts."

I had to get my mind off Glenn for a few minutes. I started thinking about what the other lawyer told Anna – that she had to get out of her office now and then or she'd go nuts. I felt the same way, but I was surprised to hear it from a thirty–something lawyer.

Technology had made practicing law so impersonal. We do everything remotely now. Just a few years ago, we went to real buildings and met with real people. We turned paper pages in real books. Now it was all online.

I'd go days without seeing anyone outside the office. I could be sentenced to home confinement with an ankle bracelet and still run a busy law practice. Nobody would know. If you asked to meet physically with young lawyers now, they'd react like you suggested knocking off early and firebombing the White House.

A middle–aged lawyer friend told me that one of his young associates had a desk fifteen feet away, but would communicate with him only by tweet. My friend would print out a response and send it over to the associate by remote–controlled toy car. It was a generational technology duel. They only spoke if they were in the elevator together, and recognized each other.

Part of the fun and education used to be meeting clients and other lawyers in person. Treat an older lawyer to a two–drink lunch and you could learn as much about practicing law as you did in six months of law school. Nobody had time for that any more. You need some human contact, even if the client is a

Mr. Bennett. Maybe that wasn't human contact, but at least it was primate contact, I think.

Anna was back. The only downside of having Anna in the office was that you didn't get a chance to finish a lot of daydreams.

"You can stop by the probate client's house at 6:00 tonight, but he has to leave by 6:30 for a meeting. Then you can see the real estate client at 7:00 at the coffee shop next to her house. It's only a few minutes from your first stop, so it should be all right. I'll have everything ready for them to sign. And I told them Glenn was away for a few days."

"Perfect. The 6:00 will only take fifteen minutes. I hope the meeting he's going to is AA. The file says his wife died of acute alcohol poisoning and she probably wasn't drinking alone. Anna, you set up a meeting for me at a coffee shop? It scares me how good you are."

She shrugged.

"You work with someone twenty–three years and you get to know a few things about them."

Maybe not, or not enough. I thought it was closer to twenty years.

She left to make a phone call, and I resumed daydreaming. Maybe I'd have Anna coordinate with Aoife on the Ireland trip. Two Hall of Fame fixers working together. It could be a training film for student fixers. And after Anna and Aoife got all the trip details in place, they could put in an extra hour or so and get the Middle East all straightened out.

Anna materialized again.

"Yo, Michael. You're still daydreaming. Let's go. We have to get these documents finished."

Maybe Anna and Aoife wouldn't take the whole hour to clear up the Middle East.

Meeting clients at a coffee shop is so civilized. Legal documents and cappuccinos make a nice combination, if you keep a respectful distance between them. The probate client was going to an AA meeting. His wife drank herself to death and he was going down the same road. Good for you, taking control of your life, I told him. I hoped I was strong enough to do the same.

The evening caffeine worked its magic. I couldn't sleep, so I started putting together a list of things Anna and I should finish up before I left for Ireland. There was nothing too urgent. My practice now was mostly probate work. It was more of a cult, really, a dwindling but devoted following of dead people. I liked dead clients. They don't break appointments and don't complain that you didn't return their calls. I was glad I met Glenn's client. You want to meet some people who aren't afraid to look a demon in the eye and slap its face.

CHAPTER FIVE

I invited Anna to lunch the next day. I needed to talk to her and I didn't want any interruptions. Glenn and I occasionally had lunch with Anna, but she usually preferred to work straight through lunch and catch an earlier train home. Sometimes Sara would stop by on a slow afternoon and the four of us would go out for pizza and beer.

Sara and Anna got along well, although they were so different. Anna was tall, dark–haired and often too quiet. Sara was much shorter, blonde and extroverted. But it worked. They made time every month or so to go shopping with Anna's daughters, and Emma often joined them. Sara didn't get to know much about Anna either. She said Anna could talk intelligently about anything under the sun, from art to politics to where the extraterrestrials were hiding. She would never talk about herself.

I had asked Anna to pick the restaurant. She chose a Hungarian restaurant near our office. It was in an alley that I walked by every day and I no idea there was a restaurant there. I didn't see any signs. I guess if you had to ask, it wasn't the place for you.

The dining area was very dimly lighted. Maybe they didn't want you looking at the food, or maybe their patrons were working drug deals or affairs. Anna ordered for us without even squinting at the menu. And she did it in Hungarian, much to the delight of our waiter. Even in the dim light, I could see he was thinking how nice it would be to have Anna for his own lunch.

Fragrant, spicy dishes appeared at our table. Anna described each one as it came out. She said cooking was her creative outlet, and she definitely knew her Hungarian cuisine. I wished we had all afternoon, but I had to ease the conversation away from food.

"I'm glad we're doing this, Anna. We should have done things like this more often."

There was a long silence.

"Michael, are you hitting on me?"

Not what I expected. I was glad now that the lighting was dim, but she sounded so serious. Shit, well so much for Michael's smooth conversational segues. This was one I had to take off the table right away. It was also time to start being more honest, in all areas of my life. This could be a tough juggling act.

"No, Anna. I can't even see you, so I'd be guessing where to hit. If I had met you before Sara, yes, and you know that. I was happily married when you walked through our door and I'm happily married now. But you've been such an important part of my life for twenty–three years and I want to learn more about you. Is any part of what I just said an okay answer?"

"A perfect answer. You and Sara belong together. I would never do anything crazy and risk losing what we all have. I'm so sorry. It was a stupid question, but a wonderful answer."

I was glad to hear it. If Anna ever did decide to do something crazy, it would be hard for any man of sound mind to say no. Best never to find out if I was one of them.

"You wanted to talk, Michael, and it sounded like it was important. If you're not hitting on me, are you firing me?"

Now she was joking, right? At least I hoped so. If it wasn't Bad Anna, I could never tell for sure.

"It is important and we'd never fire you. It's been such a joy knowing and working with you and Glenn all these years. I regret not saying that more often. But nothing is forever. Glenn's sick, and I'm sick and tired. It's not clear to me how much longer we have. We need to think about those things and be ready. We owe it to each other. Glenn and I are not going to pull the rug out from under you. When the time comes, I have friends who will hire you, no questions asked. I'll make sure of it."

"It could never be the same. I'll be fine. Michael, everything you said today, every single word of it, means so much to me. I never told you much about my life. I'm not very interesting and a lot of it is still painful. I'm ready to bury that part, starting here, right now.

"So I'll make you an offer, counselor. I heard from Mrs. Boyle a while back that you might be connected upstairs. Make Glenn better and I'll tell you anything about me you want to know, within the bounds of decency, of course, and specifically excluding two nights of youthful indiscretion at the Lincoln Memorial. Deal?"

"Deal. You have become quite the lawyer, Anna. Someday I'll ask Lincoln if he remembers you. I'll bet he does. And I do have some people I can talk to about Glenn. Well, they're not actually people any more, but I'll see what they can do."

"Great. Lunch is on me. It's the least I can do. I'll remember this day for a very long time, Michael, and I'm so happy you want to know more about who I am. Not many people ever did."

She smiled a smile I had never seen before, and the crabby angel did his even–the–German–judge–is–blown–away backflip. And the rest of lunch was pretty wonderful too.

There must have been beautiful women I met along the way who were relieved to find out I wasn't hitting on them. Anna was the only one who said thanks by treating me to a fantastic lunch. And I had learned a few more things about her. She was a good cook and visited national monuments at night. I admired people who knew how to thoroughly enjoy our country's history. This honesty thing wasn't so bad after all. I might do it more often, maybe gradually increase the dose.

I couldn't stop thinking about what might have been. It burrows and it surfaces and it never really goes away. Honesty gets complicated. Maybe Grandpa Tom would have understood.

CHAPTER SIX

On Friday morning, Glenn walked in like nothing had ever happened.

"Good morning, people. The prodigal son has returned. It's a bit chilly today, isn't it?"

Anna and I looked at each other. The only question was who was going to do it. Anna did.

"Office meeting, gentlemen. I'll lock the front door."

We went into the conference room. There was no sense beating around the bush. It was my turn.

"Glenn, you had us worried out of our minds. Were you really in Montreal? What happened?"

"I was in Montreal, after a few days at the Mayo Clinic. Damn cool in Minnesota for July. I told you, there are some heavy hitters trying to figure out what's going on inside me. They're in agreement it's a malignant tumor, an aggressive one. Radiation and chemo won't work long. They have to get it out. And I was told down here it's inoperable because of where it's sitting.

"But there's a surgeon in Montreal who knows more about these tumors than anyone else. I met with her and she tells me it might be operable if a lot of things go well. My odds went up from zero, so I guess I had a good week. She wants to go in soon to take a look. If she thinks it's removable, she'll try to get it out then and there. It's a dangerous operation. This woman is the best and she's my only hope now. She wants a few more tests, and I'll have them done here. I'm thinking about scheduling the operation for the middle of next month. It can't wait any longer than that."

"Glenn, give me thirty seconds to talk to Anna. Cover your ears."

It only took fifteen seconds. I pulled Glenn's hands off his ears.

"Anna and I want to be there when you have the operation. I'll be back from Ireland by the 10th, and I'll come back earlier if I have to. There's nothing to discuss. I'm putting it to a vote and you don't have the votes to stop us. All those in favor of having Anna and Michael in Montreal for Glenn's cure, please raise your hands."

Anna and I raised our hands. Glenn smiled, then slowly raised his own hand.

"Thank you, Anna. Thank you, Michael. I'm outvoted, as usual. I wish I knew what to say."

"Just schedule the damn operation. Do it this morning and tell your surgeon not to do any rock climbing until it's over. And I'm lining up some help for your doctor. No reason to go into the details right now."

CHAPTER SEVEN

Sara and I had a comfortable flight to Ireland, arriving the day before we were to meet Aedan. We flew business class. Hey, Aedan wanted that. Nice big seats. The flight attendant said she could tell the ones who haven't flown business class. They sit down and immediately scrunch into a tight little ball.

Right after we reached cruising altitude, she brought us a box with a green bow and ribbon. There was a crooked red shamrock drawn on the box. It contained what I recognized to be a two–hundred dollar bottle of Irish whiskey, and a note from Aedan.

Please enjoy this with my compliments. I believe your Surgeon General advises against operating heavy equipment while consuming it, so it's best you do not take the controls of your plane unless it is a real emergency. I've crash–proofed the bottle.

Aoife will be waiting for you at the airport. She'll drive you to the B&B and leave the car for you. It's about a hundred and thirty kilometers and you are not used to driving on the other side of the road. It would be a shame if you had an accident and we could not meet. Especially so if this bottle is empty when you land. Our gardai are strict about such things.

But Aoife is an excellent driver and they all know her.

Sláinte, Aedan

I tried to imagine how we would recognize Aoife. I pictured a tall young redhead talking on two smartphones at the same time. Sara thought she would be about thirty, with a white lace blouse, eyes which shone like diamonds, and hair tied up with a black velvet band. Sara spent too much time at Saint Patrick's Day bar singalongs.

We were both wrong. Aoife was tiny, fiftyish and Japanese. She was holding a sign that said 'Michael and Sara, cead mile failte'. It had a crooked red shamrock drawn under the names. Aoife bowed when we introduced ourselves. She spoke perfect English with a British accent. In an hour or so, we were at the B&B. Aoife also knew how to work an accelerator.

She had negotiated everything in advance, and handed Mrs. Carty an envelope. Mrs. Carty opened it, slowly counted the bills inside, stared up and down at Sara and me, studied our passports, then nodded her head. As Aoife walked out, she winked at me and rolled her eyes.

Mrs. Carty was the grandmother you didn't much care to visit when you were young. And when your parents dragged you to see her, you made sure you kept your hands visible at all times. There was no warm and fuzzy "Treat my house as if it's your own" vibe.

Mrs. Carty didn't care for strangers in her house. That must have made it difficult to operate a B&B. She started by laying out the rules. Breakfast at half seven or you go hungry. And no smoking or weapons allowed on the premises. I told her we liked to eat at 7:30, didn't smoke and weren't packing. Mrs. Carty didn't look convinced. I had learned from Mrs. Boyle when to play the ace. I asked her how to get to the nearest Catholic church.

65

I knew it was only two blocks away, and the only way Sara and I would see the inside of it would be if we had a bathroom emergency walking past it to a pub. The ice was broken. Mrs. Carty smiled and handed Sara extra towels.

After an hour or so of listening to Mrs. Carty tell us how the world was going to hell in a handbasket, Sara and I excused ourselves and walked down the street and past the church, to the local pub. I wondered why there was always a pub within sight of a church.

Some local musicians were setting up to play trad. Sara requested the song about the girl whose eyes shone like diamonds and kept her hair tied up with a black velvet band. The musicians loved it. They asked Sara if she knew the girl in the song was a pickpocket who got an innocent man drunk and deported to an Australian penal colony for receiving stolen goods. Sara hadn't known, but it made her sing the song even louder. We slept well that night.

I asked Mrs. Carty if she would join us for breakfast. We had a nice conversation, mostly about Aedan. Mrs. Carty was fond of Aedan. He had helped her through a rough patch or two. He respected his elders. And even though he was wealthy now, Aedan never forgot where he was from. He put on no airs and had no use for Satan's toys. Apparently, Satan's toys did not include two–hundred–dollar bottles of Irish whiskey. The pity of it was, Aedan was going to burn in hell anyway. He had turned his back on Holy Mother Church. Mrs. Carty prayed for him every day. It might take a miracle, but she wouldn't give up.

66

It was hard not to respect Mrs. Carty. There were no gray areas in her life and she was genuinely concerned for Aedan. We excused ourselves before she could ask which services we would be attending tomorrow. Sara wanted to take a few pictures in the early morning light, and I wanted a last run–through of some family history folders.

And then it was time to meet Aedan Burns.

CHAPTER EIGHT

We headed out to the White Stag, arriving just ten minutes early. It had taken an hour to drive eight miles. Until the American brain is re–wired to stay on the left side of the road in Ireland, you keep pulling over, planning out the next quarter–mile, and forcing your hands not to move right.

It didn't help that we encountered a flock of sheep not willing to give up either side of the road. A border collie herding them finally felt sorry for us and neatly moved the sheep off the road. Maybe back home we should pay border collies to direct traffic at road work sites. They don't stand there texting and drinking coffee, and don't demand six–hour minimum shifts.

It was raining gently, a "soft day" the Irish call it. How do they grow anything here except fungus? Should I go in a few minutes early? Sara suggested I wait in the car until exactly noon. Aedan was a stickler for punctuality.

The White Stag overlooked rolling fields, with far–off mountains appearing and disappearing through swirling mist. Sara said she could easily fill up five hours doing sketches under her umbrella. She had her full field pack. It always held a good book and a flask of bourbon, in case she ran into a snake. I never met many snakes who weren't running for office, so I wasn't sure how it worked. Were you supposed to have a drink with the snake so it wouldn't bite you? And another drink to neutralize the venom when it did? Unless Sara ran into a lot of snakes and had trouble walking back, she'd join us for dinner at 5:00.

68

She said she would wait in the car for twenty minutes after I went in. I'd call her to let her know I had met Aedan and everything was okay. We agreed on code words to use. If she didn't get a call using the right words, and another one at 2:00, she was calling the police. There was a garda station less than a quarter–mile away, but I didn't want her to make things worse by driving there on the wrong side of the road.

Sara was enjoying this. She loved spy novels and it was an exciting break from our daily ruts. She said if she saw a large trash bag being thrown into the dumpster in the next hour, she was driving to the police station. We had decided double–lined trash bags might be an economical way to dispose of our mortal remains when the time came. Sara thought if you double–bagged and didn't overfill the bag, they'd pick it up curbside. Good burial plan. Hey, if I had to pay a few bucks extra to put Sara into two or even three bags, she was worth it.

I didn't think I would be seeing the inside of any dumpsters. I had checked Aedan out online and made a few calls to Ireland. I talked to a dean at one of his universities. He told me that Aedan was a bit strange, but legit, and I was in for one of the most interesting experiences of my life.

At noon, the convent bells across the street rang the Angelus. I felt like Gary Cooper in 'High Noon'. So I guess Sara was Grace Kelly. She was flattered by the comparison, but I had no idea if she would be as good with a gun as Grace Kelly turned out to be. It didn't surprise me. Grace Kelly had Mayo roots.

I walked into the pub with the Angelus bells still echoing. The place was empty except for a bartender setting up stools. The pub was just opening. I told him I was there to meet Aedan Burns. The bartender nodded, pointed to the back door and said, "Out yonder." I could see a deck and umbrella through the door window. "Out yonder?" Maybe this really was a western, a western Irish western. Should I spit on the floor before walking outside?

The bartender said Aedan had ordered lunch for us. It would be served at 1:00, after drinks and some small talk. My drink would be brought out in exactly five minutes. Aedan thought that was enough time for proper introductions. He knew I would show up right on time.

There was only one person on the deck. He was sitting at a table near the railing, his back to me, gazing out at the fields and singing softly. His table umbrella was down, but he had set up a miniature umbrella in a potted plant to cover his drink and an ashtray. There was a lighted cigar in the ashtray. I could see that the man was wearing glasses, but no jacket or hat. The back of his long–sleeved white jersey said, 'Top of the morning to ye'. It had a hand–drawn red shamrock.

"Excuse me, would you be Aedan Burns?" As if it could be anyone else.

The man rose and turned to greet me. He was taller and more angular than I expected. The shock of white hair alone would have made him visible from quite a distance, and he appeared younger than I knew he was. The glasses were sunglasses. He studied me and smiled.

"Yes, indeed, Aedan it is. Doctor Tiernan, I presume?"

"Only a juris doctor, but Michael Tiernan I am. I've looked forward to meeting you, Aedan."

"And I you. A most hearty welcome to Ireland. You are punctual. I like that. It signifies respect. Something sadly lacking in the world today, as I'm sure Mrs. Carty told you. Did you have any trouble identifying me?"

"Not really. There's nobody else on the deck. The dark glasses in the rain and the 'Top of the morning to ye' jersey helped narrow it down even more. And the Angelus bells made it easy to get here right on time."

"Ah, yes, the Angelus bells, a revered part of our culture. They tell an Irishman when it's acceptable to have the day's first drink. Since this is our red—letter day, I cheated and started a bit early. The jersey was bought from a Russian street vendor just for your benefit. I'll burn it later so nobody else ever sees me in it. I trust Sara is with you?"

"She is, thank you. The weather today is not conducive to outdoor painting, so she's off photographing and doing some pencil sketches. I hope she hasn't run into many snakes. Would you mind if I gave her a call to let her know we've met, and to join us in five hours?"

"Please do. Tell her I am anxious to meet her. I'll sit here quietly and see if I can figure out your code words. There is nothing to fear, you know, but better safe than sorry. Reassure the lovely Sara, and then please join me in a drink. And tell Sara not to worry about snakes. The good Saint Patrick drove them all into the English Parliament. The few that remain are mostly bishops. Give them some money for green fees and they'll move on."

I called Sara on my mobile phone. "Hi, honey. I've met Aedan and we'll be having lunch. We look forward to having you join us at 5:00. Remember, a wet parachute never destroyed a flock of inebriated Bolivian geese."

"Michael, what are you talking about? What the hell is going on in there?"

Our code word that I was okay was 'honey'.

"I'll call you again later, honey. No worries and happy photographing. If you see any snakes, just give them a few bucks. It's an Irish custom. Hangnails and gout, over and out."

Aedan examined his fingernails.

"So the code word was 'honey'. I've noticed couples of a certain age never use terms of endearment except as code. I suppose the words could have been 'inebriated Bolivian geese', but that's so overdone and would be rather beneath you. Tell me, Michael, what's your first impression of me?"

"Well, I already had a first impression of you from our communications and what I was able to find out about you before I came here. I have to say, the visual was pretty striking."

"How so? Should I be flattered?"

"Yes, I think so. Look at this through my eyes. I see a man sitting alone in the rain with his table umbrella down. The man has set up a flowerpot with a smaller umbrella to protect his drink and a lighted cigar. The man is wearing dark glasses, with no hat or jacket, and has his back to the door. So the first thing I see is a 'Top of the morning to ye' jersey with a crooked red shamrock. And the man scheduled the meeting so I wouldn't be seeing the jersey until just after morning ended. Can you see why someone might consider all of that striking?"

"I'm not sure. I didn't think the shamrock was crooked. So it's the flowerpot umbrella, isn't it? This is a good whiskey and the cigar is a Cuban. A prudent man covers his assets."

"Okay, you've got me there. I guess I had never seen a flowerpot with a drink umbrella saying 'Welcome to Jamaica, mon'. But dark glasses in the rain?"

"It makes perfect sense, and it's not considered rain here until sheep look up with mouths open and drown. When the sun next comes out, I won't have to go looking for my dark glasses."

"Aedan, I researched this. The sun comes out here about once every three months."

"So I'll be ready for it, won't I? I certainly don't want the sun sneaking up on me. The squinting and such, that's how you get baggy eyes. It's very logical. Here's what we'll do, Michael. In deference to your narrow definition of normalcy, we'll move inside to a table near the fireplace in a few minutes and continue our conversation. The fire will dry us out quickly.

"I must finish this fine cigar first. I've taken the liberty of ordering for us, and our lunch will be ready by that time. They have quite a good lamb stew here. It's really lamb, if you know what I mean. I've also ordered colcannon. It's a bit early for kale, so it might not be in top form. But it's a house specialty and worth the wager. When Sara joins us, I think we'll have crubeens. They are always tasty here. And then some Clare Island salmon for our entrée, unless you and Sara are not fish–eaters. Are you familiar with any of those dishes?"

"I'm familiar with what I always thought was lamb stew. And I've had colcannon, although I'm sure it was not as good as the White Stag's. Sara and I both love salmon. I must confess, I've never heard of crubeens."

"Let that be a surprise then. If you knew what they were, you might never try them. They are usually enjoyed as a pub snack later in the evening, but they make a fine appetizer as well. Don't bring any preconceived notions to the table, Michael. It's a good rule in dining and life.

"If you care to join me in a Cuban cigar after lunch, as I hope you will, we'll have to come back outside. We'll have more privacy here. It was a sad day in Ireland when they banned smoking inside pubs. The most productive meetings are those attended by fine whiskey and cigars. Do you not agree?"

"I do. We run the same type of meetings in Boston. The second hour is always more productive than the first. I'm no stranger to the whiskey, but I've never been a cigar smoker. This might be a good day to start. There are no preconceived notions for Michael Tiernan at the White Stag."

"Excellent. While we're inside, I'll have the barkeep dry off this table and raise the big umbrella. I'll also have him put a 'Reserved' sign on the table to add to your visual impressions. We may or may not get to some specifics as to why I asked you here. The main purpose of this meeting is for us to get to know each other better. That's important to me. I need to be absolutely sure you're the right man for

74

what I have in mind. I can only do it by conversing face–to–face. It won't hurt a bit. And if it does, I trust Mr. Green and some distinguished peated single malt will dull the pain.

"Tell me more about your aversion to cigars. It seems unnatural. A beautiful woman and a good cigar are two of life's great joys. I believe you already have the beautiful woman. Is your cigar aversion due to health concerns?"

"Probably. Also, they're expensive, and until recently we couldn't get Cuban cigars legally in the United States. President Obama re–established relations with Cuba, so it should be much easier now."

"Smart fellow, that Obama. Do you think he did it because he smoked them himself? Make them legal, you know, and perhaps avoid another scandal? Didn't one of your presidents get into some trouble with a cigar?"

"He wasn't smoking it and I doubt it was a Cuban. And yes, President Obama is a very smart fellow. He has Irish blood, you know."

"I do know. County Offaly. There are good people there. Your Mayor Walsh comes from even better stock. His people were from Connemara, County Galway. That's the best of Ireland, Mayo excepted. You don't have to worry about Galway or Mayo people putting sticky tape on their fingers and pretending to drop money into the collection basket. If you and I are fortunate enough to make it to heaven, we'll see streets full of men and women from Mayo and Galway. And I'll wager a few from Sligo will find a way to get in through the back door. But you'll look long and hard for an Ulster man,

Michael. The Good Lord won't send an Ulster man to hell. He can't bring himself to do that even to Satan. So he sends them back to Ulster as pigs. It's an upgrade for most of them.

"While I finish up this cigar, let me put your mind at ease about the ill effects of indulging in a Cuban or two. Did you study chemistry at university, Michael?"

"I did, but I wasn't very good at it."

"Nor was I. They use the letters C, H and O too much. Those are boring letters. I much prefer F, U and K. You get more predictable reactions from them. However, I did learn one useful fact. Do you know what you get when you mix Cuban cigar smoke with Irish whiskey?"

"I don't know. Emphysema? Liver disease? A messy divorce?"

"No, Michael. Such nonsense is what the medical and legal establishments would have you believe. It pays for their yachts. The truth is, when you mix Cuban cigar smoke with Irish whiskey, you get carbon dioxide and water. Perhaps a little vinegar on the side, acetic acid the chemists call it. That's why you shouldn't overdo. Too much vinegar roils the stomach. I limit myself to four cigars and five glasses of whiskey each day. I make exception for special occasions, naturally. Everything in moderation and the body adjusts accordingly."

"I'm surprised I didn't remember that from college chemistry. Does the whiskey have to be Irish and the cigar Cuban?"

"There's good research being done now on the whiskey part. Early findings suggest the better single–malt Scotch whiskies might work also.

Lesser spirits break down into embalming fluid or the chemical equivalent of cow urine."

"I have a law partner in Boston who might like to participate in those studies. And the cigar?"

"Oh, the cigar has to be Cuban, no doubt there. There's some special ingredient in Cuban tobacco that science does not yet understand. Non–Cuban cigars are deadly, Michael. You might just as well hold a gun to your head and pull the trigger. There's no taste in them anyway. Imagine smoking a turd wrapped in a sheet of yesterday's newspaper. You've got to give the commie bastards some credit. They have studied their chemistry.

"But let's move inside, shall we? Our barkeep Declan has signaled that lunch will be served in fifteen minutes. Very fortuitous timing. This cigar has exhausted its possibilities. You really should wear a hat in the Irish weather. You'll catch your death.

"We're getting to know each other, Michael. It's pleasant, isn't it? Please finish your drink. A younger, fresher one awaits you with lunch. Some of the best things in life are younger and fresher. Others require some age and seasoning. It's a wise and happy man who can distinguish them.

"Let me share my first impression of you, Michael. I knew you to be a lawyer, of course, with a touch of the frustrated Irish poet. When I turned to greet you, I knew right away you were a Tiernan. Did you wonder why I had my back to you? I needed to see it all at once. You have the unmistakable look and bearing of a Tiernan, one hundred and thirty years after your ancestors left Ireland. I have known a few

Tiernans and could have picked you out of a crowd. That alone makes it worth meeting you."

We moved inside to a wooden table by a cozy fire. A waiter brought out a basket of bread. Aedan spoke to him in Irish, and the waiter smiled and bowed. It reminded me of my lunch with Anna, except the language was different and the waiter wasn't leering. I could get used to this.

"Please, Michael, have some warm brown bread. We'll talk as our meal permits. Can you guess why I favor this pub, the White Stag?"

"I know the symbol of Saint Aedan is the stag, and you have a distinctive mane of white hair. Are you the White Stag?"

"You astonish me, Michael. I am lunching with Sherlock Holmes himself. Are you a fan of the great detective? I've thought of your White Stag theory and wish it was so, but alas, it is not. This establishment was already named when my hair was black as Cromwell's heart."

"I am a Sherlock Holmes fan, Aedan. I try to think the way he would, without the cocaine. It can drive Sara crazy. She uses other parts of her brain. If it's not because of your name, why the White Stag?"

"This property was a horse farm when my father Liam was a boy. They raised and trained racing ponies here. Some had considerable success throughout Europe. My father needed work to help feed his family. His own father John seldom worked, and mother Mary was sickly. My father was a small and surly lad, and seemed not too bright. It was a wonder he found a family willing to take him in. If he was growing up today, I suppose he'd be considered autistic or mentally challenged in some way, and there might be professional help for him. Back then, who would hire such an unsavory little misfit? Well, the farm owners here did. Good Catholics they were, in the best sense of the word, willing to give a troubled boy a chance. Many was the night they fed and warmed him at this very table before sending him home.

"My father's job was to clean out stalls and exercise the ponies. He loved those ponies and I think he almost became one of them. He surely looked like one. Liam could communicate with horses by a form of mental telepathy. Lord knows, he couldn't communicate with humans. He'd say something rude, and the womenfolk would smack him a good one. The men would try to cut him a new arsehole.

"Liam was afraid to get up on horses, so he'd exercise them by racing the ponies on foot to the hedges you saw from the deck. Quite a distance, it was. Word got out that a wee strange lad was testing his legs against the best racing ponies in Ireland. People came from far and away to watch and to wager. In Ireland, many folks will not watch anything without placing a wager. I've seen men in a pub wager on which person at another table will get up first to go for relief. A word to the wise on that one, Michael. Place your bet on the biggest woman. The size of the female bladder is inversely proportional to the size of everything else. It's another useful fact I learned in anatomy class at university. You'll pay for your drinks many times over.

"The all-knowing city folk would always wager on the pony. How could such a tiny boy beat a horse on foot to yonder hedgerows? The smart locals would put their money on my father, with very favorable odds. There seemed to be a jet engine tucked up his arse. It probably came from years running away from the gardai. Police seem to need twenty meters to reach their top speed. By the time they did, my father was in the next village selling what he had stolen. His credo was if you run fast and sell fast, you'll never wind up in Belfast. My father had to seek other work when the gardai started using dogs. Dogs are fast starters too, and better equipped than a portly garda to remove pieces of a young thief's buttocks. My father found honest employment right here, training and racing the other horses.

"Liam would be halfway to the hedgerow before the poor horse knew what hit him. And he knew which ones he could reach before each horse. But my father always let the horse almost catch him. It was partly so the horse would not get all depressed and consider taking its own life. It was also so the city folk would think that my father got a wee bit lucky, and keep betting against him. Some thought Liam even had an arrangement with the horses. Lose by a respectable distance, act upset, and there will be extra oats for you tonight. The locals would give my father a share of their winnings and he also got paid for exercising the horses. Liam was able to take good care of his own family growing up, and then mine after he took a wife.

"My father never forgot what he learned here, Michael. The value of hard work, taking responsibility, and how to separate pompous fools from their money. What better lessons could there be for a twisted lad? He would not have learned as much at Trinity or Oxford.

"The owners of the farm passed away, and their son turned the house into this pub. There's no farm here now, but he kept the fields, hedges and walls intact as tribute to his parents. It's a good son who honors his parents. I often sit on the deck and stare out over the fields. Sometimes I think I see my father, racing a pony and counting his money. And the pony never quite catches up.

"That's why I favor this pub, Michael. Whatever they paid my father, I've paid their son a thousand times in food and drink. This building probably floats on what I've put into the urinal. It's well worth it. Except for what the owners of this place did for my father, I'd be a petty thief today. Instead I got to study law and become a grand thief. I'm pulling your leg, of course.

"Thanks to my father's fast feet and ability to work out deals with other species, I was able to attend university. I was the first and I expect the last in my family to do so. I have no wife or descendants. The Burns line dies with me, Michael. That weighs heavily on me, very heavily indeed.

"I loved studying history when I was at university, especially the history of Western Ireland. I still do. I hope you won't think me vain if I tell you I know more about it than any other person alive. My parents wanted me to learn something they thought was more useful. Leave the graves undisturbed. If you won't be a priest, then study accounting. My father told me that's the next best thing to thinking like a horse. One ignores words of parental wisdom at one's peril, especially when one's parents are paying the tuition.

"I took a degree in accounting to make my parents happy. It may also have been because there were some lovely girls in my accounting classes. I married one of them. But I soon learned that I don't care for numbers. That can be a drawback for an accountant, don't you think? I much prefer words. I became a solicitor, as you did. Words are our stock in trade. We have so much in common, Michael.

"It was hard for a young man to resist the siren song of the law. Now I wish I had been tied more tightly to the mast. When you finally see the siren up close, you realize she's a vicious little whore with bad teeth and worse breath. I soon tired of trying to help despicable people take unfair advantage of other despicable people. I was able to build a steady practice handling real estate transactions for the Church. My mother accepted that I was in the service of God by putting together his land deals. Frankly, I thought it unfortunate that God would have to buy back what he had created. To be honest, I was a devout Catholic at the time and also saw myself serving God. They always asked for a discount on fees, but the clergy I dealt with seemed pious, genuinely committed to living by the Good Book. I considered myself more of a real estate broker for God than a solicitor.

"Then I came to see that Satan had infiltrated the Church, at least at some levels. Terrible things were being done to our young people and it was all denied and covered up. My firm tried to get compensation for two of the poor victims. We sought no criminal penalties, just remuneration for lives shattered. I was

82

perfectly willing to hate the sin while loving the sinner. Alas, some in the Church hierarchy seemed unable to so compartmentalize. I was branded a Judas. Legal work from the Church stopped. So I left the Church, as it had left me. It was a most difficult time for me professionally, personally and spiritually. It had been less than a year since my wife Fiona died in childbirth, and my infant daughter Maeve passed some months later. I sought comfort in drugs and I contemplated suicide. In a stupor, I believe I did pull the trigger one time, but the gun jammed. It was probably made in Ulster. My life since has been a quest for redemption, for closure, for purpose.

"When my parents passed away within the next year, it was two more crosses to bear, but the cloud had an unexpected silver lining. I was left very well situated financially. I was amazed to see how well my father had done. He kept it all hidden. He had the rare ability to think both like a horse and an accountant. And he loved going to work every day, although his office was a racing oval. Liam died on the job, last race of the day, a smoke and three winning tickets in his cold dead hand. My mother passed a month later, from boredom, I think.

"I found myself free to devote full attention to the work I really love, the history and mysteries of Western Ireland. As you know, I've written three books. The first was just a collection of stories I heard growing up. I suppose you would call them ghost stories or fairy tales. To my great surprise, it became a bestseller. I used the money to write two more books, scholarly works which were well received in the academic community. I was forced to buy tweed jackets and a pipe, and learn to look bemused. I'm now considered to be a somewhat bizarre but respected historian and my life has regained some purpose. I have achieved part of the redemption I sought, but not yet all of it. And that is where Michael Tiernan comes in.

"There is another quest I must complete. It revolves around the story of Grace O'Malley. Some of my friends in academic circles say it's a fool's errand. I don't believe them. I know things they don't know. I don't want to give you too much information to digest in one sitting. A mystery which has lasted more than four hundred years can wait another day or two if need be.

"I do ramble on, don't I? I hope you're finding this interesting. If not, take comfort in the fact that you're being well paid to listen. That's more than my students can say. I have a question before we lunch. Are you a writer yourself, Michael?"

"I want to be. It's a deferred dream of mine. I have too many deferred dreams. I've started to write several times and I always got distracted. I'm finding more time now, and I cling to the hope there's a good book in me waiting to come out."

"There probably is, but don't just wait for it to happen. You have to push it out, as if giving birth to a baby. And write something worthwhile, not something you piss out in a day or two to make a fast dollar. You are shaping your legacy. The world needs no more coming of age novels, the mind—numbing dreck about young girls who wake up one morning and are shocked to discover they have titties. Formulaic crap written by software programs. Then the authors get all teary about how they have

84

suffered for their so—called insights, and now it is the world's turn to suffer, for a fee. Most of us come of age quite successfully without marketing our pain. It's called life, Michael. We experience adversity and we rise above it. Even worse are the vampire novels. The lowest circle of hell is reserved for writers of vampire novels. It's getting quite full, so much so that bishops and serial killers get promoted to a higher circle."

"I'm not doing a vampire novel, and it's certainly not being written by a computer. Maybe that's why it's taking me so long. Aedan, wasn't Dracula written by an Irishman?"

"Indeed, Mr. Bram Stoker. Born in Dublin, although the book was written after he moved to London, so he gets no full credit from me. I must say, though, he is not to blame for how his work was abused by shameless profiteers. It's quite good. A clean point to Michael Tiernan on that exchange.

"Remember you're not a better writer or better person because you revel in exaggerated angst, self—created tragedy or tortured sentence fragments. There is no disgrace in using the English language as it was meant to be used, not imitating a drunk chimpanzee that stumbles onto a word processor. Think Ernest Hemingway. And there is no shame in the happy ending, in life or on paper. We shall be graded mostly on the ending. Some pain and poor choices along the way are simply part of being human, much like breathing or taking a dump. To paraphrase one of your very finest writers, we are not put here to wallow in self—pity and endure. We are put here to prevail and to prevail with some dignity. What sort of book is it that you wish to write, Michael?"

"I'm trying historical fiction. I've been fascinated by what I've learned about my ancestors in Ireland, before and after they emigrated to America. I hear their voices. They're talking to me. I don't think my own spirit ever really left Ireland. Sara thinks I'm crazy. I don't know who I am, Aedan. It worries me and it worries Sara. Should we be worried?"

"No, and yes. Sorry, but that's the way it is. Most writers hear voices. I do. It could be the songs of the past I'm hearing. The past communicates with us, but it alone chooses when and how to do so. The important thing is that the past must never dominate the conversation. It can consume you one small bite at a time, and you won't even see it happen. I have sometimes thought the Irish curse is not schizophrenia, but an unhealthy obsession with the dead. If you learn nothing else from me, Michael, learn this. Respect your past, but never become it. It is easier said than done. If the past starts to overtake you, do what my father would have done. Turn around quickly and give it a hard kick to the privates. Then finish the race and collect your winnings.

"In Irish folklore, Michael, fairies can be good or evil, and they are difficult to distinguish. Perhaps it is the fairies you are hearing. And do you know when they are most likely to howl? It is during periods of great change. If you are hearing them now, you are changing. Is that merely a legend? Perhaps, but it's never the smart way to bet.

"You and I have asked ourselves the same questions. That may be another reason why the fates

86

have brought us together. I believe we are going to do some great work. The work is its own reward, but the story will make a fine book and you shall write it. It is your legacy. You cannot choose not to write it. And this book shall make no reference to the brooding undead or adolescent titties.

"But I see that the stew and colcannnon are making their way to our table. Good food, good company and good conversation. Who could ask for more?"

"Aedan, am I being interviewed for something? It's been a long time and I've forgotten how to do it."

"Good. Then your answers will not be trite or rehearsed. We all interview for something or other every day, do we not? We don't call it an interview. I prefer to think we are learning from and about each other. And what have we learned so far? We share Mayo roots, a love of history and writing, respect for our past, somewhat similar career paths, and perhaps much more. People whose lives will be intertwined should know each other, don't you think?"

"Yes I do, Aedan. I certainly do."

CHAPTER NINE

Aedan was quiet during the first part of our lunch. He made some comments about the food, but his head was in another place. After twenty minutes or so, he snapped out of it and apologized. Our getting–to–know–you session resumed. I told Aedan about my work, Sara's artistic endeavors and Emma's academic plans. Aedan had tried painting, but said he didn't have the ability to transfer what he saw and heard onto canvas. He thought that, unlike writing, artistic ability was something you either had or you didn't, and if you didn't, no amount of hard work could make up for it. I was a little taken aback to hear him admit there was anything he couldn't do.

I warned Aedan that Sara was looking forward to discussing their female pirate ancestors. Not surprisingly, Aedan knew something about Jeanne de Clisson. Jeanne predated Grace O'Malley by a few hundred years, but Aedan thought that Grace might have been somewhat inspired by Jeanne. They were both educated noblewomen before they went rogue. They both retired undefeated and rich. Jeanne favored decapitation and targeted French nobility, while Grace was more inclined to the pistol, and targeted anyone who had something she could acquire. Grace usually didn't take prisoners. Jeanne would often let one or two captured sailors make it to shore to tell people what had happened. Good PR. Whatever their stylistic differences, these were not the women you wanted to see sailing over the horizon if you were the captain of a cargo ship.

At 2:00, I excused myself to visit the bathroom, but it really was to update Sara. Our code word for the second call was 'delicious'. I ducked around a corner behind the bar and made the call.

"Hi, Sara. Aedan and I are having a delicious lunch and getting to know each other. He's ordered a surprise for dinner, so bring your appetite."

"Forget lunch. What has he told you about the O'Malley Protocol?"

I wondered if she had seen snakes and self–medicated.

"Nothing yet. You read too many spy novels. He doesn't want us to be a black ops team."

"How do you know if he won't tell you anything? When do we get to liquidate some Russian spies? I'm a woman of action, like my pirate ancestor. Aargh!"

"You're not handling this well. It's only been two hours. Aedan has a plan and he's unfolding it at his own pace. I don't think it involves offing Russian spies, but I'll ask. You may get a chance to take out a Russian street vendor."

"Who is probably a spy. Aren't they all? Okay, big guy, we'll do it your way for now. If he doesn't break soon, I'm kicking that door in and he'll talk."

"Sara, take a pill. Have a drink. Throw away whatever you're reading. Just be here at 5:00."

When I returned to the table, Aedan was studying his fingernails again. I could see it coming.

"I trust the bathroom was clean enough for you. This meal is quite delicious, isn't it? I've always admired the word delicious. It's a reassuring word. I don't know why I thought of that. I do hope Sara is having a relaxing afternoon. I'm more anxious than ever now to meet her."

How does he keep doing this? Maybe he really is in black ops.

By 3:00, we had finished lunch. Aedan ordered liqueur and we talked more about politics, sports, and what hallucinogenic drugs James Joyce was on when he wrote *Finnegans Wake*. I told Aedan I had tried three times to make it through the book and had failed miserably. It was Aedan's favorite. He re-read it often and said it inspired him. Aedan gave me a tutorial on the Irish wake, and also the American wake, the "wake" for the Irish emigrating to America, never to be seen again. I could get into the idea of a wake for the living. I told Aedan it almost resembled a vampire funeral. He rolled his eyes. I was getting nervous now. It was almost 4:00 and not a word about the O'Malley Protocol. I was afraid I'd look over and see Rambo Sara kicking in the door.

Aedan suggested we move to the outside deck. Finally. Surely now I would find out why he asked me to come here. But there was no rushing Aedan. It had stopped raining. He studied the sky and proclaimed it to be perfect weather for a Cuban cigar and a proper drink. I was starting to wonder if any weather wasn't. Aedan signaled the bartender with a series of hand motions which seemed too elaborate for ordering two drinks. That was a little worrisome. Aedan probably had never been a third-base coach. I expected to see Irish ninjas jumping over the bar.

He opened his humidor and took out two Cuban cigars. He offered me one and gave me a brief lecture on the correct way to light it. Aedan couldn't not be a professor. After the lighting ceremony, he spent a few moments watching the smoke curl and drift away. He was a happy man. Two drinks appeared, neither served by a ninja.

"We should get down to brass tacks now. First, Michael, tell me something. Do you enjoy being a lawyer?"

"The short answer is no. I've been a lawyer for thirty–four years. The first ten were good. The next twenty started somewhere around okay and ratcheted down to barely tolerable. Now I'm filling time. I can't say I wake up with sharp pains in my stomach at the thought of going to work, but there's no fulfilment either. You try to convince yourself you're as good as you ever were, but it's a lie. You're burned to a crisp and everyone sees it except you. I've decided to wind it down soon and do things that light a fire in me."

NOW will you tell me?

"Excellent. You have defined the problem analytically and started to address it. I think what you described is common. We get stale. The work gets stale. People change. My own progression was more accelerated and I did feel the stomach pains. I can only imagine how bad they would have been had I stayed in accounting.

"But I don't think that one can ease out of law or any other profession. When the time is right, take your sword and plunge it into the siren's heart. Twist it to make sure the bitch is dead. Then walk away, head erect, eyes straight ahead. You'll find it exhilarating. And by the way, you'll be completely forgotten by your colleagues in a matter of weeks."

"That's poetic, Aedan. I'll keep it in mind."

"Please do. Now tell me something else. You have dual citizenship and I know your brain has spent thousands of hours in Ireland over the past ten years. How much do you really know about your family history in Ireland? Do you have any Irish, spoken or written?"

"No on the language. You're accurate about the time. I have the names, dates, places, but I wish I had more context, backstories. When my mother was with her Irish friends, they spoke Irish. When I came into the room, they switched to English. Please teach me Irish, I asked. No, you're American, you speak English. One of the reasons I had to work so hard on my family history is because my parents and grandparents told me so little of what they knew. Write your own story, they said, ours is not important to you anymore. Aedan, I didn't even know that my family was from Mayo until after my mother died. Sometimes it washes over me in a giant wave, my imagination runs berserk, and that's when I wonder if I'm still more Irish than American. Why else would any sane person spend so much effort trying to reconstruct the 1500s?"

"Well, perhaps you are not that sane, and there are many like you. Your parents were well–intentioned, never to be confused with being correct. Now to business. Did you do as I asked and transfer your files from your Connacht ancestry to a flash drive?"

At last.

"I did. I have two copies."

"Do you have them with you right now?"

"Yes. I transferred everything I had. Ten years' worth of research on one little flash drive. It may not be as organized as you'd prefer, because it's a work in progress and I use abbreviations."

"No problem. We're all works in progress and I'm good with abbreviations. I'm declaring this non—interview over. I'm prepared to offer you the job. Congratulations and condolences."

"Thank you. Does that mean you'll tell me the connection between Grace O'Malley and my ancestors? I sure can't see one, which is the whole point of what we're doing, right?"

"Perhaps you see but you do not yet observe. I'm afraid Sara must be patient for one or two more days. And you as well, of course. Let us enjoy the journey without focusing only on the destination. That will come soon enough. First, I must be convinced we can fully trust each other."

"How do we do that? If I didn't trust you, I wouldn't be here."

"Agreed, and you certainly wouldn't tell me that you had the flash drives on your person. I might have muscle in the next room waiting to take them from you and dispatch you to join your ancestors. On the other hand, how do I know you have the flash drives, or there is anything on them? Or that you didn't take out critical parts and replace them with Irish recipes? We are both somewhat at each other's mercy, aren't we?

"We are both clever men, Michael, but I do not yet know who is more clever. We are both distrustful by heritage and by profession. If we cannot trust each other, there is no sense working together. Therein lies the dilemma. I believe that a Mayo man will never take unfair advantage of another Mayo man, but do you?

"However, I think I have a solution, in the form of an offer. I don't expect an immediate answer. Please discuss it with Sara.

"I am prepared to purchase one of your flash drives for the sum of one hundred thousand U.S. dollars. And I will do that without first verifying what is on the drive. I will pay cash if you prefer, but that will cause you a problem at Customs. So I expect you'll want to give me some bank routing information and I'll have the money wired into any American bank you choose. When you have confirmed receipt, hand me the drive. You see, Michael, I trust you that the information is really there and I am not purchasing expensive dessert recipes.

"But you must trust me as well. How do you know that I will not find the information I am seeking, end our relationship, and use your information to open a treasure chest which may be worth a hundred times more than I paid you?

"You don't, so without mutual trust, our relationship must fail. I shall have an equal partnership agreement prepared for you to review and sign before we finalize our exchange. As lawyers, we both know those agreements might as well be written on toilet paper. I would rather we shake hands, look each other in the eye as Mayo men, and promise to be honest with each other. If we cannot do that, it means neither of us has found the man he was searching for."

"And if we do everything as you proposed?"

"Then I spend the night reviewing what you gave me. If it does not contain the clue, then you have made yourself some good money and I hope we shall exchange Christmas cards. If it does contain the clue, I'll recognize it. And then we shall meet again without delay to formulate a plan of action. The lock must be opened with two keys. One, I hope, is on the flash drive. If so, it will tell us where to find the other one. And I believe the other key is in your possession also, but not on the flash drive. Locating it may take good detective work and reflection on your part, but I should be the one guiding you. That's why this puzzle can only be solved by the two of us together. I do so love being vaguely sinister and inscrutable."

"You're good at it, Aedan. I love the symmetry of this. I told you I wouldn't be here if I didn't trust you. I'll go with my gut. I'm willing to accept your offer right now. There's one thing you should know before you commit. I went over every single file, line by line, and there is nothing that pointed me to any Grace O'Malley connection."

"As I said, you would not have identified it. Remember what Mr. Holmes taught us. The best hiding places are in plain view. The more space it takes up, the better it is hidden. I know what I'm looking for. Not everything is stored in an online database, Michael. The answers are not all sitting there in neat little packages waiting to be opened.

"But please discuss it with Sara before you give me your final answer. She may want to run it by her CIA friends. Oh, and you should never use those inexpensive mobile phones if you want privacy. They seem to always be on speaker and you don't even know it. Little voice transmitters they are, and the acoustics in here are quite good.

"If you and Sara are comfortable with my offer, we shall conclude the exchange on Monday at this time and place. Your banks will be open then. Perhaps you can use tomorrow to take in the beautiful Irish countryside. I hear there will be sun and you may never see it again here. Please tell Mrs. Carty you will be meeting me for church services first. She'll bring out the best towels and pastries for the rest of your stay.

"If you're a puzzle man, I'll give you another. I'm glad you share my appreciation of Sherlock Holmes. One of the Sherlock tales suggests a clue as to the nature of our venture. And I assure you again, everything we shall do is perfectly legal. Inspector Lestrade will not be needed."

"Aedan, I have two questions. I'm more than a hundred years removed from Ireland. You want to deal with another Mayo man. Are you saying I'm one even today?"

"You'll have to tell me. It's not just where you were born. A Mayo man hears our songs. He observes the Five Core Commandments, even if he does not attend church. And he makes difficult choices, often bad ones, and lives with the consequences. If all of those things describe you, then I suppose you could still be a Mayo man. And your second question?"

I thought about changing my question to ask about the Five Core Commandments, but there was something I wanted to know more.

"Why the red shamrocks?"

"Because Aedan likes to drop a clue every now and then, and everyone does green these days. A shamrock can also be red clover. There was a lot of

96

red clover in the fields where my father became a horse and plied his trade. I am color—blind and can't easily tell red from green, so it makes little difference to me. You know, Michael, there were two other questions I thought you might ask. You'll think of them at some point, I'll wager, and then we'll know better if you are a Mayo man.

"Now I believe I'll go freshen up. Take off this awful jersey and change into something more appropriate for dinner. Sara might be coming through that door any time now and I wouldn't want to get her upset."

CHAPTER TEN

Sara showed up a few minutes early. She came through the door in conventional fashion, using the doorknob and closing the door behind her. We were off to a good start. She had somehow found a way to change into a white lace blouse and dress slacks I had never seen before. That was probably an interesting story. Thankfully, no black velvet band.

Sara and Aedan hit it off immediately. He was genuinely interested to hear how Sara's people came down from Quebec to work in New England textile mills, as mine had come from Ireland to work in other mills just a few miles away. Sara had her own family history agenda. She wanted to get right to the important question – whose pirate ancestor was numero uno. Aedan was diplomatic. Jeanne de Clisson would, of course, be a worthy opponent in any maritime cage fight. But Grace O'Malley would win because she'd cheat.

Sara's stock with Aedan went even higher when the crubeens were served. Crubeens turned out to be broiled pigs' feet, eaten with bare hands. I recoiled when the platter appeared. Maybe they were the remains of Ulster men.

Sara's reaction was, "Oh, yummy." She told Aedan that she grew up with French–Canadian cooking, including pigs' feet stew, ragoût de pattes de cochon. She dove in.

But Sara really scored points when the subject turned to art. She didn't know as much about Irish artists as Aedan did, but she held her own. Aedan told her he had seen her work and was especially impressed by her Irish mountain scenes. She thanked him and asked why. Where we lived, she didn't get to paint mountains very often.

"Because your paintings tell our stories. Those mountains have watched over us for thousands of years. They share what they have seen with those who listen. You have listened. I no longer enjoy works that tell no stories. They are little more than exercises in self–indulgence. Do you remember when figure skaters were scored on their ability to trace circles and figure eights? It was such a waste. I much prefer a freestyle performance to render the audience slack–jawed, even if it does not succeed. You and I seem to share an artistic vision, Sara, although my medium is different. Have you ever tried to articulate what that vision is for you?"

"Well, I don't like the phrase artistic vision, Aedan, but I can't think of a better one. I heard someone say vision is the art of seeing what is invisible to others. Maybe that's close to what I try to do."

Aedan put his napkin down and looked at Sara. His smile disappeared.

"Remarkable, Sara. It was the Irish writer, Jonathan Swift, who said that. Let me show you something."

He reached into his briefcase and pulled out a stack of papers held together with a binder clip.

"These are class notes for courses I will be teaching at university in a few months. I've been working on them for the past several weeks and nobody else has seen them. Please look at the second page. I've never done a page in such a format."

Sara opened the notes to the second page. There were three inscriptions after the Foreword. The second inscription was what Sara had just told Aedan about vision, attributed to Jonathan Swift.

"I am more convinced than ever, Sara. The three of us meeting today is fate. I have made Michael a business proposition I want him to discuss with you before deciding. If you both accept my proposition, I expect there shall be another one later, a bit more long–term. And I'll predict it will have a very happy ending. I like happy endings. I wanted to meet you both before we set the wheels in motion.

"As I have told Michael, one of my gifts is judging people. I am seldom wrong. And I know I have today met two people with whom I wish my life to be interwoven."

"Thank you, Aedan. It's an honor to meet you as well. The pigs' feet were an unexpected bonus."

"Sara, do you consider yourself religious?"

"No. I was raised Catholic, of course, but the Church always seemed sexist to me. I wanted to be an altar girl, but was told there were no altar girls. Many priests looked like fat men with sweaty hands who couldn't do anything else. I do consider myself to be spiritual. An artist has to be spiritual. As far as religion, the Golden Rule says it all to me. Everything else is just fundraising. I hope I haven't offended you."

"Not at all. I somewhat agree. Our priests run less to fat, but many do have sweaty palms. It must be the grease. Or perhaps sweat glands are the only glands they are allowed to use. Most priests here are sincerely trying to do God's work, I think. The problem is more at the higher levels.

"I don't want you to think I'm playing a game of Twenty Questions, Sara, but as one who was raised

100

Catholic, you know the Ten Commandments. I believe only five of them need be followed. The others are so much religious rectal itch. Can you guess which ones I consider important? If you get four correct answers, there shall be more crubeens delivered to you."

Aedan and Sara were laughing so loudly now that other people were starting to look over at our table.

"If you don't mind, Aedan, could it be another drink instead? Pigs' feet go straight to my hips. Okay, let's see. To start off with, we can throw out the ones about not taking the Lord's name in vain and having to go to church on Sundays. I'd keep the ones about honoring your parents, not murdering anyone and not committing adultery. Those are big ones. I'd drop the one about bearing false witness against your neighbor. It can be fun at a party and the neighbor is probably doing it to you. I've never coveted my neighbor's wife, so it can go. See what I mean about sexism? I'm reserving the right to covet my neighbor's goods. If people didn't covet goods, our economy would collapse. So we're down to choosing between not stealing and not worshipping false gods. I'd keep the one about not stealing and get rid of the one about not worshipping false gods. Some false gods are pretty cool. Is my answer worth a drink, Aedan?"

Sara had reached cruising speed and it was only 6:00.

"Your answer, Sara, is worth the whole bar. You are indeed a nuanced Catholic. Michael, please accept my compliments on convincing Sara to marry you."

"Thank you, Aedan. I did get more than I deserved. Somehow I never thought of Sara's religious views as nuanced."

"Then you have learned something tonight, the Gospel according to Sara. Now to our main course. I've chosen the Clare Island salmon. Do either of you have an idea why it may be appropriate?"

Sara shook her head no. It was time for me to re-enter the conversation. Aedan and Sara had been yukking it up almost an hour.

"Clare Island in Clew Bay was Grace O'Malley's home and base of operations. The ruins of the Clan O'Malley castle are still there. Some think Grace is buried nearby in the Cistercian Abbey. I'll pass on the pigs' feet, thanks."

"Splendid, Michael. Exactly right. I am glad to see you've done your homework."

We ate and drank for another three hours. The conversation flowed as smoothly as the drinks which magically kept appearing. At Aedan's table, an empty glass was a personal insult to him.

Then Aoife appeared, greeting us again with a deep bow. She would lead us back to the B&B in her car, making sure we did not run afoul of the gardai. Aedan swore the police waited in the bushes across from the White Stag and targeted strangers as they came out. But the gardai knew better than to mess with Aoife. She had full immunity to escort Aedan or his guests anywhere they wanted to go, no matter how many pints or glasses they had quaffed. Screw with Aedan or Aoife and you could kiss your next promotion goodbye. After making sure we were safely delivered back to Mrs. Carty, Aoife would return to the White Stag and drive Aedan home.

Before we left, Aedan handed Sara a small bundle of hand–drawn maps, showing her how to get to some vistas he said were worthy of her consideration. Sara asked him to pick his favorite, and she would give him the best painting she could do of it. Aedan was delighted and immediately picked one.

"This has been a momentous day, my friends. Please talk things over. I suggest we meet here at 14:00 on Monday. If you accept my offer, I shall have Aoife wire the funds and then you can give me the flash drive. I'll review it in the afternoon and evening. If it contains what I'm looking for, we shall meet again Tuesday as early as possible, to formulate and commence a plan of action. And Sara, I may need your paramilitary assistance dealing with an artistically challenged Russian business acquaintance. He is giving Ireland a bad name. I believe your actions will be considered an exception to the relevant Core Commandment. We can discuss the details."

"Paramilitary assistance, Aedan? Whatever are you talking about?"

Aoife and Sara visited the ladies' room before we left. I thanked Aedan for his hospitality and offered to pay for dinner. He wouldn't even discuss it.

"You know, Michael, I may be losing my touch. I made a mental wager Aoife would be the first to visit the ladies' room. She has a bladder the size of a peanut. They went in together. I guess it's a wash, so to speak.

"While they are away, let me ask you a serious question. Please do not hesitate to tell me if I am out of line. Are you and Sara as happily married as you appear?"

"We are, I hope. I have to tell you, the road had deep potholes and the wheels almost came off. In the early years, Sara had a former boyfriend who had a hard time accepting she was married. They worked together at an art museum. I guess he never got to the Commandment about not coveting your neighbor's wife, and I didn't think Sara was doing enough to discourage him. I thought she enjoyed the attention he gave her and led him on. Then they had to do some traveling together on work assignments. My eyes got pretty green and I said ugly things I still regret. I was an idiot. Sara resented that I didn't trust her. It escalated, and we separated for almost a year. We were both so young and angry, Aedan. I didn't realize back then how important trust is. I deserved to lose Sara, but I hope those wounds are healed now. Maybe men shouldn't be allowed to have pretty female co–workers. Lead us not into temptation and all the rest."

"I know you are not serious about enforcing attractiveness standards in the workplace. What's sauce for the goose is sauce for the gander, is it not? I've seen online pictures of Anna Danos. Lead us not into temptation, indeed. She's quite stunning."

So he was researching Anna too, and he made sure I knew it.

"Among many other things. There was never anything between Anna and me. I can't say I wasn't tempted, and if I had met her before Sara, maybe a whole different ballgame, who knows? Like you said, you make your choices and live with the consequences, and you don't always get it wrong. I have a lot of baggage, Aedan, but infidelity isn't one of the suitcases. We're all observing the Core Commandments, at least I hope so."

"Good. I have a somewhat similar story, Michael. I did cheat on my wife, but not with another woman. I became married to my work and had nothing left for family. I have even wondered if my daughter Maeve was really my own. Such a lovely name, isn't it? It's an old family name. My wife died and we never got a chance to work things out. We both knew I deserted her when she needed me most. Now she and Maeve are gone, and so much of my life died with them. I try to find ways to make amends, but who is left to make amends to?

"Ah, but the ladies are returning, with light hearts and lighter bladders. I don't believe I've ever seen Aoife laughing so hard. What happens in the ladies' room stays in the ladies' room."

We walked to our car with Aoife. She greeted the local policeman standing about ten feet away. He tipped his hat to her and opened our doors for us. We drove slowly back to the B&B, Aoife in the lead. I knew Sara wasn't going to wait until we got back, so I gave her the details of Aedan's offer.

"Holy crapola, Michael. Are you serious? Jesus, Mary and John. A hundred Grover Clevelands for your family history files? What's in them? Where does this joker get his dough?"

"Stop talking like Edward G. Robinson, Sara, and I think it's Jesus, Mary and Joseph. I don't know what he's looking for. I couldn't find it. He's got the money because his father ran a successful hedge fund, and how did you know whose picture is on a thousand dollar bill?"

"*New York Times* crossword puzzle. We're going to do this, right?"

"Right. I trust Aedan. He thinks we're both honest Mayo men. But I want to talk to Glenn first. We're in uncharted waters on the partnership agreement. And I distinctly heard you tell Aedan you'd keep the Commandment about not stealing."

"Maybe some Commandments have wiggle room, but I wouldn't steal from Glenn. A woman has to stand for something, even when she can barely stand. Get his blessing, big guy."

"Sara, don't you have one more pill left you can take? Some weed, maybe?"

"After drinking this much? Are you trying to kill me? Remember, I kept that Commandment in the Core Five. If you don't mind, I'll sleep. Let's take a drive tomorrow and do some painting."

After we got back to the B&B, I called Glenn. We had an unusual partnership agreement. We each put half of our gross office income into a partnership account. We used the money to pay expenses and Anna's year–end bonus. It was a bonus for putting up with us for another year. If there was anything left over, and there usually wasn't, Glenn and I split it equally. I told Glenn about the offer. I'd put half of any money I got from Aedan into the partnership account. We had never had a client quite like Aedan.

"Don't be ridiculous, Michael, it's yours. You did the research on your own time. All I did was make fun of you. Besides, if I took half of your deal, I'd have to put half of my new office couch into the partnership account, and I don't know if they have deposit slips for furniture."

"Thanks, Glenn. Aedan specifically told me he wanted to be considered a client for our first meeting."

"Which is over. He was never an office client. He was just looking for a confidentiality shield. Look, I don't want any part of whatever fell out of any envelopes or anything else you get from Aedan Burns. If it would make you feel better, put whatever you want into the partnership account and designate it specifically to be added to Anna's bonus. I'll match it. I don't want to send more rain your way, but this might be a good year to jack up her bonus."

"I'll do that. We're going to prevail, Glenn. You're okay as Mayflower spawn go."

"Have another drink and get some sleep, Michael. You need it."

So we were going to do it. Coming at you, Grace O'Malley. And Jeanne de Clisson would clean your clock. They all cheat, Aedan. They're pirates, for God's sake.

CHAPTER ELEVEN

When we joined Mrs. Carty for breakfast the next morning, we told her we'd be meeting Aedan for church services, then heading out to do some painting. I went over all the Core Commandments in my head and didn't see anything that flat–out prohibited lying, except maybe about your neighbor.

Mrs. Carty blessed herself, looked at the ceiling, and murmured, "Thanks be to Christ for answering an old woman's prayers." Then she cooked a feast. It was too bad Sara didn't have much of an appetite. She had a splitting headache, probably a reaction to something she ate, she thought. Right, something she ate. Mrs. Carty was happy to give Sara a cup of tea with whiskey. Good for the headaches, you know. Sara had two cups and said she was feeling better. I wasn't sure that was the best medicine for what ailed Sara, especially at 7:30 in the morning.

We drove out, slowly, to the place most highly recommended by Aedan. Fortunately, it was only ten miles away. Sara set up her easel, took a few photographs and got to work. There was a magnificent mountain in the distance, bathed in dancing bright clouds and dark shadows. Aedan had a good eye too. And I had a backpack full of Grace O'Malley materials to go over again. I set up camp and started reading, hoping for an "ah–ha" moment. It never came.

Sara finished her first rough painting. She could fill in the details later from memory and photographs. But she wouldn't show it to me until a second one was done and she could look at them next to each other. After a quick picnic lunch, she was back at work on the second painting. I could see the shadows moving across Sara's field of vision, but the shadows weren't moving at all in my Grace O'Malley backpack. Sara told me to give it up. If my files contained the clue, Aedan would tell us what it was. He was paying us enough for it.

By the time it started to approach dusk, Sara was done with her second rough painting. Good. I wasn't ready yet for night–time drives in Ireland. We decided to go back to the B&B and walk to the pub for a late dinner. First, I asked to see her two rough paintings. Sara put them next to each other on some nearby rocks and we studied them together.

I liked both paintings. They were looser than usual for Sara, but I thought they captured the mountain. Or mountains. The painting she did in the morning showed two mountains, and the painting she did in the afternoon showed only one. I looked out into the distance. There was one mountain. I asked Sara if painting two mountains was artistic license.

"No, I definitely saw two mountains in the morning. Someone must have taken the other one while we were having lunch."

I told her I would be surprised if that had happened. The more plausible explanation was nature and Mrs. Carty's medicine took longer to undo the effects of our evening with Aedan than Sara expected. She acknowledged that might be a possibility. In any event, she preferred the painting with one mountain. The other was a little too loose. She said it resembled a baked Alaska. I was starting to understand what Sara meant when she told Aedan vision is the art of seeing what is invisible to others.

One more dinner with Aedan and she'd be painting mountain ranges nobody else would ever see.

We made it back to the B&B uneventfully and had a nice time at the pub. But there would be no falling asleep early. Mrs. Carty had gospel prayer group at the B&B late into Sunday night, and the singing got loud. So I guess we did attend Sunday church services in a way.

I looked over my files one last time and thought I heard a faint voice calling out when I got to the Sligo ancestors. There were so many people screeching downstairs, I couldn't be sure. I fell asleep reading and woke up at 3:00 a.m. My notes had been put back in order and all the lights in our room were turned off. Sara must have done it, but she said she hadn't when I asked her about it in the morning.

We met Aedan at the White Stag a little after 2:00. He was a few minutes late, for which he apologized profusely. He had run into Mrs. Carty. She insisted they hold hands and give thanks to the Lord for the new lamb in his flock. Aedan let her pick the words. It had been a long time since he last talked to the Lord.

"So, my friends, do we have an arrangement?"

"We do, Aedan. Sara and I most appreciate your kind offer."

"Excellent. I've had one of my solicitor friends prepare a simple one–page agreement memorializing it, and stating we are equal partners in whatever financial benefits accrue. Here it is. I have already signed it. When you are ready to sign both originals,

Michael, we shall proceed. Do you have the flash drive with you today?"

"I do. I'll sign right now. I wouldn't know what makes an Irish contract enforceable, but it looks like what I expected, and I trust you. May I borrow a pen?"

"Of course. I'll call Aoife now and have her transfer the funds. Is this the wire information? I expect you may call your bank in a half hour or so to confirm receipt. Aoife will make sure the necessary government forms are filled out."

He took out his cell phone and asked Aoife to come in from the next room.

"Fire away, Aoife. Here is the wire information. Try not to hit any inebriated Bolivian geese."

Aoife bowed and left.

"I deserved that, Aedan, but I hope you'll explain it to Aoife."

"No need. She disregards most of what I say except the actual instructions. One learns from experience. Now, I believe we have time for a quick lunch. I hope you will not consider me rude, but after we have completed the exchange, I shall be most anxious to get back to my rooms and start reviewing the contents of your flash drive. I suggest we meet again here tomorrow, same time, for lunch and I hope some intense strategizing. If your files contain the key, we must strike while the iron is hot. I may have another business proposition for you, and perhaps more crubeens for Sara."

"Thanks, Aedan. Do you really want me here? I know so little about the work you and Michael are doing."

"But you and Michael are a good team and it would be more enjoyable for me if you were here. Also, you may learn something about Grace O'Malley, perhaps a weakness you can pass along to Jeanne de Clisson in case they ever engage each other in the afterlife."

"Since you put it that way, how can I say no? Thank you again, Aedan. I have a rough painting I'd like you to look at. It's not done, but these are the bones. It will be for you. I want you to be honest. If this painting isn't going anywhere, I'll scrap it and do one right."

She opened her portfolio and showed him the painting of the one mountain. Aedan studied it.

"It's extraordinary, Sara, and I'm being quite honest with you. I know this mountain well. I have heard it speak, but I never heard what it told you. The mountain took you into its confidence. Does this make any sense?"

"To an artist, it makes all the sense in the world. You have paid me a high compliment."

"And you have paid me the same. I shall be honored to own it, Sara."

I was tempted to share with Aedan what the other mountain started to tell Sara, but maybe the mountain should tell its own story to the person who kidnapped it while we were eating lunch.

Aoife called Aedan to tell him the wire had gone through and every Bolivian goose was accounted for. Lunch was being served. Fish and chips and Guinness all around, culinary perfection. As we finished, Aedan suggested I call my bank to confirm receipt. I excused myself and stepped outside. I recognized the voice on the other end of the call.

"Hi, Kathy. Michael Tiernan calling from Ireland. Did any money just get wired into my account?"

"Let me check. Okay, I'm pulling it up. Is Sara with you? I hope you're both having a great time. Yes, one hundred thousand dollars arrived a few minutes ago and it's safely in your account. Throw down a Guinness for me."

"Consider it done, Kathy. You're my favorite banker."

"It's confirmed, Aedan. Here's the flash drive. Let me know if you can't figure out any of my shorthand or if you have any questions."

Aedan put the drive into his briefcase and raised his glass.

"To the partnership."

Sara and I raised ours. Sara said it for us.

"Hear, hear. To the partnership, and jolly long lives to the partners."

Aedan stood up, smiling.

"Hear, hear. You must excuse me now. I have much homework to do before our next meeting. But please don't run off. I've told Declan to honor your every request, and your money will never be accepted here. I take very good care of Declan. Perhaps you might celebrate our new venture by enjoying these on the deck."

He handed me two Cuban cigars, a cutting tool, and a book of matches from a Havana hotel.

"I'll see you both tomorrow, same time, same place." And he was gone.

Sara looked at the cigars. I don't think she had ever seen one so close. It was the same look I had given the pigs' feet.

"You don't have to do it, Sara."

"Pig's butt I don't. We made ourselves a hundred Grover Clevelands, cowboy. Let's step outside and have ourselves a cee–gar. Tell Declan to leave the bottle."

"Sara, never call a Cuban a cee–gar. Life is about respect. I'm starting to worry about these mood swings of yours, not to mention seeing mountains not really there."

"They were there. You didn't see them. Don't worry, I'm having the time of my life. We are so doing the proper thing. Michael, I hope you're feeling it too."

"I am. And to think I could have sent the second envelope back to the courier. We never would have known. It makes you wonder what other things we passed on along the way."

"Life gets weird, right? I've thought the same thing. But you nailed this one. Hey, I've got a female pirate ancestor too. Do you think anyone would pay me a lot of money for a flash drive?"

"Maybe.You'd have to load the drive first. Ask me again in ten years. That's how much time it took me."

"Oooh, take that, Sara. Is it true you saw nothing connecting your family to Grace O'Malley? You're so thorough, and you spend so much time on this. Something should have jumped out, if it indeed existed."

"Nothing jumped. I ran all my files by name, location, time period, occupation, everything I could think of. No luck. For now, I may move to Aedan's other puzzle and curl up with a little Sherlock

114

Holmes. First, do you want to have a cigar and celebrate by plundering a ship or two?"

"I'm ready to shiver your timbers, matey. Dibs on executing the captains. Let's have a drink and a cee–gar, then go set off some fireworks. The seventeenth great–granddaughter of Jeanne de Clisson will be respected or the hounds of hell will be loosed! Declan, more grog here if you value yer life."

The game was afoot, at last. Sherlock Holmes or Grace O'Malley, I needed one of them to tell me what was going on.

CHAPTER TWELVE

Sara and I returned to the White Stag Tuesday afternoon at 2:00. Aedan was waiting for us on the deck, but with no cigar. And he was drinking coffee. There must have been a problem with the Angelus bells.

"Good afternoon once again, partners. Michael, I believe I have confused you with my coffee cup. I grant you, it is not something you will often see in front of me past noon. I fear I may not be the man I once was. I stayed up the entire night and through this morning reading your files. I sit before you happy, but exhausted. And I have a matter of some importance I must attend to in Dublin, one which will keep me there overnight. I'm afraid our brainstorming session will have to be postponed for a day. Perhaps we can regroup here tomorrow, say at noon? I extend my deepest apologies."

Aedan looked awful. Whatever he had to do in Dublin must be very important.

"Sara and I are at your disposal, Aedan. We'll be here and please don't apologize. When you say postponed, I hope that means you found what you were looking for."

"And more. It is clear to me now what I must do. Only the details need be worked out. Your flash drive was worth every penny I paid for it. Friends, you must think I am trying to keep you in perpetual suspense. I assure you that will end tomorrow.

"But I believe I can make today's visit to the White Stag worthwhile for you. I am offering you another business arrangement, an extension of what we already discussed. I suppose the proposal is to

116

you, Michael, but Sara must agree to it. I respect our partnership, and yours.

"Michael, I found your work to be illuminating. It took me down familiar roads, but also roads I had forgotten existed or never knew about. It is not often Aedan Burns pulls an all–nighter. Your narratives soared. You infused your work with vitality, context, and reverence. Sadly, you also infused it with many inaccuracies, but it was not entirely your fault. It is difficult to do such work from three thousand miles away. It was a most productive night. Did you know the sun still comes over the horizon in the morning? I had not seen sunrise since I was at university, returning from a night of revelry.

"So here is my proposition. I wish to engage your services to work with me on finding Grace O'Malley, bringing her back to life. Most of your work can be done in America, but I would be happy to have you return to Ireland at my expense whenever it would serve your purposes. The period of employment is five months starting today. That will take us through the end of the year, which may or may not be enough time. I expect we can communicate mostly by email, telephone or videoconference, although it might dismay your local courier.

"I will not insult you by asking for time sheets. I know you will expend the appropriate effort. I shall pay you in advance for the entire five months. Your compensation for the term is four hundred and twenty–five thousand dollars total, paid immediately. Even if we solve the puzzle in the first two days, the full sum is yours. If we have not

117

solved it in five months, then we decide together where to go from there.

"I hope you have noticed two things so far. First, I trust you. And second, the compensation is a multiple of my lucky number eighty–five. I want to give us every advantage. I believe you have referred to it as hedging one's bets. That is good business, and it was the green hedgerows of Ireland that made it possible for me to send Mr. Green to extend my greetings.

"My solicitor friend has prepared another one–page agreement for your review. Sign it, and within five minutes Aoife will be sending another four hundred and twenty–five thousand dollars through the ether to your bank account. Feel free to confirm receipt while you are here. I shall wait a few minutes while you do, and while Aoife brings the car around. With these tiresome business details out of the way, you can have a nice lunch, but I'm afraid I must be on my way. We can discuss more specifics tomorrow."

I looked at Sara. Her jaw had dropped. Aedan was saying this in such a matter–of–fact voice, like he did it every day.

"Aedan, I know I shouldn't negotiate against myself, but aren't you being far too generous? How much do you know about me and what I can do to help you?"

"I know more than you think and I learn more each day. My father's blood runs through my veins and his ability to make good wagers runs through my bank accounts. You are the man to help me complete my unfinished business.

"Michael and Sara, I am getting older. I have no wife or children. I have more money than I can spend. Those are just plain facts. And I am a man of simple tastes, whiskey and cigars excepted. I could spend this money on a villa I would never use, in some dreadful country where they think white wine is an acceptable drink. Or I can use it in the service of my passion, to cement my legacy and help create a legacy for you. For me, it's an easy choice. I hope you will trust me on everything, but at least trust me on this. Aedan Burns knows how to play the odds. It is the most valuable thing he inherited from his father. If you require a few moments and some privacy to discuss this, I'll excuse myself and get another cup of coffee. It will amuse Declan no end."

I looked again at Sara. She nodded her head yes.

"We don't need more time, Aedan. We're in, and we can't thank you enough for everything you've done. I won't disappoint you. I'll sign the agreement right now."

"Wonderful. You are very decisive. I am sure I will not be disappointed. Are you sure you can do this and keep up with the other responsibilities of your office? That is another partnership I must respect."

"Yes. Glenn, Anna and I take care of each other. I have to keep several days free in about two weeks, to help Glenn get through a medical issue he's having. Except for that, I'll spend whatever time it takes to get this done. You can absolutely trust me."

I signed both originals and handed one back to Aedan. He had already signed them. I thought I saw a tear in his eye as he put the original in his briefcase. Then he called Aoife on his mobile phone.

"We have ignition. We have lift—off. Please bring the car around in thirty minutes."

Sara and I both stared at him.

"Well, I enjoy coded messages also. I always wanted to say it and never found the right opportunity."

I guess it was better than "Houston, we've had a problem."

Aedan insisted Sara try the lamb stew and colcannon, because they were the White Stag's signature dishes. So he ordered again for us, but just a cup of oatmeal and more coffee for himself. He said he was too tired to eat much and wanted to be off to Dublin as soon as we confirmed the wire transfer. Sara and I ordered coffee as well. We weren't going to let him drink alone. The Irish used to make far and away the world's worst cup of coffee. They probably tortured prisoners by threatening to make them drink it. It's a lot better now.

Aedan was quieter than the day before, but still controlled the conversation.

"Sara, are you happy in your work?"

"Yes, I am. There are days I wonder if I'm hiding from more important things, but mostly I get to choose from interesting possibilities every day. Sometimes I don't get them right, and I want to throw in the towel. Then I try to learn from my mistakes and grow. It never really gets old."

"Nor will you. Do you see, Michael? An historian and an artist whose work fulfils them, and two

120

lawyers whose work did not. May one draw conclusions? Here is one I have drawn. Reading your narratives last night convinced me you must spend more time writing, Michael. It is in you."

"Thanks, Aedan, I will. I want to leave footprints. I don't want my legacy to be he always answered his text messages quickly."

"Well, Emma is a good legacy, never forget. But I see your point. A book is part of your legacy, even if only a few people ever read it. However, they must be the right people. Now perhaps this would be a good time for you to confirm your money has made its way across the pond. And please say hello to Kathy for me."

I excused myself and went outside to call the bank. How does he keep doing this?

"Hi, Kathy, Michael Tiernan one more time. Did more money from Ireland land in my account this morning?"

"Hi, Michael. Yes, it did. A little more than four hundred and twenty–five thousand dollars this time, after the exchange. You and Sara must be having a very good time over there."

"We are. And I had a pint for you, maybe more than one. Thanks, Kathy."

I told Aedan that I was now officially on his payroll, and he smiled.

"Splendid. You must excuse me now. Aoife is waiting outside to bring me to Dublin. I shall return in the morning with wonderful stories to share about Grace O'Malley.

"But please don't leave because I must. I suggest you have a drink or two, something more satisfying than French Roast. And Declan keeps a supply of

121

my Cuban cigars if you care to indulge. Sara, I hope I do not offend you by offering you cigars?"

"Not at all, Aedan. Thank you for opening my eyes. You were right when you told Michael, those commie bastards certainly know their chemistry."

"And so does Aedan Burns. But remember, my friends, everything in moderation."

Aedan walked away, too slowly. You're getting old for all–nighters, partner. I insisted on carrying his heavy briefcase for him. Aoife was sitting in a car outside, talking to a policeman. Nothing to see here, officer. Please move along now.

By the time I returned to the table, Sara had gotten us real drinks, nothing ground from beans, and had picked up three cigars from Declan. Three? Maybe she was imagining other people now, not just mountains.

"Michael, whenever we come to the White Stag, we have wonderful food and Cuban cigars, and we make a pile of money. Can we keep coming here? What was in those files?"

"I wish I knew. I think he found something he wasn't expecting. And Aedan said you'd enjoy the White Stag. You should finish up his painting before this good living makes you soft and lazy. Haven't you told me that a good artist has to stay a little hungry?"

"And a smart artist adapts to changing circumstances. You're right. Why don't we drive back to those mountains tomorrow after you meet with Aedan?"

"I think you mean mountain. I don't know if we'll have time. I hope it's a long meeting, and Aedan wants you there too. You seem to inspire him."

"I'm glad you think so. He's changing me, Michael. I never would have smoked a cigar if I hadn't met him."

"That might be a good epitaph for you, matey."

Before we returned to the B&B, I called Anna. Everything was under control at the office, and Glenn was confirmed for surgery two weeks from yesterday in Montreal. His surgeon didn't want any more delay. Glenn's only living relative was his sister Patricia, who lived a few miles from Glenn. Anna overheard Glenn call her. Patricia told Glenn it would be impossible for her to make it to Montreal for the surgery. She had so many other things scheduled. She'd try to check on him when he got back, and would he please excuse her now? She was late for spa. You like to think when the chips are down, blood rises to the occasion. Families don't always work the way you think.

Glenn had to check into the hospital the Friday before the operation. Anna was going to go up a few hours later with her older daughter Kata to make sure everything was in place. Glenn wanted to go to Montreal by himself to meet with his doctor before any of us got there. I'd fly up Saturday morning. Sara had a gallery opening she had to attend on Saturday, but she'd fly up at night or Sunday morning. Anna would book a hotel room for herself and Kata, and one for Sara and me. I'd get someone to cover the office for a few days. At least Glenn would have the whole team there for him.

Anna asked how things were going in Ireland, but she was just being polite. I told her I was in meetings with Aedan Burns about working on a project together. The details could wait. Anna didn't push it. She did say Glenn was happy we would all be in Montreal for the operation, and his surgeon was somewhat encouraged by the results of Glenn's last tests. But this was a horrible tumor and she couldn't promise anything.

Except she wouldn't do any rock climbing before the operation.

CHAPTER THIRTEEN

We had breakfast with Mrs. Carty on Wednesday morning. She was in a good mood. Aedan appeared to be coming back to the Lord since Sara and I arrived. It was not for her to know why, she said, she was merely an old foot–soldier in the army of Christ. But the Lord certainly did work in mysterious ways. She had probably noticed the cigar sticking out of Sara's jacket pocket. I told her yes, there was no doubt that Aedan, Sara and I were all experiencing the power of Grace. Another pile of fresh towels and a plate of pastries appeared.

Before we left, Mrs. Carty handed me a pack of crucifixion prayer cards to give to Aedan. He was sitting alone on the deck when we arrived. There was a muffin and a pitcher of water in front of him instead of coffee, and he looked more awake than he had yesterday. He was gazing out over the fields and singing softly, as he had been when I first met him.

"Good morning, my friends. I see that you have brought me a gift from Mrs. Carty. I do look forward to receiving her religious propaganda. It makes grand kindling. I'm not sure why she thinks pictures of a man nailed to a cross are her best recruiting materials. It doesn't matter. She's a very good woman. She cares for people. I'm fond of her, actually.

"Michael, before we begin, are you reading your Sherlock Holmes? Have you deciphered my clue as to the red shamrock?"

"I've started, Aedan. Eight stories down, fifty–two to go. Nothing yet, unless you are really the Hound of the Baskervilles."

"Heavens, no. Phosphorous makes me itchy. It is interesting that you considered the possibility I was trying to frighten you to death. As you pointed out, my name means stag in Irish. In life, one gets to be the stag or the hound, but not both. So I'm afraid you'll have to keep reading. Do you and Sara have any plans for the day after our meeting is concluded?"

"We thought we'd drive back to the mountain and Sara will continue to work on your painting."

"Very good. I must be uncharacteristically brief. I shall not burden you with too much information at any one time. I have been working on this for more than twenty years and you have not. I shall lay it out a chapter at a time, as I do with my students. Please reflect on each chapter. I recommend you do so in the company of Mozart and a glass or two of good whiskey. You may find before the eyes close, they open wide and the truth reveals itself for just a moment as you sink into slumber. And please remember something else Mr. Holmes observed. When you have eliminated the impossible, then whatever remains, however improbable, must be the truth.

"The main character in our play is Grace O'Malley, the Pirate Queen of Connacht. Born in 1530, died in 1603. Was she really a pirate? Most definitely. At the peak of her career, she had at least five ships and more than two hundred men under her command. Grace was the only known legitimate child of a powerful Gaelic chieftain. She was a literate noblewoman of the Irish clan system, reputed to be a red–haired beauty who could kill a man with her looks as easily as with her sword. She

126

was also acknowledged to be vicious and greedy. She was a patriot, a pragmatic politician, a fierce warrior and a devoted friend as it suited her purposes. And as chief of Clan O'Malley, she was a painful thorn in the English arse until the day she died.

"King Henry VIII had declared himself King of Ireland and vowed to bring us under the royal boot. One would have thought the son of a bitch was too busy killing his wives, interviewing whores and feuding with Rome to worry about us. The Gael clans were occupied fighting each other, and did not offer much unified resistance. We Irish have always been our own worst enemies, and Henry and his toadies were masters of divide and conquer. A plan and some cunning will usually beat cunning alone.

"One by one, the clans submitted to English law in return for impressive–sounding titles and pittances of stipends. Grace resisted, while sometimes pretending to cooperate. She fought for Ireland, surely. Was she fighting more for herself or did she have a larger vision? We do not know for sure. She bought us time, but not even Grace could hold back the English tide. The whole of Ireland came under English rule and the Gaelic order disappeared. It was a shameful time in our history and the opening act in a bloody drama that lasted more than four hundred years. Grace survived by working every side against each other. She died a wealthy woman in spite of England's efforts to make her a pauper. So one wonders, is there still O'Malley treasure hidden out there? Yes, I think. Gold, but perhaps other sorts of treasure.

"Grace had two husbands, and if the tales are true, many lovers. Her second husband was Iron Richard Bourke, another chieftain. They married in 1567. It was a tumultuous marriage, but it lasted in some form until Richard died in 1583. In 1580, Iron Richard agreed to accept English law and pay rent to the Crown. He was ennobled as Lord Bourke. Now the Pirate Queen was in the somewhat awkward position of being Lady Bourke, while at the same time terrorizing English shipping off Western Ireland.

"I mentioned some legends depict Grace as a woman of mesmerizing beauty. Other tales depict her as homely and stout. I suppose it depends upon whether one believes the Irish or English. The truth is the world does not know what she looked like because there are no identified portraits of her. Indeed, there is much the history books cannot yet say about Grace.

"We do know of her successful meeting in 1593 with Queen Elizabeth, daughter of Henry VIII, to ask for the return of her captive sons and her confiscated lands. Picture it. The two most powerful women in England and Ireland, conversing in Latin as equals. Our Pirate Queen and the resplendent Gloriana, face to face. What a sight it must have been. Grace's own account of the meeting would be priceless. And if it exists, I intend to find it, with your help.

"Legend has it Queen Elizabeth offered Grace the title of Countess, and Grace refused, saying one queen could not lawfully ennoble another. Can you imagine anyone else addressing the Queen of England in such a manner? I think Elizabeth saw

128

much of herself in Grace and they got along famously. The tales also have it that on the way to her meeting with Elizabeth, Grace was made to walk past the rotting carcasses of executed pirates, kept displayed in cages as a warning to others. Grace never flinched. She didn't lack for courage.

"Much of what we think we know about her is just a collection of tales, songs and rambling poems, almost certainly exaggerated. The real Grace was neglected by historians of her day, and even today. I used to walk by her statue in Westport and promise her I would set her record straight. My resolve became greater when I discovered I was directly descended from her. Yes, part of Grace O'Malley lives in Aedan, literally and figuratively. Who better to tell her story?

"Now, partners, you have the background. Here is the assignment, the quest. There is a portrait of Grace O'Malley out there. I know this in my heart. It is mentioned in the tales and songs. I choose to believe poets, musicians and artists rather than certain close–minded academics. And Ireland must know what the woman who symbolized her looked like. The portrait was probably created between 1580 and 1583, while she was Lady Bourke. Nouveau nobility loves to create images of itself. I suppose it could be an earlier, flattering rendition of the beautiful red–haired pirate temptress. When we locate the portrait, I hope it will lead as well to a treasure trove of historical documents. I believe Grace hid them so they would not be read by Sir Richard Bingham, the English Governor of Connacht and Grace's tormentor. I believe they exist and may reveal themselves to the person who knows what to look for.

"I would not get my hopes up the trove will include a map to buried gold. Grace had a big payroll and may have measured wealth in cattle and land. But who knows? There are rumors to this day of at least one treasure buried in Howth. I must confess I have walked the beaches there, looking for a glint of gold in the afternoon sunlight. The treasures I seek now are historian's treasures. Portraits, documents, original records, the lifeblood of history. Finding them will be the crowning achievement of my professional life. Now, let me give you some specifics I believe to be relevant.

"Elizabeth appointed Sir Henry Sidney as Lord Deputy of Ireland, to complete the Irish Conquest. Henry acted as her agent until he was recalled in 1578. He had a son, the highly–regarded Elizabethan poet, Philip Sidney. Grace was ever the opportunist. In 1576, she arranged a meeting in Galway City and offered her naval services to Henry Sidney on a contractual basis. The services were to protect Galway from foreign attack. No long–term arrangement was ever reached, but through Henry, Grace met Philip. Philip was entranced by her. A good deal of what little we know about Grace is from letters Philip wrote. Those letters suggest there was a relationship of some sort between Philip and Grace. There is more.

"I know from my research that Philip Sidney made several trips to Galway. They are well documented. He may have been on English business, but I believe he enjoyed Galway because there was a wealth of folk stories and a community of kindred artistic spirits. I learned he became associated with a young Irish poet, possibly as a collaborator or apprentice. The name looked as though it could have been MacTiernan, but part of the brittle document was torn off. There was no first name and I could not even be sure of the last name. It was tantalizing, but I needed more.

"As you know, Michael, one sept of the MacTiernans or Tiernans was in County Sligo at the time, with others living near Blacksod Bay in Mayo. As I started to peruse your online postings, I surmised you were descended from those MacTiernans. Then you mentioned in response to an online query that you had identified a branch of your family in Mayo going back to the late 1500s, and earlier to Sligo. My guess was confirmed. You said you had thousands of pages of research notes, so of course I wanted to meet you. Specifically, I was looking for any MacTiernan Galway connections circa 1576, during the period Philip was there. In reading the files on your flash drive, I saw an entry for one James Tiernan, born in Sligo around 1556, and listed as being 'in the service of Seadhna Pilib'. Did you see it, Michael? And if so, what did you make of it?"

"I did see that name. I didn't pay much attention because James was the brother of my ancestor and I try to focus on direct lines. I suppose it meant he was a servant in a wealthy Irish household."

"And well might you have thought so. Michael, it's really a shame your mother did not teach you more Irish. The name translates to Philip Sidney. And 'in the service of' was often used at the time to describe something other than a servant relationship.

131

It could also be a way of describing an apprenticeship or some professional collaboration. And so I theorize I now have my missing name, with an identified link to Philip Sidney. I shall elaborate in a few moments.

"Here is what I think happened. Philip Sidney and James Tiernan remained friends and colleagues after Sir Henry Sidney was recalled to England in 1578. Philip stayed in contact with Grace O'Malley. They could be useful to each other. Philip was an English diplomat, you know. Or they might have become lovers. Maybe Grace and James were lovers too. Or James and Philip. One's brain gets weary wading through the Elizabethan muck. After Iron Richard Bourke sold out and accepted English rule, Grace became Lady Bourke. She then commissioned at least one portrait of herself for Philip Sidney. Why? Well, it's what nobility did and still does, and Grace was not lacking in vanity. I think it was more. It was a calling card to the English aristocracy, to Elizabeth herself. Look at me, I'm not just a scurvy Irish pirate now, I'm one of you, a player, so take me seriously. Grace might think along those lines. It was a most useful card for her to play if she wanted something, and Grace O'Malley always wanted something.

"And with the portrait, I believe Grace might have given Philip personal papers, possibly for his own literary use, possibly for safekeeping. Grace never felt her talents were properly recognized, and she now had a mesmerized and powerful ally in England, an ally in Elizabeth's innermost circle.

"A portrait may have eventually made it to England. I believe such was the intention. If it did, I don't know why it would not have surfaced by now.

132

Philip may have given Grace's papers to James Tiernan. Those papers could endanger Grace's life and his own if they fell into the wrong hands or perhaps he was smart enough to know he should have an insurance policy in case Grace betrayed him. Hedge the bets, Michael, never forget to hedge the bets.

"If I am correct, then all of this would have taken place between about 1581 and 1586, when Philip died in battle at the young age of thirty–one. There is no evidence any portrait or documents were in Philip's possession at the time of his death.

"There you have what I think happened. It is logical and consistent with everything we know about the parties and their activities. The problem is there is no proof. But we have now connected James Tiernan to Philip Sidney, and in Galway, an excellent start. We must build on it, else my theories are so many historical smoke rings blowing in the wind. And if we cannot prove the most logical scenario, then we may be reduced to hoping we stumble across papers and a portrait at a yard sale. And of course, we would not recognize them. We are on a very narrow path, my friends. However, let us not despair. We shall see how good we are.

"Michael, what was the source of your file notation to the effect that James Tiernan was in the service of Seadhna Pilib? Your notes mention it came from a family record, someone named Brigid?"

"It's not much, Aedan. My father's sister Brigid did a lot of family history work. She spoke Irish. She wasn't a trained historian, but she was a government librarian, worked at an army base. Brigid was really

133

quiet and intense, didn't mince words. She died when I was about ten. Her papers got passed down in cardboard boxes to her only surviving child, a son. I didn't know about them at the time, and only got to see them after he died six years ago. He had stored the boxes in a damp basement for years. Most of the papers were too moldy to read. I could make out a few of her notes, including that one. Then the son's lawyer chucked all the moldy boxes before they made people sick. I had some occasional contact with Brigid's son. He was tough to talk to. He did say Brigid visited Ireland at least eight or ten times. She'd stay for months, and wouldn't talk about it when she got back."

"Interesting. Well, we must pay more attention to James now, and Brigid as well. I recommend you begin your work with two projects. First, find out as much as you can about James Tiernan, his family and his activities. Second, you must communicate again with any relatives or friends of your aunt Brigid. She seems to have known many things. Look for anything that may have been passed down to her. Books, Bibles, papers, jewelry, family heirlooms and such.

"But I think we have planted enough seeds for today. I could use more sleep and you have a mountain waiting to finish its story. May I suggest we meet here tomorrow at noon for lunch and more good conversation? The Queen shall not elude us."

As Sara and I drove off to the mountain, she asked me what I thought of everything we had just heard.

"I guess it makes sense, especially since we don't know what other information Aedan has. And it's consistent with what I read about Grace O'Malley.

134

And yet, something doesn't ring true. Why couldn't Aedan figure this out without buying my files? Why did he need to meet us and put me on the payroll for something he could probably do himself? He's good at this kind of research. And if he was stalking my online postings, he could have tried asking me what information I had. Family history researchers are willing to share information. If someone asked me what I had on the Galway Tiernans circa 1576, I would have posted or emailed whatever I had. We could have exchanged information without meeting. There's more going on here than what he's told us so far. He enjoys turning over one card at a time."

"Or maybe you're seeing things that aren't there, the way you say I do."

"Could be. It wouldn't be the first time."

"I'm glad he wanted to meet us, Michael. Maybe he doesn't do shamrocks well, but he understands art. You can't fake it. I can smell a fraud right away. And he's put half a mil into our bank account. Let him turn over those cards as slowly as he wants.

"But he threw out quite a challenge in there, didn't he? Let's see how good we are. He meant how good you are, Michael, you know that. Are you good enough to keep up with him?"

"We'll find out pretty soon. I haven't figured out exactly how good he is either. I'll tell you this, though. He hasn't seen my best. It's been a long time since anyone saw my best at anything. I'm ready now and I didn't come here to be left in the dust. He's fascinating, Sara, but he's so annoyingly patronizing. You and I learned how to handle that growing up on the mean streets of Providence. Smile. Say the wrong thing to the wrong person, and you sleep with the fishes. So stay cool until the time is just right, then strike."

"Mean streets? Lord, Michael, get a grip. You're remembering things that never happened. Neither of our families had much, but it wasn't a daily struggle to survive. We didn't have to kill rats to eat, and when we were there, the Providence River was so polluted the nearest fish were in Massachusetts."

"Okay, I overplayed it a little. But those streets were mean enough that you never forgot two things. Respect everyone, because you can't be sure what they've got in their pockets. And if you take money for a job, you'd better do the job. I'm going to teach him a lesson, Sara. Enjoy the show, or better yet, join me."

"Yes, Michael! I've been waiting so long for this. And maybe I have a few things I can teach him myself."

We drove back to the mountain and Sara finished her painting, minutes before the heavens opened. She could polish it up in our room. Sara thought the mountain had told a wonderful story and Aedan would like the painting. I thought so too. Whoever took the second mountain hadn't put it back yet.

CHAPTER FOURTEEN

Sara and I met Aedan at the White Stag Wednesday, as the Angelus bells rang. He was in a good mood. His business the day before had gone well, he said, but he gave no details. Would we join him in some celebratory broiled steak with whiskey sauce, and a nice potato soup? Of course we would.

"Michael, tell me more about your family after it left Ireland. Do you still have many Irish relatives in America? Aunts, uncles, cousins?"

"Not as many as you might think. Life was tough in America for the Irish immigrants, my family included. My great–grandfather Daniel and his family came to Boston in 1883 as part of the James Hack Tuke Assisted Emigration Program. He had four brothers who stayed behind in Mayo. Daniel qualified for the Tuke Program because he could speak English and had been promised a job at a textile mill in Connecticut. I think he learned English by doing seasonal farm work in England.

"Daniel and his wife Catherine had six children, all born in Ireland. Two died in infancy and two more in early childhood. Another adult child never married and had no children of her own. She was a nun, died doing missionary work in Africa. So it was only my grandfather Thomas who kept the line going.

"But the hardships kept coming. Thomas and his wife Mary had five children. The oldest was my father Francis, and I'm his only child. The second died at birth. The third was a railroad worker and was killed in a train accident when he was fifteen. The fourth died in the influenza epidemic of 1918, at age ten. Then there was my aunt Brigid, who had two sons, one of whom died young of rheumatic fever. The other one, the one with the moldy boxes, died a few years ago and never had children.

"I suppose the saddest part of the story is my grandfather Thomas. His wife also died in the influenza epidemic. Thomas fell apart and went back to Ireland for two years. Brigid's son told me she thought Thomas 'wasn't right'. The Irish curse, schizophrenia. He thought Brigid had it too. She spent so much time smoking cigarettes and staring into space.

"According to her son, Brigid mentioned Thomas telling her about having an illegitimate child in Ireland who was mentally and physically disabled. He died shortly after his first birthday. Brigid thought it was one of Thomas' delusions. First he told her it was a boy, then a girl, then a boy. Thomas came back to America and never remarried. He was a weird guy. He heard voices, and they were scary voices. One night, he walked into the woods in his underwear and died of exposure. I was about thirteen.

"It's odd, Aedan. People think the Irish multiply like rabbits. In my family, there were enough children, but so many died young or never had children of their own. No, I don't have a lot of Irish relatives in America. I have more relatives in Ireland, but they're distant relatives and I've never met them."

"You should seek them out. What you just told me about your family is interesting. Excepting Emma, of course, you appear to be the only living direct descendant of your great–grandfather Daniel. I don't think people fully appreciate the hardships suffered by Irish emigrants, at least the ones sent to New England. Many of the Tuke emigrants were sent to Canada or the American west. I'll wager they had better lives in the early years than the ones who went to New England. There was rich soil in Canada and Montana, more living space, and less resentment against the Irish.

"I'm glad you mentioned Mr. Tuke. He was an English hero, a wealthy Quaker genuinely concerned with the plight of the starving western Irish farmer. His timing may have been unfortunate. There were no more devastating crop failures in Western Ireland after the mid–1880s. One might wonder if your family would have been better off staying here. That's not for me to say.

"I see that lunch is about to be served. Michael, I would like you to focus your initial efforts on the matters we discussed yesterday. Please try to find out as much as you can about James Tiernan and any connections to Philip Sidney. Focus also on your father's sister Brigid. It would be interesting to know whom she was visiting in Ireland and why. It might be a long shot, but my father had good paydays from long shots. Take as much time as you need and share your findings with me as you think appropriate. Nothing good comes from haste. I daresay nobody ever asked da Vinci how many hours it took him to paint the Mona Lisa, right, Sara?"

Sara gave Aedan her painting, and he loved it. She and I had a hand signal we used when we thought someone was slinging it. There was no signal from

Sara on this one, and she had a good nose for manure after years of marriage.

As the food and drinks were frequently replenished, Aedan regaled us with stories about his classes. The best was the one about the Chinese–speaking student trying to post bail for Aedan after Aedan was arrested walking to class dressed as a Viking prince. Who knew there was a law in Galway against carrying broadaxes in crosswalks? Not Aedan. The judge made Aedan promise he'd never do it again without getting a license to carry a broadaxe. License to carry a broadaxe?

After our celebratory lunch and celebratory drinks, we repaired to the deck for celebratory cigars. Sara was getting a little too good at this. She was now blowing perfectly circular blue smoke rings with two minutes of hang time. Aedan was impressed. He thought maybe Sara should try to teach Mrs. Carty and her Bible study group how to do it. Sara thought it probably wasn't a good idea, even if Mrs. Carty did think Sara was an instrument of redemption.

At around 3:00, Aedan made a suggestion. Would we object if he had Aoife drive us all to the mountain Sara had painted for him? He would like a photograph of Sara and him holding the painting, with the mountain as backdrop. After that, we'd go listen to trad music at the pub Sara and I had been frequenting. It would give us a chance to get to know Aoife a little better, and Aedan just might have a jig move or two he could teach us. Then he'd leave us alone on Thursday and Friday so we could do our own exploring. We'd regroup at noon on Saturday, the day before we would be returning to the United States.

Sara and I couldn't imagine any better way to spend the rest of the day. I told Aedan I had to be honest with him. Glenn was up against it. The next two weeks were going to be difficult and there had to be enough time for Glenn and Anna. So instead of exploring Ireland the next two days, I'd rather go to the Galway Family History Society or NUIG, the National University of Ireland in Galway, and get started on my research. Sara would have no trouble finding things to paint or photograph. She never did. We'd do the sightseeing another time. Aedan studied his fingernails and smiled.

"It seems Glenn, Anna, Sara and I might have found the right man."

"I appreciate the kind words, Aedan. Would you mind putting it in writing for them?"

We drove out to the mountain and took lots of pictures. Sara mentioned to Aedan she was surprised there was only one mountain. It seemed like a good place for more than one. Aedan thought Saint Patrick had something to do with it. You could always give the credit or blame to Saint Patrick. Aedan said he'd have our photograph framed and hang it next to Sara's painting in his dining room.

After picking up our car at the White Stag, we headed off to the pub. The musicians knew Aedan and told him they'd be sure to play his favorite tunes. The hostess gave us the best table in the house. There were people already sitting at the table the hostess wanted to give us, but when they saw Aedan, they tipped their caps and gladly gave up their seats. Crubeens were on the house.

We learned that Aoife was born in Japan and had been adopted into an Irish family as an infant. She attended Oxford and took a degree in Fine Arts, not exactly the usual qualifications for a fixer. Sara had exhibited Japanese artists in her gallery. It turned out one was a good friend of Aoife's. Sara and Aoife became buds over a Guinness or two. Aedan chuckled and kept the drinks coming. He told me later it made him very happy that Aoife and Sara hit it off. Aoife didn't have any family of her own.

Aedan could bust some moves on the dance floor, and taught Sara and me how to do a proper Irish jig. The Irish musicians announced there were Americans in the house and in our honor, played 'New York, New York'. Close enough to America, I guess. Sara requested the song about the girl whose eyes shone like diamonds, and dedicated it to Aedan. I wished she had thought that through, but Aedan sang louder than anyone else and twirled Aoife around the floor. Then Sara got up and closed the house with a solo 'I'm Shipping Up to Boston'. The musicians raised their glasses to us as we walked out.

Aedan and Aoife couldn't remember having more fun at a pub. For me, it was another quiet night out with Sara. Que Sera, Sera.

After breakfast the next morning, I called the Family History Society in Galway City to request an appointment. I was in luck. A genealogist could meet with me at 11:00 a.m. Sara decided it would be a good photography day, so we piled into the car. It was only about a fifty–mile drive. After five days in Ireland, I could do it in two hours, maybe a little more.

I met with the genealogist, Mrs. Feeney. She was crisply efficient and knowledgeable, but we didn't find much on James Tiernan. There were too many people with the same or similar names.

Mrs. Feeney gave me a list of sources, and told me if I emailed her any new information as it turned up, she'd be happy to do more digging for me. 'Tis a noble search, she remarked.

Mrs. Feeney knew who Philip Sidney was and of his meeting with Grace O'Malley. She thought a couple of people had been in over the last several months, also asking about Grace O'Malley's activities in Galway. She had not been the one helping them and she didn't know any more.

Sara and I met for a quick lunch, and then I visited the NUIG Library to scope out their collection of old Galway records. A librarian sheepishly admitted many of their records dating to the 1500s had been relocated decades ago to protect them, and were still missing or misfiled. The remaining collection would keep me busy for at least a year, he thought. My head was pounding. I had already made copies of at least two hundred pages of material. It was searching for needles in a haystack, but I had made some progress for the first day on the job.

Mrs. Carty insisted we join her for tea and cookies that evening. She was having a good day too. Aedan asked her for more religious pamphlets, the thicker the better. He told her they helped warm his soul of a damp, rainy evening. Mrs. Carty would remember us as the visitors who saved Aedan from the eternal flames. She would not have expected God's agents to be coming from the United States. Italy would have been her guess. We told her Europeans generally took their holidays in August, so we were covering for the Italian agents of redemption. She looked skeptical, but it sounded good to me.

We decided to take a short walk before turning in.

"Sara, I should do more of Aedan's research tomorrow, but I don't want you to feel ignored. Let's face it, things are going to heat up when we get back. I've been thinking a lot about Glenn in the past few days."

"So have I. Do the research. Michael, what are you going to do if Glenn doesn't make it?"

"I don't know. And what will Anna do? And what am I going to do if he does make it? I think we're all at the crossroads here. I want to take a ride tomorrow to the South Mayo Family Research Centre in Ballinrobe. Maybe they can steer me in the right direction on James Tiernan. It's a hunch, but they helped me once before on a different question. I want you to come, but we'll have to leave very early."

"I don't mind at all, if you understand I'm going to be a computer jockey for the rest of the night. I promised Aoife I'd give her a folder of gallery information and links. She wants to open her own place someday. She's got what it takes. She only needs some encouragement. Deal?"

"Deal. Throw me the Sherlock Holmes book, will you?"

Two hours and ten stories later, the light bulb came on. I knew the story. I knew at least some of what Aedan was doing. Why didn't I see it at once? Now I had to figure out the why.

144

Sara and I met Aedan on Saturday at our usual table. He had already ordered lunch. It would be skirts and kidneys, with black pudding. Since Sara enjoyed munching on pigs' feet, Aedan thought she might like to try other parts of the pig, parts I thought any sane person would bury or incinerate. Our drinks were already on the table. Sara was quiet, because this was our farewell lunch and Glenn's situation was looming ever larger on the horizon. As usual, Aedan had an answer.

"I have another proposal, partners. Forgive me for saying you both look morose. I hope it is not the company. I know Glenn is weighing on you. Your priority now is go back and help him in his time of need. Put our respective puzzles aside until his situation is resolved. We must take care of the living before dwelling too long on the dead. Sometimes we forget that.

"My proposal is we meet again at this table in exactly two months. If it is not convenient for you, please suggest a better date. Ireland is lovely in the fall. I hope you will consider staying at least ten days, as my guests, of course. Michael, I am sure you and I will be in frequent communication before we meet and then we shall discuss our progress face–to–face. Sara, I must tell you Aoife is most excited about the prospect of you returning. I doubt Mrs. Carty will object either. She is of the opinion you have saved me, and perhaps you have. Aoife will set everything up."

I could see Sara thought Aedan had made an offer we couldn't refuse. There would be hell to pay if I didn't jump on this right away.

"We would be delighted, Aedan. You are most generous. We would also be delighted to have you and Aoife come to the United States any time as our guests. But I'm not sure what you meant when you said our respective puzzles."

"Did I say that? An old man's slip of the tongue, perhaps. Thank you, Michael, but I would prefer we meet here. I need my familiar surroundings. Tell me, did you have any success in your research the past two days?"

"I'm not sure. I met some helpful people and made a lot of copies. I didn't hear any bells ring, but it's still early."

"Yes, too early for non–Angelus bells. The answers often come in the sifting and analyzing, not the digging. You were wise to avail yourself of the historians at the family history centers. They are very good. And I see you met Mrs. Feeney. She's one of the best. You have done well for only two days. Please keep plowing along.

"I have been thinking more about your aunt Brigid. A woman who went to Ireland so many times might have had particular reasons to do so. It was no small expense. I shall be interested to learn what you find. It may be nothing. Perhaps she just had lots of frequent flyer miles she needed to use up.

"And there is another line of research I would like you to explore. Your great–grandfather Daniel was able to emigrate to New England through Mr. Tuke's assisted emigration program. Mr. Tuke was well connected to the English nobility who

146

supported his efforts, and maybe there are things about the workings of the Tuke Program we don't yet understand.

"I noticed in your ship's log records for Daniel Tiernan that when he emigrated in 1883, he stated he had been in the United States before. Why would a poor Irish farmer have gone to the United States before emigrating there? How could he afford it? Your research led you to conclude Daniel had no known relatives in the United States. Was it an employment interview? It would have been an unusual way to hire a textile laborer. Mr. Tuke or his agents usually dealt with employers directly. I have sometimes wondered whether Mr. Tuke and his patrons used the program to deliver things to and from wealthy persons who were providing the jobs and financial support, a form of quid pro quo. There is no firm evidence to support my hypothesis, but there has been speculation, some from a colleague I respect. Occasionally one must bet on the slowest horse with the best odds.

"I do not suggest Daniel Tiernan carried a portrait of Grace O'Malley across the Atlantic, but perhaps there were papers or other small items transported. It would be a good use of your time to explore possible connections between Daniel Tiernan and the owners of the mill who gave his family employment. Were those owners collectors? Historians? Irish? Is there any reason to think they received information or documents of interest to us? Sometimes the truth is tripped over in the night and trapped. What I have said may seem fanciful to you, but please keep in mind a few excellent historians have tried to solve the Grace O'Malley puzzle and failed. We must plow fields they did not discover or could not easily enter.

"I think we have done enough work for today. Let us drink to a most enjoyable and productive week in Ireland, with more to follow."

Okay, Michael, there's some nice confirmation of what he's up to. But let's give Aedan the benefit of at least a little doubt. He did just help fund your retirement. And it could be a double trap. Let's try to change the conversational dynamic and see what he does.

"To your health, Aedan. Sláinte. Oh, by the way, I think I've figured out your Sherlock Holmes clue."

Aedan put his glass down slowly.

"Do tell. And the answer is?"

"Aedan, a wise man once told me the truth is sometimes tripped over in the night and trapped. So here's what I'll do. I'll write the answer on a sheet of paper and seal it in this envelope. I'll draw a red shamrock on the envelope especially for you. Please don't open it until we meet again in October. We'll see then if I was right. This will make another nice scene when our adventure is turned into a film."

Aedan laughed. He looked at Sara and winked.

"I have met my match. And the two questions I thought you might ask?"

"I know one of them. I'll write it on the paper as well and I'll have the answer for you by October. I think I know the second question too. The answer may be a lot to get my head around. I'll have it for you by October also."

"So, in two months we shall find out if Michael Tiernan is as clever as I hoped. If he is, then I'll wager our respective puzzles will be solved."

148

I wrote on a piece of paper, put it in an envelope I had in my laptop bag, sealed it and gave it to Aedan.

"Thank you, Michael. And now it is time to enjoy some Connemara pig and Cuban tobacco. You really should let Sara draw your shamrocks for you. No offense meant, but you're a poor excuse for an artist."

And you're a little rattled now, aren't you, Aedan Burns?

We spent the rest of the afternoon talking about everything except Grace O'Malley. Aedan asked me to tell him what it was like growing up in New England. There wasn't much remarkable about it, which was the blessing. I had food to eat, clothes to wear and schools to attend. I took for granted things my ancestors might have killed for. I told Aedan the story of my life, where I went to school and what I did there, how I met Sara, Glenn and Anna. He kept asking me questions and he kept asking Sara questions. Aedan wasn't just being polite. He was on a mission. He wanted to know everything he could find out about me, Sara and Emma.

We moved to the deck, and Aedan challenged Sara to do something creative with her smoke rings. Sara thought for a moment, lit up, and blew a figure eight. Then she asked Aedan if he wanted to see a figure five. Well played, Sara.

Aedan applauded, stood up, and gave Sara a sweeping bow. He told her such self–confidence and talent are divine gifts. It was hard for me to imagine God spending a lot of time picking the right people to blow good smoke rings. Aedan gave Sara a filled travel humidor to bring home. I'd go to the men's room when she filled out her Customs declaration form.

On our way back to the B&B, Sara asked me what went on with the passing of the envelope.

"Did you give him the old disappearing ink trick? Blank paper with transmitting fibers embedded in the envelope seal, so you know if he opens it early? It's what the Jackal would have done."

"Sara, you've got to find better books to read. How about *Finnegans Wake*? I think I figured some of it out. He's checking what I do against what he's already done. He wants to see if I'll do and find the same things."

"You think Aedan is trying to see if you know how to do this?"

"Not really. He's followed my online postings for a long time. He has my flash drive with ten years' worth of data. He's already decided whether he thinks I know how to do this."

"Okay, what's he up to? Don't think I object to large deposits into our bank account and the chance to work on my cigar smoke rings."

"He scatters clues and watches which ones I pick up. He's studying us and testing me. The man has a monumental ego. Maybe he wants to see if I'm another Aedan Burns, which I'm not sure he or I want, by the way."

"Are you?"

"I don't know what an Aedan Burns is. I do know one of the puzzles he wants to solve is me. And us. Obviously, there's always the possibility I'm hallucinating. It could be the scent of a beautiful lunch date, or a reaction to eating pig offal."

150

"I'd go with the beautiful lunch date theory. Is he making this stuff up about Grace O'Malley? Is it a hoax?"

"No, absolutely not. He's completely serious about trying to locate a Grace O'Malley portrait and documents. But he doesn't think we'll be much help to him. We don't have enough academic training or cred."

"You're describing a bizarre chess match. Is it a match we'll regret?"

"I don't think so, but I can't be certain. He knew I would check him out to make sure he wasn't a criminal. He's not, or he hasn't been. And yet he's keeping secrets. I figure you have to take chances in life, right? Sara, we can bail on this any time if you're uncomfortable."

"No way. You and I are getting the magic back, Michael. I haven't felt like this since after we first met. Was there really a clue he found on your flash drive?"

"Absolutely. He was delighted and surprised. Philip Sidney's name in Irish was pretty important. I don't see how he could have nailed down the connection to James Tiernan without it. Still, he thinks it was something I stumbled onto without appreciating its significance. I haven't impressed him at all yet as a puzzle–solver. I might only be a good information collector. He can't be sure yet, because he found something else in those files he wasn't expecting."

"And it made him put you on the payroll for the rest of the year. Good thinking, Aedan. Okay, one last question. What do I have to do with this? I'm not a person he would have to know if he's working on a Grace O'Malley puzzle."

"Very good, Watson. He doesn't think you can help much with Grace O'Malley, but you're a person he would absolutely need to meet if he was trying to solve a Michael and Sara puzzle too. Look, you could be right. I make things too complicated. Maybe Aedan's a gentleman and he wanted to meet you because he admires your work. It's clear to me he's impressed by who you are, not only what you do, and what sane man wouldn't be?"

"Lawdy, how y'all do sweet–talk a girl. My manure–mometer is flashing red. I do hope he's at least a little impressed, Michael. He's changing me, changing us. I can feel it. Lick a pig's foot with a man and you know him."

"I'll take your word, and I'll bet you're the first person ever to say it. Sara, if it's legal, I guess I don't care what his agenda is. He's paid enough for it. But I don't enjoy being only a laboratory rat for him to study and experiment with. We've got skills too. Why don't you and I give Aedan Burns the shock of his life and solve his Grace O'Malley puzzle?"

"Michael, I am so freaking happy to be here doing this with you."

Sara stared out the car window for a long time as we approached the B&B. She didn't look 'freaking happy'. I knew what was coming.

"How's Glenn doing? It's getting close."

"I called him and Anna from Ballinrobe yesterday. They're both getting antsy. Glenn's surgeon is still saying the tests are coming back a little better than

152

she expected. But his odds aren't great, and she's not playing Pollyanna. I don't want Glenn or Anna getting their hopes up. This story isn't on track for a happy ending."

"Is she as good as Glenn thinks she is?"

"Apparently so. I printed out her biography. It's in the pocket of my briefcase back there."

Sara reached around and pulled it out.

"She's really pretty. Glenn even finds gorgeous surgeons. I'll bet she was a Miss Canada."

"I can see her as Miss Canada. 'And in the talent competition, Miss Manitoba will remove a diseased body part while singing a Leonard Cohen medley'. Glenn didn't pick her on looks, Sara, but I think she may be a little young to be so good."

"You think everyone is a little young to be good. You're an old curmudgeon now, raging against the universe."

"Experience counts. I'd feel better if that gorgeous face of hers had a few creases in it. You know, like yours."

"You might be needing her next, Michael, to remove some new creases of your own."

Aoife and Aedan met us at the B&B the next morning and drove us to the airport. It was a bittersweet farewell, even for Mrs. Carty. We'd be back in two months. Hey, Glenn can watch the office while we were away. You're on this, Mrs. Boyle, right?

First, we had to get through ten days of hell.

CHAPTER SIXTEEN

I almost bounced off the wall of tension when I walked into the office Monday. Anna and Glenn weren't even trying to hide it. I decided to stay in my office and see if one of them wanted to talk before I brought it up. Glenn did. He asked Anna to take a few things to the Post Office across the street, and then he came into my office.

"I don't know how this is going to end, Michael, so I want you to know how much you, Anna and Sara have meant to me. If things don't work out, I want you to handle things. Here's an envelope with the information you need, and a key to my safe deposit box. It should be in good order. I've had a lot of time to think things over. And if I can't make medical decisions for myself, I want you and Anna to make them for me. Here's all the paperwork. I'll talk to Anna about it too."

"Glenn, you know we'll do anything you want."

"I guess we've got things to talk about if I make it. Don't say another word. I'm trying to hold it together. Big Brahmins don't cry. Take the envelope and don't open it unless you have to. I'll tell you this, though. If I do make it, there are going to be big changes in my life. There's nothing that clarifies the thought process better than an angry fucking tumor."

He walked out and closed the door.

Anna came back, and Glenn asked her to join him in the conference room. I didn't look and didn't ask. Anna had her poker face on when she came out, but she wasn't a good poker player.

A little before noon, Kata stopped in. I had never met her. She was the spitting image of Anna the day

154

we hired her. That's a lucky young woman. And she was an emergency room nurse at one of the big Boston hospitals. I was glad she'd be in Montreal with us. Anna needed her. We might too.

There wasn't much urgent work to take care of that week. I picked away at a few files and gave up. I'd hire accountants to finish off the estate tax returns I was working on. I kept looking over at Anna and thought I saw the unlighted cigarette. Shit. As much as I disliked him, I hoped Mr. Bennett didn't walk in to settle his score. Anna would have ripped him into Krugerrand–sized pieces.

I had to get my mind off Glenn. I tried to bury myself in Grace O'Malley research for most of the next two days. I didn't think I was making much progress, but I thought about Aedan saying that sometimes the progress only appears when you sift through what you've dug up.

I couldn't find much on my aunt Brigid. Everything Brigid had, which wasn't much, had been given or thrown away after she died. I called her son's lawyer, the one who had tracked me down to show me the moldy boxes. The son died with less than his mother. There wasn't even enough to pay his funeral expenses.

Brigid didn't have many friends, and the one I was able to find didn't remember much. She did recall that Brigid told her she was doing some translating for her husband in Ireland. Translating what? She didn't know.

I spent hours digging through ship passenger records, passport documents and online newspapers. No luck. Maybe every door you can shut gets you closer to the one which leads you where you want to go. I was just about ready to shut the door on Brigid and her son, but I kept wondering about what she might have been translating.

I decided to take a closer look at Brigid's husband. All I knew about him was that his name was Leo Norman and he was a high school teacher. Brigid's friend told me that he drowned trying to swim to an offshore buoy faster than an all–state swimmer student of his. He went down like a rock, body not recovered until the salt–water carnivores were done with it days later. A real pompous ass, she recollected, and apparently not much of a swimmer. I pulled up his obituary online. The newspaper considerately omitted some details of his passing. The cause of death was listed as accidental drowning, not complications of male menopause. The rest of the obituary was interesting. There might be some leads, but tracking them down would take me out of the office, so they'd have to wait until after Glenn's operation.

Since Aedan thought the connection might be James Tiernan, I decided to focus on him. I organized the materials I had gotten in Ireland and hit every online database I could find. Why would Aedan not be giving me more information about what he had already found? If four eyes were better than two, why not use the four? Sara told me I was overthinking it. There was a second Golden Rule in life. He who has the gold makes the rules. She was probably right. After all, I had a week of lunches and dinners with Aedan, and I had never once been given a menu.

Before I knew it, it was Wednesday. Glenn decided to head off to Montreal to rest for a day and

156

then check into the hospital. I told Anna not to come in Thursday or Friday. She and Kata needed time to get ready. They'd head up to Montreal Friday after Glenn had talked to his doctor and been admitted for final workups. Anna had taken care of our flight and hotel reservations. Glenn insisted on paying for everything. He said he saved some money by not renewing his Celtics season tickets for the fall, in case he wasn't able to use them.

Sara's plans had firmed up. She could leave the gallery reception Saturday afternoon and make it to Montreal that night. But she wanted me to go up before her. There might be things to take care of. Sara would take a cab from the airport and meet us for a late dinner if we wanted. It would give her a chance to use some of her growing–up French. I hoped she didn't wind up in Saskatchewan because she didn't remember enough of it. Maybe none of us would have an appetite anyway.

On Friday night, I got the call from Anna. Glenn had been admitted and was in good spirits, but she was a wreck. Glenn's surgeon wanted to talk to his health care agents before the operation. It sounded serious.

"Michael, she wants to do it tomorrow if at all possible, while Glenn is having his final tests. I feel terrible asking this, but is there any way you could be at the hospital by 3:00? I need you here with me. I'm not strong enough to do this alone."

I booked an earlier flight Saturday morning and made it to our Montreal hotel by 1:30. Anna and Kata's room was three doors down from the one Anna had reserved for Sara and me. I knocked on the door, but they weren't there. So I left a note and headed over to the hospital. It was only a few minutes away.

Anna and Kata were sitting in the lobby waiting for me. We took the elevator to Glenn's room, nobody saying a word. He was about to be taken for his final tests, and was talking to his surgeon. She was even prettier than her picture. She and Kata could have passed for college roommates. We were going to wait outside, but she motioned for us to come in. Glenn was happy to see us.

"Bonjour, I'm Sylvie Lepine, Glenn's surgeon. Are you his family?"

Before we could answer, Glenn said, "Yes, they are."

We introduced ourselves. Doctor Lepine gave us a dazzling smile and even better, she had a nice strong handshake. You want that in a surgeon.

"Okay, mon ami, the orderlies are here to take you away for final exams. Get some good grades for me today. They'll page me when you're done."

Glenn smiled and was rolled away. Doctor Lepine took us into a family conference room.

She wasn't smiling now.

"I have to be frank with you. Tumors like this are about the worst. If I can't remove it, he won't live very long. And it's a dangerous procedure. The overall success rate is twenty percent at best. You have to know all of this. You should discuss with him what his wishes are if we can only keep him alive by machines."

Anna looked shell–shocked, so I asked: "Doctor Lepine, suppose you open him up and see that it's inoperable?"

"Then I close him up. I'm not going to have him bleed to death on the operating table. But he wants me to try to get it out if I think there's any chance I can. I've explained the risks to him.

"I know it will be awful for you sitting in the waiting room on Monday. I've been in that room myself. You could be there for a long time and I won't be able to send anyone out to update you. If it's a long operation, that could be a sign it's going relatively well, but I can't keep him under indefinitely. We've got to catch a break. The only thing I can tell you is that I'll have the best surgical team in Montreal behind me and I've worked very, very hard to become the surgeon Glenn needs. He'll get the absolute best I can give. God bless you all."

Doctor Lepine didn't look quite so young to me anymore. Glenn picked a winner.

It had been a draining hour. I asked Anna and Kata if they wanted to get an early dinner. We could rest a bit and come back later to visit Glenn. Anna wanted Kata to see some of the city while she had a chance. Kata had never been to Montreal, so she decided to go for a sightseeing run through downtown. Anna said she could use some decompression time alone, but maybe we'd visit Glenn and have dinner with Sara later. We walked back to the hotel lost in thought. I was glad my room had a well-stocked mini-bar.

But no ice. That was at the end of the corridor. I walked by Anna and Kata's room and heard loud crying inside. I wasn't sure what to do, so I knocked on the door. Anna answered. She was in full meltdown. She grabbed my hand, closed the door and pulled me close to her.

"I'm so scared, Michael. I don't want it to end like this. He's going to die."

Anna's tears washed over me. I held her hand and stroked her hair. She hugged me and buried her head deep into my shoulder, sobbing. I wanted to comfort her and tell her everything would be okay. She pulled me closer and closer, wrapping me tightly in perfume and tears. My knees started to buckle. This was out of the comforting zone now and into the Core Commandments danger zone. Anna knew it too. She brushed her hand against my cheek and we pushed each other away. The calculus of risk on this one wasn't very good, not that logic always prevails.

"Michael, I'm sorry. I had no right to do that, but I needed you to hold me close. Please forgive me and please go."

She eased me out the door and closed it softly.

My heart ached for her. Except for her daughters and us, Anna was alone. God damn you, Mrs. Boyle, are you getting my messages?

What began as a simple trip to the ice machine turned into the Temptation of Saint Michael. Saint Michael stood strong in the end, if barely. Isn't that worth something, God? Do you really want Glenn now? I went back to my room and had a whiskey, neat. Ice machines in this hotel were too dangerous. Maybe I'd take a shower too. I wondered if there's a County Mayo in Hungary.

Sara got in late, and she and I went out to dinner by ourselves. When Kata had come back from her run, she found her mother still crying. Kata gave

Anna a sedative and put her to bed. Anna hadn't slept in a long time. Kata said they'd order room service.

I filled Sara in on Glenn's prognosis, but not Anna's meltdown. I told her that Glenn was calm. He knew there was no better surgeon anywhere, so let's get this over with.

"I'm glad. I'm glad you're under control too, Michael. I was worried about you earlier in the week, but Anna's composure seems to have rubbed off on you. I need you to be my rock. This is starting to sink in."

It wasn't Anna's composure which had rubbed off on me. The Five Core Commandments withstood an unexpected assault, and I had learned something. Grandpa Tom was a lunatic in more ways than one. Actions have consequences, and twelve–year–olds have to grow up sometime. Maybe it takes a few years, or in some cases, decades.

Except for separate visits with Glenn, we slept or rested most of Sunday. It had been a mother of a week and the worst was yet to come. How on earth do the Sylvie Lepines do this?

CHAPTER SEVENTEEN

Sara, Anna and I were at the hospital by 7:00 Monday morning. Kata stopped to pick up some croissants and arrived a few minutes later. Glenn was being prepped for surgery in a room down the hall.

Doctor Lepine sent word that she planned to begin at 7:30 sharp. She was reviewing Glenn's films one last time and going over the game plan with her surgical team. She'd be out to see us right after the operation was over, whatever the outcome.

Anna had regained the Anna composure. There was nothing to do now but wait. Wait and watch the clock, and the door to the operating room. 7:30 turned into 9:30, 11:00, noon. Maybe that was a good sign, but it didn't make things any easier. The hospital chaplain stopped by to give us some reassurance. It didn't work, but I was glad he tried. He seemed like a good guy. He told us if there was a surgeon around who could pull this off, it was Sylvie Lepine.

A few minutes after 12:30, Doctor Lepine came through the door. The five seconds it took her to reach us took a lifetime. I reckoned I was good at reading faces, but I couldn't read hers. I thought she was walking a little too slowly.

Then she flashed that smile.

"I have great news. We got it out. Glenn's doing fine."

Then she eased us into one of the family rooms. Anna and Sara were sobbing and holding onto each other. It was finally over.

162

"I'm so happy for you. I don't get to say that very often in these cases. I'm not sure what happened. Three weeks ago, the tumor was wrapped around critical blood vessels in a place we couldn't quite reach, almost certainly inoperable. Either our tests got it wrong or that tumor moved, not much but enough. I think Glenn will make a full recovery. He'll need follow–up treatment to be sure the cancer's gone, but he can have that done in Boston. I don't want him to have visitors today. Go celebrate. I'll tell him you're popping a few corks for him, and I'll try to discharge him Friday if nothing changes and there's no evidence of bleeding or infection. In six months, this will be only a bad memory for you."

Anna spoke for all of us.

"Doctor Lepine, it will be a wonderful memory, thanks to you."

"That's so nice of you. I'd love to claim the credit, but I think we were getting outside help. These tumors don't give up easily and they don't move. There are a lot of things I don't understand. One of them happened today."

Maybe she didn't understand, but I did. Thank you, Mrs. Boyle. Now rip up those bills and have a snort for me, okay?

Celebrate we did. One of the best restaurants in Montreal was around the corner. The menu was in French, but Sara thought she could handle it. Please, God, no. How's the fried umbrella today? As it turned out, Anna could handle it better. Her mother grew up in Paris, she told us, and taught her French.

Anna and Sara ordered for us. I wasn't sure what I was eating and didn't much care. To see those two women so happy, I would have licked pigs' feet for the rest of my life. I gladly paid the largest restaurant bill I would ever see in my life. Whatever we ate, it must have been good, or at least endangered.

Three hours and many bottles of champagne later, we wobbled across the street to a little park. Sara pulled out four of Aedan's Cubans to cap the celebration. How many women could reach into their purses and do that? I thought Anna or Nurse Kata might be appalled, but I was wrong. We lit up with gusto and Kata pulled a loaded flask from her purse. She was proving to be a very agreeable addition to Team Glenn.

Bad Anna taught us some bawdy French songs, which we sang in the off–key of too much champagne. Maybe not so off–key that a group of young men sitting nearby couldn't understand the lyrics and wished they could do what we were singing about without getting arrested. They stared at me, a let's say mature guy sitting on a park bench with three good–looking, cigar–smoking, flask–passing, bawdy–French–song–mangling women, wondering what I knew that they didn't.

Oh, Canada!

CHAPTER EIGHTEEN

It was time to get our lives back on track, although we knew there were big changes coming. We met with Doctor Lepine Tuesday afternoon. She thought she could discharge Glenn late Friday morning, but then he'd need ten days of bed rest and daily monitoring from visiting nurses. I emailed Aedan an update. There was an immediate response: 'Magnifique!'

Sara and I would fly back to Boston Tuesday night, but Anna and Kata insisted on staying in Montreal until Glenn was discharged. They'd bring him home. Glenn talked to another Son of Mayflower and arranged for a private flight back. It would be less stressful and still cheaper than a funeral. Doctor Lepine agreed, as long as Kata was there to keep a watchful medical eye on things. She told Glenn he was a lucky guy to have so much family looking out for him. Glenn told her he was starting to realize how true that was.

We wanted to give Doctor Lepine something to remember us by. I couldn't think of anything else, so I bought an autographed Leonard Cohen poster which proclaimed 'Hallelujah!' We had a picture taken in Glenn's room, him holding the poster and us holding a banner that said, 'Hallelujah and merci, Doctor Lepine'. She appreciated it but told us to call her Sylvie. Doctor Lepine sounded pretentious. She used to sing "Hallelujah" in the shower, but not very well. I didn't believe that, at least the part about *not well*. The Sylvie Lepines of this world can't do not well.

On our flight to Boston, Sara asked me, "Things are never going to be the same as they were, are they?"

"No. How many warning shots can we ignore?"

"Do you think Glenn will bag his law practice?"

"Oh, sure, and soon. It looks to me he's got plans he's mulling over."

"You say you have the power to read a man's mind. Do you know his plans?"

"He didn't tell me, but I hope I know some of them. I read female minds too, by the way."

"In your dreams. It would scare me to death if I thought you did. You might realize that you can occasionally be a long–in–the–tooth chick magnet, maybe Sean Connery."

Uh–oh. Did she read my mind on Anna's meltdown? I hope she saw the ending. The endings are what matter, even ones which might have gone the other way if the story was just a little longer.

"You have a gift for the back–handed compliment, Sara. Thanks, I think. And no worries, I've already found the chick for me. Good thing for me, she seems to agree, although she could do better."

"I hope her name is Sara. That means you'll have to think about what you want to be when you grow up. One assumes."

"Her name *is* Sara, and I've been thinking a lot about that. It may be possible to pull it off without having to grow up. I'll see what I can do."

"Are you happy with the choices you made in life, Michael? I mean, the big ones."

"Absolutely. I found the right woman and convinced her to marry me. I have a wonderful daughter. I worked at something I loved for a long time. The first two make me happy every day. It's time to deep–six the third."

"I'm happy too. We hit some turbulence in the early years, but nobody fell out. I'm glad we held on. I wouldn't ever want to be that young and confused again. So what now?"

"First, we have to crack the O'Malley Protocol. That will keep us busy until at least October. Then we've got some decisions to make, all of us. And you should go cold turkey on the Cuban cigars until we get back to Ireland. It can get to be an expensive habit, and they'll turn your teeth brown."

"So I'll have a good pirate's teeth. If I stop too soon, I'm afraid I'll lose the smoke ring training effect. Tough choice. I think I'll start a Boston chapter of Cuban Cigar Smokers Anonymous. We'll support each other through the withdrawal process."

"You're seriously going to quit?"

"Definitely, but not for a while. I just want them to give me their unsmoked cigars. I'll destroy them, of course, but in my own way. Maybe I'll give a few to Anna. She looked like a natural in that park. I think I'd want her and Kata on the cover of my cigar smokers' magazine. Do you think Anna's been practicing in your office ladies' room?"

"I wouldn't know. I don't go in there much. Anna's been surprising me for years. Why wouldn't she surprise me again in Montreal?"

So it was back to you now, Grace O'Malley. Did you miss me? I had to spend some time with another woman who knows how to cut a man open. Then she brings him back from the dead. And no disrespect here, but the people who thought you could kill a man with your looks should have seen Sylvie Lepine.

I hadn't done any research on Leo Norman. He was the spouse of an aunt, and I didn't usually go that far out into branches of the family tree. He died before I was born. Brigid and my father never talked about him, although I vaguely remembered my father referring to his brother–in–law as "that feckin' obnoxious peckerhead." Something told me I should find out more now.

I discovered that Leo Norman was not your typical high school teacher. Graduated Cornell in 1933 with double majors in math and English, enlisted into a top–secret Army intelligence unit for three years, wrapped up a Ph.D. in English Literature at Yale in less than four years, authored six major academic papers. He was hired right away as a tenured full professor at a tony prep school in Providence. I knew it as a place where young princes and princesses of privilege go to be with their own kind and start making contacts. The kind of place that my Irish ancestors kept nice and clean. Chill, Michael. That war is over, they say. Doctor Norman's field of interest was Elizabethan poetry. Philip Sidney was one of the most prominent Elizabethan poets. Coincidence? Probably. Maybe someone at the school could shed some light on that.

I called the school Wednesday morning. The bored–sounding person who answered put me through to a young reference librarian named Carol DiStefano. She hadn't heard of Leo Norman. Her computer told her he died in the 1940s. Carol would see what she could find out and call me back.

Reference librarians enjoy getting their hands dirty and learning new things. I liked Carol right away.

The return call came two hours later. Carol had put together a package of what she found on Professor Norman and would be happy to mail it to me. I told her I'd be even happier to come and pick it up, to thank her personally. Great, she replied, and if you're coming down here anyway, you might see if you can talk to Professor Emeritus Lester Sackett. He was in his mid–nineties now, but still kept an office at the school and dropped in most days. He lived alone and missed the academic action. Leo Norman had been an outside mentor on Lester's Ph.D. dissertation. It was a comparative analysis of works by an English poet named Philip Sidney. Thank you, Carol, and thank you, gut. Carol gave me Professor Sackett's telephone number. He might be in now, because she had seen him walking by the library earlier that morning.

I called Professor Sackett. He picked up on the first ring. I told him I was doing family history research, and that I was related by marriage to Leo Norman. Did Professor Sackett recall him?

"Oh yes, I certainly do. He was most helpful to me on my dissertation and was the reason I eventually came back to this school. Leo died young and tragically, you know. A great loss. I'm afraid the drinking eventually exacted its terrible price. You already knew that, of course."

I did now. And I knew I'd learn a lot more if I could meet with Lester Sackett.

"Professor, may I meet with you, at your convenience? I have seen Leo's name used in connection with Philip Sidney and want to find out as much as I possibly can."

"Yes, I would enjoy that. I like meeting new people. I could even do it today. Would it be possible for you to come to the faculty dining hall at, say, 2:30?"

Would it ever.

"Your uncle Leo was a respected authority on Philip Sidney. He redefined rising star. I fear I never rose to his level as an academic. I'm rather irrelevant these days, a relic of a bygone era, collecting dust in my office. I have some fond memories and I will be pleased to tell you everything I remember. That might not be as much as you would hope. It was so long ago."

"Professor Sackett, I can't tell you how much I look forward to meeting you."

I arrived at the faculty dining hall right on time. A student greeted me and brought me to meet Lester Sackett at his table. This was what a film director had in mind for a professor. Rimless glasses, neatly-combed gray hair, herringbone blazer, pressed gray slacks, polished wing–tips. He looked twenty years younger than he was. Lester Sackett didn't have the appearance of a relic taking up space.

"Thank you again for meeting with me, and so quickly, Professor."

He smiled.

"Delighted. Will you join me for lunch? One of the perks of professorship here is free meals as long as one lives, for faculty and a guest. They must be hoping I'll die soon. Now, what can I tell you about Leo Norman? Or shall I tell you all that I remember?"

170

"The latter, if it's no imposition."

"No imposition at all. Leo was a complicated person. A troubled spirit, but a genius, capable both of extraordinary generosity and extraordinary arrogance. Leo never could accomplish everything he thought he should accomplish. I suppose no person could. The darkness overtook him. Over a period of years, I sadly watched him sink into an unhappy life of paranoia and self–destruction. He thought other people were trying to get information from him and kill him. One would not have thought Philip Sidney was so controversial. There was so much he kept to himself.

"I was a student here, but I never knew him at that time. My interest then was American literature. In senior year, I decided to pursue college and graduate work in English literature, which led me to Elizabethan poetry. A graduate professor suggested I write my dissertation on Philip Sidney. Well, the next thing I knew, I got a call from Leo Norman, offering me guidance and mentoring. We had a chuckle over the fact that we had spent four years on the same preparatory school campus without meeting each other. And now we would be working together, Leo based in Providence and I at Columbia. I accepted his offer gratefully. I cannot begin to tell you what a giant Leo was in his field."

"Professor, did Leo Norman ever mention traveling to Ireland to conduct his research?"

"Please, call me Lester. Yes, indeed. He went several times with Brigid. On two trips, I accompanied them. Leo was doing research on Philip Sidney in Galway. He was exploring his theory that seminal works of Philip Sidney were inspired by western Irish folklore. Leo trusted only primary sources. I have photographs of us taken on those trips. Leo gave them to me right after our second trip, and made me promise I would hold onto them. I don't know why, but he was adamant and I honored his request. He made me promise if anyone ever asked me about him or his work in Ireland, and mentioned the name 'John Taylor', then I should give the person the photographs and any of Leo's red research binders in my possession. Isn't it strange? Brigid spent her time in Ireland researching her own family and translating for Leo. She was fluent in Irish Gaelic."

"Did they mention an ancestor of Brigid who might be connected to Philip Sidney?"

"Yes, most definitely. Leo was not interested in Brigid's family history. Yet I have a clear memory of him being intrigued by one of his wife's Irish ancestors possibly knowing Philip Sidney. If I ever had the name, I've long since forgotten it. He was a poet, I believe, and Leo thought he might have been a major influence on Philip. He was focusing his research along those lines.

"Leo was anxious to complete his work and publish his findings. Leo and Brigid spent long days poring over documents in dark archives somewhere. They would leave before the sun came up and return in late afternoon. My job was mostly as errand boy and secretary, and I helped Leo organize and transcribe some notes. I didn't mind, because I got to work on my own dissertation during the day, with pay, and Leo made time to help me at night."

"Did Leo and Brigid tell you exactly where they spent their days? Did you ever accompany them?"

"No, I was not invited. Leo kept many of his activities secret. I do recall one thing I thought unusual. Sometimes a young gentleman would appear at our apartment early in the morning, and he would leave with Leo and Brigid. Leo introduced him as an academic colleague. I recall his last name being Carroll, because my roommate in graduate school had the same name and was from the same part of Ireland. It turned out they were not related. The gentleman had a definite military demeanor. He was not in uniform, but the erect posture, polite formality, content–free clipped speech and darting eyes gave him away. I come from a military family and it's easy to recognize. I once walked in on them unannounced, and saw Leo and Professor Carroll going over sheets of numbers. Leo seemed startled and told me they were working on a numerical system to catalog their research. But I've not seen such a system, and at my age, I've seen them all."

"If you'll indulge me, Lester, I have only a few more questions. Did Leo or Brigid ever mention an Irish pirate named Grace O'Malley?"

"I could not give you a particular name. On several occasions, over a glass or two of wine, I recall Leo remarking what a unique man Philip Sidney must have been to be able to negotiate with heads of state and pirates, while still finding time to produce great literature. Leo seemed to become more and more intrigued by what he called 'Philip's many hats'. Philip may have been the only intellectual equal Leo ever encountered.

"Would you care to have me make a tape for you, with all my recollections? My memories of Leo, his work and his musings, including our summers in

Ireland? I will also give you our photographs from Galway. Nobody has mentioned John Taylor to me in seventy years, so I suppose they should now live with one of Leo's relatives. I'll look through my papers to see if I have forgotten anything. That was a happy time in my life and I'm pleased to share what I know with you.

"Leo died a year or two after our second trip to Ireland and his research there was never published. To be honest, I wondered about his death. He was in superb shape and an excellent swimmer, and yet they say he drowned. But I will always cherish the long hours he spent helping me with my dissertation. It was accepted with highest honors. Leo was so generous of his time and expertise with me. He said he believed it would benefit him down the road."

"Lester, you have also been so generous with your time and memories. I would love to have the tape and photographs. Do you know of any other possessions or papers of Leo Norman's that might still be around? Books, documents, research notes, perhaps a portrait?"

"Not really. Brigid wanted nothing from his office. Leo kept so little there anyway. Unlike most academics, myself included, he was no hoarder. He left one shelf of ring binders containing his life's work. Leo did love his ring binders. They were custom–made, his personal symbols. Every bit of his research went into two–inch ring binders, black for data, white for analysis, nothing out of place. I never saw any red ones. Brigid offered his binders to the school, but her offer was not accepted. Had I known, I would have come from New York and taken them back with me. Brigid probably looked through his

174

papers for anything related to her own family history and discarded the rest. I don't think she would have understood his notes. Leo used a most curious shorthand.

"It's tragic, Michael, a lifetime of hard work thrown away. If anything survived, I doubt it will be found some seventy years later. I'll send you my tape and the photographs."

Unbelievable. The key to Aedan's puzzle might have wound up in a prep school dumpster, with no back–up. Life before technology wasn't always better.

After lunch with Lester, I stopped in the school library to pick up the package Carol had waiting for me. I gave both Lester and Carol a wine and cheese basket, a small enough token of my appreciation for what they had done. It turned out that Carol and I both spent some teenage years in the same town. It's a small world, especially in Rhode Island. Ugly school blazers and syrupy smell of trust funds aside, this was an impressive place. Grace O'Malley would have done well here.

I emailed Aedan as soon as I got back to the office.

The reply came in ten minutes.

This is a most important development, Michael. It is disappointing, of course, if relevant information might have been found and discarded. You are to be congratulated. You have fully confirmed the connection between James Tiernan and Philip Sidney, very useful to me in pursuing other lines of inquiry. I trust you now appreciate what I meant

175

when I said our work cannot easily be done from three thousand miles away.

I am most anxious to review a copy of Lester Sackett's tape and the Leo Norman information. They are credentialed academics. Hearsay may not be admissible in a court of law, but credentialed hearsay is often the best we can get in the court of history.

Very well done indeed, Aedan

No, Aedan. It wasn't just an important development. It was a game–changer and you know it. And what is this drivel about needing the blessing of trained academic historians at every step? Either we find Grace O'Malley or we don't, right? Everything else was style points. We had added several new actors to the cast, and who knows what fruit it might bear?

I recalled one of the first murder trials I had seen. The grizzled beat cop testified he came across a man who had been stabbed to death. The earnest young defense attorney asked how he could be sure without a medical background that the death wasn't a suicide? The cop replied he found the decedent lying face down in a pool of blood, hands tied behind his back, with a meat cleaver sticking out from between his shoulder blades. He didn't need a medical degree to ascertain the cause of death.

I would have thought letting alcohol destroy your life, then drowning in an ocean of middle–aged ego, was relevant to the issue of one's professional judgment and credibility. Maybe it's the difference between thinking like a lawyer and thinking like an historian. A Yale Ph.D. trumps a lot of bad life choices. I still wasn't sure where all this was going, but I wasn't going to get too excited about today until I saw what Lester Sackett sent me.

Anna called from Montreal Wednesday night. Sylvie Lepine was ready to discharge Glenn Friday afternoon. Sara and I would meet the plane and make sure Glenn got to his home in Cambridge. We hadn't heard anything from Glenn's sister, Patricia. Glenn hadn't, either. So Anna, Kata, Sara and I would make sure Sylvie's magic was not wasted. And the package of Anna, Sara and Kata sure looked to me like a nice straight—up trade for a sister who couldn't be bothered. Glenn would have to decide.

I never liked giving Anna orders. She was our partner, whether she was willing to admit it in public or not. But she had been through the wringer. She was going to take ten days off, no discussion. Get out of Dodge and take some unadulterated vacation. I told her I'd change the office locks and call security if she even walked by our building. Anna protested, as I expected, but seemed relieved. Sara and I would do the checking on Glenn, even if Glenn might have preferred Sara, Anna and Kata. Glenn had to understand miracles come with a price tag.

"Thank you, Michael. It will be so many days away from the office. Promise me you won't hire someone to take my job."

"Anna, of all the things you could possibly have to worry about in life, being fired is by far the least likely to happen. You're on the hiring committee, remember?"

She called back in an hour, excited. Kata had extra vacation time and her other daughter, Vica, could

177

get time off from her job as a social worker. Vica needed a break too. They were going to take a family vacation, something they hadn't been able to do for years.

"And do you know where we're going?"

"Please don't tell me Las Vegas. If I ever see a picture of you with Elvis, I'll vomit."

"And if you ever see a picture of me with Elvis, you'll know I was kidnapped. No, we're going back to Montreal. It's my new favorite city. Vica has never been there, and Kata only got a chance to see a little bit of it. My mother took me there a few times when I was growing up. Now I want to bring my own daughters. I think we'll avoid one park where they might recognize us. Glenn and I will both be back in the office a week from next Wednesday, just like old times."

It wasn't going to be like old times. It would be the start of better times. The Bradley and Tiernan Last Waltz had begun. I wouldn't have guessed it would start in an operating room in Montreal. Life does get weird. The endure part was over and good riddance. They say adversity makes you stronger, and I guess it does, up to a point. Then it grinds you into fine dust. You blow away like you never existed. It was time to gorge on the prevailing.

Since things were quiet, I threw myself into Grace O'Malley research on Thursday. And I told Anna if she wasn't on her way to Montreal by Saturday morning, I'd start running ads for young, pretty multi-lingual office fixers. I think Anna liked the way I phrased it. She gave me one of those probably—a—compliment in Hungarian. It's such a beautiful language when you don't understand it.

I was still inclined to give Aedan the benefit of the doubt, but only for a little longer. It took Thursday and most of Friday to re—research ship passenger logs and possible Tiernan family connections in New England. I scoured records from every East Coast American and Canadian port from 1850 through 1883. If Daniel Tiernan had been to the United States before 1883, I couldn't find it. All I knew for sure was the Daniel Tiernan family arrived in Boston in May 1883, and he reported for work at a cotton mill in Connecticut two days later. A year on, Daniel was working at a silk mill in New Jersey, and a few years after that, he was laying railroad tracks around New England. I'd head down to Connecticut on Monday to see what I could find on those textile mill owners. I called Sara and asked her if she wanted to ride shotgun.

"Sure, there's always something for me to do. But I already miss the White Stag and the food, drinks and cigars with Aedan. I'm glad my parents didn't live long enough to see what I've become, thanks to you. We've got to solve this puzzle. I need more celebrations at the White Stag. Every pig in Ireland must die."

No pressure, Michael.

Glenn's flight arrived in Boston Friday night, right on time. He was moving well and looked a lot better. Anna and Kata navigated him through Customs and we got him set up in his house. A nurse would be by in an hour and would stay around—the—clock for five days. It was Glenn's idea. He had been through too much to take chances now. Then the

179

visiting nurses would drop in three times a day, and Sara and I would fill in any gaps.

Bienvenue, Glenn. Au revoir, Anna, Kata and Vica. Have a great vacation. You earned it.

CHAPTER NINETEEN

Monday was a long, frustrating day in Connecticut. The mill where Daniel Tiernan worked had been torn down, and local libraries and historical societies had few records. Mill owners in the 1880s liked Irish workers because they worked hard for short money. Mr. Tuke made sure his emigrants had another advantage. They spoke English.

I found nothing suggesting that anything might have been delivered from Ireland to the mill owners. These textile mill owners were hard–assed businessmen, not historians, collectors or aristocrats. And they sure weren't Irish. A local museum had a chilling exhibit on a day in the life of the 1880s textile worker. Fourteen–hour shifts, six days a week, in oppressive mill heat and toxic air. The machines could chew you up if you got distracted for just a moment. No work for any reason, no pay. No child labor laws or OSHA. Long days, short lives. This was the better place the Tiernans had come to. To them it was better, and they would make it better still by refusing to give up. They looked up, down, and side to side, but they never looked back. I was humbled, but Michael Tiernan was getting tired of wasting precious time.

The package from Lester Sackett arrived at my home that night. Lester must have started working on it the day we met. A note on his tape joked he no longer had the luxury of being able to procrastinate. Lester did everything in true academic fashion – a statement of his background and credentials, followed by ninety minutes of detailed recollections of Leo Norman and his work, including the trips to

Galway. He left out any references to Professor Carroll or John Taylor. Maybe he felt a little guilty about giving me the photographs of Leo and Brigid in Ireland. These were the photographs he promised Leo he'd always keep. I'd hold Professor Carroll and John Taylor in reserve for now and not blow Lester's cover.

Five of the photos were marked on the back with dates and the word 'Galway'. One was undated and marked 'Carroll Street, Galway'. I made two copies of the tape and would mail the original to Aedan first thing in the morning. I knew he wouldn't want to wait for mail. So I called Lester and left a thank-you message on his voicemail. Then I scanned the photographs, transcribed the tape and emailed everything off to Aedan just after midnight.

I immediately regretted doing so. Aedan was tethered to his email and I had forgotten about the time difference. He responded less than two hours later, saying what I sent him was better than he expected. Does this man ever sleep? He thought Lester obviously was a trained and credentialed academic, so his opinions must be given considerable weight. Will you stop putting me down, Aedan? I told him I needed to study the Sackett materials with fresh eyeballs. Could we talk later? The reply came back, 'Will call 10:00 tonight your time'.

I was back on the case right after dinner. Let's step back and look at the big picture. What do we know with some confidence? Leo Norman spent five months over two years in the Galway area, chasing down Philip Sidney's Irish connections, and those were only the trips we knew about. Leo and Brigid were skilled researchers. Would they have spent so much time there if they weren't sniffing something out? I didn't think so, unless they had another agenda in Galway.

That top–secret military intelligence thing still nibbled at me. Leo trusted only primary sources, and he and Brigid were spending long days in archival dungeons. They wouldn't tell Lester where they were working. Why didn't they want him to know? Brigid was helping Leo translate from Irish, so some primary sources must have been in Irish, which wasn't surprising. And Leo's original notes likely were buried in a Rhode Island landfill. How could I reconstruct anything now? I couldn't, unless there was a wild card in the deck. Leo thought those photographs were important.

Look at them, Michael. What are they telling you? Leo insisted Lester keep them. Leo knew Lester would never discard them. And Leo told Lester someone might start using the right words, and should be given the photographs. Nobody did, so I got them.

What was so special about them? I lined up the six photographs next to each other and started comparing them, like I had seen medical examiners do on television. I took out the big magnifying glass Sara and I used to check each other for ticks. The photos looked like nothing more than surprisingly clear shots taken at different locations and different times. It was sunny in three photos and cloudy or raining in the other three. Shadows in some, no shadows in others. Five of them showed just Leo and Brigid in full frown. No smiling for the camera, but they were an attractive couple in their day. The sixth photo showed Leo, Brigid and Lester. They were all smiling and I could recognize the location as being the Galway Spanish Arch. That photo was probably the outlier, the one that made you look more closely at the others to see what was different.

There was something else in all of the other photographs of Leo and Brigid. It might be important if it was there. The detail was so small. I checked over and over with the magnifying glass until my eyes got blurry. Yes. I was seeing it right.

Sara stuck her head in to see what was going on.

"A little help here, partner. Every pig in Ireland must die, correct? We're showing Aedan how good we are, correct?"

"Please, Michael, it's *Game of Thrones* night. Can't we do this tomorrow?"

"Tomorrow and tomorrow and tomorrow, creeps in this petty pace from day to day. Sara, we've got our own *Game of Thrones* going here."

"Okay, twenty minutes now, more tomorrow morning."

I told her what I thought I had seen in the pictures. She went back and forth with the magnifying glass for a few minutes.

"You're good. I wouldn't have noticed it, but it was intentional. It's not clear to me how much it means, though."

"Read Lester's report between your medieval bloodbaths."

"Sure. There might be something else interesting about those pictures. Give me fifteen minutes alone with Mr. Magnifying Glass."

She moved back and forth among the pictures, slowly, then quickly, then slowly. She started absent–mindedly scratching the back of her neck. That was a good sign. It's what Sara did when she saw something.

Then she put down the magnifying glass, dropped her bombshell, and went off to binge on *Game of Thrones*. Mother of God, how did she ever see that? She was so good at this.

Aedan called on the stroke of 10:00, middle of the night where he was. Actually, he was fifteen seconds off, inexcusable for him, but he probably had to push extra buttons to get the call to Massachusetts. I asked him what he thought of Lester's materials.

"They provide some additional confirmation of the connection between James Tiernan and Philip Sidney. So now, we have the major players connected, and in Galway. I am not sure how much more they do. But nailing down the connection beyond any doubt is not just another brick in the wall. It is a cornerstone brick."

"If the brick in the wall is a musical reference, Aedan, then I'm impressed. Doesn't it suggest also there might be a stash of documents related to Grace O'Malley hidden somewhere in Galway?"

"You've made quite a leap, Michael. With all due respect, it's a hallmark of the untrained mind. Lester never recalled hearing Leo speak of Grace O'Malley."

"True, but he remembered hearing Leo say Philip Sidney was negotiating with both heads of state and pirates. Grace was the big cheese pirate in Galway. Who else could it have been? Maybe Leo found a connection in whatever he was researching in Galway, and maybe he found out a lot more. We

185

know Grace O'Malley met Philip Sidney in Galway."

"But we do not know how many times, for what reason, or who might have been present. If Leo did discover relevant documents in Galway, who is to say they are still there? And why would he not tell anyone, even Lester? And if Brigid was translating Irish, how do we know she was translating it correctly? There are dialects, and the Irish language has changed since the 1500s. It's an interesting theory, Michael, but without more information and rigorous historical analysis, there are not enough bricks in the wall. And it was a musical reference.

"Michael, if the documents existed, how would we know where to find them? Many have explored the most likely locations without success, including one Aedan Burns."

"I thought you'd never ask. Look closely at those photographs, Aedan. In particular, the five photographs of Brigid and Leo. They were each taken in Galway, two during one summer and two others the next summer. The fifth one is undated and says 'Carroll Street, Galway'. The sixth is only a tourist photo of Leo, Brigid and Lester. I think there's a law you can't go to Galway without having that very picture taken at the Spanish Arch, so you can disregard it for now. Is there anything you notice about the other five?"

"Well, as you said, each one shows only Brigid and Leo. He's such a dour fellow, must be Scottish. I presume they got a passer–by to take the pictures in each location. I don't immediately recognize any of them, but I would guess they are in or close to Galway City. None of the locations looks like a

186

tourist destination, and at least one was taken on Carroll Street. Perhaps they were strolling through the city and wanted to remember various neighborhoods they liked. There's nothing else remarkable about them."

"You're saying pretty much what I thought when I first looked at them. Then I saw something, and I asked Sara to take a look. She knows more about staging a photograph than anyone else we'll ever meet. She saw something else, and I think the two things together are important. Let me start with what Sara saw, or rather, what she observed.

"She's sure the five photographs of Brigid and Lester were taken at almost the same location, only from different angles. There are no street or building signs or obvious telltales. They appear to be ordinary shots taken at several locations. But there's a small tree in each picture, more of a scraggly bush. You need a magnifying glass. It's near the corners in four pictures and close to the middle in the fifth. The photographs were staged so you wouldn't notice a small tree in the background. Your eyes don't focus on a dull, busy background. You zero in on the people. It's the same tree, Aedan. Sara is sure these five photographs were taken within thirty yards of each other."

"And so one would think they were taken on Carroll Street. Interesting, but what would be the significance of it?"

"In the five photos, Leo is carrying an open shoulder bag. In each photo, you can see something sticking out of the top of the bag. It shows best with a magnifying glass, and it's easier to see in the sunny photos. I'm sure it's a ring binder. In the

187

photo marked Carroll Street, it's two ring binders, one black and one white. Lester said Leo always entered his research notes into ring binders, black for data, white for analysis. In every photo, the ring binders were carefully positioned in the bag so you could see exactly what they were if you looked closely. Doing it that way took some effort. Sara says you stage the important elements first, then work out from them. These photos taken together were meant to tell someone where Leo and Brigid were doing their work.

"Aedan, tourists don't carry ring binders. In the Spanish Arch photo, Leo has the same shoulder bag, but with no ring binders sticking out. You can see an umbrella, a newspaper, and what could have been their lunch, but no ring binder. Sara also tells me every good picture is set up to draw the eye to something and away from something. You have to force yourself to look where your eyes don't want to go. The tree and the binders are visual fingerprints.

"And here's something else. My father used to play a similar game with me when I was a boy. I had to group pictures from a pile by identifying a small similarity in them. He said it would train me to use my eyes. Brigid liked the game, and she sometimes played it with us. She was damn good and played to win, always. I never once beat her. My father was the only one who could beat her, and it drove her nuts. I think she might have been playing the game again in Galway. Even if I'm right, we'd still have to find the location."

"Did you not say it was Carroll Street?"

"I checked street directories, old maps, everything I could find. There is no Carroll Street in Galway

188

today, and I can't find any evidence there ever was one. Maybe the name changed along the way. I have to research it more."

"And if there never was a Carroll Street?"

"Then it was code. Here's something I don't think you know. Before he got his doctorate, Leo Norman had top–level military access and security clearance for three years. That was no surprise. Then I asked a friend with some murky connections to do a little poking around in the files. Some of them even he couldn't get into, but he discovered both Leo and Brigid had top–level security clearance between 1941 and 1943. Pretty odd for a high school professor and a research assistant, don't you think?"

I didn't share with Aedan that my mole also told me the security clearance file jacket was cross–referenced 'Dominican'. Best to keep that under wraps for now. It was probably code for the group contact person or project name. I needed a few more days to try to put all this together. The scent was getting stronger.

"So Michael believes Leo and Brigid uncovered information relevant to Grace O'Malley, and the task now is to locate where they were working. And he believes the photographs were intended to provide enough information to do such, notwithstanding they seem to point to a street that never existed."

"I know what you're thinking, Aedan. It's a lot of implausible dot–connecting. What do we have that's any better? You have no idea how strange my family is. It's the sort of thing Brigid and Leo might have done."

"Then I shall look into it also. I have access to my own local resources. Please send me the originals or the highest–resolution scans or duplicates you can create. If you are correct, why do you think Leo and Brigid felt the need to tell someone where to look?"

"I have no idea, but I don't think Lester understood the significance of the photos. He would have told me. Something, that mysterious something, told him he should give them to me so many years later. Maybe I'm grasping at straws. Leo and Brigid's focus in Galway was Philip Sidney, not Grace O'Malley. Their puzzle wasn't our puzzle."

"True, but puzzles can overlap. What you have told me tonight is intriguing, if not yet clearly relevant. Coincidence is seldom causation, but we shall go where the facts take us."

I was able to find a 24–hour print shop, and emailed Aedan the highest–resolution copies they could produce. And I left the originals to be cleaned up and enhanced. I'd send the originals to Aedan when I got them back. At least I had his full attention now.

Early Wednesday night, I got a call from Lester. Something amazing had happened that afternoon. His school received by wire transfer a two hundred and fifty thousand dollar gift from one Professor Aedan Burns in Ireland. The gift was to be used for research stipends to deserving students, and for a two thousand dollar prize to be awarded at every graduation ceremony. The prize would be called the Lester Sackett Medal for Excellence in Literature. The only conditions were that Lester choose the recipients and personally present the award at graduation, for as long as he was able. Lester didn't know why it happened, but it was a great honor and he knew it must have had something to do with our conversation.

I emailed Aedan and told him his gift had gone over very well. Aedan replied people like Lester must not be allowed to fade into obscurity. He had earned his legacy, and he should be able to stand in front of the graduating class and hear their applause. The students should know who Lester was, what he looked like, and that he still mattered. Lester was a winner by any measure.

Aedan was telling me something else too. A quarter–mil check in Lester's name was a much bigger thank–you than my wine and cheese baskets. What Lester sent us must have been very important, and Aedan wanted to make sure I understood it.

I told Sara what I thought. She asked me how many mountains I saw coming up with it. Not everything in life has a hidden meaning. Sometimes people like to play around with camera angles. We couldn't rule out that the photos were nothing more than an exercise in perspective and staging. Sara said she did it a lot to keep the skills sharp. Sometimes what you see is all there is. As if she would know. I didn't get the impression that Leo and Brigid were the kind of people who played around with anything. There was always a purpose.

I told Sara if I ever wrote a book about cracking the O'Malley Protocol, I'd probably have to kill her character off in the first few chapters. She wasn't working out. Sara was okay with being killed off, but thought I should run it by Meryl Streep first. She had decided Meryl would be playing her in the film.

And Sara wanted creative control over the death scene and any memorial service. I was afraid to ask. I told her Meryl Streep's career would probably survive Sara dying in my book. But I couldn't kill Sara's character off now. She had discovered a major piece of the puzzle. Meryl would have to live with another Academy Award nomination.

I was starting to develop some theories of my own. Maybe I could channel both Sherlock Holmes and my own rumbling gut. Sara thought I needed meds. I might have to agree with her this time.

"Michael, I'll give you the logic part, but the stomach twinges when you think you hear some door opening? It's over the top. Try a good antacid."

"You don't understand anatomy. The intestine is a highly evolved cerebral cortex. They even look alike in a laboratory. Haven't you ever eaten tripe?"

"I know more about anatomy than you think. Cerebral cortex and intestine only look alike if you live on potato chips, so maybe for you, it's true."

"Sara, have you ever started to lay down a brush stroke, and then something moved your hand and it turned out better than what you intended? Serious question."

"Sure, and it's often when I'm working my way through a bottle of wine. The wine is doing it, or more likely, the law of averages. I don't understand exactly how inspiration works."

"It isn't the wine and it isn't the law of averages. It's something inside you nudging you in the right direction. That something knows when to push and when to hold back. In your case, it might be coming from the creative part of your brain. In my case, it's the stomach lining. Gut feelings are usually correct if you marinate them in bitter experience and season with a dash of logic."

"You need help, Michael."

So maybe the best way to handle Aedan was to play his game right back at him. He seemed taken aback but smiled when I handed him the sealed envelope and told him not to open it until October. Aedan enjoyed a good game. It was something he would have done. If Aedan expected me to recognize veiled messages, let's see if he could do it too. I might have the advantage there. I was married to Sara.

There was another research project I wanted to begin first thing in the morning. Aedan casually mentioned he was a descendant of Grace O'Malley. I didn't pick up on it as being important, but he said it twice. It was time to run the Grace O'Malley line of descent forward and the Aedan Burns line back. There might be some surprises there. For a guy who talked a lot, Aedan didn't make much idle conversation.

CHAPTER TWENTY

I had blocked out several days for trips to Connecticut to see if I could turn up more information on the Connecticut mill owners, but decided not to do it. After looking at what Lester had sent me, it would be a waste of time. There was no connection between the Tuke Program and Grace O'Malley. I had given Aedan enough benefit of the doubt. On Thursday morning, I spent a few hours drafting a report of what I had done and found in Connecticut, or more accurately, done and not found. I emailed it to Aedan and told him I needed to talk to him again. The reply came in ten minutes. He'd call me at 6:00 that night. Good. I wasn't going to let this one be another Professor Burns lecture. I wasn't in college anymore.

"That was a very thorough presentation, Michael, but trees do not grow fruit overnight. I don't believe you have yet exhausted a possible Tuke Fund connection. I would like you to spend another week or so on it. Slow and steady wins the race. I would welcome any updates."

"No, Aedan, I'm not going to do that, unless you have specific information which would help me. You said a colleague of yours speculated that the Tuke Program emigrants might have been a delivery service. What details do you have? I want to be fair to you. Surely you didn't pay me a lot of money only to add information to my own family history folders."

Aedan was startled. I could feel it through the phone line.

194

"That wouldn't seem to make much sense, would it? You must concede we can't always predict where useful information comes from. We have seen that with your aunt Brigid. Thanks to a casual remark by a competent librarian in Providence, we have been able to establish beyond doubt a Galway link between James Tiernan and Philip Sidney, and perhaps more."

"You're right on that one. It surprised me as much as it must have surprised you. But I would have eventually realized that Leo Norman was someone I should know more about, and maybe things would have turned out exactly the same way. Look, we're trying to find Grace O'Malley. I don't have time to take it slow, and nobody has ever called me steady. I'm not one of your star–struck students, Aedan. I'm pretty good at figuring things out too, and I've eaten a lot of dirt to get good. When clients give me money, they expect results, and I expect to deliver them. I'm only a cynical lawyer, not a trained historian or academic, but I'm not going to waste more of my time or your money. There is no Tuke Fund or Connecticut mill or Daniel Tiernan connection, full stop. The answer is hidden somewhere in what Lester sent us. Fire me for insubordination if you want. I'll send back every damn penny you paid me, and good luck getting the answers on your own."

"I think I just got some of them. Cynicism is a virtue each of us should strive to perfect. I will accept that your time now is better spent on Leo and Brigid, and James Tiernan. However, we must proceed in an orderly, academically disciplined manner, laying one confirmed brick at a time. We cannot race off willy–nilly in all directions. Are you capable of doing that, Michael?"

You know, I think when I see you again in October, I'm going to kill you, Aedan. My brain doesn't work that way, never has, never will. Be cool, Michael, be cool. Then strike.

"Good advice, Aedan. I'll try to put a saddle on my brain. Should I pursue further communications with Lester? You'd enjoy meeting him, by the way."

"I have met him, at least by videoconference and email. Yes, he is a delightful fellow and still in possession of a razor–sharp intellect. Let me deal with Lester. I have asked him to prepare a chapter on historical research for my upcoming course materials, with proper attribution, of course. He is a thoroughbred, Michael, and needs exercise."

"You're the expert on that. Out of curiosity, when you chatted with Lester, did you happen to mention Grace O'Malley again?"

"No. You did and I see no reason to pique his curiosity by beating a drum. Even professional colleagues must keep little secrets from each other, wouldn't you agree?"

You don't know the half of it, Aedan, but thanks for making this easier. Let's show Aedan a few face cards.

"Indeed. I do that myself sometimes. Trust has to be earned, right? I can tell you this. Lester is extremely happy that Aedan Burns came into his life."

"As I hope you are. My best to Sara, Glenn and Anna, and please wish Glenn a speedy recovery. Is there anything else you wish to discuss this evening?"

196

"Yes. You should be looking into a Professor John Carroll at Dominican College on Taylor's Hill, Galway, in the early 1940s. I think you'll find especially relevant information."

There was stunned silence on the other end.

"Michael, what are you talking about? Upon what do you base this?"

"Maybe it's only the haphazard ramblings of the undisciplined, untrained mind. I can't give you the details right now. Confidentiality issues."

"Certainly, Michael. I'll see what I can find out."

That was fun. Actually, it wasn't that hard, but a good magician makes the trick look more difficult than it is. I had the words "John", "Taylor", "Carroll" and "Dominican" to work with. Run the combinations through an internet search engine, screen the results, and it was a short hop to Dominican College in Galway. There were a lot of Carrolls around there, so it seemed logical that John might be his first name. And eureka, there was a Professor John Carroll at Dominican in the 1940s. You weren't expecting this from the other side of the pond, were you, Aedan?

I could almost feel him smiling. He was starting to enjoy our match. The competition might be turning out a little better than he expected, But why is it a competition? Aren't we supposed to be on the same team?

Running the Grace O'Malley lines of descent took two days. I didn't like to trust research that other people had done. But some respected genealogists had posted the O'Malley lines, although with gaps. There wasn't enough time for me to verify everything independently. I thought it strange that Aedan had not posted any of his own family trees. I'd start by running the Aedan Burns line back as far as I could, and then run Grace O'Malley lines forward, to see if there was any overlap. I'd begin with Grace. Ladies first, even if the lady is a pirate.

I wasn't able to find a link between Aedan Burns and any known descendants of Grace O'Malley and Iron Richard Bourke. Grace had a previous husband, Donal O'Flaherty. That marriage produced three children: Margaret or Maeve, Murrough and Owen. The Murrough line was well documented, but there was nothing there. The Maeve and Owen lines were cloudier. There were missing or weak links in the chain. If Aedan was a direct descendant of Grace O'Malley, it would have to be through one of those lines. As usual, Aedan had thrown me a clue to see if I'd recognize it. It wasn't an immediate priority. There was a bigger fish to catch first. Why hadn't I been able to trace Aedan's ancestry back more than one generation?

You're not that good after all, Michael. You've run into this before. You should have realized right away what was going on. Wall, say hello to your new brick. Now how can I prove it?

CHAPTER TWENTY–ONE

Glenn had a setback on Saturday. He was light–headed and more fatigued than he thought he should be. The visiting nurse called his primary care physician in Boston. An answering service transferred her to the coverage doctor, who put Glenn "on watch" without even talking to him. I guess "on watch" means watch me tell you to call back Monday when the office is open. Glenn insisted on calling Sylvie Lepine. He thought she wouldn't be too busy to talk to him.

She wasn't. Sylvie called back in less than twenty minutes. She talked to the visiting nurse and then Glenn, and told him she thought the symptoms were normal. Glenn's body was putting itself back together after a surgical assault. It would take time. She gave Glenn her private cell phone number and told him to use it anytime if something worried him. If he felt any worse, don't be a macho man. Get to a hospital right away and have someone there call her, night or day. Glenn was still her patient, and those self–important Boston doctors better not be thinking they could fluff her off because she was a polite Canadian. Glenn had found himself one hell of a surgeon.

Sara and I decided to stay with him for the weekend. He apologized for putting us out, but he wasn't. Sara and I both had things we could work on. Glenn's house was big, but felt empty. He wasn't much on toys or look–at–me baubles. He only kept things that mattered. Sara was happy when she saw that included several of her paintings.

By mid–afternoon, Glenn was feeling better and even asked if we could get him a pizza. Then he bitched about it not having enough anchovies. Not enough anchovies was a difficult concept for my brain to process, but I guess this was another good sign. Bitch away, my friend. Who cares if your road to recovery is paved with sardine fragments? We'll get you another one with a mound of anchovies. They can use the leftover ones to make tires or fill potholes.

Aedan's clues were flying around like tumbleweeds in a sandstorm. I grew up in Rhode Island and had never actually seen a tumbleweed flying in a sandstorm. But I liked saying it and I had watched a lot of cowboy shows on television.

I spent most of the day grinding through Tiernan message boards and blogs. I got to say a virtual hello to some people I had met online, but found nothing I didn't already know. Now what? Well, I liked to occasionally re–check my 'possible leads' shoeboxes as new information came in. Today would be a good day for that.

Over the years, I had photocopied or printed out thousands of pages of research notes. If anything started to look promising, it got promoted to the computer files. Otherwise it was stuffed back into 'possible leads' shoeboxes, real cardboard shoeboxes, to be looked at again later on. My home office was a technology Jurassic Park.

Emma always rolled her eyeballs when she saw the overflowing cardboard shoeboxes. Hey, at least what was in them didn't vaporize if I upgraded to a better shoebox. I told Emma that if she really wanted me to stop, then maybe she should stop buying so many damn shoes. I could see the logical flaw in that even as I said it, but maybe Emma wouldn't. I had heard the adolescent brain isn't fully developed until the age of twenty–five. Sometimes it takes longer, Sara told me.

I stumbled across a page I had photocopied five years ago from an Irish genealogy magazine which had since gone out of business:

INFORMATION WANTED, regarding MacTiernan siblings believed to be born Sligo circa 1550: Caitriona born 1551, John born 1557, Richard born 1558; parents unknown. Reply to Box 255.

That was interesting. It had never been promoted to the computer files because those names and dates together didn't send a clear signal. I knew Tiernan and MacTiernan were variant spellings of the same family name. This John MacTiernan would have been a few years younger than Philip Sidney, which seemed like a plausible age for an apprentice. Maybe these three siblings had a brother James. My direct ancestor was named Richard and my family was concentrated near Rosses Point on Sligo Harbor. The Reply Box number was a multiple of eighty– five. Just more coincidences, right?

I had spent the equivalent of months trying to expose Tiernan roots in Sligo. Early records there weren't very good and there were so many people with the same or similar names. I had only been able to sift out one definite James Tiernan and one James MacTiernan near Rosses Point. The first was born in 1510, probably too old to have been Philip Sidney's apprentice or colleague. The other was born in 1569, definitely too young. I had nothing on any John or Caitriona MacTiernan. Maybe it was worth another shot. It was the right county and right time period, and what else did I have?

Then I remembered something Aedan mentioned. Did he hand me an instruction manual to see if I would be smart enough to use it? The local clergy sometimes have records that never make it into databases, he said. Spread a bit of grease on clergy palms and you may be surprised what they'll show you. And even colleagues keep secrets from each other, don't they? If I went back to Ireland before October, Aedan would find a way to know I had done it and why. The guy had an intelligence network that Putin would envy. There was a better way. I'd hire a local gun.

It was easy to find professional genealogists near Sligo. Every other person in Ireland is a genealogist. There was one in particular who had good reviews. His name was Patrick Ruddy, and he had been doing this for almost thirty years. We exchanged emails and videoconferenced. I could tell straight away he was good. I liked that he didn't resemble me and would be hard to describe physically. I agreed to hire him for three full days at his daily rate plus expenses, and we'd go from there. I'd wire Patrick his full fee up front on Monday, with an extra thousand euros to be held in escrow. I told him I wanted him to drive to the Rosses Point Abbey and speak to the Mother Abbess. The Abbey went back to the 1400s, and the MacTiernans must have known it well.

Patrick was to hand the Mother Abbess one hundred euros, avoid giving his name and find out if

202

the Abbey had any records on Caitriona, John or Richard MacTiernan in the 1500s. Cash never goes out of style in the Catholic Church and nuns never throw paperwork away. If Mother Abbess delivered the goods, Patrick was to give her another two hundred euros, with a note saying, 'For God's work, with deepest appreciation from the White Stag'.

I was playing a hunch. If Mother Abbess drew a blank, I gave Patrick the names of two other medieval abbeys within thirty miles to check out, and asked him to repeat the process. Those were the only three abbeys or cathedrals in Sligo that were active and old enough possibly to have what I was looking for. Patrick promised me a report within a week.

Glenn was feeling much better by Saturday night. He even started talking about getting back to the office a day early. Sylvie wanted him to rest at least through Tuesday, so Sara told Glenn she'd tie him to the bedposts if she caught him trying to leave the house before next Wednesday. Glenn joked that having Sara tie him to the bedposts might lift his spirits and speed up his recovery. She told him his recovery wouldn't be helped if she then strangled him, which she fully intended to do. It was great having the real Glenn back.

Anna called later from Montreal. We didn't tell her about Glenn's setback. She was having a wonderful time with her daughters and asked if she could stay an extra two days. Holy Hungarian goulash, Batman. She thinks she has to ask? Anna wanted to know again if she would have a job when she came back. I told her that would be up to the pretty young replacement sitting at her desk. She was working out well. Even Mr. Bennett liked her. I didn't want to carry it too far, just in case Anna was really worried. Twenty–three years and she was still hard for me to read. So I told her the truth, an unusual first option for me. Stay as long as you want and have a terrific family vacation, but we miss you, so don't be reading any Canadian help–wanted ads.

In the middle of the night, another thought bubbled up, something Aedan had said about his father, which should be easy enough to check out. My brain was getting disturbingly active after midnight since I started following Aedan's suggestion to reflect on things with a glass or two of Irish whiskey. I wondered if that was how Leo Norman started to unravel. From now on, I'd limit it to once or twice a week, just coffee in–between. Special occasions excepted, of course.

Patrick Ruddy emailed me from Sligo on Tuesday. His visit with Mother Abbess had gone well and he wanted me to know a few things right away. The Abbey did have private records. Patrick could confirm that the three MacTiernans were siblings. They had each been born in the years stated in the magazine query and christened at Rosses Point Abbey. The father's name was faded, but it was the same name for the three and it clearly began with an R. It was probably Richard. So far, so good.

Patrick thought there was some other name confusion. The entries for the siblings Richard and Caitriona were easy enough to read because the lettering was darker. He had doubts about the John. The big letter J was legible, but there was a water or acid stain on the other letters. The name could be John, but Patrick didn't think so. He thought it was more likely James. Time and moisture aren't kind to stored documents, so Patrick was making an educated guess, based on years of experience. There wasn't much other information on the male siblings which Patrick took to mean that they had not married or been buried at the Abbey.

Caitriona was the more interesting story. Apparently, she never married and renounced her Catholic faith to become an Anglican nun in 1582. She spent the next fourteen months in Saint Elizabeth Anglican abbey in Dublin. By the grace of God, purred Mother Abbess, Caitriona saw the light, rejected her false gods in 1583 and returned to Sligo. She took the vows of a Catholic nun the same year, and lived in Rosses Point Abbey until she died in 1585.

When she signed up to take her Catholic vows, Caitriona listed one James Tiernan formerly of Galway as a relative. Caitriona's religious name was Sister Fidelma and she was buried in the Abbey cemetery. Patrick thought James MacTiernan in Sligo and James Tiernan in Galway were probably the same person.

The Mother Abbess recalled that another man had come to the Abbey four or five years ago, asking many of the same questions. She didn't remember much about him except he thought Caitriona's story was inspirational. He must have thought the name he was reading on the birth and christening records was John, not James. Then the magazine query was posted. Hello, Aedan Burns.

Patrick didn't know if what he found was enough information for me, so he had given Mother Abbess one hundred euros as an extra offering, plus my note. He would send me copies of the records he had found. What did I want him to do now? Send back the unused money? Give some to the Mother Abbess? See if he could get more information at the other two places? He had called both of them. The person he talked to at the first abbey told him that their old records were destroyed in a fire set by the feckin' Protestants in the 1700s. The headstones in the cemetery would be worn smooth and of no use. The person he talked to at the other place said that any records had been moved somewhere else for storage, then just disappeared. I had run into the same filing system in some American courthouses.

I told Patrick he had done his job and then some. He should keep his fee plus half of whatever was left of the thousand euros, and send the other half to the Mother Abbess with another note reading, 'In memory of Caitriona MacTiernan and the Saint Dermot Orphanage'.

I asked Patrick to please keep his communications with me a secret until further notice. And if his visit with Mother Abbess ever became part of a film, who should play him?

It was time to rattle Aedan's cage. I sent him an email.

Hello, Aedan.

Glenn is on the road to recovery and I am back on the trail of Grace O'Malley. I have uncovered some interesting information at an abbey in Sligo. I am evaluating it now. Sara sends you best wishes and an electronic smoke ring.

Regards, Michael

206

The response came in minutes, as usual. It just read:

Impressive, Michael. You do amaze me.
Cheers, Aedan

Sara sometimes told me the same thing, and it wasn't always a compliment.

Of course he'd contact her. He'd drive up there tomorrow and she'd remember him. Aedan would unleash the charm and the checkbook, and Mother Abbess would sing like a black–robed canary. She'd describe Patrick to him, but he'd have no idea who Patrick was. Patrick hadn't given his real last name and there must be thousands of Patricks in Ireland with absolutely no distinguishing features. God, this was getting fun. Sara will love this.

"I love it, Michael. Is there really a Saint Dermot Orphanage? And why does it matter?"

"There is, or there was. It was near Castlebar and it's been closed for years. Here's why it matters. Aedan told me his father Liam was raised near Castlebar. Then he said a young boy as unsavory as Liam was fortunate to find someone to take him in. At first, I thought it meant the family which owned what's now the White Stag. After all, they gave him a job and a lucrative career. But it seemed like a funny way to phrase it, the part about taking him in. He worked there, but he still had his own home to return to at night, right?

"So I wondered if it was somebody else who did the taking in. And then I had trouble running Aedan's ancestry back. It's happened to me a few times over the years. Often it turns out to be a name change breaking the research chain, and sometimes names get changed without being legally changed. I started looking at databases for orphanages near Castlebar during the relevant period. Sure enough, there was a young boy named Liam from Castlebar who spent a few years at Saint Dermot's. And I couldn't find any other Liams. It was a small Catholic orphanage, and the only one near Castlebar.

"This Liam left the orphanage and was taken in by John and Mary Burns when he was about seven. I'm not sure whether it was a legal adoption or a placement. Aedan told me Liam's parents were John and Mary Burns. Everything matched up, and it was all from information Aedan gave me. He wanted to see if I could put it all together."

"So Liam's birth name wasn't Burns?"

"You're right. I don't know for sure what his last name was when he went into the orphanage. It's hard to get those records unless you have legal standing, and I don't. What I think I know is Aedan's father was in Saint Dermot Orphanage until he was six or seven years old, and then went to live with John and Mary Burns. He became Liam Burns, officially or unofficially."

"Will you tell me Liam's real name when you find out? It's so cool. This is turning into a real–life spy novel."

"I'd like to tell you, but aren't you afraid someone will torture you to get the information? I'd hate to see your fingernails pulled out. How do I know you won't break?"

"I carry a cyanide capsule, and someone else has been torturing me for years, so I know I can take it.

208

Michael, I'm struck by how you remember what people say to you, at least other people."

"Thanks, I guess. I've decided I'm not going to kill you off in the novel. You're good comic relief and I want to hear Meryl Streep do your Rhode Island patois. It might be tough, even for her."

"Suck the big quahog, Michael. Is that authentic enough Rhode Island patois for you and Meryl?"

CHAPTER TWENTY–TWO

On Sunday night, it was time for my scheduled meeting with Sherlock and Mr. Jameson. I needed to pick up the pace. Sherlock would call this a three–pipe problem, or in my case, a three–glass problem. I was only doing this once a week, special occasions excepted, right? Eliminate the impossible, Michael. Let the truth reveal itself.

The question I had written in the envelope I gave Aedan was whether we were related. Sure, we're all related if you take it out to twentieth cousins once removed. Therein lies madness. Aedan would know what I meant, and the answer was yes. He dropped enough hints about how much we had in common. Where was the connection? I knew my direct ancestry lines back to the 1500s and had never come across the name Burns. Aedan knew that. And I couldn't get back past Liam in Aedan's line because I didn't know Liam's real name.

Maybe the answer was in front of me. Aedan told me there was a clue in my aunt Brigid. But how much could he have known about her at the time? He probably knew nothing about Leo Norman, and he certainly knew nothing about Lester Sackett. No, the clue Aedan meant was probably related to something I had said to him, something which had triggered a spark. I tried to remember what I had told him about Brigid. I told him about her frequent trips to Ireland. I mentioned that Brigid told her son my grandfather Thomas had an unknown child when he went back to Ireland for two years after his wife died. A sickly child who died young. Is that the Hallelujah Chorus I'm hearing?

210

It had to be. Liam was born a Tiernan, the illegitimate son of my grandfather Thomas. The poor little kid whose name nobody knew. Liam didn't die young. He disappeared into an Irish orphanage, which sometimes was almost the same thing. You didn't have to be an orphan to wind up in an Irish orphanage during those years. Maybe you were "slow", or had parents who couldn't or didn't want to care for you. And a father who returned to America and pretended you were dead. Aedan thought Liam was autistic or worse. Back then, it was "retarded". There wasn't much inclination or ability to diagnose precisely. They probably gave him the name Liam in the orphanage. And they cared for him when nobody else did.

Liam was a Tiernan when he went in and a Burns when he came out. Aedan and I had the same grandfather. That's why the old picture of Aedan I had seen before I met him was vaguely familiar in a way I couldn't quite place. Aedan's crooked smile in the picture looked like Grandpa Tom's demonic grin. Were the voices Tom heard the cries of his abandoned son?

I needed proof rather than a grin. Those records were sealed and might not even exist. This had been handled quietly through the Church. I had asked for information, and was told I wouldn't have a response for at least a year, if ever. There was nobody left in my family who could tell me except Aedan, and why would he tell me? Colleagues keep little secrets from each other, don't they?

If Aedan and I were both right, then it wasn't only Aedan who was a direct descendant of Grace O'Malley. I was too. Sara would be pretty upset.

211

Another pirate descendant in our household, and maybe I had the baddest–ass blood. We'd better find a way to keep Emma on land. With her genes, she might plunder and Davy Jones a harbor sightseeing cruise. That would be a newspaper clipping worth saving.

I remembered some other things Aedan threw out there. Except for Emma, it appeared to him I was the only living descendant of my great–grandfather Daniel. He told me his parents were deceased, that he was an only child and that the Burns line would die with him. I put all of it together. Aedan was telling me I was his closest living relative, which explains a few things about why he contacted me.

I had first thought the other question Aedan expected from me was whether I was related to Grace O'Malley. No, not if I had the other question right. The answer to the first question would dictate the answer to the second. So Aedan was expecting another question. Was it how we were descended from Grace O'Malley?

I thought I might have figured that part out too, at least generally. Aedan talked about his late infant daughter, Maeve, and told me Maeve was a family name. It was a common first name in Ireland, but I had never run into it in my own family research. Maeve was the daughter of Grace O'Malley and her first husband, Donal O'Flaherty. I didn't see any other way to get from Grace to Aedan and me except through Maeve. I couldn't be sure, but it wasn't something I needed to nail down immediately. There were bigger fish to fry, and the clock was ticking.

I spent the rest of the first glass rolling James Tiernan around in my brain. Aedan had suggested the clue he found, the one he paid Sara and me the stack of Grover Clevelands for, was my file notation about James Tiernan being "in the service of Seadhna Pilib." He seemed disappointed that I hadn't realized the significance of it, but he wasn't surprised. He had told me I wouldn't recognize the clue, and I had confirmed to him what he thought were my limitations.

Aedan knew about Philip Sidney and his meeting with Grace O'Malley, and he was the one poking into the MacTiernans in Sligo. He was closing in on the truth, slowly and from different directions. Okay, Aedan made a mistake reading James as John, if Patrick Ruddy was right. On the other hand, he was smart, organized, liked doing historical research and had deep pockets. He'd trap the truth eventually. So again, why did he need me?

But there was something else Aedan never would have found on his own. What surprised him, and dropped from heaven into his humidor, was Lester Sackett and what he told us. Aedan had sent me a signal that what we got from Lester was worth a lot. Even deep pockets aren't bottomless. Lester gave Aedan new information, not just confirmation of things Aedan already suspected. Aedan put me on the trail of my Aunt Brigid instead of sending me down more promising trails, and wound up catching lightning in a bottle. What was he thinking?

My first glass finally exhausted its possibilities, as Aedan would say. Sara walked into my man cave. She thought she smelled something burning, but it was only Michael in deep thought. She announced she was going out to meet her pimp, and would be back in a few hours. I hoped she was saying that just to see if I was listening, but she was styling pretty good for a Sunday night.

I told her to have a good time and call if she was going to be late. I couldn't let even Sara distract me now. The synapses were crackling. Pieces of the puzzles were snapping into place. Sara was going to get her victory celebration at the White Stag. Bad news for the Irish pigs.

I had probably laid enough bricks now to earn a C–plus from Professor Burns, but we hadn't found Grace O'Malley. Stay on task, Michael. Let's come at this from a different angle. I could use some outside help. I set up an extra chair for Sherlock and poured him a drink. We had to discuss this man to man, or man to whatever. If she ever saw this, Sara would agree I needed outside help.

Right after he read the files I gave him, Aedan mentioned having important business in Dublin to take care of immediately. Castlebar to Dublin was about a hundred and thirty miles, and Aedan looked dead on his feet. His business must have been important. And whatever the business was, it had turned out well, because we partied hearty when he came back. But a stickler for organization like Aedan would have scheduled his important business well in advance, especially that far away. He told me earlier that, after he reviewed my files, he wanted to sit down right away to brainstorm. There was no time to lose. Then he read my files and something changed. Suddenly, he had to be in Dublin, and we lost almost two days.

So the business in Dublin was something he couldn't or didn't want to do electronically or by telephone. There wasn't much you can't do today electronically or by telephone. Maybe he thought it would be more private if he did it in person. In my experience, that meant a delivery or an inspection. If it was a delivery or an exchange, the parties could have met closer to Castlebar. I was leaning in the direction of an inspection. Of what? So many questions, so little whiskey.

One possible scenario jumped up from inside my glass. When Caitriona MacTiernan decided to become an Anglican nun, she went to an abbey in Dublin for fourteen months until Holy Mother Church reclaimed her. Connection or coincidence? I'd put it to a vote. Were Caitriona going to Dublin, and Aedan going to Dublin centuries later after reading my files, somehow related? Sherlock nodded yes. I nodded yes. Two votes in the affirmative, none in the negative. I would pursue the scenario further. And I might never criticize Sara again for seeing imaginary mountains.

Okay. The most obvious explanation, if there was one, has Caitriona transporting something to Dublin. Could it have been a portrait of Grace O'Malley or maybe some of her papers? Too obvious. And it probably meant Grace gave something to Philip Sidney, who gave it to James Tiernan, who gave it to Caitriona MacTiernan, who took it to Dublin. You don't want that many hands touching a secret delivery.

It would have been a long, difficult and dangerous land journey from Western Ireland to Dublin in the 1500s. The Gael tribes still controlled much of

Western Ireland and wouldn't have been favorably impressed by an Irish Catholic lass schlepping off to Dublin to shake hands with the devil. The English controlled the areas closer to Dublin. They wouldn't have believed Caitriona, because who could believe an Irish whore?

Thieves and liars the Irish were, to be dealt with by the sword. There would have been awkward searches and seizures, and heads would have rolled, literally. So there had to be some other scenarios to consider. I had a detective friend, not a fictional one, who swore the answer is always in the logistics. Don't ask what you would do. Ask what *they* would do.

But the eyes so wide open a few hours ago were starting to close. Good meeting, people. Let's get together again next week. Thank you for presiding tonight, Mr. Jameson. We are adjourned. Now, I think I'll go see what Sara's up to.

CHAPTER TWENTY–THREE

I spent the whole day Monday poring over every bit of information I could find on James or Caitriona MacTiernan. They came from a family of flax farmers in Easkey, a fishing village in County Sligo. I had been able to trace my roots back to about 1530 in the same village, so I could be reasonably sure it was all the same family.

James' brother Richard was born near Rosses Point and was a farmer there until he moved to County Roscommon in 1600. James lived with his family in Easkey until he was about twelve. Then he just disappeared, and surfaced again in Galway City around 1573. Caitriona lived on the family farm until she left for Dublin in 1582. The MacTiernans looked like typical hardscrabble farmers, dirt poor, grubbing out a subsistence living until the soil gave out and they moved on. There was nothing that mentioned Grace O'Malley.

It was time for a videoconference with Aedan. I set it up for Tuesday night. Aedan might still be smarting a bit from our last exchange. I was, therefore, expecting a long session of thrust and parry. Fun, but I had to step up the pace. Glenn and Anna would be back in a few days and I'd have to return to the twenty-first century.

"Good evening, Aedan, I hope you're well. I wanted to debrief you on what I've found and not found."

"They are often equally important, Michael. I am well, thank you. Oh, and please accept my compliments on tracking me back to the Rosses Point Abbey. Mother Abbess was quite pleased by

217

your generosity. I had to up the ante significantly to get her to talk to me. It seems we are now in a bidding war for her information. That was a fine piece of detective work. Mr. Holmes would be proud of you."

"Thanks, I'll tell him you said so. And perhaps you'll tell me by how much you had to raise the ante, in case I ever go back. We don't want Mother Abbess buying herself a Porsche on you. But Aedan, I think you had a name wrong in your magazine query. It was James MacTiernan, not John."

"I believe you are correct. I studied those records again, and I must defer to the expertise and younger eyes of Patrick Ruddy. It was a touch of hubris on my part to think I could decipher such faded and stained names. You may have been the only person to read my magazine query. There were no responses."

"And so it appears I must also congratulate you on a fine piece of detective work, Aedan. I went through considerable trouble to keep Patrick's identity a secret."

"You did a fine job. He's so ordinary looking, isn't he? I'll wager his own mother would have difficulty locating his table at a pub. He rented a car for his journey that day and drove it past the Abbey's security camera. For an additional offering, Mother Abbess let me see the film. A few telephone calls and I had the name of the person who rented the car. They didn't remember him, as you might expect. Nobody would. It must be useful to be able to render oneself completely invisible. However the rental office photocopied his identification. It is sad, Michael, that religious buildings must now rely on

218

security cameras for protection. Perhaps Mother Abbess also had a nine–millimeter secreted in those flowing robes. I always wondered what they hid in there."

"Sad indeed, Aedan. In my day, the Catholic school security system was a cocked ruler. It was very effective."

"My knuckles recall those days as well. And expressing your thanks to Mother Abbess in the name of Saint Dermot's was a stylish touch. How did you know?"

I told him.

"You're beginning to frighten me, Michael. You sit in your comfortable chair and apply pure, sweet logic to arrive at correct answers."

"Not logic, half a lifetime of work experience sticking my hand into dark holes. I appreciate your compliment, but you gave me most of the information I needed. I only had to listen."

"You are far too modest. That would be like saying the person who told Sir Isaac Newton about apples deserves credit for explaining gravity. I gave you very little information. You sorted through it, built upon it and went where the evidence took you. Were you surprised to discover that Liam was abandoned by his birth parents and raised later by John and Mary Burns?"

Okay, Michael, this is as good a time as any for the Hail Mary. Go long or go home.

"I guess I was. I'm glad someone helped him. Those were difficult times in Ireland, I know. There but for the grace of God go any of us. What really surprised me was to discover Liam Burns was born a

Tiernan. I had no idea Sara and I were going to Ireland to meet my cousin Aedan."

"I thought that might surprise you. Now I am truly awed. Those records are confidential, although I suppose nothing is confidential these days if the price is met. I doubt our grandfather Thomas told you anything. He would not have known Liam's first name. The orphanage named him, and Liam told me he had no communication ever with his birth father. So pray, how did you discover all of this?"

"I didn't. You just told me. I suspected it, but I had no way of proving it. Confirming what we think we know is a big part of our work, isn't it, cousin?"

"It is. Touché and well done. It appears my years as a solicitor were wasted, but yours were not. You realize, of course, the significance of Liam Burns being Liam Tiernan?"

"I do, or I think I do. It seems I am your closest living relative."

"Why do you qualify it by saying it only seems so?"

"Because I'm not sure I believe anything I've ever heard from my family. Who knows how many other relatives I might have out there, about whom I know nothing?"

"Good point. Truth is not an absolute with the Irish, so perhaps I lack certainty as well. I suppose we should phrase this as men of law would and say that, based upon the record before us, the preponderance of evidence suggests that Michael Tiernan is the closest living relative of Aedan Burns."

"Works for me."

"And it works very well for me."

220

"Aedan, we have to speed this up. The days are getting shorter. We are trying to track down Grace O'Malley, aren't we? I need to know for sure what Sara and I are doing. Otherwise, we're taking money for nothing, and you deserve better than that."

"Thank you. I agree that I have been too mysterious. It's a problem I have. One of the puzzles I wished to solve was the Michael Tiernan puzzle. I have done so to my complete satisfaction. So now, let us turn our undivided attention to the Pirate Queen. I have been honest with you about what we are looking for. I shall now tell you what I know and where I think it leads. First, I must know if my cousin has any theories on where that might be."

"Okay, you asked for it, Aedan. Here's what I'm thinking. It's nothing but logic, logistics and instinct, but those are my only tools. I am blissfully unencumbered by historical knowledge and training. We're an odd couple, but maybe that's what this puzzle needs.

"I think at least some of the answers are hidden with Brigid and Leo. There are things about them we don't know yet. Those photographs told us a story, and I think Grace O'Malley is part of that story.

"What do we know right now? The MacTiernans in Sligo were poor and illiterate farmers. James drops off the radar and shows up years later as a Latin–speaking poet in Galway, and most likely a colleague of one of the most accomplished English poets. How does that happen? I think it happens only if James joined the household of a wealthy, educated family with connections to the Sidneys. It could even have been the Sidneys.

"We don't know much about Caitriona except she was a Catholic farm girl in Sligo. Then she's an Anglican nun in Dublin. And after that, she's a Catholic nun back in Sligo. All of this took place within fourteen months, and it was the same fourteen months you think Grace O'Malley might have been delivering her portrait and documents to someone for safekeeping. That's a little too much religious back–flipping to ring true. Caitriona had another agenda.

"To my great regret now, Aedan, I never studied cigar and whiskey chemistry in college. I did take courses in logic. I remember Occam's Razor. The simplest explanation is usually the best one. James Tiernan was a colleague and confidant of Philip Sidney. Caitriona was James' sister. If there is a portrait of Grace O'Malley and a document stash, I think they and Caitriona went together to Dublin. The documents and portrait were placed somewhere for safekeeping or for another delivery, probably to Philip Sidney. After things looked secure, Caitriona returned to Sligo. She had as much of a calling to become an Anglican nun as Sara would have had. The delivery service we talked about when we first met wasn't Daniel Tiernan or the Tuke Fund. It was James Tiernan and Caitriona MacTiernan. There might have been someone else with them, someone Philip Sidney thought he could trust. I haven't figured that out, if there's anything to figure out.

"But the Caitriona connection would make sense for another reason. Any documents being transported were likely written in Latin. You told me Grace spoke and wrote Latin, but nobody is sure whether she spoke English. Latin would have been a

222

safer language for her to use in case those documents fell into the wrong hands. And Latin documents would fit right in at a church or an abbey, wouldn't they? Hidden in plain view, readable by only a few. As far as any portrait, I think it would not identify Grace O'Malley by name. That could be a death sentence for the delivery person. The portrait had to be disguised in some way, but not so well disguised that someone on the other end couldn't recognize it if he knew what he was looking for.

"Then it gets even more complicated. What happened next? Maybe any documents or portraits were re–delivered to someone else, or maybe they're still sitting in Dublin today. Or maybe they're gone forever. When her job was done, Caitriona switched teams again and disappeared into a remote Catholic abbey, the medieval Witness Protection Program. But as Sara will tell you, I have a very active imagination, and I have nothing which tells me why Caitriona would ever have gotten involved with something like that."

"It's an ingenious scenario, Michael. The broad strokes paint a persuasive picture, but some of the details trouble me. If Caitriona delivered documents to Dublin, then what was it you think Leo and Brigid were examining in Galway? It seems that important documents would have been kept together. And why Dublin? Would it not have been safer and less complicated to get documents or portraits directly to England, if that was their ultimate destination? It all seems a bit overly complicated.

"Now let me show you that Aedan's imagination can take wing also. I agree a land journey from Western Ireland to Dublin was fraught with peril. So what if the delivery was made by sea, perhaps on a Grace O'Malley ship? And what if James MacTiernan became a refined young gentleman by serving in the O'Malley household itself? He certainly would have learned his Latin and Irish folk tales there.

"As for Caitriona's motivation, what if the sweet Irish maiden had become infatuated with the young and dashing Philip Sidney and did his bidding? Perhaps this was a case of unrequited love, ending with the spurned Caitriona pining away in a Sligo convent.

"Now, is this a bit fanciful, the stuff of pulp fiction? Perhaps so. And yet, Caitriona took the religious name of Sister Philippa in Dublin. You did not know, did you?"

"I did not. That's some nice research, and a good screenplay. It hangs together, especially since Caitriona later took the religious name of Fidelma. First Philippa, then Fidelma. Maybe it was her way of saying she would always be faithful to Philip. I like it. It sings to me. How can we ever prove any of this?"

"And once again, you have identified the problem. Unless we find specific references in a primary source document, it's nothing more than pure conjecture. Interesting details, to be sure, but details nonetheless. We must keep a sharp focus. There are only two questions before us. Are there Grace O'Malley portraits and relevant documents in existence today? And if so, where?"

Good. At least we could now agree on some things.

"Michael, I think you are spot on with respect to several points. There was a delivery of some kind to Dublin by or on behalf of Grace O'Malley. James and Caitriona were involved. I believe you are correct Caitriona moved too casually between faiths and there is more to it than meets the eye. And I think James and Philip were literary colleagues, but more than such. I leave the possibilities to your fertile imagination.

"Philip was not just a superb poet. He was a political operative, an ambassador without portfolio, a trusted godson and advisor to Queen Elizabeth. He was Gloriana's fixer, if you will. Elizabeth and Grace were strong and pragmatic women, each with a refined sense of how to grab, consolidate and retain power. It would not surprise me if this turned out to be a tale of political intrigue at the very highest levels. Perhaps that was part of the attraction to Caitriona, but she was betrayed and cast aside. We may never know. There is still much work to do, Michael."

"There is, and October will be here before we know it. But Glenn and Anna will be back to the office tomorrow and there are some big decisions for us to make over here. I'm afraid Grace O'Malley can't have my undivided attention for the next week. So I have a sporting proposition for you tonight, Aedan. How about an equal exchange of information? It might keep us on the straight and narrow path. We each ask each other one question, and get honest and complete answers. Are you game?"

"How can I resist? Please, Michael, you go first."

"When you invited Sara and me to join you in Ireland, did you know I was your closest living relative?"

"Yes. Remember, I had access to years of your online postings. You are not the only person who spends so much time staring into a computer. You might say it was relatively easy for a trained historian to unearth the truth. And now my question, in two parts, I'm afraid. Once a lawyer, always a lawyer. I have not opened your envelope. What was the Sherlock Holmes tale I alluded to, and why do you think I chose it?"

"It was The Red–Headed League. The red shamrocks were a clue of their own, I guess. Then I realized you were paying me well to do make–work projects, research that might benefit me but wasn't likely to help you. Red herrings wrapped in crooked red shamrocks. The tip–off was when you stressed nothing illegal was happening here. In the Holmes story, the make–work project was copying an encyclopedia to distract from a bank robbery in progress.

"I know we agreed on one question, Aedan, but if I had a second question, hypothetically speaking, it would be whether you have stopped giving me make–work projects. Are we finally working together now only to find Grace O'Malley? No other agendas?"

"Three questions for the price of one. You have out–lawyered me once again, but you earned them. Yes, Michael, you are now my full research partner and more. You are correct on the Holmes story, and yes, our only goal now is to find Grace O'Malley. There are other loose strands I need to tie up along

226

the way, but they require no further effort on your part. I freely admit, when I contacted you and Sara, I did not expect you to be much help finding Grace O'Malley. It was a calculated long shot. I simply had no idea the two of you would be as good at this as you have turned out to be."

"High praise indeed from the head of the Red Shamrock League. Thanks, Aedan. Sara keeps seeing things I'll never be able to see. And I'll never be in your league, whatever you call the league. Maybe digging runs in our family."

"It seems to, but putting what we unearth into proper perspective is the hard part, which can take a lifetime. I look forward to seeing you in October, and we'll chat many times before then. You have given me much to think about in the last several days. Now you must take some time and work everything out with Glenn, Sara and Anna. A man can have more than one family, you know. You are fortunate, Michael, perhaps more fortunate than you yet realize."

CHAPTER TWENTY–FOUR

I got to the office extra early on Wednesday. Glenn and Anna would both be back in a few hours, and I had a feeling it would be a day we'd remember. Glenn had negotiated a deal with Sylvie Lepine. He'd come in mornings only until Friday, then relax at home for three full days over Labor Day weekend.

Glenn showed up first. He was still pale, but looked much better than he had ten days ago. He wanted to talk.

"Michael, we have to make some changes. I've been given a second life and I won't piss this one away. I'm closing down my law practice. Three months from today, earlier if I can do it without hardship to you and Anna. I've got some ideas there too. I can stay as busy as I want on charity work. Money is like bullshit, works best if you spread it around. You're familiar with bullshit, right?"

"I've read about it. I hear the Mayflower brought the first cargo of bullshit to New England. I'm not shocked, but I hope we can agree our partnership was one of the good decisions we made. Have you told Anna?"

"Not yet. I'd like to take her to lunch today and tell her then. We can work things out so it's better for all of us. And our partnership here was the best decision I ever made, before I got sick."

"When Anna thought you weren't going to make it, Glenn, in Montreal, she fell apart. Sara wasn't far behind. Neither was I, and you missed one hell of a resurrection party. The park police are probably not finished interviewing witnesses. So if you meant it when you told Sylvie we're your family, it's something we're happy to be. But I don't see how you pissed away your first life."

"There are things you don't know, and some you never will. And I meant what I told Sylvie. Thanks, Michael. I don't have your gift for words, but you can see what I'm thinking. You always do."

"Not always, but this time, I'm hoping. Don't talk yourself out of it. There's a nice Hungarian restaurant Anna likes in an alley right around the corner. Bring a flashlight. I won't mention anything more to her until after you get back."

Anna arrived an hour later. There was something different about her. What was it?

"Michael, I thought there might be someone sitting at my desk when I got here. Will she be in later?"

"No, she's been delayed. Until hell freezes over. That's what you get when you ride the Green Line."

Glenn asked Anna if he could see her in his office. He said it would only take a minute and it did. He must have been inviting her to lunch. Anna was back staring at her desk, lost in thought.

"I promise you, Anna, nobody has sat there since you left for Montreal. I was kidding, pinky-swear."

"Okay, I believe you, but it's not what I was thinking. Give me a few minutes to settle in, then I'll help you undo any damage you did around here while I was away. Glenn wants to take me to lunch. It has to be on the early side, so he can keep a deal he made with Sylvie Lepine. Let me know if there's anything I can do."

"There is, speaking of deals. Can you meet me in the conference room at 10:00? It will take about twenty minutes, and it's not what you're thinking either."

Anna walked into the conference room a few minutes early and closed the door behind her.

"Let me say something first, Michael. It's bothered me for weeks. I'm so sorry I threw myself at you in the hotel room. Everything hit me at once and I completely dissolved. It was awful. Will you please forgive me?"

"No, I won't. There's nothing to forgive. Anna, I'm glad you thought of me as someone you wanted to hold on to when you were suffering. I wish I could have sucked your pain into me. So lose the guilt, you're starting to sound Irish. Everything ended the way it was meant to end.

"But we made a deal over lunch a while back. It was your idea. I make Glenn better, and you tell me about yourself. I did my part. I'm calling in the deal. If we're family now, then I need to learn more about my family members."

"Am I missing something? Wasn't it Sylvie Lepine who made Glenn better?"

"Don't be a lawyer, Anna, you're better than that. Okay, she handled the scalpel, but I handled the arrangements. I set everything up with those connections of mine, the ones who used to be people. I'll let Sylvie take the credit, but maybe someone else was pulling the strings in Montreal."

"You say the most wonderful things and the most bizarre things, and within twenty seconds. I'll give you the benefit of the doubt. Do you want to know more about me?"

"Shoot."

"Maybe a poor choice of words, but here goes. My brother and I had a happy, uneventful childhood. Our father was well off in Hungary, not so much

230

here. Right after I graduated high school, my parents insisted I marry the son of one of my father's friends. We knew each other in high school, but we never dated. He was a good Hungarian boy from a family with money, a trophy son–in–law. I don't recall anyone asking me what I thought. It was an arranged marriage. We never loved each other, but he seemed decent enough at first.

"I was pregnant within a few months and again two years after Kata was born. His attitude changed. I wasn't giving him enough attention, I only thought about my babies. He started drinking too much, and he'd hit me. He hit me a lot, and hard. I miscarried once after he hit me in the stomach. And then he started slapping Kata. My parents didn't want to get involved. My father said I must have done something to provoke him."

She stopped for a moment.

"Michael, to continue this story, I'm afraid I'm going to have to show you one of my body parts. Is it a problem for you?"

"There's no good answer to that, is there?"

"You just gave a pretty good answer. Relax, it's my arm."

She rolled up her sleeve. The jagged scar looked even worse to me than when Mr. Bennett stormed out. It ran almost all the way from her wrist to her elbow.

"It's a souvenir of my marriage. The day my husband died, he had the usual liquid breakfast and left for his construction job around the corner. He slapped me on his way out the door and I screamed at him. He smashed a bottle and hit me with it, here. He was already half–drunk. I couldn't call anyone. I

231

must have provoked him, right? I stopped the bleeding and decided I was taking my girls and getting out for good. I had a friend we could stay with, one he didn't know about.

"It would take only a few hours to get everything together. He wouldn't be back until it was time for me to pour him his lunch, but in case he came back earlier, I had my pistol ready. I was raised Hungarian, Michael. We learn to shoot when we're young, and my father was always afraid the communists would come back to get us. If my husband showed up and laid a hand on me or my girls, I would have shot him dead, and it would have taken only one bullet. I can shoot the flame off a candle at thirty feet.

"But it didn't play out that way. A few hours later, he toppled a piece of construction equipment onto himself and was crushed. I wouldn't even go to his funeral. My parents didn't speak to me for years. I had shamed our family. The only things I ever got from the marriage were my two girls and this scar."

"Anna, this has to be painful for you. I had no idea. Let's stop now, okay?"

"No, I have to get this out. I've kept it bottled up so long. I was free, but I was scared, scarred and broke. I had two daughters to feed and no skills. My husband's brother once told me all I had was some looks and I should rent myself out to make money. I didn't think my looks were anything to write home about. Did I have anything at all going for me?

"Then I found you and Glenn. Now there were two slightly strange but kind men in my life, men who respected me and valued what I thought. I didn't know how to handle that because it had never

232

happened. I went into a shell and stayed there for years. I was afraid I'd mess things up again. It wasn't only my arm that was scarred.

"My fucking husband got into my head, Michael. There were men who wanted to date me, even one who wanted to marry me. How could I let myself get close to a man and maybe have it happen again? I didn't see the first one coming, why would I see the next one? And so I let my girls grow up without a father. I may be a coward, but at least I'm not a whiner. I made the worst scars heal, the ones you can't see, but it took more than twenty years."

She put her head into her hands. God, this must hurt. I had to say something to try to make her feel a little better. Geez, Michael, when you make a deal, be careful what you wish for.

"Understand this, Anna. We value you because there's so much to value. We're not idiots. When you walked through the door, Glenn and I both knew something big had entered our lives, and I'm not talking about your height. We had no business hiring anyone. We were barely breaking even, talking about splitting up. Things started to get better in every way as soon as you joined us. It wasn't a coincidence. I don't believe in coincidences any more.

"And on behalf of men everywhere, let's not go nuts here on your lack of looks. They weren't why we hired you, but you definitely have them. Deal with it, okay? Don't you ever wonder why Glenn always puts his files on the top shelf of the cabinets? He likes to watch you stretch up to get them."

Anna laughed through the tears. Good. You're clumsy, Michael, but at least you mean well.

"Then you two should have gotten taller cabinets. There wasn't much stretching. I'm pushing six–one in my bare feet and I'm not in bare feet much around here."

"I noticed. Listen, Anna, leave this lack of self–esteem crap for people with nothing to have self–esteem about. You're giving them false hopes. And I know current workplace guidelines discourage commenting on a co–worker's looks, so I hope you won't report me."

"And I hope we're a lot more than co–workers. I appreciate everything you said, but it's ending now, isn't it? I think that's what Glenn wants to tell me."

"There's no way it's ending. It's only beginning, but there will be changes. The Bradley and Tiernan Law Office may fade away, but Bradley, Danos and Tiernan are here for the long haul. We do have to rearrange pieces of the puzzle, and we'll have to see a new and improved Glenn, Anna and Michael. I'm betting we've got the Glenn."

"And starting today, we've got the Anna. I hope improved, but definitely new. You'll never catch me looking over my shoulder again."

"I'm counting on it. And here's something else I need to know. How did you happen to walk into our office that first day? We weren't advertising for help."

"I'm not sure. I had dropped off a job application up the street and was walking back to catch the train. When I walked past your building, a gust of wind pushed me into the doorway. Boston is always windy, but it was really howling. I went into the lobby to let the wind die down. A man I had never seen walked by and said if I was looking for Bradley and Tiernan, you were on the third floor. Why would he say it to me? But I figured why not, even though I had never heard of you or Glenn. I was in the building anyway. It was like something was pushing me in the direction of your office. Am I sounding too Twilight Zone?"

"No, I was hoping to hear something like that. Remind me sometime to tell you what it means when the fairies howl. Anna, did you mean what you told me in Montreal?"

"Every word of it. Did you mean what you told me in the Hungarian restaurant?"

"Every word of it."

"Good. I'm glad it wasn't the yellow onions talking. Is there anything else I can tell you this morning?"

"Would I be correct in assuming the Lincoln Memorial is still off the table?"

"You would be."

"What about your special tool?"

"Don't you have some work to do?"

"Okay, but thanks, Anna. This must have been hard for you. I hope I didn't open up old wounds."

"No, you healed them, you and Glenn and Sara. My past is dead, and today I threw the last shovelful of dirt on it. The Anna who died twenty–five years ago is alive again, and she's not a scared little girl."

We stood up.

"We're not quite finished, Michael. Get over here right now. Don't make me come and get you."

"Whoa. Is this part of the new Anna?"

"It certainly is."

She hugged me. A very nice hug, but not one to threaten a Core Commandment. I was tall enough to see straight into her eyes. I knew that look now.

"Michael, thank you."

"I didn't do anything."

"That's part of what I'm thanking you for, and I have no intention of ever apologizing for this hug. It will probably happen again, so deal with it, okay? Report me for harassment if you want. I don't much care."

"I'm not feeling harassed, Anna."

This new Anna might work out. But I hoped Bad Anna was still around somewhere. She was fun.

I watched her walk back to her desk and realized what was different. The graceful stride exuded confidence. Different eyes, different gait, different Anna. She finally realized how good she was. Our human Secretariat was getting ready to air it out. This would have been the easiest bet Liam Tiernan ever placed. And her husband and his brother were two seriously stupid pieces of Hungarian shit.

Glenn and Anna left for their lunch. Glenn would go home right after, and Anna had some errands to run. They had a lot to talk about, and I had a lot of research to do.

The email arrived from Aedan mid–afternoon:

Hello, Michael.

I have glorious news. Thanks to you and Sara, I have unearthed original, important documents relating to Grace O'Malley. They answer many of our questions. I must have them authenticated, and I need to protect our claim against poachers. It will take a week. If I am correct, our quest will have been a great success, whatever else may turn up. For security reasons, I shall send you my report by courier when it is ready. Watch for red shamrocks. Well done, partners.

With great joy, Aedan

This was turning into quite a day. I fired back:

Good evening, Aedan.

Great news, and I look forward to reading your report. How did you know where to look? Will you tell me now? It will be hard for Sara and me to wait.

Michael

His reply came in less than two minutes:

All in good time. Please be patient a bit longer while I secure and authenticate. You and Sara were correct. The answer was in the photographs. Wonderful details to follow.

Your partner in victory, Aedan

Glenn called late in the afternoon. Would Sara and I join Anna and him for lunch tomorrow? He had some ideas on implementing Operation Lazarus. The O'Malley Protocol. Operation Lazarus. Nuns selling secrets to the highest bidder. Life around here was getting too HBO. Glenn suggested the same restaurant. I told him we wouldn't miss it for all the tea in China. My mother used to say that. It made no sense, but she liked it and I did too.

Was the air conditioner malfunctioning again, or was I hearing the sound of pounding hooves?

CHAPTER TWENTY–FIVE

Anna came into the office early on Thursday morning and started acting strange. She kept putting things on my desk that I didn't ask for. She was wearing a pretty green blouse. The old Anna didn't do colors, and the blouse was short–sleeved. This was going to be a good day.

"Okay, Anna, what's going on? There was something a little different about you yesterday, but I figured it out. Today there's something a lot different."

"I'd like to hear what you think you figured out. You like to play detective, so you tell me what's different."

I stood up and looked her over. Up and down. Front and back. Twice. She giggled. The old Anna never giggled.

"Sorry, Anna, it's the way we detectives have to work. Measure twice, cut once. Well, a few things are obvious. Your hair is slightly under one–sixteenth of an inch shorter than it was yesterday, so I deduce you went to the hairdresser for a trim. About 4:30, judging from how your kind of hair grows. And your new perfume tells me you have recently spent time in Istanbul, the northwest quadrant of the city, if I'm not mistaken. Your scent is only sold there, and in late summer. I've written a small monograph on the subject.

"Beyond those trifling details, I observe little, except you're wearing a new rock on your finger that would choke a Shetland pony, and you haven't waved files in front of my face for years. It appears congratulations are in order. I hope I get to meet the lucky guy."

She laughed the most wonderful laugh.

"Brace yourself, Michael. Hug incoming. Yes! You're right, and you've met him. He's been your law partner for years. He wanted to surprise you and Sara at lunch today. But I wanted to tell you myself. I want you to say you're happy for me. I really need you to say it and mean it."

"I couldn't be happier, Anna. Are you asking for my blessing? I'm touched."

"No way. You're too unpredictable. I so want you to be happy for me and for Glenn."

"I was hoping for this, Anna. I never could understand why it took Glenn twenty years to line up a three–inch putt. You'll invite me to the wedding, I hope. Probably on Nantucket if you let Glenn help decide. Will I have to buy lime–green pants?"

"Actually, I was thinking Las Vegas in an Elvis wedding chapel, especially for you. Wherever it is, you and Sara have to be there, and Emma too. Michael, we want you to marry us and I want Sara as my best lady. She's your best lady. I want her to be mine too. It's going to be a very small wedding. Vica's helping me plan it. You've never met Vica, have you? I think you'll be impressed. Kata says Vica got most of the brains and looks."

Lord have mercy. Maybe I wasn't ready to meet Vica. Maybe nobody was.

"Sara and I will be there any way you want us. If it's not a tacky question, did he ask you or did you ask him? It's for some research I'm doing on thoroughbreds."

240

"Whatever that means. It may have been both, or neither. I told Glenn about my Montreal meltdown, that I was so scared and couldn't imagine life with him gone. It must have been pretty clear to him where I was going with it. I was trying to work up courage to say the words. I never got a chance. Glenn reached into his pocket and pulled out this ring. It had been his grandmother's, then his mother's, and he said now it should be mine, but I had to spend the rest of my life with him to get it. He'd been carrying the ring around trying to work up his own courage. Come to think of it, I don't think the word marriage ever came up. It may have gotten lost in the excitement, because I knocked over our table saying yes. We did discuss a wedding, so I guess there was no misunderstanding.

"Michael, I've been so ashamed and embarrassed about my scar. I needed Glenn to see it before we got married, so he could change his mind if he wanted. I showed it to him at the restaurant. Do you know what he did? He showed me the scar on his leg from Vietnam. He said our scars almost matched, a sign from the gods it was meant to be. Romantic, aren't we? I hope the other people in the restaurant got a break on their bills for having to watch it. Michael, you have to be the one to marry us."

"It's the honor of a lifetime. Of course I will."

"And there's something else I want to tell you if you haven't guessed. I would have married you in a heartbeat, but you were taken and Glenn wasn't. It sounds awful when I say it that way, so please understand. I only want Glenn and me to be as happy as you and Sara are."

"There are no losers here. Only the happy endings matter, and you're getting a pretty good consolation prize. Seriously, Anna, if Glenn couldn't get his act together, why didn't you ask him years ago? Why did this have to wait for a tumor to make it happen?"

"Good grief, Michael, did you see the women he dated? Beauty queens with doctorates. When I looked in the mirror, what did I see? A scarred beanstalk who never got to go to college. Except on a basketball court, how could I compete with them? I would have made a fool of myself."

"They could never have competed with you, and not only in rebounding. Glenn knew from the beginning who was right for him. For some reason, he couldn't act on it, but that's over now. Have you picked a date?"

"We will in the next day or so. It's going to be as soon as possible, so you'd better get working on your ceremony."

"I will. I hope I don't get overcome by emotion or the endless toasts, and pass out before I ask you and Glenn to exchange vows."

"I have every confidence you can hold it together for a very short time. If not, we're hoping to have a doctor from Montreal there. She's good at reviving people."

"Anna, you and I didn't think this through. Maybe we should have a written backup plan. In case something happens to Glenn and Sara, you and I get married. In case anything happens to you and me, Glenn and Sara get married. A succession plan, like in European monarchies. I wonder if Sara realizes I would have asked you to marry me if I hadn't met her first. It doesn't come up much in conversation."

242

"Of course she does, you moron. Women know such things. But she knows you love her and neither of us would do anything to violate it. And speaking of tacky, isn't discussing a written marital succession plan at an engagement celebration pretty tacky? We'll probably be in nursing homes by then."

"Even better. Think of the money we'll save on catering. Only prunes, oatmeal and protein shakes. And I don't think it's tacky. Sara probably already has her own succession plan."

"I doubt it. If anything happened to you, I see Sara going into a convent and mourning the rest of her life."

"Where have I heard something like that before? I'll take it as a compliment. I'm trying to pull up mental images of Sara mourning in a convent, probably smoking a cigar. The screen is going blank. And if you think I'm happy for you and Glenn, wait until you see her reaction. Glenn will never hurt you in any way, Anna. I promise you."

"I know. He'll never have to wonder where I hide my pistol."

We had a celebratory lunch to match the one in Montreal. Better, actually, because Glenn paid for it. Sara cried when Anna asked her to be best lady. Then Anna ordered lunch for us. There was no way we were letting Sara try to order in Hungarian. Maybe the next day, I'd go to a Chinese restaurant alone, ask for a menu and order my own lunch. I wasn't complaining, though.

Glenn came in early the next morning. He wanted to talk again.

"We had quite a lunch yesterday, didn't we?"

"We sure did. You're full of surprises, Glenn."

"I've got more. Operation Lazarus is in full swing. When are you and Sara going back to Ireland?"

"October 15th. It was supposed to be a week earlier, but Aedan told me he needed to nail some things down, so we pushed it back to play safe."

"Good, because Anna and I would like to get married on Saturday of Columbus Day weekend. Will it work for you, Sara and Emma?"

"We'll make it work. What should I know?"

"It will be a small wedding, only about twenty people. I told Anna if she wanted, I'd close down the Palace of Versailles for her and we'd get married in the Grand Salon."

"You can close down Versailles?"

"As it turns out, no. I got a little carried away there. Fortunately, she decided on a nice little winery out on 495. She and her daughters went to the vineyards there for picnics. Anna told me those family picnics are her best memories. She wants to pass on a fairy princess wedding and give the money we save to a group that helps abused women."

"No surprise there. You seem to be pretty good at picking doctors and life partners."

"Law partners too, don't forget that. I have someone coming in today at 9:00, another lawyer. He's going to take over my files and any new cases, unless you want them. And I'm in the process of setting up a foundation, the Bradley Danos Charitable Trust. Anna and I will be running it together. It should be ready to roll by the first of the year."

"Thanks, Glenn, but no thanks on the cases. The Charitable Trust sounds like a great idea. I'm dancing pretty close to the exit myself."

"Maybe I can help. Our lease here is up the end of December. I'm planning on renting better space right above us. It has extra offices. I'll be signing a three–year lease to begin January 1st. I'd like to offer you a three–year sub–lease on any office there you want. I made sure there's one with the same view you have now, so you can keep looking over at the dock where the Tiernans landed. That means a lot to you. Now this is bigger and better space, so your share of the rent will have to change too. I'm thinking one dollar per year, payable up front. I'll need three dollars by the end of December, uilities included. Can you handle it? If Sara wants an office too, it's hers, same terms."

"Glenn, what are you doing? Has the heady brew of love made you go crazy?"

"God, I hope so. It's not only my idea, Michael. Anna wants to do whatever it takes to keep us together. If you'd like to be involved with the Charitable Trust full–time or part–time, we'd love to have you. We can end the law partnership whenever you want. But whatever you want to do, you'll have plenty of space. I can do this. The inheritance trust funds have had a good run. Remember, it's like bullshit, works best when you spread it around. And there isn't enough money in the world to repay you and Sara."

"That's so generous, Glenn. I'm overwhelmed. I accept, but only if you agree to revisit the rent issue as soon as we wrap up the partnership. The most important thing now is that the four of us stay together."

"Agreed. It's a deal. After Anna and I return from a wedding trip to Hungary, we'll be living at my place in Cambridge. There's a guest cottage out back, and we're hoping Kata or Vica or both will live there for as long as they want. No more cramped apartments for any of them. And family should be close to each other, right?"

"Right. Glenn, why did it take so long? I mean for you and Anna. Don't answer if I'm being nosy."

"Do you want the simple truth? Okay, it's time. I was scared shitless. Not of rejection. When you've been shot at halfway around the world, you can put being shot down in perspective. I was scared what might be inside me. Both my parents had major depression issues, and my father was a violent man. He committed suicide, but was smart enough to make sure it's not what the death certificate said. My mother talked about ending it too, and she tried, twice. She was never a good finisher. Their money did them no good, Michael. But the real nightmare began in Vietnam.

"It happened on patrol. Two Vietnamese boys were walking in my direction. One reached into his pocket and started to throw something my way. I thought it was a grenade, but it wasn't. It was a piece of fruit he wanted to give me. I had less than a second to react. I panicked, guessed wrong, and killed both of them. I had eight men to protect, Michael. I know, there really were kids throwing grenades at us in that shithole, but it doesn't bring these two back to life, does it? Why the fuck were we even over there? I screwed up, and they died.

They were probably twelve years old, not too much younger than I was.

"For years, I woke up at night screaming. They were two friendly kids, some mothers' sons. I see the horror in their faces every day, and I'll have the nightmare until I die. How could I ask Anna to spend her life with a human bomb that could go off any time?

"But wait, there's more. Since I only seem to open up every thirty years, I'll tell you the other reason. I had an affair with a married woman, a summer fling. All the unmarried women I dated, and I had to go after one who was off limits. I thought she could help me with the pain. She seemed to have it all together. It was years ago, but I still can't believe how stupid and selfish I was. And I could see Anna was in pain too. She deserves total commitment, complete happiness. How could I promise her I wouldn't cheat on her, with my track record? How could I be sure? Maybe it's in my blood, my brain. Bad genes are a bitch, Michael.

"So I did nothing. I was gutless. I wasn't afraid she'd say no. I was afraid she'd say yes. And then I got sick. It finally dawned on me if I had even one happy year with Anna, it might be one more happy year than either of us ever had. You can't be too scared to live, Michael. When I got my life back, I told her everything and she told me everything. Thank God, she felt the same way. There won't be as much room in my head now for the nightmare."

Lord, Michael, you have got to stop asking questions around here. But I had found out more about my partners in the last two days than in the twenty years before that. The fairies' howling was getting deafening.

"Glenn, it's a wonder any of us survive being young and clueless. I got to be pretty good myself at a few of the seven deadly sins. I guess we all strapped in and got things right in the end. And don't ever call yourself gutless around me again, okay? You don't know what the word means."

"Thanks, Michael. I needed to tell you. It's been too long. Did I just go to confession?"

"Technically, no. Sorry. With the raging currents and deadly sins around here, it's a miracle we ever got any work done. I thought we were the law firm equivalent of Leave It to Beaver."

"If you say so. We did get it correct in the end, didn't we? So maybe you and I really were Wally and the Beav, but we had a hot Hungarian younger sister."

"That's a disturbing image, Glenn. And Wally never married his sister."

"It's an imperfect analogy. I only wish it hadn't taken twenty years to write my happy ending. That's longer than it's taken Mrs. Boyle to pay you."

"She did pay me, and threw in a nice tip. I forgot to tell you. One last question, I promise. I've been thinking a lot about how you and Anna and I got together way back when. It didn't just happen. Do you ever hear strange voices saying things you don't quite understand?"

"Only yours, Michael, and it never stops."

CHAPTER TWENTY–SIX

Late that morning, I sent Aedan an email:

Hi, Aedan.

Glenn is recovering well and we've gotten some things worked out over here. I have my own glorious news. Glenn and Anna are getting married. I'll tell you about it when we get to Ireland. I need some guidance. If you think you have answers now, where should I be digging while I wait for your report?

Best, Michael

I heard nothing for several hours. That was unusual. Then he responded, by encrypted email:

Hello, Michael, and I am sorry for the delay getting back to you.

I was keeping a doctor's appointment. There is too much dust and mold in those archives, but it is a small price to pay. That is splendid news about Anna and Glenn. I shall send you a case of a libation I reserve for the most special occasions. Perhaps you and Sara will be kind enough to raise a toast or more on my behalf.

My work here proceeds more quickly than I expected. I was fortunate to recruit talented students to assist with the sifting. Blood–sworn to secrecy, and happy to accept a generous research stipend and my highest grades for the current term. We have been able to identify and catalog many documents and the authentication process for them is underway. There are so many more. I am working on it full–time, and hope to have an interim report to you within ten days.

We are bringing Grace O'Malley back to life, but with facts, not tales. I can tell you now that Grace O'Malley sailed from Western Ireland to Dublin with something we are seeking. The voyage took place in August 1582. James and Caitriona accompanied her, but neither returned with her. I see no evidence that Philip Sidney was on either voyage. All of this information came from primary source documents, thanks to you and Sara.

Michael, you have an ability I cannot fathom. I care not whether you call it logic, experience, intuition or indigestion. We approach problems differently, but you grind information like peppercorns and draw conclusions that usually prove to be correct.

For the next ten days, I would like you to apply your gift to what I just told you, what you already know, and what you can deduce. What or whom was Grace transporting? If there was a delivery, to whom was it made? Does it still exist?

I am sorry to sound like Professor Burns giving a final exam to his class. But indeed, this may be our final exam. If we answer those questions, our puzzle is solved.

Warmest wishes, Aedan

So Aedan finally had his primary source documents and I had my final exam. Figure out how Grace O'Malley was trying to hide the truth, and herself. Think like a lawyer, think like a pirate. How different could it be? I could probably get Sherlock to weigh in.

250

Should I also ask Sara? That gave me an idea. She would be attending an artist workshop in New Hampshire on Saturday and Sunday, and wouldn't be back until Monday afternoon. Labor Day weekend would be a weekend of solitary labor for me.

All I had to do in the next six weeks was to solve the O'Malley Protocol, write a wedding ceremony and figure out the rest of my life. No pressure!

Sara picked up Chinese takeout on the way home from her gallery on Friday night. She needed time to pack and I needed time to review my notes and think. Over something that may or may not have been pork, we discussed Aedan's recent emails.

"I'm glad he's finding answers, Michael, and that we were able to help. But I'd sure like to hear how he did it. Did he see something else in those photos that we missed?"

"We'll find out soon. A few more days means nothing to a guy who measures time in centuries."

"Michael, I'm going cold turkey on cigars and whiskey right after we get back from Ireland. They're fun, but I don't want to make you a widower too soon. Who knows what crazy things you might do?"

"I'll miss you this weekend, Sara. I mean that."

"I'll miss you too. We did okay, didn't we?"

We shared a long Crab Rangoon kiss, or maybe it was a Cat Rangoon kiss.

"We sure did. Do you remember that pirate outfit you wore to the Halloween party a few years back? When you get home Monday, would you put it on for me? I think by then I'll be able to tell you some of what Grace O'Malley was up to. Before I talk to

Aedan, I'd like to run it by Jeanne de Clisson. A little pirate peer review. I felt twinges this afternoon and it wasn't indigestion. I hadn't eaten this stuff yet."

"Aargh! You never cease to amaze me, Michael. Sure, let's do some role–playing. Jeanne de Clisson will gladly give you her professional opinion, and then you may expect her to take you prisoner. How will I ever be able to concentrate on my workshop?"

I woke up at 3:00 Saturday morning. I needed to get started. Was 3:00 a.m. last night or was it this morning? If it was last night, pouring a glass of whiskey might be acceptable. If it was this morning, it could be flashing a developing problem. It was dark out, but I'd go with coffee. The Leo Normans don't get that way overnight.

Use your logic, Michael. Aedan must have discovered shipping logs or maritime journals of some kind. How else would he know who was on the voyages and when and where the ships sailed? But that didn't make sense either. If Grace was transporting something or someone she didn't want intercepted or discovered, why would she tell the truth on shipping logs or maritime journals?

Part of it seemed obvious, but the cheese in the trap is obvious to the mouse too. Grace wanted to make sure that Caitriona and maybe something else important made it to Dublin. James must have been helping Grace. She wasn't running a maritime taxi service. And with due respect to Mr. Occam, it was too obvious, too clever by half. Think like she would have, Michael. She had five ships and two hundred men under her command. She wouldn't try to do this

252

with one ship. That wasn't enough muscle. Grace was sailing into English–controlled territory. They hated her, and the Pirate Queen wasn't about to have the story end with her head on a pike singing "I ain't got no body."

So I'd presume Grace left Galway with more than one ship. And that would attract attention. English power in Ireland was concentrated in an area around Dublin, referred to as the Pale. It was heavily fortified, with good surveillance. Grace's power was in the west, or "beyond the Pale." Grace wouldn't risk going into Dublin proper. She had been imprisoned there for more than a year in 1578. People would remember her, and escape routes would be easily cut off.

Whatever Aedan was reading, it was wrong. Grace never went into Dublin proper. Maybe she stayed outside Dublin and deputized James Tiernan or someone else to make sure Caitriona made it to her abbey. Since James only had a one–way ticket, Grace could then return to Western Ireland right away. Quick in, unload, quick out. So the landing place in eastern Ireland would have been someplace close to, but not in, Dublin, in waters Grace was familiar with, but where she should be unrecognized. And it had to have multiple escape routes in case things went wrong. I studied a 1500s Irish map and went over the possibilities. One jumped off the page. It was Howth, a suburb of Dublin and a busy fishing village in the 1500s.

Are you with me so far, Mr. Holmes? Sherlock didn't look convinced. Maybe he wasn't an early morning person. Or any kind of a person. I kept forgetting that.

I'd spell it out for him. Howth is on the northern edge of Dublin Bay, about nine miles from Dublin center. It had a big harbor and easy access to open waters. Grace O'Malley knew it well. The tale was that in 1576 she landed in Howth and requested food and supplies from Lord Howth. Those were customary hospitalities, routinely offered by one Irish noble to another. Grace was turned away. Lord Howth was dining and couldn't be bothered with unexpected visitors. So Grace kidnapped his grandson and brought him back to Clew Bay in Western Ireland, her base of operations. As ransom, she accepted Lord Howth's promise that guests entitled to hospitality would never again be refused, and there would always be a place set at the table in Howth Castle for unexpected visitors. You couldn't deny the woman had a sense of humor. Howth seemed the logical choice. Maybe Grace would bang on the door of the castle to see if her old friend remembered her, and if her place at the table was set. Good times.

Aedan had mentioned Howth too. He used to go there looking for treasure which Grace was rumored to have buried. Interesting.

Sherlock shrugged and nodded agreement. My theory held water, so to speak. Like Aedan said, sometimes you don't discover the whole truth at once. You surround and trap it. And Grace would have done something else besides have dinner with a friend. She needed an insurance policy that could be cashed in quickly if things didn't go according to plan. Grace couldn't be hauling keel back and forth from Clew Bay to take care of problems. She had a business to run. What would a good pirate do? Sure.

254

A sixteenth–century variation on what some of my corporate clients would have done. Jeanne de Clisson would have to agree before I ran this by Aedan. Sometimes it actually is indigestion.

If I was right, then Grace, James and Caitriona sailed to Howth. James and Caitriona continued into Dublin to the abbey, and Grace returned to Western Ireland ASAP. So what happened to James after Howth? My guess was he met up with Philip Sidney in Dublin. But it was only a guess. If there was a damn portrait, where was it? It was going to be a busy weekend.

That was enough for one night. It was almost dawn. My head was aching and I had to get some sleep. I'd schedule another meeting with Messrs. Holmes and Jameson for Monday night. I had some research to do first. Get a little sleep yourself, Sherlock. You're looking pale.

CHAPTER TWENTY–SEVEN

On Saturday, I decided to play another hunch. It still made sense to me that James Tiernan met Philip Sidney in Dublin, and I had no later information on James. But I had only been looking in Irish records. What if James accompanied Philip back to England and never returned to Ireland? Maybe I could find something in England and work backwards into my theories.

I started plowing through English records. It took the whole day and part of the next, but I was able to reconstruct it. What a rookie mistake I had made. When you're researching Ireland, check England and Scotland too. People moved around.

By late 1582, James was living close to Philip in Kent, England. James died and was buried there early in 1583. Shortly thereafter, Philip took a teenage bride, Frances Walsingham. He died in battle in the Netherlands in 1586, at age thirty–one. A few months after Philip married, Caitriona returned to Sligo.

I figured James met Philip in Dublin in 1582. They continued on together to England and stayed there. There were lots of interesting possibilities there. Did it mean Grace's portrait went to England in late 1582 and just disappeared? As Aedan asked, if the portrait was going to England, why did it have to go to the Dublin area first? Pour and ponder, Michael.

Sara returned Monday afternoon. It had been a good workshop. She was getting back to doing portraits now, something she had moved away from several years ago.

"Michael, I have an idea for one of Glenn and Anna's wedding presents. I'd like Anna to sit for a portrait, if she's willing. She told me about her past. I was completely stunned. But she's so happy now, so radiant, so sure of herself. I want to try to capture it on canvas. Faces tell much better stories than mountains."

"It's a wonderful thought, Sara. She and Glenn will treasure a portrait. You'd better unpack now and dig out your pirate outfit. The mentors' meeting is on for 8:00 and it's rude to be late."

"I'm a damn pirate. I can show up whenever I want."

But Jeanne de Clisson walked into the room exactly at 8:00. She was prettier than most pirates, but I didn't think you were supposed to say such things out loud. It could cost you an ear.

"Michael, do pirate outfits make me look short?"

"You are short, and you're disgracing the profession even asking. Remember, for the next hour, you're not Sara. You're Jeanne de Clisson. There's a chair and a drink for you right there."

"Thanks, I brought my own drink. Why is there another empty chair in here with a drink in front of it?"

"It's not empty. I'll explain later. Now, please state your name and occupation."

"I am Jeanne de Clisson, the Lioness of Brittany. I am the most ferocious pirate ever to sail European waters."

"Well, maybe. Pleased to meet you, Ms. Lioness. Say hello to Mr. Sherlock Holmes. He's helping me too."

"What? Where is he?"

"Never mind. I'm going to tell you my theory about a voyage Grace O'Malley took in 1582. I'd like you to listen to it and tell me if I'm thinking the way a pirate would, the way you would."

I told her, and she listened attentively.

"Well, it's pretty much what I would have done. When the French nobility were chasing me, I'd make sure I stuck to waters and ports I knew. Hug the shoreline, then sneak up behind them and blow them through the gates of hell. I wasn't in the delivery business. Plunder and revenge were my games. There's no feeling like warming your hands in front of a burning cargo ship on a crisp fall day. You mentioned an insurance policy. Do you want me to tell you what it was?"

"I think I already have an idea, but I'd like you to verify it."

"You don't know. You make this shit up."

"There's a big difference between not knowing and making shit up, Lioness. Here's what I'll do. I'll write down what I think happened on this piece of paper and put it face down next to your drink. Which, by the way, I would have expected to be grog, not a Southern Comfort Manhattan. You tell me what you would have done, then turn over the piece of paper."

"Okay. I would have taken one man and buried a stash of gold or silver. It would be an underground ATM if I had to make a withdrawal. Now ordinarily, I would have killed the man right after the burying, but that would defeat the purpose here. The man was James Tiernan and he had to know where the treasure was buried in case he had to pay someone. Then I would have slaughtered a few people,

258

displayed their heads at the village gates as a warning, and set the docks on fire. The usual pirate stuff people expect of us."

"I'm starting to fear for Emma. The usual pirate stuff sounds delightful, Lioness, but a little time–consuming when you're trying to get away quickly. Why don't you look at what I wrote down?"

She turned the paper over. It said, 'Bury some treasure just in case'.

"Close enough, I guess. You left out the fun parts."

I called for a vote as to whether to run this by Aedan as a working theory. The vote was 3–0 in the affirmative. So I sent Aedan an encrypted email the next morning and told him what I was thinking. Whatever Grace was transporting, it went to Howth, not Dublin, but Caitriona and James continued on to Dublin. I didn't tell Aedan the mentors who agreed were a reincarnated pirate and a fictional detective. There was no sense making this more complicated. The answer came back within minutes, also encrypted.

You've done some good work, Michael. Everything you surmised is very much consistent with what I am finding here. Your chronology supports my notion that Caitriona was indeed a victim of unrequited love. I suppose we shall never know for certain, but Philip was reputed to be a charming young man, as Protestants go. And I had not traced James into England. That is a fine brick in our wall.

You have persuaded me the delivery was to Howth, not Dublin. And I believe now the delivery did not include Grace's papers. There was less reason for her to travel with incriminating or embarrassing documents when there was James Tiernan to tell her story to people who mattered. Grace and James obviously were very close. I had not fully appreciated it. I believe now the delivery included a portrait of Grace. But why, and where did it go?

Perhaps you should take some well—earned rest while I continue to sort through and assess the documents I am discovering. Each box I open seems to yield some treasure. I can imagine what Howard Carter must have felt when he entered Tutankhamun's tomb. We are adding much information to what is known about Grace O'Malley and how she lived. It probably means that my report to you may not be ready for a few more weeks. I assure you the wait will be worth it.

There is so much for me to finish, and time marches on. My ragtag brigade of student research assistants is a great help, but there are things only I can do.

If your brain requires more exercise while you await my report, please cogitate on our last big remaining question: if there exists a portrait of Grace O'Malley in or near Dublin, where should we look for it?

Kindest regards to you, Sara, Anna and Glenn,

Aedan

I had wondered if Aedan knew where the portrait was, and was just testing me again. Now it was looking like he didn't know for sure. Maybe he had some ideas, though. I could sense some frustration in his communications. Sure, he found some primary source Grace O'Malley documents, and was ecstatic about it. But he wouldn't be satisfied until we found the portrait. Neither would I.

Aedan knew it was out there somewhere. That was good enough for me. Maybe my grade was up to a B–plus now, not good enough. Grace O'Malley, you can run, but you can't hide. I'll get into your head if I have to. I've been to scarier places. And remember, I live with a pirate who wants to kick your butt.

I scheduled a mentors' meeting for Saturday night, and spent the rest of the week cleaning up some of my office files and outlining a wedding ceremony. Glenn and Anna were writing their own vows, but the rest of the ceremony was up to me. How could I put into words what I felt for them? At least it took my mind off Grace O'Malley and Aedan. Let the brain rest a little before the last big push.

Anna had agreed to Sara's portrait and left around noon every day for sittings. Anna told me she was starting to feel like royalty. It was about time. Sara told me Anna was becoming the sister she always wished she had. Life does get weird.

By Friday, I was back thinking about Grace O'Malley. I needed some scenarios to run by the mentors the next night. I'd start with what Aedan now believed. There had been a portrait of Grace O'Malley delivered to somewhere near Dublin, probably Howth. The portrait was likely intended for Philip Sidney. Maybe it was a lover's gift, but it didn't seem like Grace's style. I liked the theory about it being an oversized calling card to advance some mutual interest of Grace and Philip. The why wasn't important, because I wasn't likely ever to know. For me, only the where mattered.

The portrait might have been hidden in the abbey with Caitriona. It would be easy to arrange. Philip was an influential Protestant whose father had been the Queen's Lord Deputy for Ireland. The portrait could have been passed off as an Anglican sugar mommy or a powerful friend of Philip's. Whoever called the shots at the abbey wasn't likely to refuse a request from Philip Sidney. Caitriona could watch over the portrait until Philip came back to get it, and her too.

If my thinking was right, then the portrait probably showed Grace as a force, a noblewoman with money, power and chips to play. She was, after all, Lady Bourke. Give them a little get–out–of–my–way gravitas. Blend in with the other movers and shakers. They didn't want a picture of a pirate cutting someone's throat hanging in their chapel. Then again, maybe a slasher was okay with Anglicans if the slashee was a heretic or demon. I'd ask Glenn.

The Dublin Scenario was a tidy little package and the abbey was still there, although parts of it had been destroyed and rebuilt. Aedan should check it out for portraits or records of portraits.

There was another scenario, the Howth Scenario. The portrait never made it out of Howth. It was the old fake handoff play, some playground razzle-dazzle. But if a portrait stayed in Howth, why, and where did the portrait go? I was grasping at straws, and could only think of one plausible answer, Howth Castle. When Grace stopped in on her old friend, she brought him a little gift. Lord Howth owed her one. Hold on to the portrait until a named somebody came to take it. The portrait may even have been hung in the dining hall, so Grace could look down at her table setting and over at Lord Howth. Nice payback. My stomach lining was tingling, but there were so many possibilities. The team had to weigh in. I asked Jeanne de Clisson to attend the next meeting. Sara thought I was insane now, so I may as well confirm it.

I ran the two scenarios by the mentors. Sherlock went with the Dublin Scenario. It was logical, but he admitted he didn't have much experience with pirates. I went with my instinct and Howth. Jeanne de Clisson would be the tie–breaker. That was a terrifying thought. We'd better solve this soon. It was getting other–worldly in here.

"I'm going with Howth. We pirates don't like to give up control. She'd want to do the delivery herself, and Dublin was risky. Lord Howth wouldn't screw with Grace again. If she gave the portrait to James and then left, she wouldn't know for sure it was ever delivered. She'd wonder if James double–crossed her. We pirates don't trust anyone. Then she'd have to kill him and the rest of his family, and you wouldn't even be here tonight talking to your imaginary friends."

"Strange words coming from a woman wearing a pirate costume and sipping a drink with three cherries. And yet, I think you may be right. The next Shirley Temple is on me, Lioness."

"Shirley Temple? Avast! I'd have the curly–haired little twit for lunch if I didn't think all the sugar would make me diabetic. Rum and sheep's blood for me, if we're out of Southern Comfort."

"Lioness, how do you do this? See the one little thing the rest of us miss?"

"I have a mentor too. Mine is the Jackal. I do what he would have done. Of course, the Lioness must be forgiven certain space–and–time inconsistencies." At least.

"But the Lioness has a delivery question. If the portrait was intended to make it to England, why would someone warehouse it in Dublin or Howth?"

"Very astute, Lioness. I think Philip Sidney wanted to keep the portrait in Ireland because it wasn't the right time yet to bring it to England. There was something going on over there that had to be wrapped up first."

The meeting adjourned. I thanked Sherlock and put him on unpaid leave. I'd run this by Aedan, but I wanted to check something out first.

I contacted Patrick Ruddy on Monday. I had another assignment for him. It would be a nice road trip and completely on the clock. I asked Patrick to arrange for a personal guided tour of Howth Castle. Take close–up pictures of any portraits of females from the sixteenth century, and anything with the names O'Malley, O'Flaherty, Bourke or Sidney. Pay the guides handsomely for their time and information. I'd make it worth Patrick's while. And find out whether an Aedan Burns had been there recently asking similar questions. I told Patrick I'd wire him a fat retainer, and don't worry about driving past any security cameras. In fact, he should be as visible as someone like him could be. Smile into the cameras and wave to Aedan. Even better, wear a Boston Red Sox sweatshirt while doing it.

I heard from Patrick in three days. The guy was a pro's pro. He got the guides to show him every room in the Castle, even ones that were closed to the public. There was only one portrait of a female dating from 1550 to 1600, and it was identified as Lady Howth. He took pictures of it, and didn't see any of the names I gave him anywhere else. He was absolutely sure he had seen every portrait in the Castle.

And it was the strangest coincidence. A man had been in only yesterday, chatting up the guide about tales of Grace O'Malley treasure buried in Howth. He wanted to see the same portraits Patrick was asking about. A tall man with unruly white hair, but his name wasn't Aedan Burns. It was Aedan Finnegan. Strange coincidence indeed.

I waited until the following Tuesday to contact Aedan again, by encrypted email.

Top of the morning to you, Aedan.

I have a plotline I'd like to run by you. The Queen delivers the picture to a friend at Howth Castle. She buries an insurance policy nearby and returns home. Caitriona and James go alone and empty–handed to Dublin. They were decoys. James meets Philip in Dublin, and they continue on to England as lovers. Neither returns to Ireland again. Caitriona feels betrayed, goes into a convent, and dies of a broken heart. Too pulp fiction?

But Aedan, I think I struck out. I've checked out every portrait in Howth Castle. There's only one female from the right time period, and she's been authenticated as Lady Howth. The Queen isn't there, unless you found her when you stopped by last week.

Regards, Michael.

The unencrypted response did not arrive for a week. It surprised me, but I welcomed the break.

Touché again, my friend.

There's no need for encryption at this stage, a bit too self–indulgent now. My apologies for not responding sooner. You gave me many leads to explore in just a week. Our quest is taking on some urgency now, so I will share with you my current assessment of our puzzle. I have the advantage of seeing documents you have not seen.

Grace's portrait went to Howth Castle and a treasure of some kind was buried nearby. James and Caitriona were more than decoys. They were given a message from Grace to deliver to Philip. When the time was right, Philip would go to Howth Castle and pick up the portrait. For some reason, he never did. It stayed in Howth Castle for several more centuries.

You may know Howth Castle remained in the ownership of Lord Howth's direct descendants until the early twentieth century. It is now owned by more distant relatives. The recent owners did not recognize Grace's portrait. It and some lesser sixteenth–century portraits were moved to other family estates in the early 1900s. Her portrait is now in the home of a family relative in Howth. By eliminating the impossibles, I located it. There is no name or identification on the portrait, but there are enough clues to make me certain it must be she. And I have Sara and Michael to thank for pointing me to her.

I look forward to sharing the particulars over a well–drawn pint at the White Stag. There will be formal authentication, of course, after which the owners say they are willing to sell Grace and have her displayed publicly in perpetuity. I have no desire to see my Holy Grail displayed with a label saying, 'Might be Grace O'Malley'. So authentication shall proceed, but I have little doubt. This is Grace.

I told you the day we met that our puzzle could not be solved except by the two of us working together. I was wrong. We required the eyes of Sara the artist and one other pair of eyes, which I shall explain to you later.

One step at a time. First I must authenticate the documents. I am meeting this afternoon with a group of respected historians to present my findings and conclusions for their consideration. I shall contact you this evening and tell you how I found the documents.

Please give my best to Patrick Ruddy. He must be highly thought of to get a three–hour private tour of the Castle. I must say, I had not expected to see him smile for the camera and give me the finger. I'm starting to like the chap.

Best, Aedan Finnegan

So Aedan found the portrait and Sara and I helped him. Good. His legacy was assured and I'd get to meet the Pirate Queen. For me, there were higher priorities to take care of first.

I was ready now to finish writing the wedding ceremony. But I was thinking about other things too. Glenn, Anna, Sara and I had become so much closer in the past few months. We spent unrushed time together, talked about important things and shared feelings with each other. We sometimes finished each others' sentences with an easy intimacy that respected boundaries. An invisible line had been crossed. We were a real family now, the good kind, the kind none of us had much of before. Why did it take so long?

Aedan gave me the answer. We had all obsessed on the past and lost sight of the future. Glenn and Anna had horrible parts of their lives to bury. It took time, probably too much time, but they sucked it up and did it. I let a hobby turn into what Aedan called an unhealthy obsession with the dead. I ran away from real life and real family. An addiction is an addiction is an addiction, whether it's in a computer screen or in a glass.

At least Anna and Glenn beat a past that really happened. My video–game past existed mostly in my head, and I did something even worse. I came dangerously close to blowing it with Sara by not trusting her when it mattered, and dwelling on those roads not taken, one road in particular. Life doesn't give you a do–over, or maybe it does. You got it mostly right in the beginning, Michael. Your instincts were good for a while. After the dead weights of youthful omniscience and blaming everyone else stopped getting in the way, you figured things out. Maybe it only happened by dumb luck, but better to be lucky than good. You're not perfect. You never were and you wouldn't know what to do with it. Play the hell out of the cards you're holding now, because you may never be dealt another hand. You've been given a second life, like Glenn and Anna. Don't piss this one away.

I went into the conference room to polish up the only wedding ceremony that would ever be written there. It wasn't to be. Five minutes later, Glenn knocked on the door.

"Got a minute, Michael? I'm writing my wedding vows and could use some spiritual guidance."

"You've come to the right place, my son. Please, sit down and tell me what's troubling you."

"Michael, do you believe there's a heaven, a place people can go to?"

"Sure. But you and Anna are getting married at the winery, right? Heaven's a long way for a destination wedding and I think you have to book it far in advance. And then, you'd have to redo all the invitations."

"No, it's the winery. They've cashed the check. Here's why I ask. I'm going to promise to love and cherish Anna for the rest of my life and for eternity. The rest of my life part is easy, but I need to flesh out the implications of eternity. Anna was raised Catholic but no longer practices it. I'm a Christmas–and–Easter Anglican. Are we excluded from heaven? I'm not sure you can love and cherish someone forever in hell. It seems to defeat the whole purpose of hell."

"I'm glad you've come to me today, Glenn. You're confused, but it's never too late to achieve spiritual closure. Would you please tell me why you think you and Anna might be excluded from heaven? Are there specific things you wish to confess today?"

"Nice try, but let's stay macro. We'll start with Anna. She's an attractive woman, right?"

"The word attractive doesn't begin to describe Anna."

"I agree. So she had to be an attractive teenager, right?"

"Right. We're moving into confessable territory here, Glenn."

"Not yet. We didn't know her then. What troubles me is the Catholic idea of the near occasion of sin, especially the impure thought rule and its effect on salvation."

"It can be a difficult concept, my son. Many Catholics spend their whole lives studying it. The devil is in the details, as they say. Can you give me an example as it relates to Anna? Perhaps a very carefully worded example?"

"Sure. Suppose, for the sake of argument, the teenage Anna walked by a Catholic boys' high school in shorts and gave a whole bunch of pimply sophomores boners. You can grasp what I'm talking about here? It could have happened?"

"Grasp what you're talking about. Carefully worded indeed. Glenn, something like it almost certainly did happen. What's your point?"

"That is my point. It almost certainly did happen. So was Anna the instrument of their impure thoughts and whatever they did afterwards? Was she an accessory before the fact, sharing in their depravity and therefore condemned to eternal fires? Without regard to her intent or participation, of which I presume there was none?"

"Knowing Anna, I would think that's a fair assessment, as to intent and participation. You've raised the essential dilemma of Catholicism. How close can you get to the sin without becoming part of

270

it? And the stakes are high. Now it is possible Anna confessed what she did and received divine forgiveness. But how would she even realize the full extent of what she did? Now if she circled the block five times, that would raise other issues. Holy Mother Church does not condone torture. But perhaps I can answer all your questions at the same time. Why do you think you might be excluded from paradise?"

"I'm not Catholic. Outside the Church, there is no salvation, correct? No Anglicans need apply?"

"You've been listening to the wrong people, Glenn. Charlatans who got their spiritual training after answering a late–night television ad. I am trained in Irish Catholicism, the grain alcohol of Christianity. I understand subtleties of faith you might not.

"I have good news for you and Anna. You are both eligible for heaven. As I understand it, if either of you had died before 1962, you would have gone straight to hell. Lack of intent was not a good defense. Then we got an enlightened Pope who tidied up some doctrinal messes. The Jews didn't kill Jesus. Personally, I think it was the Albanians. Masses don't have to be in Latin. And it's okay for girls like Anna to wear shorts when walking by a Catholic boys' high school. She could even wear patent leather shoes with a skirt, as long as she didn't polish the shoes. The good news for you is, as of 1962, non–Catholics may enter heaven also. We figure if you were thinking straight, you would have wanted to be Catholic. I think it's called baptism by desire. There are still yearly quotas on non–Catholics going to heaven, so plan your death.

Early in the year would be best. Holidays can get pretty busy.

"But the bottom line is you and Anna may pledge your troth to each other for eternity without having to buy fireproof clothing. And Glenn, on the off chance I have imperfectly understood Church teachings, look at it this way. If heaven excludes people like you and Anna, who the hell would want to go there?"

"You've comforted me, Michael. I had no idea there was a different set of rules for salvation after 1962. I'm lucky to have a knowledgeable Catholic like you as my spiritual advisor."

"My pleasure, and I'm glad I could bring you solace. I enjoyed being able to eat meat on Friday, thanks to the enlightened Pope. High school without daily cheeseburgers and fries isn't much fun. Now get out of here and let me finish your ceremony. And it's probably best if you didn't share this conversation with Anna. It's the seal of the confessional."

"Understood. Did you happen to go to a Catholic boys' high school, Michael?"

"I did. Get out of here, Glenn."

CHAPTER TWENTY–EIGHT

There was a long email waiting for me when I got home.

Good afternoon, partners.

I am now able to share more information. You must forgive my reluctance to say too much too soon. My historian colleagues have confirmed we struck gold.

You knew, Michael, that the National University of Ireland in Galway has maritime records going back to the 1500s and earlier. You did not have time to plumb the depths of NUIG on your last trip, but told me you would try to do so in October. I was not optimistic. It is a gargantuan task. But you and Sara provided an unexpected key. The key was in your Galway photographs. I would have dismissed them as just so many touristy photographs of boring streetscapes, and filed them away. You and Sara observed what was invisible to Aedan and Lester. Sara saw they were taken from almost the same location, and Michael grasped the significance of Leo's ring binders. But where were they taken? Carroll Street?

I first established there never was a Carroll Street in Galway. I considered the possibility Carroll Street might be an unofficial name used by locals, but after talking to people who would know and examining old maps, I disregarded my theory. Michael surmised that the street might be near Dominican College on Taylor's Hill. I am most curious to learn how you knew. Frankly, I thought

273

you might be bluffing, throwing me your own red herring.

So I showed the photographs to a colleague at university, an authority on Irish urban architecture. This is a man who would have difficulty locating his car in a small parking garage. He looked at the photographs and, within three minutes, announced he knew where they were taken. One of the buildings had a very unusual architectural feature he recognized. However, the building was not in the photograph marked 'Carroll Street'. More on that later.

The street indeed is in the Taylor's Hill section of Galway, near Dominican College.

You were right, Michael. Carroll Street was code.

In 1941, NUIG leased a building on the street for three years from a trust administered by a professor at Dominican. It was part of a secret effort to protect historical documents from the ravages of war. Ireland was officially neutral, but perhaps not sufficiently so in the eyes of the Axis. Boxes of historical documents were moved with great speed and in the dark of night to locations throughout Galway. Many of those boxes were never returned, for reasons not entirely clear. There should have been better records kept, but there was a war in progress and time was an enemy as well.

I was able to locate the building, still occupied by the professor's descendants. The professor's three-roomed library contained more than sixty file boxes of 1500s and 1600s records transported from NUIG. Many boxes were commingled with other stored historical documents, and the professor's personal effects.

274

The professor died in 1995. Under the terms of his will, the house remains in his family's ownership until 2020, at which time it will be conveyed to Dominican College. The will also provides that the library is to remain open to scholars for study, research and writing.

Our professor's grandson now uses the library rooms as a getaway nook to write his novels. Dreadful potboilers they are, but at least not vampire stories.

Fortunately, the grandson was familiar with my own published works, and was kind enough to give me exclusive use of the rooms for several weeks in return for some editing and critiquing services. The mind recoils in horror.

It soon became clear that what I have been examining were not all the documents stored there at one time. The rest disappeared, or perhaps made their way back to NUIG or another hiding place.

I found more than twenty-five boxes of records related to shipping and maritime activity into and out of the port of Galway from 1550 through 1600. There are rich historical details to be gleaned from such records. Many of them relate to Grace O'Malley. Some have her notes. There are references to her meetings with Henry and Philip Sidney. I can well see why Leo and Brigid spent so much time here. And I would never have found these records had it not been for you.

Aedan

Okay, Taylor's Hill. Looking good so far, Michael. What do you suppose was the professor's name? Aedan never said it, and there were so many Carrolls in and around Dominican College. Call it petty ego, but I had to find out.

I went online to check out Dominican College and the surrounding neighborhood. I couldn't see where the photographs were taken, but the neighborhood must have changed a lot. I'd spend a few hours on it later. Time to get back to Aedan.

Good afternoon, Aedan.

Thank you for your interesting email. May I share this information? I'll be having lunch Friday with Lester and Carol DiStefano, and I'm sure they would be delighted to learn of your success. In your honor, I'm taking them to an Italian restaurant called Cervo. It means Stag.

If it is not inappropriate, would you mind telling me the name of the professor from whom NUIG leased the building?

Best wishes, Michael

Pour coffee, take three sips, read reply. Please, let it be John Carroll.

Certainly, Michael. You are considerate to think of Lester and Carol, and I shall soon be contacting Lester myself. I would like to engage his services to help me put my findings into proper form for publication. Did I neglect to mention the professor's name? Please accept my deepest apologies. I'm getting so absent-minded. It was John Carroll.

Enjoy Cervo, and may your bartender be named Declano.

Cheers, Aedan

276

Sloppy, Michael, very sloppy. There was something else I should have done right away to try to track down Leo's research notes. I just forgot. When Lester told me the school had refused Leo's papers, I never followed up to confirm that. I called Carol to see if she had time to look into it. I promised her another lunch, any restaurant she wanted. Carol would be happy to do it, but if I kept this up, she'd have to renew her gym membership. She promised she'd have the information by the time we met for lunch on Friday.

So the professor's grandson had a getaway nook where he could quietly get work done. It was like my man cave at home. It was another long shot, but I may as well ask. I fired off an email to Lester. I was looking forward to seeing him and Carol again, and would he please give a little thought to one more question? Did he recall Leo Norman having a getaway nook, a quiet oasis he could escape to when he needed to concentrate? Lester had told me that in Ireland, Leo would sometimes lock himself in the bathroom for hours when he was writing, to Brigid's great annoyance. Leo could probably find a better getaway nook than a bathroom.

I ran everything by Sara when she got home. She was a little exasperated that Aedan hadn't told me exactly how he identified the building, or the name of the street.

"I'm happy he found the portrait, Michael, if he did. Something in his approach is changing now. He's rushing things, no more methodical one brick at a time. I understand how badly he wants this, but identifying Elizabethan portraits can be tricky. He's moving outside his skill set, and I'm getting too old

277

to have him feed us information like crumbs to a pigeon. Why don't I hop a plane and wring it out of him?"

"Sara, it's not how the Jackal would play it. Be cool. Let the game come to you. You've been right so far on the important stuff. Show him you're bigger than he is."

"I'm not bigger than anyone except Aoife, and I'm not who I appear to be. I'm the Lioness of Brittany."

"And a fine Lioness you are, but give this a little more time. Leo and Brigid are not who they appear to be either. John Carroll had a background in military intelligence, like Leo Norman. I don't think it's a coincidence."

"Too many threads here for me to keep straight. This Grace portrait thing is bothering me now. I used to spend a lot of time on Elizabethan art. Do you remember what I was doing when we first started dating? I'll give you a hint. I had recently finished my Master's in Art History and was working as a conservator at the MFA. You kept walking by my desk and conned me into believing you appreciated fine art."

"I did. Those tight jeans of yours were a twentieth century masterpiece."

"Well, art means different things to different people. I kept dropping things and bending over to pick them up whenever you walked by. We didn't know how lucky we were, did we? We almost threw it away. Maybe I had an okay ass, but parts of my brain weren't working very well. I guess it's how nature divides things up. We've got to get it all back, Michael, and I think we are."

278

"We are, Sara. My brain was pretty messed up too, and I never even got the good ass."

"Quit while you're ahead, Michael, but thanks. Look, Aedan has a definite time period for the Grace portrait, around 1580. I'm going spend the next week re–acquainting myself with late sixteenth–century Elizabethan art. I hope it's like riding a bike. We have to live in the real world now."

Amazing, Lioness, simply amazing.

Carol got back to me the next day. She located copies of two letters. The first was from Brigid, offering Leo's papers to the school. If the school wasn't interested, she requested permission to dispose of the papers as she saw fit. The headmaster politely declined the papers, with sincere condolences. The school didn't have enough space, but the headmaster was sure the papers would be of interest to a university with a larger library. If not, Brigid was free to keep them.

Cripes, how many universities would that be? Which is exactly what Brigid would have thought. She probably did what everyone else in my family did – threw up her hands and headed for the nearest trash bin or incinerator. My father used to laugh about that. The Irish here saved little. They had gotten used to moving around, often on short notice. Pack fast and travel light. Another door had closed, unless Lester had somehow stuck his foot in it.

And he had. Lester walked into the restaurant Friday with more than a little impish swagger, twirling a schoolbook bag like a ninety–five year old high school freshman. He handed it to me with an exaggerated bow.

"I have a gift for you, Michael. I was able to recall one time I was invited to Leo's sanctum sanctorum, a grim little crypt in the bowels of the old school library basement. I remembered it was next to the boiler room. The building has since been put to other uses and the heating system relocated, but Carol was able to locate plans showing the old layout.

"Leo's desk was still there, covered with decades of dusty old yearbooks and building maintenance records. But underneath it all, Carol and I found six of his research binders. Three are from the Galway years, and two of those binders are red. I thought you might want them."

The other binders were black, for recording Leo's observations. Talk about Harold Carter entering King Tut's tomb. I thanked Lester and Carol, asked them to please order drinks and lunch for us, and raced into the bar. I had to email Aedan immediately.

I am speechless, Michael, absolutely speechless. At your very earliest convenience, please make a copy of each Galway binder. Send the copies to me by the fastest secure means of delivery possible and place the originals in a safe.

There shall be a substantial expression of my thanks coming your way by Christmas.

I shall also arrange for something to be added to Lester's and Carol's Christmas stockings. You have assembled an exceptional team.

With astonishment, Aedan

I made Carol and Lester promise we would keep getting together, and I'd pay the next two years of

280

Carol's gym membership. I could just imagine the two of them slogging through dust and hacking through cobwebs in the prep school catacombs, trying to help me out.

We sealed the deal with espresso and pastries. Carol and Lester had earned every calorie and I'd make sure they and Aedan knew it.

CHAPTER TWENTY–NINE

Saturday morning, I made two copies of Leo Norman's research binders and got a set off to Aedan by international express courier. I kept a set and put the originals in my safe. Then I found an escape nook in the basement of the local public library and finished writing the wedding ceremony. It was only a week away, and we'd be in Ireland a few days later. I made time on Sunday to read through Leo Norman's three Galway binders.

As Lester had warned, Leo's writing was hard to decipher. He used abbreviations followed by numbers, and some strange chicken–scratch shorthand. If Lester was transcribing, I wondered why these materials hadn't been turned into something the rest of the world could easily read. Maybe Leo didn't want Lester to see them, or maybe Leo didn't want them easily read.

The contents of the binders were well organized, everything arranged by date. Two of the inside covers were marked TH Galway, which I took to mean Taylor's Hill. The third was marked NUIG.

For each date, there was a list of documents examined, with a short summary of the document and a note or two. Most of it was legible. Leo assigned every document a number from one to ten, possibly his assessment of its importance? Each binder contained more than three hundred pages, some with two or three summarized documents.

I could identify one notation as being the language in which each document was written. Most were written in Irish, some in Latin, only a few in English. No wonder it took several summers. Two things jumped out. One binder was dated the year before Lester's first trip to Galway with Leo and Brigid, so Leo and Brigid spent more than those two summers in Galway. And at the end of each red Taylor's Hill binder, there were fifty or so pages of numbers in four columns, with pencil lines connecting some of the numbers and marginal notes in Leo's chicken–scratch shorthand. Leo had told Lester he was working on a numerical system to catalog his historical research. If this was it, it was one strange system. It had the appearance of a game or mathematical puzzle.

I saw notations for PS and HS, which could have meant Philip Sidney and his father Henry. There was an occasional GM notation. Maybe it referred to Grace O'Malley, using her Irish name. I'd leave that to Aedan and the experts. I went through the other binders. Only the two red Taylor's Hill binders had the pages of numbers at the end. You're wasting more time, Michael. This is about Grace O'Malley. Forget the numbers and see if you can find anything in those notations.

Anna knocked on my office door Monday morning.

"Michael, the wedding is only five days away, but I have a big favor to ask if you'll do it. It's something I just thought of. Promise me you'll say no if I'm being a jerk."

"You haven't been one in twenty–three years, so it's a yes. What is it?"

"Glenn and I are visiting Hungary on our wedding trip. I've never been there, and I've never learned my family history. I'd like to see some of the places we came from. If I give you the information on my parents, would you have time to go back a little ways and tell me where those places are?"

"This is a real rush job, Anna. For you, I can handle it, but I'm going to have to charge a little more. Suppose I do it and put a report in a sealed manila envelope for you. Will you agree to open that envelope in front of me using your special tool?"

"That's a steep price, maybe for both of us. Are you sure you can handle seeing my special tool?"

"I'll only know if I see it. I did pretty well on my last cardiac stress test."

"Okay, you win. I think it's appropriate that the last man who will ever see my special tool is you, Michael. It's a deal."

I reached into my desk, took out a sealed manila envelope and handed it to her.

"I anticipated this. Sara might have told you, I have the power to read a woman's mind."

"And to cloud it. This is a trick, isn't it?"

"Not at all. I have traced your ancestry back to Ferdinand III, King of Hungary in the 1600s. The blood of royalty flows through your veins, and I can't say that surprised me. It's all in here, names, dates, places. It's my only way of doing another portrait of you. Now would you kindly open the package?"

Anna slowly reached into her purse, pulled out a knife and popped the blade. It was a serious knife, not something you'd put on a keychain to open a beer bottle. She carefully cut the top off the envelope, slid out the contents, and slowly flipped through the pages. I had put a lot of effort into this portrait of her and she knew it. Then she pressed down on a legal pad in front of me, carved a deep, neat 'Z' into it, and folded up the knife.

"After my husband died, I promised myself nobody would ever scar me again. Zorro doesn't need her blade anymore. It's just another part of my past I can throw away."

She walked over to my wastebasket and dropped the knife into it. Anna's mentor was a Fox. Sara's mentor was a Jackal. Maybe these two really were sisters.

"Michael, I'm glad you can read my mind right now. I could never say it out loud."

She smiled and walked out. I looked down at the 'Z' she had carved. There was no way El Zorro could have carved a better one.

CHAPTER THIRTY

The wedding was magical. I used most of the ceremony I had written, but improvised as emotions overtook me. You can get away with that at a wedding. Anna and Glenn were a breathtaking couple. Sylvie Lepine was there with her husband, who turned out to be an accountant. Maybe I'd rethink those preconceived notions about accountants. After Glenn and Anna exchanged vows, they both raised a toast to Sylvie and thanked her for this wonderful day. Surgeons can cry too. That toast, and many which followed, were made possible by Aedan's special libation. It was probably the most expensive spirit I would ever raise to my lips. I was thoroughly convinced now of the power of spirits, at least this kind.

Vica was every bit as beautiful and engaging as advertised, and Kata glowed almost as much as her mother. They may have grown up without a father, but Glenn would soon make them forget that. Emma sat with the big girls and melted a few eyeballs herself. I kept looking at her and seeing Sara twenty–five years ago. It's been a good life, Michael. It should be easy to live with the consequences of your choices.

Anna's father had passed away four years earlier. Her mother was there, and also her brother and his family. Anna's mother was quiet and looked sad the whole day. I hoped it was for the right reasons or she was going to be a lonely old woman. Honestly, I didn't care that much. She had made her bed. Anna's brother and his wife were pleasant. They lived in England now, and Anna didn't see them much. Except for her daughters, that was Anna's whole family.

Anna gasped when Sara unveiled her portrait. It was perfect. How did Sara capture the new Anna so well? Maybe it was because she was starting to know Anna better. What a gift Sara had, and what a gift Anna and Glenn now had.

Every beautiful day has to have a dark cloud. Today, it was Glenn's sister Patricia. She came by herself because, as she made sure to say several times, her husband DeWitt was an extremely important banker, attending a meeting in Geneva. If Patricia's nose got any higher in the air, it would have required FAA clearance.

Seating Sara and me with Patricia must have been Glenn's idea. He wanted to watch how the other kind of chemistry works, and I was guessing he'd see a dramatic reaction. Anna and Glenn were safely married now. I had only promised Anna I'd hold it together until vows were exchanged. And Sara was still upset that Patricia blew Glenn off when he was sick. Glenn never mentioned anything about that to us, but he didn't have to. The chemicals were in place. It would take only one little spark.

Patricia and bankster DeWitt split their time between New York City and Cambridge. Not just Cambridge. Brattle Street, don't you know. Patricia said it was one of the few little islands of American civilization outside New York City. DeWitt was Crimson to the core, and Patricia regaled us with insufferable stories of tailgating with Fortune 500 CEOs every year at The Game with Yale.

As Patricia brattled on about herself, Sara made her slinging–it gesture, as if I didn't already see it.

287

Smoke rings of condescension wafted across the table. You'll pay for this, Glenn. The only question was whether Patricia would pay first. Maybe the dark cloud would pass.

"Michael, I understand you work with Glenn? Are you in debt collection and the like? Chasing the old ambulances?"

"No, Patricia, Glenn and I work together on some sensitive matters. I'd love to give you details, but you'd have to show me a Level 5 security clearance. It's that hush–hush. Let's leave it at this. If you ever hear of Operation Lazarus or the O'Malley Protocol, it was us. I wouldn't try to get any more information until everything is declassified. You and DeWitt might be visited by some scary dudes, even scarier than Yale men."

"Is there anything scarier than a Yale man? How very exciting. I had no idea brother Glenn was a spook. And Sara, you've done such an interesting portrait of Anna. She's a beautiful woman, in an unconventional way. Of course, DeWitt and I know nothing about her family and educational background, and I would have expected Glenn to get married at a more elegant location than a farm. He has the money. I must say, your portrait almost looks like her. I love the liberties you took with her eyes and nose. I'm an artist myself. I study with Federico Bosh–Lillis in New York City. Have you heard of him? He doesn't leave the Apple much. Why would one, I suppose, when it's where most good art is being done today."

Well, another question answered. Patricia would pay. I glanced over at Sara. She took a sip of her drink, put it down and studied the cherries for a

288

moment. I was starting to feel sorry for Patricia. Rattlesnakes rattle. Cobras spit. Sara studies the cherries in her drink. And it all ends the same way. I had watched so many ego freighters break apart in the Straits of Sara. Another one was about to hit the rocks.

"Thank you, Patricia. Often when I do a portrait now, I do try to make it resemble the subject. How very perceptive of you. Yes, I'm familiar with Federico. He and I co–curated a show at the Salmagundi Club on Fifth Avenue a few years ago. Please do say hello to him for me. His en plein air landscapes remind me of Monet in the early years at Giverny. But to be honest, Federico's style now seems to be influenced more by the contemporary painter Anders Frank Tutweiller, wouldn't you agree?"

Patricia was a little uncomfortable, but she was boxed in.

"Oh, of course. Tutweiller is one of my muses as well. He really must spend more time in New York."

"I would love to see your work, Patricia. Could you send me samples? I'm sure I'd recognize Tutweiller's influence. His attention to finish detail is just amazing. Did Glenn tell you he was looking into having this ceremony in the Grand Salon at the Palace of Versailles? They told him it was unavailable, but Anna is from the Hungarian royal family and silly Glenn never mentioned it. Nothing cuts red tape like blue blood, and the Hungarian royal family is so highly regarded in France. One hopes they will be renewing their vows soon at Versailles.

"It was sad Anna's family going into exile after the communists came to power. Fortunately, Princesses Kata and Vica were able to make it today. Aren't they lovely? And I'm told there have been several gatherings of the royal family at this winery, so it's quite a meaningful location for them. It's why Anna chose it, one assumes. Tradition, you know, rather like you and DeWitt cooking up those hot dogs in a crowded parking lot, then watching some good, smash–mouth Ivy League football. Such fun, Patricia. Go, Crimson Tide!"

Crimson Tide? Wrong conference, Sara. They play different football down there.

"And I believe Anna had tutors, in the manner of eastern European nobility. No overrated education factory ships for them. Anna doesn't brag about it, or anything else. That's a sign of intelligence and class, don't you think? She'd never tell you she speaks four languages fluently, or she's a world–class pistol shooter who probably would have qualified for the Olympics if not for an untimely arm injury. I've heard she can still shoot out a candle flame at thirty feet.

"But please send me those samples of your work, Patricia. I know Anders Frank Tutweiller, and he would love to know he inspires you. Perhaps he'd even show you some of his techniques. He's from Cambridge now, not far from Brattle Street. I'm seeing more and more of his work all around Boston. If I were you and DeWitt, I would consider collecting some of it as an investment."

"I agree, Sara. I shall discuss that with DeWitt when he returns from Geneva. And I shall also send you samples of my work as soon as I can pull some together. You are very gracious, and I certainly had no idea about Anna. Would you please excuse me now? Nature calls."

As she strutted away, I asked Sara to tell me what had just happened. Was this guy Federico Bosh–Lillis really reminiscent of Monet? That's good, right? Even I knew a little about Monet.

"He's reminiscent of Monet in the sense they both used paint. The similarities pretty much stop there. Federico's work is garbage. He was interesting for a few years, then he developed a following of society matron prunes. Now he cranks out pretentious manure and they pay him big bucks to shovel it up. Pimp–and–whore art. I did curate a show with him in New York. I didn't meet him, though. He couldn't be bothered showing up when the other curators did. Too busy giving interviews, don't you know."

"And what about that Anders Frank Tutweiller? Is there such a person?"

"Oh, sure. I don't make this stuff up, Michael, at least most of it. Anders is an excellent painter. Patricia never heard of him and she's Googling him at the moment. She'll discover that Anders paints trucks at a body shop near Harvard Square. She must walk past it on her way to those precious little shops. Anders does particularly good work around door frames. One of the women in my gallery swears by him, and I've met him bringing her to and from his shop. I think Federico and Patricia could improve quite a bit if they studied with a talent like Anders."

"That's my Sara. You can take the artist out of Rhode Island, but you can't take Rhode Island out of the artist. Do you ever wish you had a society prune following?"

"I've got the following I want. A lot of them are here today. And lay off Rhode Island, okay? You grew up there too. Gilbert Stuart was from Rhode Island and he painted a pretty good portrait. He almost made George Washington look like himself."

"Point taken. I know Anna is fluent in English, Hungarian and French. What's her other language?"

"Spanish. We went to a Spanish restaurant last week after a portrait sitting. She ordered for us in Spanish and had a long conversation with the waiter about the ingredients. She had him eating out of her hand by the time she was done."

"I suspected she might be Olympics–level with her pistol. She's pretty good with a knife too. I wouldn't want to mess around with her."

"I hope not. She is too modest about her abilities, Michael."

"I know a few people like that. Care for another drink? Oh look, Patricia's walking to her car. She looks a little crimson. I hope she hasn't taken ill."

There was an email from Aedan waiting for me when I got home.

Good evening, Michael.

I hope you and Sara are thoroughly exhausted after a memorable wedding celebration. It is only four days now until we meet again, and we shall have a celebration to match the nuptials of Glenn and Anna. So please rest.

The research binders you sent yielded new treasures. Many relevant documents Leo and Brigid examined no longer reside at Taylor's Hill and may be lost to us forever. Fortunately, Leo was meticulous in describing what he saw and well—trained in historical assessment. So what we have is the best we could hope for if we never see the documents themselves.

Please tell Sara to bring her appetite and her considerable charm. I shall provide the food, whiskey, cigars, music, rambling tales and old—man eccentricities. I shall also unfold more details on our successes and how they were achieved.

Your flights and accommodations are arranged, and Aoife will have your car waiting for you. A courier will be at your office Monday morning with a package.

Dare I say just like old times? And this time, we have prevailed.

With much anticipation, Aedan

Maybe we had prevailed, but I wished people would stop saying it was going to be like old times. We were all starting to switch gears and move on. Aedan found his documents and the missing portrait of Grace O'Malley, and I found the missing portrait of Michael Tiernan. Not a bad two months!

CHAPTER THIRTY—ONE

Sara and I boarded our Aer Lingus flight on Wednesday. As I was asking Sara whether she thought another bottle of Irish whiskey might be delivered from Aedan, it appeared. A flight attendant serenaded us in Irish as the bottle was presented, and she filled our glasses. It was still morning, but Aedan believed time ceased to exist above thirty thousand feet. It was part of Einstein's Theory of Relativity, something he had also studied at university. One of the flight attendants told us the song was an Irish lament about a man who gave up drinking and suffered tragedies for the rest of his life. Aedan thought it was a good cautionary tale. I asked the attendant if she'd join us in a toast to Aedan. Oh, such would be against airline policy, she replied, as she poured herself a small glass. Aedan was bigger than Aer Lingus corporate.

Aoife was waiting for us at the airport. This time, we got a bow and a hug. Sara had agreed to spend a day or two with her on this trip, coaching her on how to open and run a gallery. Mrs. Carty was happy too. Aedan was much more pleasant to deal with since he met us. He might even be taking the yoga now, twisting himself into the downward—facing pretzel to release bad humors. Downward—facing pretzel. That would do it, I told her.

Mrs. Carty told us we should make ourselves at home for the next week and just ask anytime we wanted fresh towels, pastries or tea. Aoife handed her a stuffed envelope and Mrs. Carty didn't even open it. Yes indeed, trust is a wonderful thing. Then Aoife handed me a note from Aedan.

Please get some rest after your long journey. Mrs. Carty and Aoife will see to it that you are well taken care of in the next week. To the victors belong the spoils, and nothing must spoil our next week.

What say you to dinner and drinks at the White Stag this evening at 18:00? Please let Aoife know.

Cheers, Aedan

Sara and I arrived at the White Stag exactly on time. Aedan was sitting at the same table by the fireplace. Maybe this part was just like old times. He gave us a big smile as he stood up. But he was pale and had lost some weight.

"A hearty welcome to my partners in victory. We have much to celebrate this evening, so I instructed Declan to start exercising his skills at the bar as soon as he saw you walk in. I apologize I am not quite as ruddy this evening as your invisible genealogist. The excitement of the last month, and long days and nights in the company of mold and dust, are taking a toll. Some days, I am so deeply immersed in documents I forget to eat.

"But repose is within sight and I am under strict orders from my physician to consume with abandon while you are here. One must follow doctor's orders. Sara, your drinks will be accompanied by as many crubeens as you can put into your petite body, and I hope we shall be contacting the good people at Guinness World Records by closing time."

He slid a bag across the table to me. Declan appeared from nowhere with drinks and a huge platter of what used to be pigs.

"While I still have my faculties this evening, I would like to give you two binders summarizing my

295

recent work and the conclusions I have drawn. I am within a fortnight of completing my document review, and am arranging formal authentication of the portrait. I sent summaries to Lester and have contracted him as a consultant. He knows little of Grace O'Malley, but his academic skills are formidable and transferable.

"I can tell you this much now. Grace O'Malley had several secret meetings with Sir Henry Sidney and Philip Sidney between 1575 and 1578. Many of them related to Grace's offers to provide naval assistance to defend Western Ireland against non–English invaders. I believe she was trying to impress Queen Elizabeth. Most of the discussions were in the presence of James Tiernan. James was indeed a member of Grace's household and a trusted intermediary between her and the Sidneys. Those facts themselves are of considerable historical interest.

"But now Aedan shall drop the proverbial bomb. Grace was attempting to strike a deal with Elizabeth which would have altered the course of European history. Western Ireland would become an autonomous state with Grace as its governor and commander–in–chief. The new state would pledge substantial military and financial support to the Crown and at least nominal fealty to the Church of England. Elizabeth had a rich palette of enemies, and Ireland was strategically situated. Elizabeth needed a ruthless and effective Irish military commander and ally on her western flank. The deal included amnesty for imprisoned Irishmen and substantial reinstatement of the Gaelic clan system. I have contemporaneous notes and documents to support everything I just said. That, my friends, is what historians live for. Grace O'Malley single–handedly tried to prevent the completion of Elizabeth's Irish Conquest by making a deal. Only she could have done it.

"Was this an act of surpassing political courage and pragmatism, or was Grace a traitor to her people? History will have to be the judge of that. There was an agreement in principle, but the deal was never consummated. Why? One suspects political sabotage and treachery in England as Philip's influence waned, followed by his untimely death a few years later. The deal brokers were Philip Sidney for Elizabeth and James Tiernan for Grace. Grace's voyage in 1582 was part of an effort to conclude the deal. And Caitriona was an agent, but for whom? It is tempting to think she had divided loyalties and may have been pushed to the sidelines for that reason. The two Queens could never fully resolve their differences after 1582 and the deal withered away when Philip died. This will send shock waves through the community of European historians.

"So it has been a most productive partnership, well worth a little extra wear and tear on Aedan's body."

I slid a bag across the table to Aedan.

"Thanks, Aedan. It's been a privilege to work with you, but you did the heavy lifting. To be honest, you do look exhausted. You need to get some rest soon.

"These are Leo Norman's original research binders. You should have them. All this sliding of bags across the table is starting to look like a Whitey Bulger business deal."

"Indeed. Perhaps Mr. Bulger would have been able to conclude the deal between Grace and Elizabeth and change the course of history. For a large fee, naturally."

"But before we discuss the Pirate Queen further, I have a dinner suggestion that I hope will not offend you. I have tried to introduce you to the full spectrum of Irish cuisine, from meat and potatoes to potatoes and meat. In fairness to our chefs, every now and then they capture a green vegetable trying to escape to France. And we always offer fish and chips for the benefit of our American and English friends. Why don't I have Declan hand you menus and we'll each order what we wish? Then I must hear about Glenn and Anna's wedding. I hope you brought pictures."

This could be a trap, or another one of Aedan's tests. Sara asked Declan what he would recommend, and Declan told her the lamb was particularly good that day. Sara and Aedan both ordered crubeens and lamb ragout. I scanned the menu quickly and ordered fish and chips. With my luck, I was afraid someone would come out of the kitchen and say they were all out. I guess I now qualified as an American friend. Sara rolled her eyes, but at least I knew that one never mixes pig offal with sheep after Labor Day. That's so Rhode Island.

Aedan was delighted as we told him about the wedding. When he saw pictures of Emma, he went quiet and his voice choked a little.

"My young relative is a beautiful mix of her parents. Michael and Sara are exceedingly well matched. May I have a picture of her to keep? And Sara, what a magnificent portrait of Anna. With all her regal beauty, I am immediately drawn to her eyes. They speak volumes."

"Thanks, Aedan. I can't think of anything I've ever wanted to capture more than Anna's eyes. They've changed so much in the last few months. And I agree that Michael and I are a good match. We bring out the best and the worst in each other. What could be better?

"Aedan, I asked Emma if she would write you a personal letter. She's reaching the age where family starts to mean more and she'll listen to her mother now. I haven't read it, but here's her letter to you. She spent a lot of time on it and said she'd put some pictures in the envelope. You'd like her, Aedan. You and she are very alike."

As dinner progressed, Aedan asked us if we had any special plans for the week. Sara told him she wanted to spend a day or more with Aoife. I told Aedan I'd like to see where he was working at Taylor's Hill, and maybe drive up to the Rosses Point Abbey to pay my final respects to Caitriona. And, of course, visit Howth Castle.

"I was hoping that was part of your agenda. Perhaps I can suggest a plan for the next few days. Aoife is driving me out to Taylor's Hill early tomorrow morning. Will you both join us? Sara, it would give you and Aoife some quiet time together for artistic conversation while I introduce Michael to many strains of our fine Irish dust. I should rest tomorrow evening, but we could drive out to Howth on Friday. There's a woman there I'd like you to meet. It took me a long time to track her down. After you and Sara have made her acquaintance, we can resume our celebrations."

It sounded like a perfect plan to Sara and me.

"Michael, I rather enjoyed our last game of ask–each–other–one–question. Would you like to play another round tonight?"

"I sure would, Aedan. Whose turn is it to go first?"

"Well, in the slow–motion game you call your national pastime, the visitor goes first. I believe it would be you."

"I believe you're right, so here it is. Why were you giving me make–work projects for so long? Didn't you trust me?"

"I trusted you, but I didn't know you well enough. Buying your flash drive was a good investment. I could see no other way to confirm quickly the link between James Tiernan and Philip Sidney in Galway, and on to Grace O'Malley. I was playing the odds. There was no other Tiernan who had spent as much time on family research, and I had hit the brick wall, so to speak. The make–work projects were a bit ridiculous, I grant you, but I reckoned they might give you new information for your own files, and they gave me an opportunity to take the full measure of the man I had already identified as my closest living relative. Your abilities were clear to me. Your passions were not. Yes, Michael, you were being interviewed. My very serendipitous mistake was thinking Brigid was nothing more than another make–work project. In fact, what you and Sara turned up changed everything. Live and learn. And now, my question. I hope it does not strike you as odd, but I have good reason to ask.

"When we first met, you came to Ireland on your Irish passport. Did you use the same passport this time?"

"No, I used my American passport. I'm glad you asked. I am the visiting team, Aedan. I'm American, not Irish. I've spent a great deal of time thinking about it lately. I'm not a Mayo man and I never was. It was a fantasy I turned into reality. My parents and you were right. Don't look back. Respect the past, but don't become it."

"It's not so easy, Michael. We can never discard completely who we are. Perhaps a fair analogy is you must mount and ride your past like those unbroken American ponies, what do you call them, fucking broncos?"

"Bucking broncos, Aedan."

"As you wish. In any event, I respectfully disagree with you as to who you are. So it seems I may never again see Michael Tiernan the Mayo man, and the next few days must be Michael Tiernan's American wake. That is no reason for sorrow. I have been given the rare opportunity of seeing what my own Mayo family became after they left, and I could not have written a more satisfying ending.

"Michael, you wondered what your Irish ancestors would have thought of you if you had met them hundreds of years ago. I wondered the same thing. They would have had little use for us. Their entire universe was yesterday, today and tomorrow. They would have cracked our heads open with spades if they thought it would help them get to the tomorrow.

"Oh, there was the occasional person with a larger universe, the James Tiernan or Grace O'Malley. But most of our people did not sit around sipping port and discussing current events. Their only goal was survival. Through the fog of time, we have endowed them with qualities they did not have. The truth is, most of them were venal rodents. The individuals are not important, and yet the context of their lives is very important. You should know where you are from to appreciate where you are, within limits. Most of us should stop right there. Much darkness and self–deception lies therein. As in Sara's world, perspective is all–important.

"I held out hope for Grace O'Malley as an exception to the depressing rule, but even she may only have been interested in advancing her own agenda. A fascinating woman, to be sure, but as her history is rewritten, historians may judge its face to be covered with warts. I think about her night and day now, trying to reconcile in my own mind the apparent contradictions. And I must reach final conclusions on her before my research is published. I am attempting to bring her back to life. I am not Dracula, Michael, but rather Frankenstein, and Grace has become my monster.

"Enough of such gloom. We are here tonight to celebrate the successful conclusion of our quest and to begin Michael Tiernan's wake. Sara, would you please pass this note to Declan? He'll keep the food and drink coming. We should make it to our beds at a decent hour this evening. A long day awaits us. But the evening is unseasonably warm for Ireland in October. Could it be the fairies' way of suggesting we repair to the outside deck for a cigar after dinner? Dare we risk offending the fairies? I think not."

We talked about everything imaginable at dinner. Aedan was looking forward to immersing himself in Emma's letter before going to bed. We told him she had started graduate school and was thinking she might make a career of research and teaching.

Aedan liked that. He thanked Sara for taking Aoife under her wing. Aoife had been talking about our return since we left in August. Then Aedan turned to me and solemnly stated that a man with my interest in solving puzzles really should give *Finnegans Wake* one more try. I thought Aedan was one or two drinks over the line. I had told him before that I tried to make it through *Finnegans Wake* three times. In the slow–motion game we call our national pastime, three strikes and you're out.

We moved to the outside deck. I thought I could hear singing coming from somewhere, or was it howling? I didn't know and I didn't care if anyone else heard it. I did. This was my wake, and I finally knew what they were saying to me.

CHAPTER THIRTY–TWO

We headed off for Galway right after breakfast the next morning. It should have been just more than an hour's drive, but Aoife did better than that. That's something you can always count on, Aedan told us. We pulled over and parked on a street on Taylor's Hill, which was amazing to me. In Boston, the only available street parking we ever saw was in movies. The building in which Aedan had all but lived for these many weeks was in plain view. Did we see it? It wasn't in plain view to me. Sara was squinting, looking up and down the street. She didn't see it either.

"Sara, does this neighborhood look familiar to you?"

"Not yet, Aedan. Reality is much more disorienting than photographs. The tree is gone and the shadows today are of no help. Let me quickly walk up and down the block."

She did, studying Leo's photographs.

"It's hard. I'm guessing, but I think one of the photos was taken from about where the green truck is parked. Brigid and Leo were standing on the other side of the street, so the building is probably over there too. At least that's how I would have set it up and I don't have enough reference points. I have no idea how anyone could have identified the street from what's shown in the photos. It looks like so many streets we drove down today, and this was happening more than seventy years ago."

"You are correct that the building is on the other side of the street. What enabled my colleague to identify the street is the drab building behind the bus stop. Its style is called Dutch Billy. It's not as common here as in Dublin, and that particular building was later modified in an unusual way. It blends three different architectural styles, not very well according to my colleague. Any of the three styles alone would not have given it away. However, he said the three mashed together make a signature entry in the annals of ghastly architecture. How many of them could there be? This is how urban architects view the world, Sara, with offended hyperbole. They should get out more often. Yet, as you did, he saw something the rest of us did not see, another visual fingerprint. And so the artist's eyes and the architect's eyes joined forces to lead us to the street.

"But there are more than a hundred buildings on this street, and Leo and Brigid worked in only one of them. Which one? I researched Galway property records and discovered one of the buildings was leased to NUIG for three years in the early 1940s. In Galway, all historical research roads run through NUIG. The lessor was a blind trust titled with numbers only, which struck me as an effort to conceal something. Then I realized the numbers were Professor Carroll's birth date listed in his biography. An old tax record listed one 'Carroll Jay' as agent and contact person. I knocked on the door and Professor John Carroll's grandson answered. The rest, as they say, is history.

"Now, Sara, I suggest you and Aoife walk over to that nice little park on the corner and you can share with her your gallery expertise. My plan to show Michael the records I have been bathing in, and give him literally a taste of one dusty day in the life of an archaeologist historian. There is a Portuguese restaurant next to the park. Why don't we meet there at 15:00?"

As Aedan and I walked to the building, I told him I had two more questions, and they couldn't wait.

"How much do you know about John Carroll? You checked him out, because you knew his birth date and much more besides. Nice detective work there, by the way."

"Thanks. One tries. To be honest, I had not given John Carroll much thought until I was able to connect the names Carroll and NUIG on Taylor's Hill. Thank you for your cryptic clue there, Michael. I look forward to learning someday how you discovered that.

"In any event, I did more research, starting with Dominican College. Carroll is quite a common name in Galway, and there were three professors named Carroll at Dominican in the 1940s. Only one was named John. Professor John Carroll taught mathematics both there and at NUIG in the 1930s and 1940s. Fortunately for Ireland, the mild–mannered professor had a secret life.

"The files remain impounded. But, like you, Michael, I have friends in the shadows always up to a paid challenge. John Carroll was in Ireland's G2 intelligence service in the early 1940s. He was a cryptologist, reporting directly to our legendary codebreaker Richard Hayes. Mr. Hayes was Director of the National Library, but his real job during the war was to decode German ciphers. Many in Ireland were sympathetic to the German cause. They harbored Nazi agents who communicated with each other and Berlin using an ever–changing series of numerical ciphers. Professor Carroll's team was put together to decipher coded messages, then send fake messages luring German forces into ambushes. They were quite successful, so much so that the Germans put substantial bounties on their heads and offered rewards for capturing their codebreaking manuals. And the Carroll team did it all without computers, using only caffeine, adrenaline and brainpower.

"This may be a feature of additional interest to you. Professor Carroll's team used old maps of Galway and surrounding waters, dating to the 1500s, as keys to separate codes they created to communicate among themselves. They were using maps which Grace probably used herself. Isn't that a coincidence?"

"No, it's not, Aedan. Nothing is. Leo and Brigid were G–2 also, both of them. The codebreaking operation was being run from Taylor's Hill, from the very rooms where Leo and Brigid were working. They were spies. That's the significance of the pages of numbers in Leo's binders."

"Very good, Michael. I found photocopies of old Galway maps in those rooms, each with a page or more of those numbers attached. As Director of the National Library, Mr. Hayes had access to NUIG records. It may be why so many boxes of historical documents were shipped to Taylor's Hill. There was scholarly research being done in those rooms, to be sure, but it was cover for a cryptology cell operating in the middle of a quiet neighborhood. The academic credentials of Messrs. Carroll and Norman were beyond reproach, so their professorial comings and goings would not have aroused suspicion. And to the untrained eye, the sheets of numbers might be accepted as an eccentric system for cataloging research. It gave the appearance of ivory–tower academics rooting through the dustbin of history. It seems to have fooled the Nazis.

"It is an interesting story, Michael, but one for someone else to write, perhaps you. I only care about Grace O'Malley and her activities."

"Aedan, I have one more question. Had Brigid and Leo discovered what you told me yesterday about Grace, James and Philip?"

"Yes, and they were beginning to realize its significance. They knew about the deal Grace was trying to negotiate with Elizabeth. It was referenced in Leo's notes. Perhaps they knew more than I did. But Leo was working as a literary scholar, and only from Philip's point of view. He may have been ordered to keep his work unpublished for security reasons. And yes, I suspected Brigid was equally involved with the nuts and bolts of the espionage. There is often more to quiet government librarians than first meets the eye, Michael, rather like Sligo farm girls. And now, here we are at Tut's tomb."

Aedan and I walked into the rooms that had gotten him so excited. I tried to picture Harold Carter doing the same. The windows were closed and the shades drawn. It was necessary, Aedan said, for privacy and to help protect the old documents from sunlight and humidity. The rooms smelled like laundry hampers in a college dorm room. Cardboard boxes were neatly stacked along every wall, with numbers and dates taped to them.

"The documents I have been working with fall into two broad categories, Michael. First, there are records of the port of Galway during the mid–to–late

1500s. The port authorities kept unusually good records. Part of the reason for that had to do with taxation, and part with self–preservation.

"Galway was a prime target for every warring faction of western Europe. The city fathers had an enlightened self–interest in knowing who and what was passing through the port. There are detailed manifests, cargo and inspection records, and ships' logs. The authorities also encouraged ship captains to file reports of where they had been and intended to go, a maritime flight plan, if you will. Grace was more than willing to maintain the appearance of running a legitimate shipping business which posed no threat to England, so she kept up with her paperwork. We are taking her word for some things, but she had little reason to mislead the authorities on most matters. I have located documents describing her specific activities. She had regular routes, both as Grace O'Malley and as Lady Bourke.

"The second broad grouping of records is what we might loosely call proceedings of Galway governmental bodies. Much attention was paid to security and defense, especially how to maintain and improve it. Both groupings of records sat buried for centuries, and wound up at the National University. There wasn't much interest in them until people like Leo Norman came along. Perhaps Richard Hayes made the historical connection, but he was busy with his other job. Most of the relevant records are not in English, which was an additional impediment to research. For whatever reason, the records were never organized or codified. They sat neglected in storage rooms, collecting the same dust we breathe today. Think of it, Michael. The dust of our Pirate

Queen is now set free after centuries of solitary confinement.

"But it is time to work. At the risk of sounding rude, your job this morning is to watch and stay out of my way. You may want to use these dust masks."

Aedan's demeanor changed. He was in overdrive now and he wasn't exaggerating about the dust. Two graduate student assistants showed up about ten minutes later. The three of them worked quickly though clouds that got thicker and moved around the room every time someone riffed through a box of records. Each person had a portable voice recorder to make notes. Aedan gave directions and documents were reviewed, scanned and moved from pile to pile. They had an academic assembly line going. I didn't have a clue what they were doing.

I didn't see Aedan take a single break in more than five hours, and he didn't say a word to me. Then the alarm went off on his phone, and the day's digging was done. The work dervish disappeared. We washed up, and fifteen minutes later, Aedan and I were joining Aoife and Sara for a late lunch.

Over a pint, Aedan proclaimed it had been a good day. He found three more documents relating to Grace O'Malley. Two of them were not very important, but the other described a delivery she made in 1581 just outside Galway. The delivery was weapons, and they were loaded onto an English ship. It was additional evidence that Grace was running guns as part of the deal she was trying to make with Elizabeth. Some confirmatory translation was needed. In Aedan's court of history, Grace would be innocent until proven guilty.

It had been a good day for Sara and Aoife too. Aoife was a quick study, and Sara had put together a manual for her on how to open and run an art gallery. Aoife and Sara were starting to really bond now. After spending so much time with Anna, Sara liked having another kindred spirit who was shorter than she was.

While we were having lunch, I got an email with pictures from Anna. She and Glenn were having an amazing time in Hungary, and she wanted to thank me again for the information I had given her. Most of the pictures were taken at locations which were part of Anna's family history. Aedan studied the photos.

"I hope they were not all taken on the same street. We should ask Sara. And a woman with eyes like Anna's should never wear dark glasses."

On the drive back, Aedan said we would have to excuse him for the rest of the evening. He wanted to rest before our trip to Howth tomorrow.

"Are you up for a little challenge, partners? Tomorrow I shall introduce you to a woman I know in my mind to be Grace O'Malley. I concede there must be authentication from the experts, but I consider it a formality. I was able to identify her from something in your files, Michael, and the Sherlock Holmes tales suggested another bit of verification. Please give it some thought and tell me on the way there what you think might have given it away."

Aedan was enjoying this. I guess he had earned a little fun.

We asked Aoife if she would like to join us for dinner at the pub down the street from Mrs. Carty's.

311

She thought it would be a wonderful way to end the day.

As Sara and I were walking to the pub, she asked the question I thought might be coming.

"Okay, I could hear the wheels turning in your head while we were in the restaurant, and you had your thousand–mile look. What were you thinking?"

"You read my mind. Leo gave Lester photographs he knew contained three separate clues: the tree, the ring binders and the name Carroll. Leo and Brigid were supposed to keep the location a secret, but needed to make sure someone could find it if things went wrong. They buried an insurance policy, like Grace O'Malley did, and they buried it in Lester's office."

"Michael, you knew those things before today, didn't you?"

"Yes, with your help. But there's something I didn't know. There was a codebreaking operation running out of those rooms. Leo and Brigid were spies, Sara, real–life, asses–in–the–sling spies. And they were defending Ireland against foreign invaders, like Grace offered to do when she tried to make a deal with Queen Elizabeth. Leo and Brigid used logic and math instead of cannons. My family history repeated itself hundreds of years later. I may need to consult with the Jackal when we get back."

"I can arrange a secret meeting. Wow, I have to hand it to you. Two months ago, I thought I was the one who had more interesting ancestors. It turns out you do."

"We don't know for sure yet. All I know is this don't look back stuff gets complicated."

CHAPTER THIRTY–THREE

On Friday morning, Aedan and Aoife stopped at the B&B to pick us up. Mrs. Carty was kind enough to make us all an early breakfast, and Aedan had a special gift for her. He had sent away for a framed Apostolic Blessing from the Vatican. With a picture of Pope Francis himself, Mrs. Carty, just for you. It would look grand hanging over your dining room table, don't you think? Mrs. Carty's eyes got misty and she moved seamlessly into prayer. Aedan told her we wouldn't be able to pray with her today. We had a three–hour drive ahead of us and it wasn't polite to keep a queen waiting. He laughed as we pulled out of the driveway.

"She's a good woman, isn't she? It was easier to get than I thought, and they take American Express. I'll not be disparaging Francis, though. I reckon Jesus approves of him. Now show us your best Grand Prix moves, Aoife. I'll wager there's a two hours thirty in you pushing to come out."

And there was a question inside Michael pushing to come out.

"Aedan, I don't want to be the one always asking the questions, but there's something I'd really like to know."

"Please proceed, Michael. I enjoy your incisive direct examination."

"It's a simple one. How did you locate the portrait?"

"I tried to approach it logically, as you would. I presumed that the portrait, if it existed, was intended for Philip Sidney and then for Queen Elizabeth. If it made its way to either of them, there should have

313

been some record. The English document everything, down to bowel movements. The fact that there was no record suggested three possibilities. First, the portrait never existed or does not exist today. Second, it exists secretly in a private collection in England, and we shall never find it. Third, it exists but never made it from Ireland to England. If we were to locate the portrait now, only the third possibility was worth considering.

"My first thought, which occurred to you as well, was that the portrait went with Caitriona to Saint Elizabeth Abbey in Dublin. But there were no records in the Abbey of any such portrait. I spent a considerable amount of time looking into everything known about the history and contents of that Abbey, and hired skilled investigators. We found nothing. Another brick wall.

"But then persistence paid off. Your theory that the portrait was delivered to Howth Castle made more and more sense, and as you say, we had nothing better. Several years ago, I spent time researching the legend about Grace being refused hospitality by Lord Howth at his castle in 1576. Was it another fairy tale?

"I was able to locate and study archival records of the St. Lawrence family, the descendants of Lord Howth. They were pleased I was working on the definitive story of Grace and Lord Howth. The family's record–keeping was exemplary back to the time of Grace, and we hit it off quite well. Then I discovered relevant documents at Taylor's Hill, including a log entry that Grace did in fact stop at Howth Castle in 1576 and was denied hospitality. The legend was at least partly true. I could not verify

314

the rest of the tale. I informed the St. Lawrence family accordingly, and walked away to pursue other avenues of research.

"I should have continued reading the family's records past 1576. It was a shipping document I subsequently unearthed at Taylor's Hill which told me Grace sailed from Galway to Dublin in the summer of 1582. I immediately examined more records in the St. Lawrence family archives, and learned Grace requested and received hospitality at Howth Castle in August 1582. There was an entry in the Taylor's Hill files that Grace's three vessels engaged two English ships near Howth in August 1582. It seemed unlikely Grace would have continued from Howth into Dublin, where she would have been quickly trapped. So I believe she offloaded her cargo, re–supplied at Howth Castle, and returned to Western Ireland immediately, before the English could chase her down.

"I have now researched all relevant historical records from Howth Castle. As I said, the operations of the castle were superbly organized and documented by time period, including castle furnishings. Only four portraits were added to the castle collection between 1575 and 1600. Two of them are unidentified males, and they remain there today. I could safely disregard them. The third portrait has been conclusively identified as Lady Howth, our Lord Howth's wife, and it also remains in Howth Castle. Only one possibility remained. The fourth portrait is an unidentified woman, and it was moved from Howth Castle to the private residence of a relative in 1925. I daresay she is no longer unidentified. There are compelling clues in the portrait that she is Grace O'Malley, and all other possibilities have been eliminated. QED. Now, my friends, it is your turn to answer some questions."

As Aoife screeched through roundabouts, Aedan asked Sara and me if we had any thoughts on how he had been able to identify Grace O'Malley in the portrait he found.

"Sara and I talked it over, Aedan. We both think that because of where it was going, the portrait won't show Grace as a pirate. She'll have the who–cut–the–cheese sneer of a noblewoman, a person Elizabeth could respect as a peer and military ally. There has to be something in the portrait that would connect it only to Grace. Sara wonders if her initials might be hidden somewhere in the portrait. I'm inclined to think there's a hidden symbol which could be associated with Grace, maybe a sailing ship, but at least something that wouldn't be obvious to the English while the deal was pending."

"Well, the English knew a thing or two about sailing ships. So Sara chooses letters and Michael chooses something more graphic. That's the opposite of what I would have expected. You are both on the right track. The portrait does contain a clue which points directly to Grace, and I look forward to watching my partners try to locate it. It took me twenty–six minutes, if one excludes twenty years of research and preparation. So twenty–six minutes is the time you must try to beat today. Before you do that, we shall take a guided tour of Howth Castle, where Grace lived in peace and obscurity for more than three centuries.

"Howth Castle is hallowed ground, my friends, an historical treasure. Drink it all in and let your

316

imaginations drift back in time. Try to visualize where Grace's portrait was hung. The English tried to hang her for years, but only our Lord Howth succeeded."

A leopard can't change its spots. Aedan's self–congratulatory musings gave us a hint what to look for in the portrait. Did Sara catch that too? She was gazing out at the blur of scenery as we rocketed along, but I knew she was thinking over what Aedan said.

My guess was Aedan's hint was buried in his casual reference to the twenty years of preparation. He was telling us it took years of preparation to identify the clue. He told us earlier he needed some information he got from my files. Put it together, Michael. Grind those peppercorns.

The light bulb went on. Not a hundred watts, maybe sixty. I had an idea what to look for. It's what I would have done, and I'll bet Grace thought the same way.

I had to be sure I'd know it if I saw it. I excused myself, went online for a minute, and memorized a few things. Aedan was right. After a certain age you can't trust the cranial hard drive. I'd be okay for a few hours if I didn't drink at lunch and saved a crib sheet on my phone.

We two–wheeled into the Howth Castle parking area two hours and twenty–five minutes after leaving Mrs. Carty's driveway, another PR for Aoife. Aedan had called ahead from the road, and a guide was waiting for us as we got out of the car. A two–hour private tour commenced.

The castle was magnificent, but I wanted the damn tour to end. We could come back on our own time.

Grace didn't live here anymore. Sara wasn't as twitchy as I was, or maybe she hid it better. There were centuries–old portraits for her to study, and study them she did. She kept returning to the portraits of Lady Howth and the two unidentified males, lined up next to each other on the same wall. She started taking pictures with her phone. Then she spent five minutes staring at each of the three portraits, but kept coming back to Lady Howth. Was she seeing something? I couldn't interpret this at all. She wasn't scratching the back of her neck, so probably not. This was Sara's warm–up stretching. She wanted to impress Aedan and slam–dunk over me when we finally saw Grace's portrait. She was on her turf, and the competitive juices were flowing. Aedan slipped into a quiet area to make a phone call and was all smiles when he returned.

"Our audience with the Queen is confirmed for 15:00. She resides only five minutes away, so we have time for a bite of lunch. I know a good place nearby."

He always did.

I couldn't eat much. This wasn't just a portrait. It was a portrait that had changed our lives. Even Sara was finally starting to show an edge. Can we skip lunch and go into Tutankhamun's tomb, Mr. Carter? I forced myself to make inane small talk over some rubbery greens. Earth to Irish chefs. Let them escape to France, where they'll be treated better. But Aedan's game had to be played Aedan's way. He always had to be in control. I wasn't going to give him the satisfaction of watching me sweat this late in the game. I'll get you back, cousin.

318

"A most enjoyable lunch. Now please allow me to take you to the Pirate Queen. Sara, there will be no need to curtsy. Michael, please do not kiss her hand or anything else, lest alarms go off and you are hauled away. Royalty must never be touched."

He stood and gave us an exaggerated bow, much like Lester Sackett had done.

It was showtime.

CHAPTER THIRTY–FOUR

We pulled into the driveway of a country estate about two miles from Howth Castle. Aedan told us the portrait was inside, hanging in the library.

A friendly older woman answered the door and identified herself as Mrs. McGill. The owners were on holiday, but left instructions that Aedan Burns and his guests were welcome anytime. Mrs. McGill would show us into the library and bring tea.

Aedan said he would enjoy his refreshments while Sara and I examined the portrait. We should take as long as necessary. I handed him a stopwatch. He smiled and wished me luck.

The portrait was covered with a purple drape. Mrs. McGill called for a tall young man to join us. He set up a portable staircase, took the portrait down and carefully laid it on a velvet cloth on a long desk. If Aedan was right, the Pirate Queen had finally revealed herself. The portrait was about five feet long and ornately framed. There was no identifying label and no artist signature.

Sara looked at it and inhaled sharply. She inspected it more closely. This was not what she had expected.

Aedan saw it, and his eyes flashed concern.

"Is there a problem, Sara?"

"Possibly, I'm not sure. Aedan, may I take a phone picture of this portrait and check out something online? This is so important to you and I have to be absolutely certain. I'm willing to give Michael a five–minute head start. He'll need it."

320

She gave me a little smile. Well, okay, then. Let's wheel those cannons to the front lines and have ourselves a battle.

"Certainly, Sara. Take as much time as you wish."

She took her photo and moved to the corner of the room where the internet reception was better. She returned in less than a minute.

If this was the Pirate Queen, she wasn't much to look at. The woman in the portrait was a fiftyish aristocrat, pinched and waspish, a little bony and pale to the point of ghostly translucence. Her expression reminded me of the grammar school librarian who would shoosh me if I started making too much noise, like breathing. I thought portrait artists were supposed to accentuate the positive. If this Grace killed men with her looks, it wasn't good looks.

She was leaning over a table, looking at a crude sketch of some kind. The sketch had a bunch of small, lopsided circles inside a half–oval, but no words. It reminded me of a cross–section of an amoeba I once had to draw for high school biology. I remembered that because I got an 'F' on the assignment and was grounded for a week, another painful memory of my adolescence. Who gives a shit what amoebas look like?

I started with the sketch and let my eyes move slowly down and around in concentric circles, like my father and Brigid taught me to do. Nothing. There was no detail in this damn portrait, just a woman with dead eyes, a bad attitude, and ugly clothes. I ran through my mental checklist what I should be searching for. Still nothing. I was whiffing on the final exam. You've got to be missing something here, Michael. Aedan is so confident of this.

Sara spent ten minutes slowly moving a magnifying glass over the portrait, then nodded her head at Aedan. I did the same. It was time for final grades.

"Michael, you had the benefit of a little extra time. Would you care to go first, while Sara collects her thoughts?"

I had a feeling Sara's thoughts were plenty collected.

"Okay, Aedan, I'll get right to the bottom line. I didn't see a single thing connecting this portrait to Grace O'Malley. I had certain things I was looking for. They're not there.

"But I'm not convinced. Elizabeth was looking for a tough military ally, someone she could think of as almost being in her league. She didn't make deals with ordinary people, and Grace knew that. Elizabeth had never met Grace. Any portrait of Grace intended for Elizabeth was a business card, to impress Elizabeth and move the deal to the next step. This portrait wouldn't do it. Look at the delicate hands. Those hands never hoisted sail, weighed anchor or slit a throat. Look at the pasty face. That face never spent a minute on the open sea. Would Elizabeth have been impressed by this? Absolutely not. This woman was merely a court climber, the sort of person Elizabeth probably detested."

"A lovely speech, Michael, but pure speculation. Give me empirical evidence. Give me facts. Give me some red meat. Sara, will you please put Michael's imagination at ease?"

322

"Actually, Aedan, I like what he said, but it's much worse. She does get points for the authoritative pose, unusual in a portrait of a woman back then unless she was near the top of the food chain.

"But the most reliable way to date an Elizabethan portrait is the clothing. The dress code was rigid, strictly enforced, and changed almost yearly. Fashion directives came down from Elizabeth herself, called Sumptuary Laws. Style defined status. It's possible to date a portrait within five years with a pretty high degree of confidence, if there are enough garments to look at.

"Here, I'm looking first at the rounded, wired collar and the kerchief with matching lace. The collar is called a rebato. You saw it between 1620 and 1640, maybe back to 1615, but that's about it. Before that, it was the Elizabethan ruff. The kerchief with lace started showing up in the late 1620s. Grace died in 1603.

"Then there are those puffy sleeves, called virago sleeves, also typical of 1620 to 1630. And there's that piece filling the gaps in the front of the woman's bodice. It's called a stomacher, and it's something else which appeared between 1620 and 1630.

"These things together are telling me that, whatever the records say at Howth Castle, this portrait was done between 1620 and 1630."

"It defies logic and procedure, Sara. An historian must rely on credible primary source records. With due respect, how can you conclude this with confidence from such a brief inspection?"

"An artist has to rely on her eyes. I'm not trying to be snippy, Aedan, but I have some historian credentials too, art history. And I've got colleagues at universities myself. One of them is the go–to expert on Elizabethan portraits. I took a seminar from him several years back. I emailed him the photo I took a half hour ago, and asked if he could help an old student of his by ballparking a date. He got right on it. Here's what just came back."

Sara held up her cell phone. It said, '1618 to 1628'.

"Aedan, by all means get a second opinion from your authenticators. I think they're going to tell you this isn't Grace O'Malley."

Aedan looked like he was about to bust a vessel, as Emma put it.

"Then we have nothing, nothing at all. Grace is lost to us forever."

It was my turn. Sara shouldn't be taking the brunt of this.

"Aedan, let's get back to eliminating those impossibles. Why did you think this was Grace?"

"There were only two relevant female portraits, and we know one of them to be Lady Howth. The clue I saw in this portrait was the map on the table. Some of its admittedly rough features could be identified by an old man who has spent his entire life in Western Ireland. It shows a portion of Clare Island at the mouth of Clew Bay, Grace's maritime headquarters. The clincher was that small cluster of splotches inside the bay, not far from what is now Rosduane and Newport. There were enough distinguishing features that I could recognize the small islands around which I used to sail as a boy.

How clever of Grace. In order to recognize the clue, one had to be a sailor as familiar with the waters of Clew Bay as she was.

"And then I engaged the services of a facial recognition expert to compare this portrait to the only known portrait of a descendant of Grace's, Maud Burke. My expert concluded there was a definite family resemblance. You may recall Sherlock Holmes employing a similar process in the *Hound of the Baskervilles*. One learns from the masters.

"I knew this portrait remained in Howth Castle until the 1900s. So I had the process of elimination, plus the opinion of a facial recognition expert, plus a sketch of Grace's base of operations in the portrait. It makes a persuasive case."

"No, it doesn't, Aedan. You and I spent a lot of years wrestling with how to meet a burden of proof. I can tell you this right out of the gate. Forget the facial recognition experts. I've used them as witnesses, and I've seen them used as witnesses against my clients. I know how it works. The computer imaging stuff they use is interesting, but when you're moving down four or five generations, you have to begin with reality and end with reality. It could be photograph–to–photograph, but it can't be portrait–to–portrait. A portrait might not be completely representational, and you couldn't tell if one this old was. Have you ever once seen a high school yearbook photo with any zits? The opinion you got is voodoo stuff, no probative value at all. There isn't a jury in the world which would buy it.

"As far as Clew Bay, same thing. Who knows for sure if it's Clew Bay? It's like abstract art or a

Rorschach test. You can read into it whatever you want. I saw an amoeba and a bad high school experience. You saw Clew Bay. You believe it, but you can't meet the burden of proof with it."

"What do you think, Sara? Is Michael correct?"

"Well, his instincts are good and he knows how to prove a case in court. I have no idea what Clew Bay looks like, but I'm going with my colleague at Yale on this one. This isn't Grace. But the battle may not be over yet. I want to go back to Howth Castle and study those three other portraits one more time. Can you arrange for that to happen this afternoon?"

"Yes, Sara, but I fear you are spinning your wheels. The portrait of Lady Howth has been authenticated beyond any doubt."

"It has been, twice. Thirty years apart, by two respected firms, once for possible auction and once for insurance valuation. The people who do that usually know what they're doing. There are big bucks, big egos and big reputations on the line. I want to look at them anyway. There's one thing now I'm looking for. Maybe it's not there, but it's definitely not here."

CHAPTER THIRTY–FIVE

A half hour later, we were standing again in front of the three portraits. Sara spent more than ten minutes studying Lady Howth, making shapes with her hands. Then she walked over to one of the two male portraits, labeled 'Courtier, circa 1578, artist unknown'. She asked that the painting be taken down and displayed on an easel in a private library room.

For the next fifteen minutes, Sara paced back and forth, looking at the portrait from every possible angle. She was in a zone, like I had seen Aedan at Taylor's Hill. Nobody was speaking.

"It is what it says it is, a male courtier from the late 1570s or thereabouts. Everything checks out. We're down to the last strike, I guess. Aedan, could we have this one put back, and the other one put on the easel?"

The second painting was titled 'Royal Guard, circa 1580, artist unknown'. Sara stared at it for fifteen minutes, nothing moving but her eyes. Then she started scratching the back of her head. She took out her magnifying glass and examined the subject's face and hands, back and forth, over and over. She was pure intensity now. Good thing it wasn't *Game of Thrones* night.

Sara looked up at the ceiling, rubbed her eyes, and zoomed in on the face and hands again. Then she smiled.

"There might still be hope. These three portraits were done by the same artist within ten years. He used different styles and colors, but the similarities in composition are unmistakable. I know this artist.

327

When I was a lowly grad school intern, I was part of a team which did some restoration work on one of his later portraits. He's English, one of the best. Now why would he identify himself on one portrait but not the other two? What didn't he want people to know?

"Here's what I think. This one isn't a man. It's a woman dressed as a man. That's what I was looking for."

Aedan was stunned.

"How can you possibly conclude this, Sara?"

"Anatomy, Aedan. Good portrait artists have to learn it, and this guy was better than good. Short hair means nothing, and you can't see this subject's hair anyway. Most men of the period were showing facial hair, but there were enough exceptions that you can't read too much into not seeing it. There are other things, though. Men usually have bony ridges above their eyes and a sloping forehead. This person has a flat, smooth and vertical forehead, no ridges. The eyebrows are high, the eyes aren't deeply set, and the nose is narrow. Those are all female traits.

"Look at the whole face. It's a weathered face, but not a square male face. And the hands – big and powerful. Male hands, right? No. The ring fingers are shorter than the index fingers. Another female trait.

"If you look just at the label, your brain tells you it's a male. You accept it. Then your eyes get drawn to the face and hands. You focus on the menacing scowl and rough hands and overlook the other features. That's exactly what the artist wanted you to do. He left enough clues that this he was a she. Now comes the hard part. We have to figure out if it's the

328

right she. Philip Sidney would have to know he was picking up the correct package."

I recalled something from my Grace O'Malley research.

"Grace did this before, Aedan. When she was a young girl and wanted to join her father's crew, she was told girls didn't have the right stuff for that. So she cut off her long hair, dressed like a male, and joined the crew. One of her nicknames was Grace the Bald."

"You are correct, Michael, I had forgotten. So let us try to discover if this picture tells even more stories. Please, Michael and Sara, give our patient a good physical examination."

The woman in the portrait was a force of nature, cold sneer on her face and a chip on her shoulder. Elizabeth would respect that. It seemed as if she could step off the canvas and break me in half without batting an eyelash, if she had one. She was standing behind a table, monster hands resting on a small globe. The background was richly detailed, full of leather–bound books and the trappings of wealth and power, but not a pirate ship, Irish sweater or leprechaun in sight.

Wake up, Michael. Sara was already prowling from side to side, examining the portrait from different angles. Where are they? Okay, there's one, but I didn't think it would be so obvious. Aedan will see that one right away, and it's not enough by itself. The payoff will be finding the other one and I don't see it anywhere. Come on, Michael, your father and Brigid showed you how to do this. The more space it takes up, the better it's hidden. Rookies think small. The pros think big.

Take a deep breath, close your eyes, count to five. Start in the middle and move around in concentric circles, first clockwise, then counterclockwise. Nothing yet. My eyes kept being pulled to that intimidating face and those massive hands. She was deciding whether to kill me. Don't forget the Sara Principle. Look where your eyes don't want to go. Still nothing. I was getting worried.

And then it jumped out. It wasn't the way I would have done it, but it was pretty damn clever. I closed my eyes for ten seconds, and looked at it again. I made a shape with my fingers and checked it three times. I was better at high school geometry than biology. Bingo. Twenty minutes on the nose. Then I wrote the answer on a piece of paper, folded it, and handed it to Aedan. As I walked past Sara, I gave her a wink and a pat on the rear end. She gave me a withering glare. Yes, indeed, just like old times.

"Here's the answer, Aedan. You shouldn't open it until we've given Sara the courtesy of trying to find it too. It may take her a while, so I'll join you in some tea if you don't mind. But please note my elapsed time. I must say, it's a fine portrait. The artist's attention to finish detail is amazing."

Another withering glare from Sara. The gauntlet was thrown. I had taunted the Lioness. She studied the portrait for another fifteen minutes, and I mean studied it. She pulled out a magnifying glass and a ruler. She stared over the edge of the ruler and moved in and out, side to side. She crouched. She started muttering to herself. Uh–oh, she's getting warm. She was scratching the back of her head. She spent another five minutes examining the middle of the portrait with her magnifying glass. I couldn't tell what she was doing. Then she told Aedan she was finished. May she summarize what she had seen? Aedan said he would like nothing better. Neither would I.

"It's definitely 1580s. The woman's features are harsh for a formal portrait. The artist could have made her look better, but he didn't, and she didn't want him to. The artist might have even made her more intimidating than she was. Michael is right. This portrait was making a statement, sending a message. The pose with those huge hands framing a little globe was meant to show power. Everything else in the portrait screams money and status.

"This artist really understood how to force the eye to go only where he wanted it to go. And he wanted it to go to her face and her hands. He put more detail into them than almost anything else in portrait. The rest of it is almost too cluttered and loose, which was also intentional. It wasn't his usual style. But there are two small areas with great detail, and I'm guessing those would be the important areas.

"One of them is around the books behind the woman. Do you see the almost photographic lettering and binding detail? The other is in certain areas of the woman's clothing. I doubt the clue would be in the books. People eventually notice and study books in a painting. So I spent more time on the details in the clothing. Every woman knows it's always about the clothes, even when you're cross–dressing.

"The most interesting feature to me is the clasp fastening the woman's cape. The cape itself is fur–trimmed silk or satin, with finely–etched big ornamental gold buttons. She's flaunting it. I would have expected the clasp to be a gold filigree chain, or maybe something with jewels. But it's not, or I guess I should say it's a knot. If you examine the clasp closely, you see it's a light twine or rope knot, made to resemble an etched clasp. I couldn't get so much fine detail into something that tiny if I tried for the rest of my life. Why would a wealthy woman making a statement be fastening her cape with a twine knot instead of a gold or silver clasp? And it's so small it's hard to believe a woman with hands so big could even keep tying and untying it. She'd have to put the cape on over her head. It just doesn't make sense. It's the only feature of the portrait inconsistent with everything else, the one detail not pulsating wealth and power. And that's why I think it's important.

"It's such an intricate knot. When Emma was studying knots at summer camp and I was trying to help her tie them, I recall the ones with all those elaborate curlicues were called sailor knots. I never sailed much, but Grace did. Could that sailor knot be the clue, Aedan?"

Aedan sat bolt upright. He asked Sara if he could borrow her magnifying glass, and studied the middle of the painting for a long time. Then he took pictures of the magnified knot with his phone and sat down, shaking his head.

"Extraordinary, Sara. Upon first glance, it does appear to be a sixteenth century Celtic Tuim knot. I shall have one of my colleagues at university who studies such things examine my photographs. If he confirms it, we may have another cornerstone brick. Now let us see what Michael saw."

Nicely done, Sara. I completely missed the knot. You asked me a while back if I was good enough to keep up with Aedan. Maybe the real question is whether I'm good enough to keep up with you. Let's find out. I think you also missed a thing or two there.

Aedan opened my note, put his hands behind his head, and stared at me for a few seconds.

"Equally extraordinary. Would you care to explain?"

"Sure. First of all, the cape itself is a clue. The fur trim is ermine. Under the Sumptuary Laws Sara talked about, only royals were allowed to wear ermine. You probably remember the famous Ermine Portrait of Queen Elizabeth in the 1580s, the one with the little ermine wearing a gold crown. Grace considered herself the Queen of Western Ireland. It would be a powerful statement to make to Elizabeth."

Like that dunk, Sara? I call it my in–your–face disgrace.

"But I was trying to find the coats of arms or crests of the Sidneys and the Tiernans or MacTiernans. I could see there was no coat of arms for Grace herself. It would have been much too obvious. The central element of the O'Malley coat of arms is a red boar. A pissed–off red pig in this portrait would stick out like a sore thumb.

"The Sidney coat of arms was easy to find. It's stamped on the spine of a book behind Grace. It's small, but you can identify it. It resembles one of those railroad spikes Daniel Tiernan might have hammered in for years. Finding it wasn't enough, but it told me I should be searching for another one not so obvious. One lock, two keys.

"Putting the Sidney coat of arms into the painting might help conceal Grace's identity by giving the impression the subject was a Sidney. Or maybe it was intended to protect the portrait and the person carrying it. Mess with us and you're messing with the Sidneys. I don't know.

"I do know you needed one more thing, and a good thing would have been a link to the Tiernans or MacTiernans in the same portrait. It's like the Dutch Billy house and the other clues pointing to Taylor's Hill. A link to Grace alone or Philip alone or James alone wouldn't be enough to identify the woman. Mix in all three, and who else could it be? Nobody would be looking for a reference to the Tiernans as a clue, except the Sidneys and the high mucky–mucks they reported to.

"So I tried to find the MacTiernan family coat of arms and crest. It wasn't immediately apparent, because the artist split up the elements to hide them. The MacTiernan coat of arms is two lions on an ermine shield, and the crest is a griffin. The woman is wearing an ermine–trimmed cape. It has a gold lion button on each side halfway down, one of those ornamental buttons Sara talked about. Only two gold buttons have lions. The griffin is a small statue over the woman's head. I think it's a bookend. Every element of the MacTiernan coat of arms and crest is in this portrait. And get this, they are each at different points of an imaginary triangle you can draw connecting them, with Sara's knot in the middle. You'd have to measure it to be sure, but it looks like a perfect triangle to me. It's the Golden

334

Ratio thingy, and there are no other lions or griffins anywhere. The entire middle of this portrait is an expanded MacTiernan coat of arms and crest. It's not likely to have happened by accident or coincidence. I think that's the clue."

Aedan got up and studied the portrait again, with both the magnifying glass and a ruler. He did some measuring. Then he leaned back and closed his eyes.

After about a minute, Sara asked.

"Aedan, are you okay?"

"Better than okay, thank you. Sara, nobody else observed the knot. You would not have known this, but one version of the O'Malley coat of arms features a Celtic knot. It is our family symbol of eternal connectedness, the knot too strong to be broken.

"And Michael, neither I nor anyone else I know saw your Golden Ratio thingy. I believe I see a perfect triangle exactly as you described it. I have seen the triangle used as a Christian symbol in Irish art, but also as a symbol of nobility. We may have the marks of Grace and her deal brokers in the same portrait and in a perfect geometric pattern. Who else indeed could this be? The cumulative weight of the evidence appears to satisfy the requisite burden of proof, wouldn't you agree?"

"Right, Aedan, but none of it can be authenticated until after you publish your research."

"Correct again. I now have much additional incentive to complete my work."

"Aedan, why did you rush off to Dublin right after reviewing my files?"

"To pick up a full–size copy of a map of Clew Bay in the 1500s. There is a shop that specializes in old

Irish maps. Your files contained such lyrical descriptions of Clew Bay, where I spent some of the happiest times of my life. Then I thought inspiration struck. The clue was Clew. I took the map I purchased in Dublin to the first portrait we examined today, tried to match up squiggles, and proceeded to draw my erroneous conclusions."

"It was a pretty easy mistake to make. I'm thinking it really was an amoeba and she was a high school biology teacher. My high school assignment will haunt me the rest of my life."

Aedan went off to make some phone calls, and Sara and I walked back to the car. I complimented her on a fine day's work. Seeing the knot was a nice dunk of her own. Aedan's head was probably still spinning.

"Thanks, and back at you. I'm a little upset I didn't recognize the fur trim as ermine. I didn't see black tail–tips, so I thought it was probably white fox. I guess we both saw things the other missed. We make a pretty good team, Michael. Like they say, it takes a village to find a pirate."

"Who says it?"

"I didn't catch their names. I have to tell you, though, that's one tough mother there. Jeanne de Clisson would have her hands full."

As we kept walking, Sara gave me a pat on the butt.

"The Ermine Portrait. The Golden Ratio thingy. Impressive, Michael. You've been studying."

"I told you, I appreciate fine art in all its forms, maybe some forms more than others. I give the credit to my mechanic. He's the Michelangelo of mufflers. And you seem to know quite a bit about cross–dressing."

"I watch a lot of television, Michael. Any self–respecting cross–dresser would be embarrassed buying her clothes in the boys' department. Maybe I'll see if I can dig out those old jeans."

"That would be nice. Sara, this has been special. We've both changed so much in two months."

"I know. I like it."

"So who do you think was in the other portrait, the courtier?"

"It's impossible to know for sure, but we're thinking the same thing, aren't we? I'll bet you just met James Tiernan."

Tomorrow, we'd drive out to Blacksod Bay and the Belmullet Peninsula. I'd stand again on the beach from which the Tiernans sailed for America. This time, I'd bury a little box I had brought. It contained some of my parents' ashes, one of my mother's Celtic crosses, a photo of the Connecticut mill, and pictures of me, Sara and Emma. I'd ask the crashing waves and howling fairies to guard my past forever, and they would.

Then I'd walk away without looking back, and we'd head over to the White Stag to resume Michael Tiernan's American wake.

CHAPTER THIRTY–SIX

By Saturday night, Aedan felt better. He asked Aoife to join us at the White Stag and told her it might be her last chance ever to attend an American wake. Aoife got us off to a good start by proposing an ancient Japanese funeral toast. The only people allowed to drink were the dead who had crossed back over for the party. She may have been making that part up, but we all looked at each other and drained our glasses.

Aedan said he would like to continue the wake with a victory toast to Sara and me. His knot expert had confirmed that what Sara saw in the portrait was a 1500s Celtic Tuim knot. Now, there's an academic specialty. And the MacTiernan coat of arms and crest were the icing on the cake. The triangle was perfect. There could be no reasonable doubt now. Aedan had purchased a two–year option to buy the portrait from the owners of Howth Castle. His university could acquire the portrait at appraised value any time during the option period, after satisfactory authentication. It would be publicly displayed as the only known portrait of Grace O'Malley.

As we sipped our drinks, Aedan suggested another round of ask–each–other–one–question. Sure, Aedan. This time, you go first.

"Michael, in August, I told you I expected you to ask me two questions. You did guess the first question. It was whether you and I are related, and we know now that you are my closest living relative. You said the second question was a larger one and you had to give it some thought. Are you ready to ask it tonight?"

"I am, although it's a two–part question, I'm afraid. The two questions do go together."

"Ever the lawyer. I see no reason why not."

"Are you real or are you a spirit?"

"Is that a serious question?"

"Yes, and you just used up your question."

"Then I assure you I am real. If there is any doubt, please feel free to pinch my arm. It's an interesting question, one I might have asked myself if I were you."

"There's no need to pinch your arm. I still trust you. So I guess here's the real question. If you're not a spirit, are you me? Are you what I would be today if my family had stayed in Ireland? And am I who you would be if your family had gone to America? Are we each seeing tonight what would have been?"

"Splendid, Michael. You have almost figured things out. As to your question, I believe the answer is yes. That is why I wanted to meet both you and Sara. I wanted to see what my life might have been had my own wife and daughter lived. You remind me of myself. You and I are very alike. Sara reminds me so much of my wife Fiona. And Emma is the young woman I hoped Maeve would become. Yes, I believe we are looking across the table at what each of us would have become, and I hope you are as pleased as I am."

Almost figured things out?

"I am, Aedan, and I hope our lives continue to run in parallel."

"Well, be careful what you wish for, cousin. It is easier to tame the past than the future. But I hope that in the very near future, Declan will appear to go over our range of dinner options. Sara, what would you think of letting Aoife choose our meals tonight? Technically, Michael cannot order dinner at his own wake."

"What a fine idea. Aedan, I wish I could have met your wife and daughter."

"Thank you, Sara. You may someday. You'll all get along famously."

While they were in the ladies' room, Sara asked Aoife what was going on with Aedan's health. Aedan was exhausted every day now, but he was not a young man and he had been working hellish hours for two months. He was obsessed with getting his Grace O'Malley research accepted for publication. Then, he promised Aoife, he would take a long vacation. He expected to have everything wrapped up in less than a month.

My wake resumed with dinner and drinks all around. Aoefe ordered five different entrées and suggested we eat Chinese–style. It sounded strange coming from a Japanese woman in an Irish pub, but a good time was had by everyone. Our only regret was the Irish fall weather had turned from warm rain to cold rain, and there would be no cigar ceremony on the deck.

I told Aedan Sara and I were going to drive up to Sligo the next morning to visit the Abbey and Caitriona. Would he care to join us? Aedan begged off. He was meeting with two historians from Dublin to go over the O'Malley documents. It would be a long day and night for him, followed by another long day at Taylor's Hill. We'd finish my wake on Tuesday. Aedan asked me to extend his best wishes

340

to Mother Abbess. I thought I didn't want to meet her quite yet. She'd be reading about Caitriona soon enough.

Sara and I left for Rosses Point before breakfast on Sunday, with apologies to Mrs. Carty. We were hoping to be at the Abbey in about three hours, and I wanted to be back before dark. Sara had called Aoife and arranged for us to meet her at the pub in Castlebar early that night, so she and Sara could continue their gallery brainstorming.

We arrived at Rosses Point on schedule. I emailed Patrick Ruddy to see if he was around. He was on holiday in Scotland, so I'd never actually meet him. Patrick told me he had thought about it, and Daniel Craig should play him in the film. That was a good choice. Claude Rains would have been better, but he was dead.

The Rosses Point Abbey cemetery wasn't very big. Sara and I wandered through it until it started to rain. We didn't ask for permission. The old gravestones were mostly broken or worn smooth, and I'd never be sure if I was looking at the right one. I left my basket of forget–me–nots in the middle of the cemetery. The card said they were for Fidelma from Philip, James and Michael.

I thought I would feel a little melancholy about my trips to Blacksod Bay and Rosses Point, but it was almost a relief. Some restless spirits might finally get some sleep now. I was glad Sara was here to be part of this.

At the pub in Castlebar that evening, Aoife had good news. Aedan's meeting with the Dublin historians had gone well. There was a clear pathway now for Aedan to get his research into publication.

Also, Aedan had received from Lester some good suggestions for reworking Aedan's rough draft of his manuscript. Aedan hadn't expected them for several days. And now he could put the Grace portrait out of his mind.

So all cylinders were firing, and Aedan thought he could see light at the end of the tunnel. He was in good spirits, but had turned in early and would be back to work before dawn. It worried Aoife that most of Aedan's days began in darkness and ended with him crashing on his bed. Aedan said he promised his doctor he'd be done with the dusty files at Taylor's Hill in less than a week. Then it was down to final re–writes and editing. He had rounded the final turn and was sprinting for the finish line.

Sara and Aoife didn't want me to feel like an ignored date, but I didn't mind in the least. It looked to me like a lasting friendship was being created, and there was a letter I wanted to write to Emma. She might not see it for years, but I had to write it while things were fresh in my mind.

As Sara and I walked back, she asked me how I was enjoying my wake.

"It's better than I thought a wake would be, especially since it goes on and on. Maybe when we get home, I'll put one together for you."

"Fantastic. Lay me out on a platter of crubeens and everyone can eat around the body. Pile the bones on my stomach. Michael, I have a serious question. So much has changed between us since we met Aedan. Are we beginning the second life you've been talking about? Is it going to work out okay for us? I'm starting to think you really can read minds."

342

"We are and it is and I can't. We've got it back, Sara, every bit of it. But we're not done here. Aedan has another surprise up his sleeve. I can smell it. He's running on fumes and he's doing what he told me not to do, living in the past and letting it consume him. It's his whole life's legacy he's finishing up now, not just Grace O'Malley.

"And speaking of happy endings, Anna and Glenn are back and they've invited us to dinner next Saturday at their place. Seeing pictures of other people's trips is usually awful, but I'm looking forward to it this time."

"Me too. His house definitely was missing something, but now it isn't."

CHAPTER THIRTY–SEVEN

We wouldn't see Aedan again until Tuesday night, the night before we'd be leaving Ireland. But he said nothing would keep Tiernan's wake from its rousing conclusion. It had never occurred to me that a wake could have a rousing conclusion. In Boston, that meant the 1812 Overture and fireworks. I'd settle for fish and chips and a parade of well–drawn pints.

I was worried about Aedan, but Sara and I needed a break too. We spent Monday and Tuesday acting like newlyweds and first–time tourists, laughing, taking goofy pictures of each other in leprechaun sweat shirts, and visiting places which had nothing to do with family history. I had thought I might want to take in some Grace O'Malley landmarks, but we had tracked her down, and it didn't seem important anymore. Sara was surprised.

"That's one way you and Aedan are different, Michael. You both like the thrill of the chase, and you both usually catch the antelope. Then you start hunting for a new antelope right away, while Aedan likes to savor the kill."

I had never thought of it that way.

"I'm glad you didn't look like an antelope when I was chasing you. For months now, I've been waking up every morning thinking about Grace O'Malley. I don't care about her much any more, even if she's my direct ancestor. She's still the biggest thing in Aedan's life now, maybe the only thing, so I want to keep helping him any way I can.

"I've learned something else from the O'Malley Protocol, Sara. I like working with you on the same things. In the second life, we should keep doing it together. How about setting up a business as forensic genealogists or historical consulting detectives?"

"Impressive titles, whatever they mean. It doesn't sound like a bad gig, as long as I can still paint and run the gallery. I'll need a Casablanca fan if I'm going to be a detective, like the old movies. And would we have to put your imaginary detective friends on the payroll?"

"Probably, but they won't use much office furniture. We'll have to decide whose name goes first on the office sign."

"We're both named Tiernan, Michael. So it's either Tiernan and Tiernan, or Tiernan and Tiernan. Think about it."

"You're right. I like them both. You decide."

The last night of Tiernan's wake was a blowout. Aedan reserved the White Stag and stationed a policeman at the door. He invited Mrs. Carty and warned her in advance there might be considerable alcohol consumption. Mrs. Carty said she'd bring her special monogrammed whiskey glass and explain to Pope Francis that she was doing missionary work.

If any problems arose, Aoife would smooth them over with the gardai and would be our designated driver. Aedan thought the police might enjoy a few bottles of his special libation, with thanks for their dedicated public service. The three trad musicians from the Castlebar pub would play until closing time, and they brought two of Mayo's best and prettiest Irish step dancers. It was shaping up as a wake me sainted ma would have been happy to attend.

Aedan served as master of ceremonies. I suppose the official term would be officiant. I didn't know much about American wakes. It brought back good memories of Glenn's resurrection celebration in Montreal – a raucous blur of eating, drinking, laughing, crying, hugging, smoking and singing, tonight embellished by Irish dancing and off–color toasts to the dearly soon–to–be–departed Michael. I had seen good hard–shoe Irish step dancing before, but never on the top of a bar with drinks being mixed around the flying feet. That would be a good Olympic event.

Mrs. Carty stayed at ground level and did an excellent job keeping up with the dancers. In her younger days, she mentioned, she had been a dancer to be reckoned with. I didn't doubt that.

An hour into the party, the policeman outside the door stuck his head through a window and motioned to us to open the door. Aoife put on her fixer face and asked him if there was a problem.

"There is, Miss Aoife, a big problem. My glass is empty and I'd like to offer a toast for the repose of Michael's soul."

I think that can be arranged.

Aedan thanked us all for coming. It had been a wonderful gathering, but like the real American wakes, it was rinsed in sadness. An Irishman was leaving for America, maybe never to be seen again. He told us to remember always that we would never again be separated, except physically.

Aedan announced he had some gifts for me to bring to my afterlife, like the ones the Egyptians put

346

into Tutankhamun's tomb. He'd send them to America directly, after he knew we had made it to the afterlife. Best to play safe. We Tiernans think the same way. But I had no intention of not crossing over, and bringing Sara with me.

The farewells were bittersweet. We raised final pints to each other and shared a long group hug. I asked Aedan if we could fold the pretty young step dancers into the hug. Sara told me not every wake is followed by a resurrection. Good point.

CHAPTER THIRTY–EIGHT

Glenn, Anna and I returned to the office the next Monday. Anna and Glenn had gotten nice tans in Hungary. I had gotten paler in Ireland. I wondered if you can even buy sunscreen there, and if you could, what you'd use it for. Then Glenn and Anna went back to work, planning Operation Lazarus. I went into the conference room to call Lester.

"Good morning, Lester. Sara and I are back and I wanted to brief you on what we found out. Aedan is grateful for your assistance, by the way. He thinks he has met his match in you."

"Good morning to you as well. From what Aedan tells me, he does think he has met his match, but it is not me. Perhaps it would be better if we chatted for a few minutes now and at greater length this afternoon. Is that convenient? I'll explain later. Is there anything of particular concern?"

"I'm worried about him, Lester. A man half his age couldn't work as hard as he's been working. He's shutting everything else out, but he says he sees light at the end of the tunnel and he'll wrap everything up in less than a month. Is he blowing smoke to make us feel better?"

"Doesn't sound like Aedan's modus operandi. The most difficult thing in academic research is knowing when to stop. But I can tell you that Aedan's draft manuscript is in advanced form. He is thorough, articulate and disciplined in his presentation, and I am doing my absolute best to help him. I received an email from him this morning asking me to review eight new pages he crafted yesterday, and he will

348

have my comments by noon. That's why it's best that we talk later.

"Michael, Aedan believes Leo and Brigid Norman already did much of the work which he is now doing, but they could not disclose it. He is pushing as hard for them now as for himself. My own debt to Leo is such that I will do whatever it takes. Aedan has agreed to my offer to consult with him twice daily until his work is ready for publication.

"And yes, I think less than a month of concerted effort will do it, but only if Aedan finishes at Taylor's Hill this week and drives away without checking his rear–view mirror. He is disappointed he has not discovered original letters or journals of Grace, but he has discovered many other primary source documents the world should see. A quest like his is seldom completely finished. I know this to be true, and I will impress it upon Aedan. Sometimes it takes one professor to prod another."

"Thanks, Lester, I feel better now. I don't want to pester him too much. I'd really appreciate it if you kept me informed."

"It will be my great pleasure. Were it not for you and Aedan, I would be sitting at my desk playing solitaire and waiting for lunch to be served in the faculty dining hall. The work may have drained Aedan, but it has invigorated Lester. I'll call you mid–afternoon."

Glenn knocked on the conference room door.

"Got a minute?"

"Oh, God, please don't tell me you need more spiritual counseling."

"No, but the last session worked out well. It was unseasonably warm in Hungary and Anna brought her shorts. Thanks to you, I was prepared."

"You're married to her now, Glenn. It's different, theologically speaking."

"Glad to hear it. Are you okay? You were the one who got us thinking about moving on to life's second act. Anna and I have done it. We're waiting for you now. Things are pretty good on the other side."

"I'm okay, thanks. I'll be busy for about a month finishing up the Aedan Burns stuff. Then Sara and I are thinking of setting up a business together. Historical detective work, maybe some forensic genealogy. I'll be writing too, and Sara will keep painting and running her gallery."

"Great. What the hell is forensic genealogy? Never mind, as long as it means we'll see more of each other. The business name is critical, Michael. Call it Tiernan Squared. It's a new world. Stuffy corporate names don't cut it anymore. Instead of the Bradley Danos Charitable Trust, I'm thinking of calling ours the Mayflower Man and Magyar Maid Foundation.

"4–MF on the logo. Serious but a little irreverent, plays to every age group. It came to me in the middle of the night. I'm running it up the flagpole for you. Do I see a salute?"

"It sounds like a property management company in hell. You married Secretariat. Let her pick the name. Although Tiernan Squared has a nice ring. We can get by with a smaller sign, and if Emma ever comes into the business, we'll call it Tiernan Cubed."

"Isn't Secretariat a horse?"

350

"In the same way a Bentley Flying Spur is a car, Glenn. Please get out of here."

Aedan called as Glenn was walking out. I didn't tell him I had spoken with Lester, but Aedan's news was even better.

"Michael, I am pleased to tell you that my work at Taylor's Hill is completed and I have forever disposed of my dust masks. I am coughing much less and my physician's frown has turned upside down. With Lester's able assistance, I expect to have the manuscript ready to submit for publication in no more than seventeen days. The peer review process will demand some revisions, which I shall make after I return from three weeks' holiday in a warm clime. Then it will be time to discuss our own book, in earnest and in person, I hope."

I didn't remember hearing Aedan cough that much. There was always an important little snippet tucked into his soliloquies. I'd email Aoife about it.

"And I have not forgotten I promised you gifts to make your afterlife more comfortable. They are being assembled and there are some for Sara and Emma as well. I neglected to tell you how much I enjoyed reading Emma's letter. She has your poetic bent, and I was most impressed and gratified by her generosity of spirit. I keep one of her pictures on my desk. She is everything a Tiernan should be, made even better by Sara's qualities. I was happy to see that. Emma is a very fine legacy.

"Michael, while I finish up here, I do suggest one last time that you re–acquaint yourself with *Finnegans Wake*. You may find it much more rewarding at this stage of your life, even if you think you are no longer a Mayo man. Now you must excuse me. Work beckons. It is time once again to become Grace O'Malley."

I fired off a thank–you email to Aedan and a more important one to Aoife. Level with me. How's he doing? Aoife wrote back that she was worried, but trying to convince herself that she was worrying too much. Aedan was exhausted, not eating or sleeping enough, and had picked up a cough in the last two weeks. But he was in excellent spirits, making progress on his manuscript, and he was talking to his doctor every day. His doctor told Aedan he should be fine if this all got wrapped up soon. It was a race to the finish and Aedan was willing himself to the winner's circle. Aoife was happy that she had seen travel brochures on his desk. Best of all, Aedan marked his calendar seventeen days out to submit his final manuscript for publication. The calendar entry had a red shamrock, a skull–and–crossbones, and a note saying, 'Knight takes Queen, checkmate'. Bring it home, Aedan.

Anna knocked on the conference room door.

"Got a minute, Michael?"

"For you, always. Are you requesting spiritual counseling today, my daughter?"

"Are you out of your mind? You're the last person I'd ask. Glenn tells me that you and Sara might be starting a detective business in our new offices. Please do it. We all need to stay together, Michael. We can't ever drift apart. I won't let it happen. There's only one more resurrection to finish up."

"Thanks, Anna. It's not exactly what people would call a detective business, but I think we're going to do it. Your own resurrection seems to be going very well. I hope those doubts you had about yourself are in a landfill somewhere with the special tool."

"They are. I got Glenn to marry me and you to say you would have asked me if things had been different. And Sara tells me I'm becoming the sister she never had. So I'm probably pretty okay after all, and I never thought I'd be this happy."

"You deserve it. You know, those are the exact words I've been looking for to describe you. You're probably pretty okay."

"If you want, I could get a swelled head like Patricia. I live in Cambridge, don't you know."

"I'm not worried about you getting a swelled head, and to Patricia, you don't live in the right part of Cambridge. Until you make it to Brattle Street, you and Glenn have only pitched a tent in heaven's parking lot."

"I wouldn't trade anything I have for everything she'll ever have. Get going on your resurrection, or I'll have to buy another special tool just for you."

I got an email that night from Lester. He had received another seven pages from Aedan to review. Aedan must be working deep into the night. Lester said he'd do the same and have his review comments to Aedan first thing in the morning.

He is doing work of the highest quality, but his pace has become unsustainable. I have contacted the other historian Aedan asked to review the manuscript.

I took the liberty of telling him that Aedan's physician wants this project completed within one week, and I will make sure that happens. At my age, I am not afraid to ruffle a few feathers.

Best, Lester

Bless you, Lester Sackett. Lester had finally been able to convince Aedan that the perfect is the enemy of the good, in this case the very good. Aedan had a manuscript worthy of publication in any historical journal. Just tidy it up a little and get the damn thing in. There's always the next publication. Aedan was on board. They were in final re–write and the manuscript would be submitted in a week or less. Maybe Leo Norman wasn't the only professor at Privilege Prep who never got some good research published.

Sara and I talked it over, and decided we'd go with the new business. With all due respect to Glenn, it was going to be called Tiernan and Tiernan. We'd tell Glenn and Anna Saturday.

She hadn't lived there very long, but Anna's personality was radiating through Glenn's house. Their house, actually, because he had already put it into joint legal ownership with her. When Anna hugged us at the door Saturday night, I could see what Sara meant. A hole in that house had been filled.

"This is so exciting. You're our first dinner guests. I hope you like French cuisine. I thought you must be getting tired of everything Hungarian by now."

Not entirely, Anna.

Glenn showed us Anna's portrait. He had wanted to put it in the foyer so everyone who came into the house would see it right away. But Anna never liked being the center of attention. So it was in Glenn's library, where he could look at it often and think about how lucky he was.

We told them about our business plan. Glenn popped a bottle of champagne, and Anna proposed a toast to new lives, old friendships and her new sister.

Sara got a little teary as she returned the toast, but I could hear something click in in her brain. I knew that click. Danger, Will Robinson. Glenn suggested cocktails and Sara jumped right on it.

"Thanks, Glenn. Anna, I've waited my whole life to have a sister like you. We have so much to celebrate. I think I'd like a Moscow Mule. I haven't had one in years."

"Sure, Sara. Let me mix it up for you, then I'll take the other drink orders."

Sara didn't like vodka. I didn't remember her ever drinking a Moscow Mule. Michael to mentor, come in please. You're back on the payroll. What's going down?

The rest of us went with whiskey. Sherlock slipped me a mental note. Oh God, she wasn't doing that, was she? Sherlock shrugged and nodded yes. I'd know for sure if she took a refill.

We exchanged stories about our recent trips, and talked about the changes in our lives. Sara was biding her time, waiting to strike. Was Glenn going to play right into her hands? Was he just another Patricia, a lamb waiting to be slaughtered? Wait, maybe not. He was studying his fingernails, like Aedan used to do. Maybe he had mentors too and was positioning himself to crush her like a bug. One can only hope. I felt like a spectator at a bullfight.

"Refills before dinner, anyone?"

We said yes. Then Glenn dropped the hammer.

"Ah, *Two Mules for Sister Sara*. Well done. I'm a Clint Eastwood fan too."

Ole. Sara looked devastated. I've underestimated you, Glenn.

"Damn. Okay, Glenn, you got me that time. I should have guessed hanging around with Michael would rub off on you. Forget the sissy drink. I'll have Irish whiskey straight up."

I was looking forward to us staying together for a very long time.

The email from Lester was waiting for us when we got home. He had ruffled enough feathers that the final manuscript would be submitted next Wednesday. Lester thought it was a magnificent piece of work. Aedan insisted Lester be credited as a co–author. Lester reluctantly agreed, but told Aedan he would ask for something in return later. Aedan agreed to whatever it was.

Best of all, Aedan would be on a flight to Jamaica next Friday to spend a relaxing three weeks with a retired colleague. He had taken a semester leave of absence from his university. Lester asked if I'd join him and Carol for a celebratory lunch in Providence on Friday, and he hoped Sara would join us. Aedan had told Lester a lot about Sara, and he wanted to meet her. Sara nodded yes, and I told Lester that we would be delighted.

Just before Sara and I went to bed, I got an email from Aedan. The man never sleeps now.

Greetings, Sara and Michael.

I trust you heard from Lester that our manuscript will be delivered for publication within a few days, and then I am off to deplete the stocks of alcohol in Jamaica. Among the many things I must thank you for is connecting me with Lester. I have seldom met a person with his keen mind and intellectual rigor. Those qualities, and his ability to crack the whip, got me to the finish line.

We set out several months ago to find Grace O'Malley and we found her. But who is the Grace O'Malley that we found? A patriot? A traitor? Perhaps both? Although history will be the final judge, my manuscript must set forth my opinions. I have concluded that Grace was a patriot. Elizabeth's Irish Conquest was nearly complete. The Gaelic order was collapsing, killed by greed and jealousy. Grace tried to make the best deal she could, for herself and for Ireland. The two are not mutually exclusive. She was looking well into the future. Had Grace's deal been consummated, Ireland might have avoided centuries of troubles. Bloody hell.

Michael, you and I share the blood of Grace O'Malley. Have you figured out how? I gave you a clue and forgot to ask if you recognized it. Would you care to satisfy my curiosity? And then, I believe, I have no more questions that need answering.

> *Soon to be in Jamaica, mon, Aedan*

I was exhausted, but had to respond.

The clue was her daughter Maeve, mon. Her daughter and your daughter, the old family name you mentioned. Have a rum punch for me. You did it. You should be very proud of yourself,

As is, Your American family

Back came the response. Aedan always gets the last word.

Maeve it was. I shall have Aoife send you the full line of descent. I am the only living person who knows it with certainty. And I am proud, but I had much unexpected help.

Until we meet again, my friend, Aedan

Aedan died sitting in a beach chair in Jamaica. His heart just gave out. He had given Aoife a sealed envelope before he left, to be opened only in case of emergency. When she opened it, Aoife learned he had been diagnosed with a terminal heart condition eight months ago. He was told he should put his affairs in order, which he had been doing every day since.

Aedan's instructions were clear. No service of any kind. His body was to be cremated immediately and his ashes scattered in the nearest ocean. He probably never dreamed it would be that ocean. He wanted Aoife to organize a celebration of his life at the White Stag, but the celebration must not take place until it was warm enough to use the deck. So Aedan never returned, at least physically, from the only warm–weather vacation he ever took.

I couldn't help thinking he would have considered it an undignified death. The man who lived in tweed jackets and lubricated his life with the finest Irish whiskey died in his bathing suit and a Bob Marley T–shirt. Even worse, he died drinking a fruited rum concoction with a tacky little drink umbrella. Maybe he was happy he was in pirate waters now, but I thought he would rather have checked out in a dusty room at Taylor's Hill, surrounded by his beloved documents. Sara disagreed. She said this was exactly how Aedan would have wanted to go, making a last statement to the world. He had prevailed and he didn't give a rat's ass how it looked. As I thought more about it, Sara was probably right.

Aedan's manuscript was accepted for publication while he was away, with only minor revisions requested. Lester took care of them. It was immediately judged to be one of the most important academic papers in Irish history. One historian remarked it was so richly detailed and textured it might have been based on interviews with Grace herself.

Lester cashed in Aedan's promise. He agreed to be listed as co–author, but only if appropriate acknowledgments were given to the other reviewing historian, Leo and Brigid, Carol, Sara and me. Lester said worthy research is always a team effort. Lester would see to it Aedan had his full legacy, as Aedan had done for him, Brigid and Leo.

Aoife didn't have many details about the death. Aedan's colleague had called her from Jamaica. The death occurred two days ago, and it took him that long to figure out who to call. Aoife was sad, but not shocked. To be honest, we probably saw it coming and tried to pretend we didn't. After we mourned respectfully for a few minutes, Aoife started giggling at the thought of Aedan sitting stone dead in his bathing suit. She was finally able to convince him to get some fresh air and sun, and it killed him. Sara joined in, and suggested we ask the Jamaican authorities for pictures of Aedan in his reggae T–shirt, and frame them for his party. I said it was probably Aedan's turn to pay for drinks and this was his way of stiffing his colleague, literally. Before long, we were laughing uncontrollably. Aedan would have loved it.

Sara made Aoife promise we'd all stay in touch. If Aoife wanted to open a gallery, Sara would help her, and she'd love to have a joint gallery arrangement with Aoife in Boston and Ireland. Aoife was excited about that. They agreed to start making plans in a few weeks.

Aedan's friend in Jamaica had already taken care of the cremation, as Aedan instructed. The letter in the envelope stated there was nothing more for Aoife to do except put together the party at the White Stag. Aedan had deposited money with his trustees to take care of everything else. He left final instructions with his team of lawyers and accountants, and we should be hearing from them soon. Aoife told us the envelope also contained eighty–five hundred euros in cash for her. It was to tide her over until his fiduciary vampires put his final wishes into effect. Eighty–five hundred euros. That's how it began with Aedan and us.

Sara and I had an early celebration of Aedan's life at our favorite restaurant. She raised a glass to his memory.

"He was quite a guy, wasn't he, Michael? Think of the lives he changed, especially ours. And those lives are interwoven, like the knot in the painting."

"That's exactly how he thought about it, Sara. It was his grand plan, his other legacy. Aedan tied a Celtic knot with himself, you, me and Aoife. As new people came into the picture, he found ways to get them into the knot. Lester, Emma, Leo, Brigid, Anna, Glenn. We're connected now in the eternal knot, too strong to be broken."

"I love it when you go mystical on me. This new life of ours may have a future."

"I think so too, and I'm going to go even more mystical on you. Remember when I asked Aedan if he was a spirit? He denied it and told me to pinch his arm if I didn't believe him? I wish I had done it, to be sure. I didn't completely trust him when he said it. I guess I'll never know."

"They don't cremate spirits, Michael. You thought he had a final surprise up his sleeve. Was it him dying, if you can accept he did?"

"No, dying would be a tough surprise to plan. Aedan was a showman. I think he had one more card to throw down, to try to make our jaws drop one last time. Maybe he wanted to see if we could guess it beforehand. It's why he said we had almost figured things out. Almost, but not quite."

"Can you guess it? I can't."

"I can't, either. He kept mentioning *Finnegans Wake* and how it would be more rewarding for me now. The setting for *Finnegans Wake* was Howth Castle, so there could be a connection. I've never made it past the first few chapters and I don't see myself trying again. So I guess he wins."

"I don't see how we lost in any way."

Sara was right about us not losing, but this still wasn't computing. You're missing something, Michael.

The letter from Aedan's three Irish lawyers arrived at my office a week later. Please accept our condolences, etc. Mr. Burns provided for you in trusts he established before his death, and attached herewith please find summaries, copies with instructions, forms to sign in triplicate and return forthwith in the envelope herein, yada, yada. God, every lawyer talks the same way. I stopped reading right there. Sara and I should go through the rest of the letter together.

"Michael, he's already been so generous, and he gave us back each other. I hope it's something personal to keep the good memories alive. I want it to be the painting I did for him in Ireland. It would mean a lot to me. I'd look at it every day and think of him."

It was the painting and a bit more. Aedan left Sara and me five million one hundred thousand euros. He left Aoife the same amount, and Emma eight hundred and fifty thousand euros, "As she is keeper of our pirate flame and future scourge of the seven seas." I'd remember to tell Emma she didn't have to endorse any checks that way. Lester, Mrs. Carty and Carol would each receive one hundred and seventy thousand euros. Everything a multiple of eighty–five. Aedan had sat with his accountants to make it work, and to make sure whatever was left would cover final bills, taxes, fees and one hell of a party, Aedan's Irish wake. And we would each be receiving personal letters.

Sara's jaw dropped and she started hyperventilating.

"Why, Michael? He didn't even meet us until a few months ago."

"I'm not sure he didn't meet us long before that. He wanted to take care of his entire family, all of his families. His family was Aoife after his wife and daughter died. Then he met us and the family kept getting bigger. Those family connections meant a great deal to Aedan. I guess this was the redemption he was looking for. Liam must have been really good at reading those ponies."

"How could he have known us before a few months ago?"

"You'd better sit down, Sara, I'm going to go full–bore weird on you. I did a lot of digging in the last week. Aedan knew I would. There were so many things not making sense.

"How did this colleague of Aedan's learn he wanted to be cremated? It's not something you chat about on a vacation. And if he knew Aedan's wishes, how could he not know whom to call? For two days? It's not the way Aedan would handle it. And Sara, there are no records anyone named Aedan Burns ever died or was cremated in Jamaica in the last month. I can't find any evidence this 'retired colleague' ever existed. Nobody has a name. The people at Aedan's universities didn't have a clue who I was talking about. Nobody did. Aedan didn't leave a name with Aoife, only a non–existent phone number. I can't find any evidence Aedan ever flew to Jamaica, and I can't find any evidence he had a doctor in or around Castlebar. Nobody has the doctor's name either. Everything we accepted as true came only from or through Aedan or his supposed colleague, but there's no evidence to back it up. Everyone trusted him, took what he said as gospel. Maybe it was all made up, and that was his big final surprise.

"The thing is, I don't really care to know. Aedan would be good at covering his tracks if he wanted to. Three months ago, I would have devoted every waking minute to trying to get the answers. As far as I'm concerned, Sara, it's not important anymore. The game is over, and you're right, we won. I'm moving on. Leave the graves undisturbed. There's too much darkness and self–deception in them. Walking away from it will be my final tribute to Aedan and everything he taught me."

"Michael, are you saying Aedan never existed?"

"No. I talked to people at his universities. He taught there. They're not making it up. But I don't know who he was when we met him. I do know he had the spirits of my ancestors in him. They were talking to him, and through him to me. Was he a spirit himself? Was he Grace O'Malley, and the first portrait we saw was just another test? Sure, I've thought about it. But I don't need to know what carrier plan the spirits use. The messages came through loud and clear, and they changed my life. I could be hallucinating again. My new business partner tells me I sometimes overthink things."

"You do, in a nice way. But there's one big choice I'm glad you made. I love her to death, Michael, but I'm happy you married me and not Anna. She would have been an outstanding second choice, though, and I know you still think about it."

Another question answered.

"I did, but not anymore. I owe Aedan for that one, too. I'm glad I married you, Sara, and I'm glad you didn't leave me for Glenn back then. I didn't make it easy for you. I deserved to lose you to him, and I just got lucky."

"Oh my God, did he tell you about us? Michael, I'm so sorry. I wanted you never to know. It happened while we were separated and I was sure our marriage was over. I was hurt and confused. I lashed out and tried to punish you, myself, anyone in sight. I broke it off as soon as I came to my senses. Glenn and I were both damaged goods, and not in a complementary way. He deserves Anna now, and for me, you were always the one. Tell me you forgive me, Michael. Please say that."

"Glenn didn't tell me. He'd never do that. I'll forgive you, Sara, but only if you forgive me for driving you away. It was my fault. You married a jealous kid who took way too long to grow up.

"Let's never look back there again, okay? Those thirty–year–olds had our names and our drivers' licenses, but they weren't us. And they're dead now. Leave the graves undisturbed. The man I am now wants to spend the rest of his life with the woman you are now. We can't let the past destroy our future. We've both got things to forgive and forget, so let's do it and move on to the next life."

"We'll never forget them, will we?"

"Probably not, but let's spit in their faces if they get too close, okay?"

"Deal. I hope Aedan's seeing some happy endings, wherever he is."

"And whoever he is. That's not important anymore, either."

CHAPTER FORTY

The letter arrived six days later. It was dated the day Aedan died. No return address, and delivered in a beaten–up manila envelope by the same courier. There were no red shamrocks this time, but the outside of the envelope had a crude drawing of a Celtic knot.

Hello, Sara and Michael.

I'm not sure where I'll be when you read this. I just hope it's not too warm, the Irish skin, you know. I expect you have already been contacted by my three solicitors, the Holy Trinity as they modestly call themselves. I trust you enjoyed their message. Whatever my new address may be, I shall be most relieved I no longer have to deal with lawyers and accountants.

But we must give Liam's accountant his due. It was he who suggested Liam purchase several hundred acres of prime land to use as a horse farm. It was a tax scam, of course. Liam had no chance of running a real business. His only skills were drinking and wagering. The land later attracted the attention of developers who saw office buildings and shopping plazas in those fields. Liam cashed a nice winning ticket, which he reinvested well in equine futures. And there you have the story of how the three wise suits appeared from the east bearing tidings of comfort and joy for my American family.

It was an exhilarating journey, was it not? We learned so many things from each other. Aoife will be sending you some notes and documents, and I look forward to reading your book, our book. And now, I shall give you a farewell puzzle, one worthy of you. You are a Mayo man, Michael, and up to the task. I may not contact you directly, but I shall be watching you with great interest. I have a screenplay for you to consider. Something that happens only in pulp fiction novels, I suspect, but you may find it amusing.

In my screenplay, the Queen does bury treasure near the castle. The person for whom it was intended has the great misfortune of dying young, and the treasure sits there today. But where? As it turns out, the Queen left disguised instructions as to the location, a copy of which made its way into a pile of dusty documents. An old professor doing arcane historical research stumbles onto the two pages of instructions and recognizes them for what they are. He is a careless old man, and somehow loses the second page. Fortunately, he has a good memory and a copy of the first page.

He becomes, shall we say, permanently indisposed, but before he does, he makes arrangements for a copy of the first page of the instructions to be mailed in a few months to a relative. Alas, what good is the first page without the second? The professor is an avid reader and realizes the missing critical information on the second page can all be reconstructed from clues in various passages of Finnegans Wake. What a magnificent coincidence, wouldn't you agree?

I realize this screenplay is fanciful and would never sell. I was even going to suggest the relative engage the services of another pirate to help him. It's quite ridiculous. Where would one find another pirate in this day and age? In any event, please think about it, as you have thought about so many other things in the past few months. I would like to believe that our brief association has already given you treasure more valuable than any bits of shiny metal. Do not squander it.

Take no prisoners, my cousin.

Aedan

64814909R00205

Made in the USA
Middletown, DE
18 February 2018